SONIC™
THE HEDGEHOG
ALL OR NOTHING

@IDWpublishing
IDWpublishing.com

ISBN: 978-1-68405-722-1
25 24 23 22   3 4 5 6

COVER ART BY
AARON HAMMERSTROM &
REGGIE GRAHAM

SERIES ASSISTANT EDITOR
RILEY FARMER

SERIES EDITOR
DAVID MARIOTTE

COLLECTION EDITORSA-
LONZO SIMON
AND ZAC BOONE

COLLECTION DESIGNER
AMAURI OSORIO

Originally published as SONIC THE HEDGEHOG issues #25–29.

Nachie Marsham, Publisher
Blake Kobashigawa, SVP Sales, Marketing & Strategy
Mark Doyle, VP Creative & Editorial Strategy
Tara McCrillis, VP Publishing Operations
Anna Morrow, VP Marketing & Publicity
Alex Hargett, VP Sales
Lauren LePera, Sr. Managing Editor
Greg Gustin, Sr. Director, Content Strategy
Kevin Schwoer, Sr. Director of Talent Relations
Keith Davidsen, Director, Marketing & PR
Topher Alford, Sr. Digital Marketing Manager
Patrick O'Connell, Sr. Manager, Direct Market Sales
Shauna Monteforte, Sr. Director of Manufacturing Operations
Greg Foreman, Director DTC Sales & Operations
Nathan Widick, Director of Design
Neil Uyetake, Sr. Art Director, Design & Production
Shawn Lee, Art Director, Design & Production
Jack Rivera, Art Director, Marketing

Ted Adams and Robbie Robbins, IDW Founders

Special thanks to Mai Kiyotaki, Aaron Webber, Michael Cisneros, Sandra Jo, and everyone at Sega for their invaluable assistance.

STORY
IAN FLYNN

ART
ADAM BRYCE THOMAS (#25 & 27-29)
EVAN STANLEY (#26-28)
PRISCILLA TRAMONTANO (#26)

COLORS
MATT HERMS (#25-29)
HEATHER BRECKEL (#26)
BRACARDI CURRY (#27)
ELAINA UNGER (#28)

LETTERS
SHAWN LEE

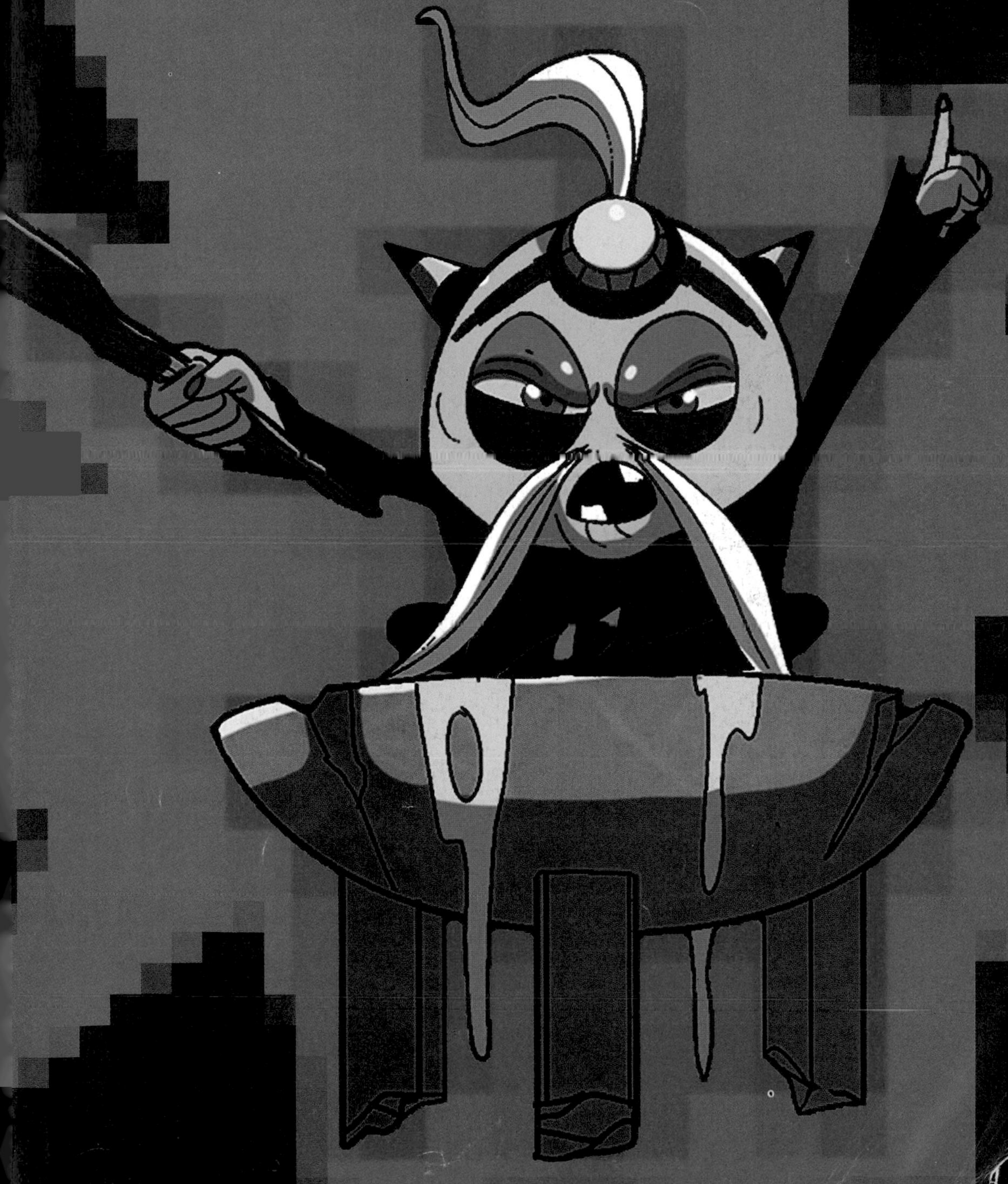

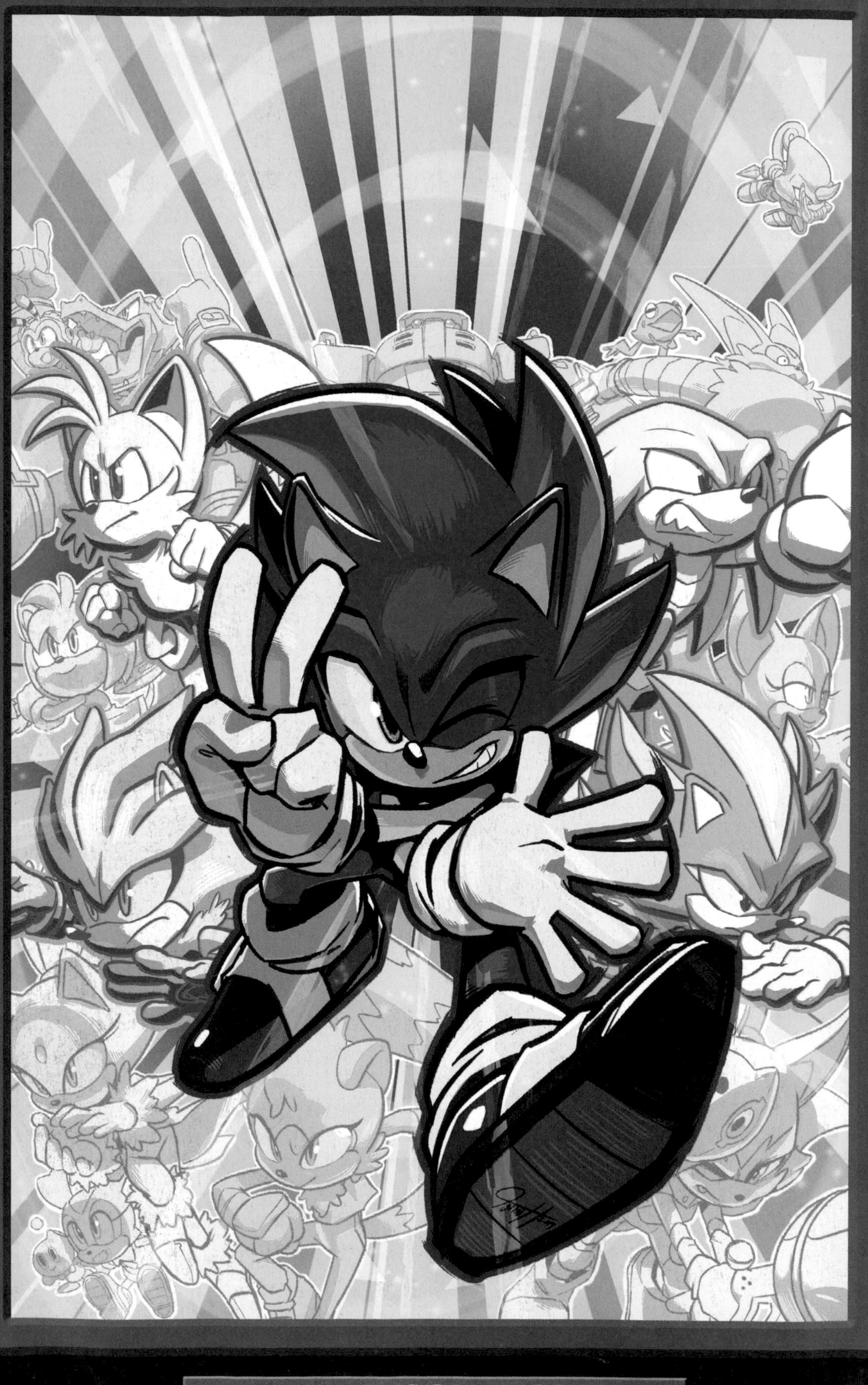

ART BY **TYSON HESSE**

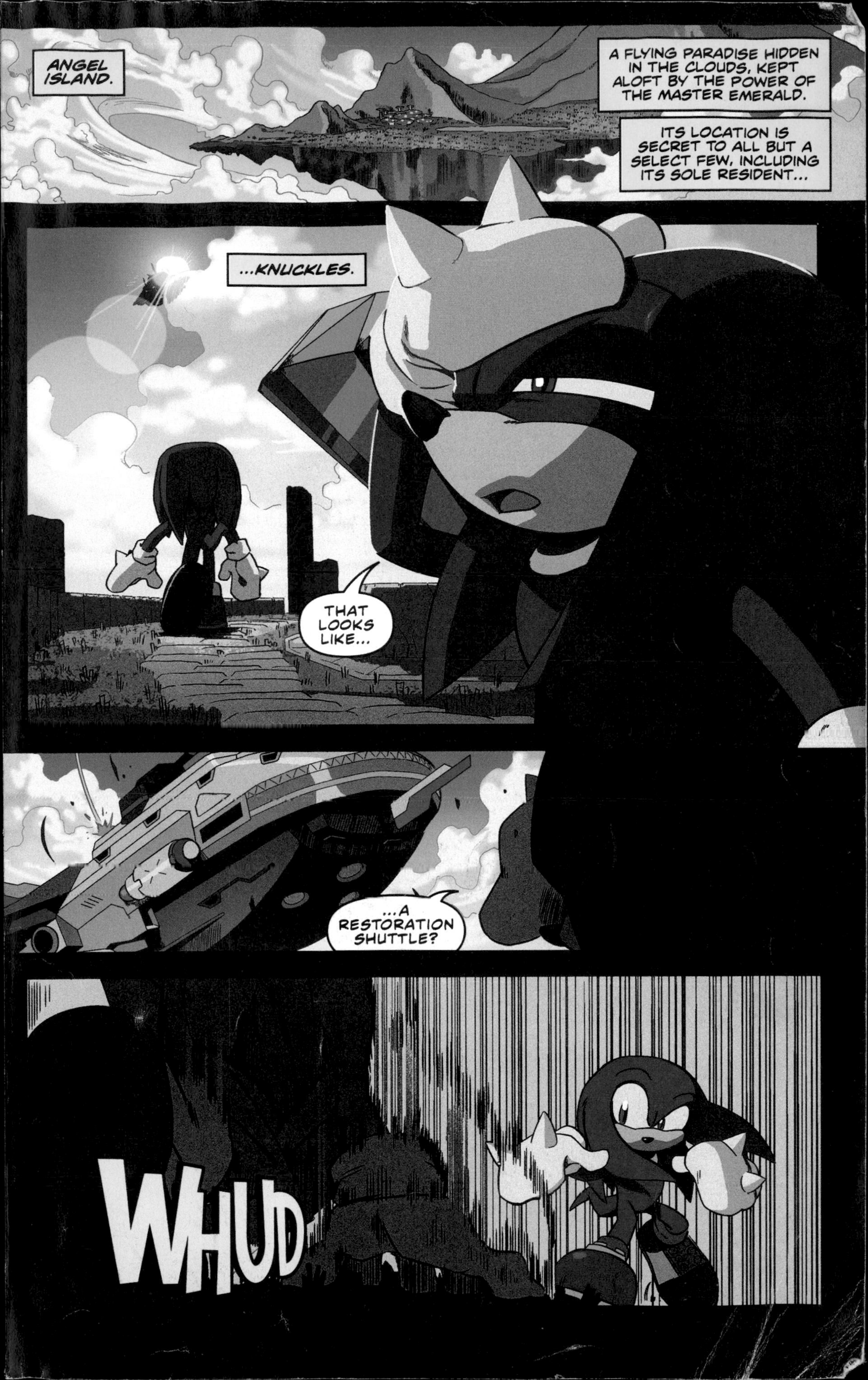
ANGEL ISLAND.
A FLYING PARADISE HIDDEN IN THE CLOUDS, KEPT ALOFT BY THE POWER OF THE MASTER EMERALD.
ITS LOCATION IS SECRET TO ALL BUT A SELECT FEW, INCLUDING ITS SOLE RESIDENT...
...KNUCKLES.
THAT LOOKS LIKE...
...A RESTORATION SHUTTLE?
WHUD

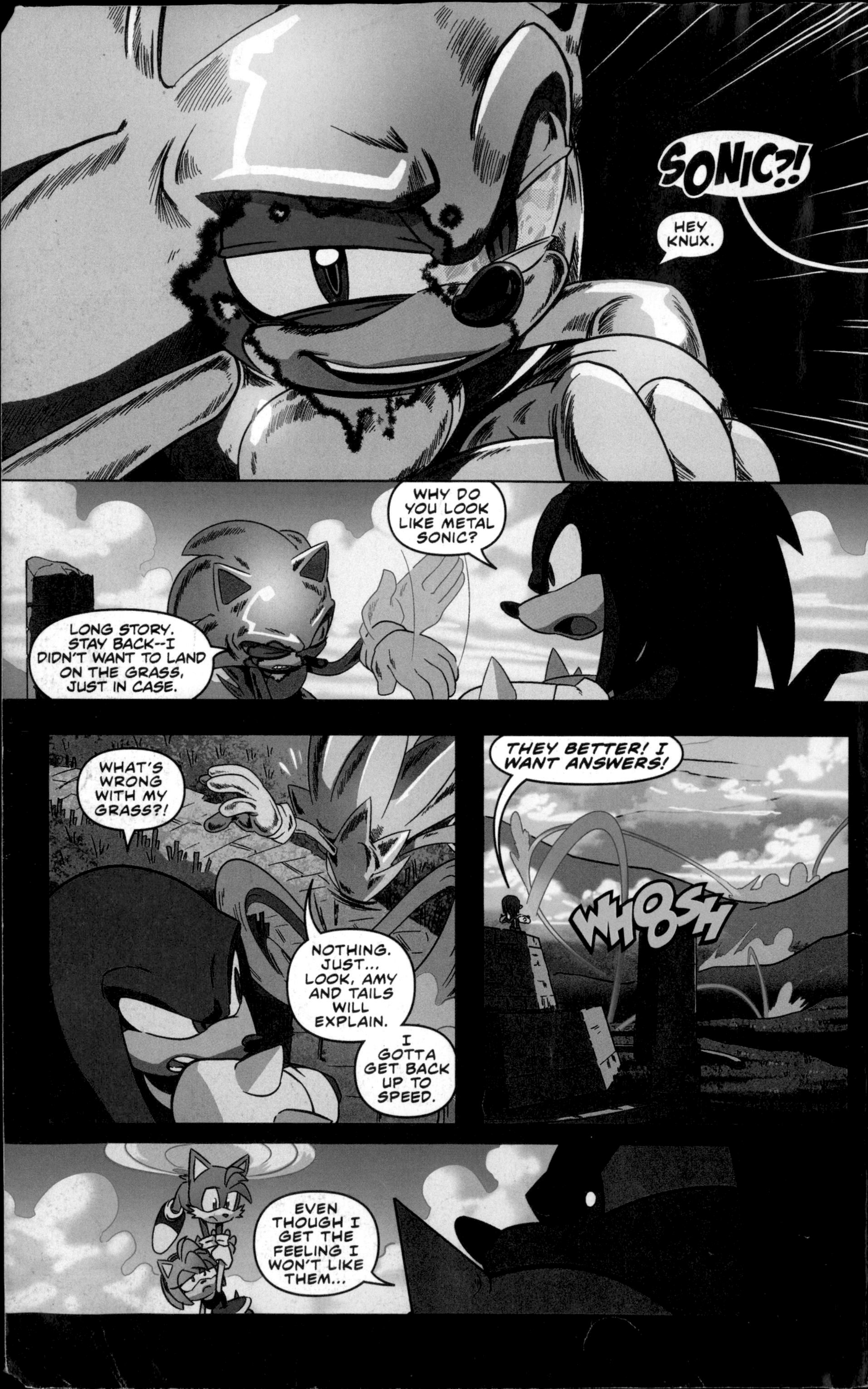

SONIC?!
HEY KNUX.
WHY DO YOU LOOK LIKE METAL SONIC?
LONG STORY. STAY BACK--I DIDN'T WANT TO LAND ON THE GRASS, JUST IN CASE.
WHAT'S WRONG WITH MY GRASS?!
NOTHING. JUST... LOOK, AMY AND TAILS WILL EXPLAIN.
I GOTTA GET BACK UP TO SPEED.
WHOOSH
THEY BETTER! I WANT ANSWERS!
EVEN THOUGH I GET THE FEELING I WON'T LIKE THEM...

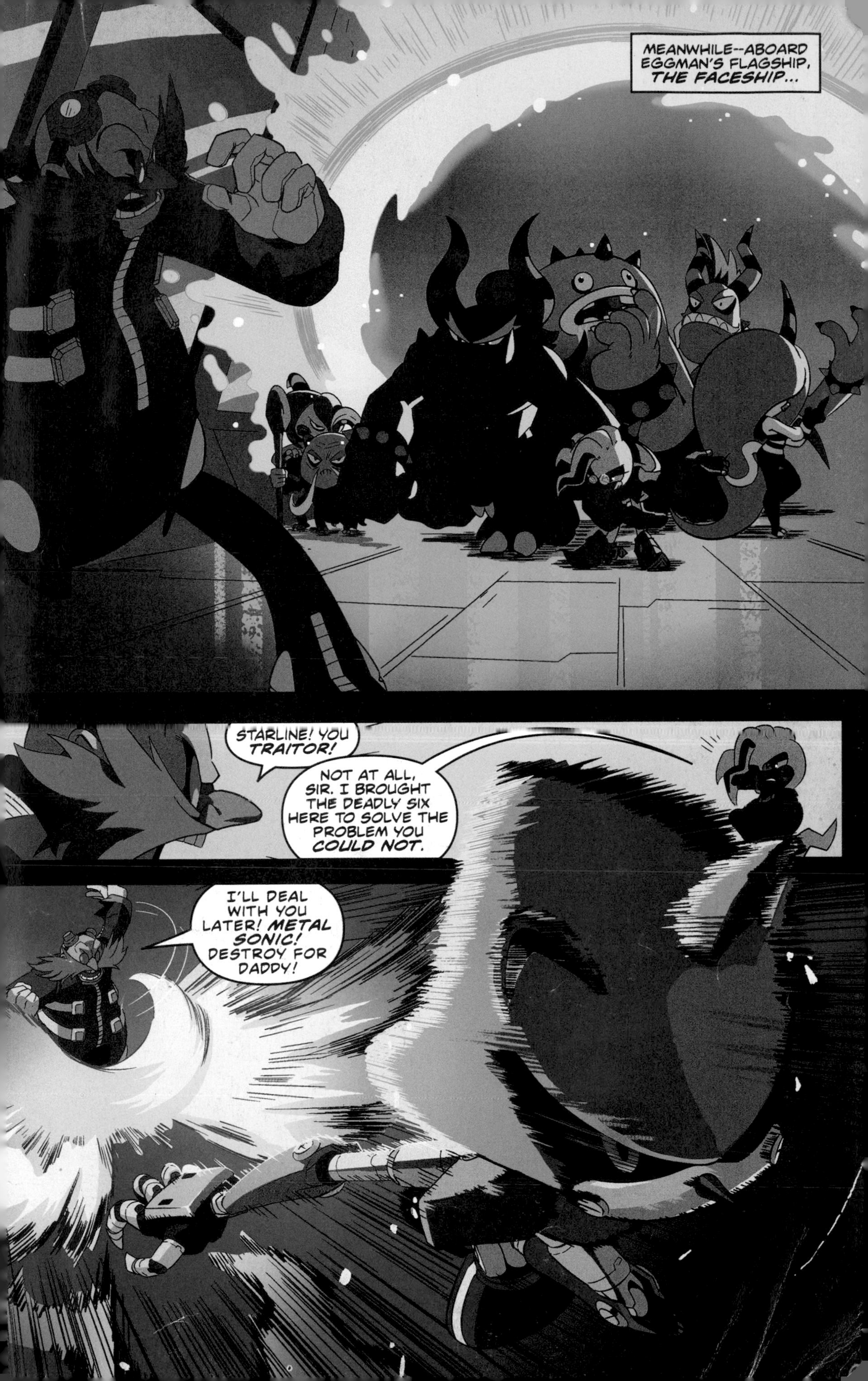
MEANWHILE--ABOARD EGGMAN'S FLAGSHIP, *THE FACESHIP...*
STARLINE! YOU *TRAITOR!*
NOT AT ALL, SIR. I BROUGHT THE DEADLY SIX HERE TO SOLVE THE PROBLEM YOU *COULD NOT*.
I'LL DEAL WITH YOU LATER! *METAL SONIC!* DESTROY FOR DADDY!

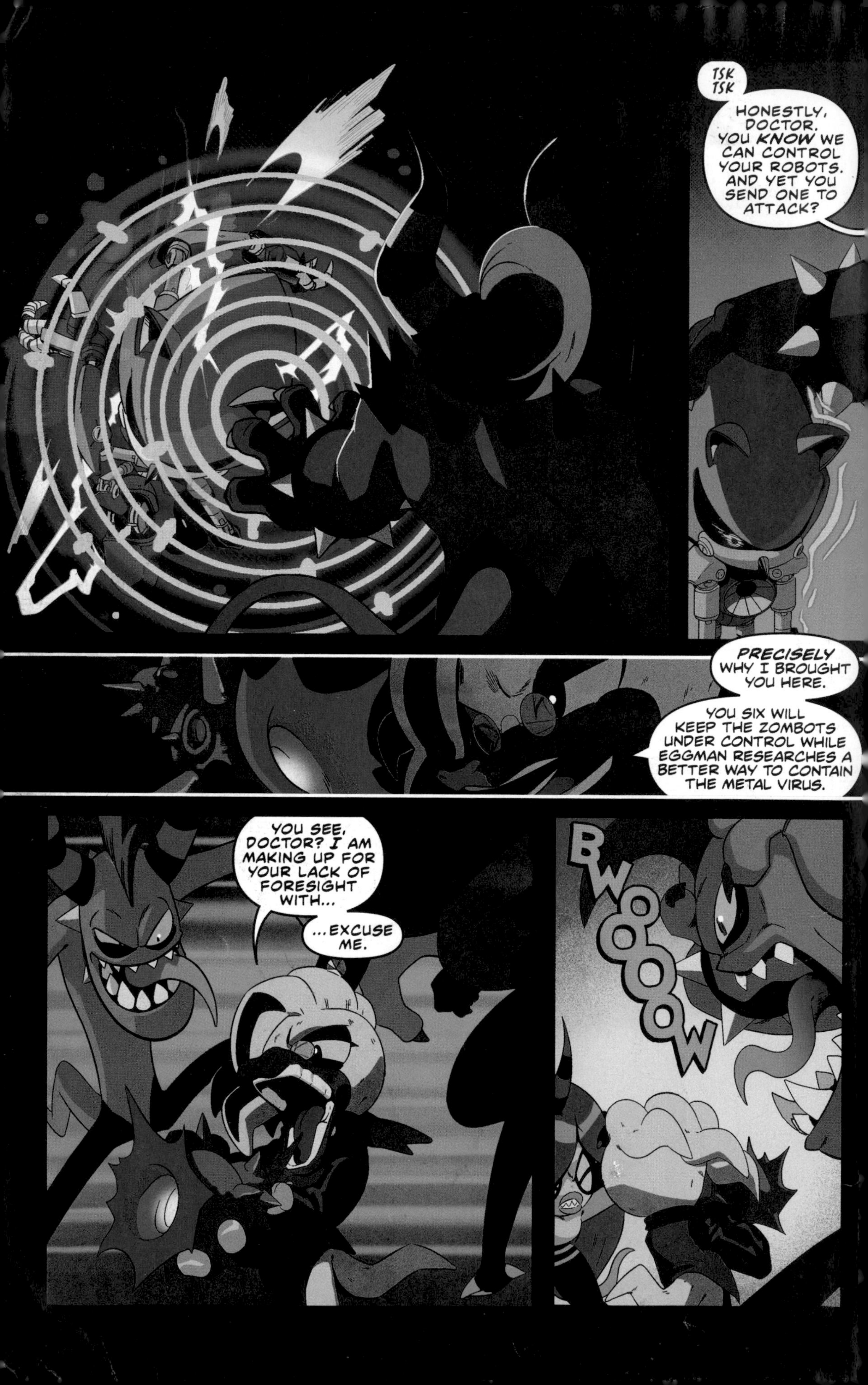
TSK TSK
HONESTLY, DOCTOR. YOU *KNOW* WE CAN CONTROL YOUR ROBOTS. AND YET YOU SEND ONE TO ATTACK?
PRECISELY WHY I BROUGHT YOU HERE.
YOU SIX WILL KEEP THE ZOMBOTS UNDER CONTROL WHILE EGGMAN RESEARCHES A BETTER WAY TO CONTAIN THE METAL VIRUS.
YOU SEE, DOCTOR? *I* AM MAKING UP FOR YOUR LACK OF FORESIGHT WITH...
...EXCUSE ME.
BWOOOOOW

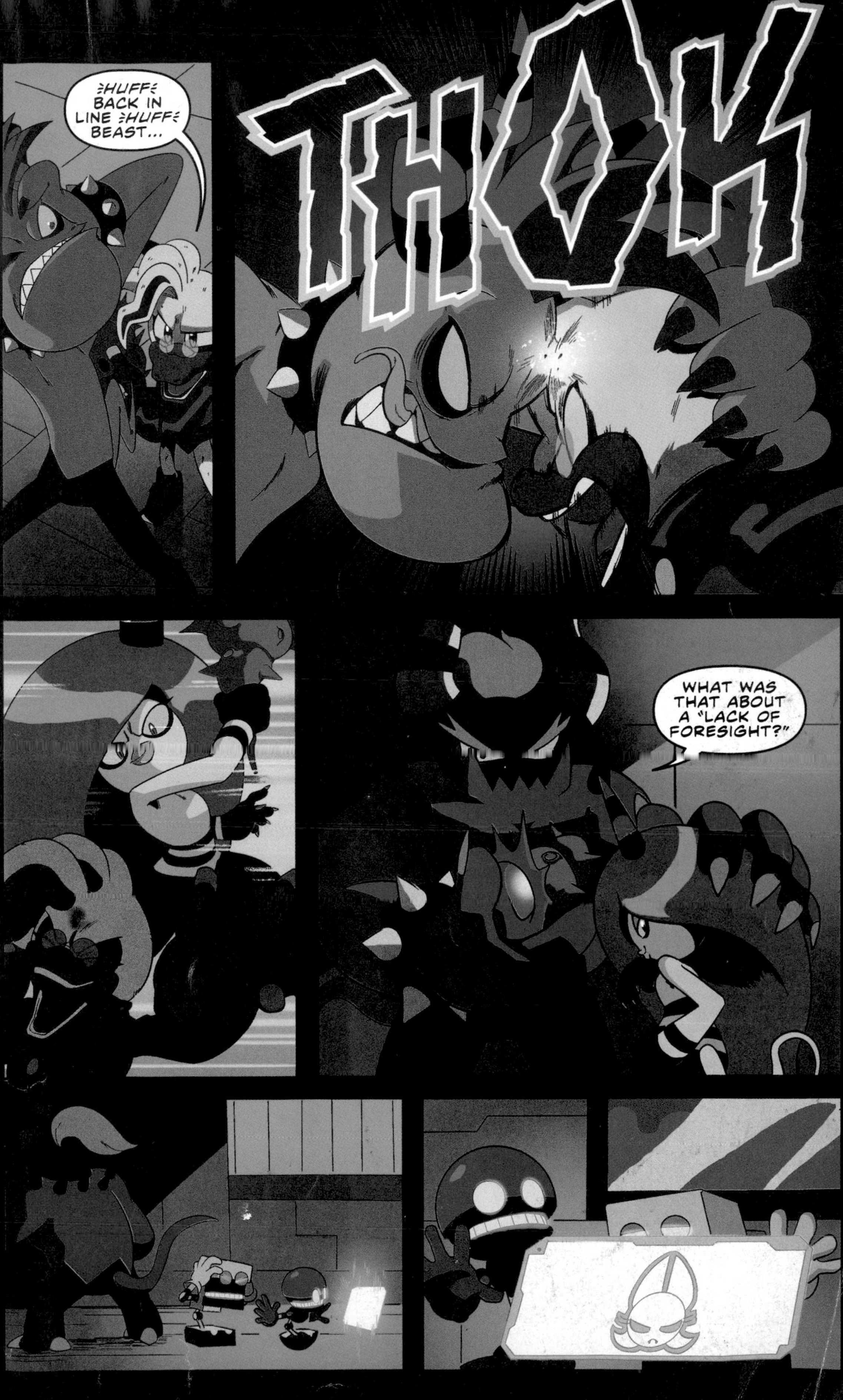

⸗HUFF⸗ BACK IN LINE ⸗HUFF⸗ BEAST...
THOK
WHAT WAS THAT ABOUT A "LACK OF FORESIGHT?"

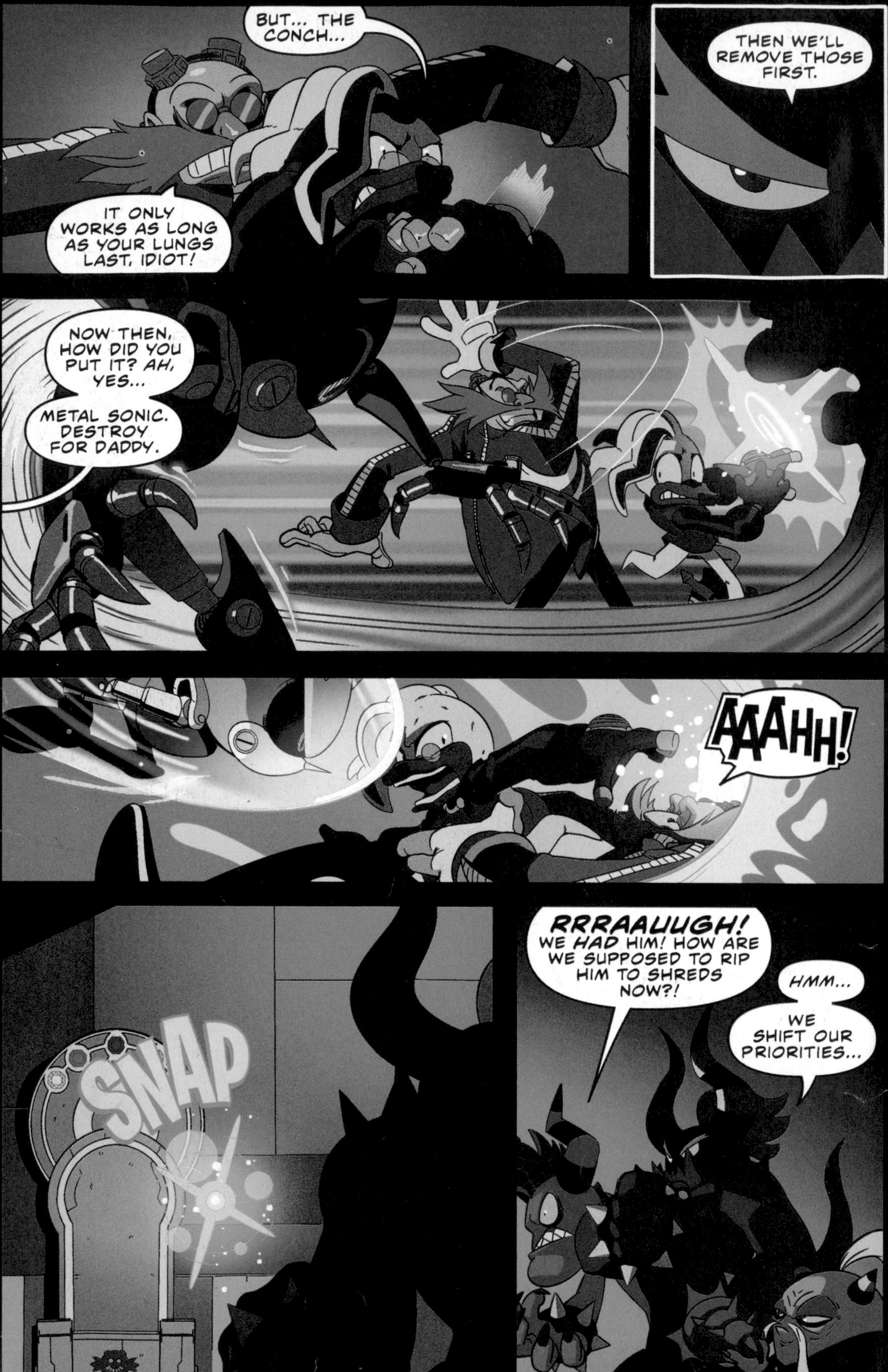
BUT... THE CONCH...
IT ONLY WORKS AS LONG AS YOUR LUNGS LAST, IDIOT!
THEN WE'LL REMOVE THOSE FIRST.
NOW THEN, HOW DID YOU PUT IT? AH, YES...
METAL SONIC. DESTROY FOR DADDY.
AAAHH!
SNAP
RRRAAUUGH! WE HAD HIM! HOW ARE WE SUPPOSED TO RIP HIM TO SHREDS NOW?!
HMM...
WE SHIFT OUR PRIORITIES...

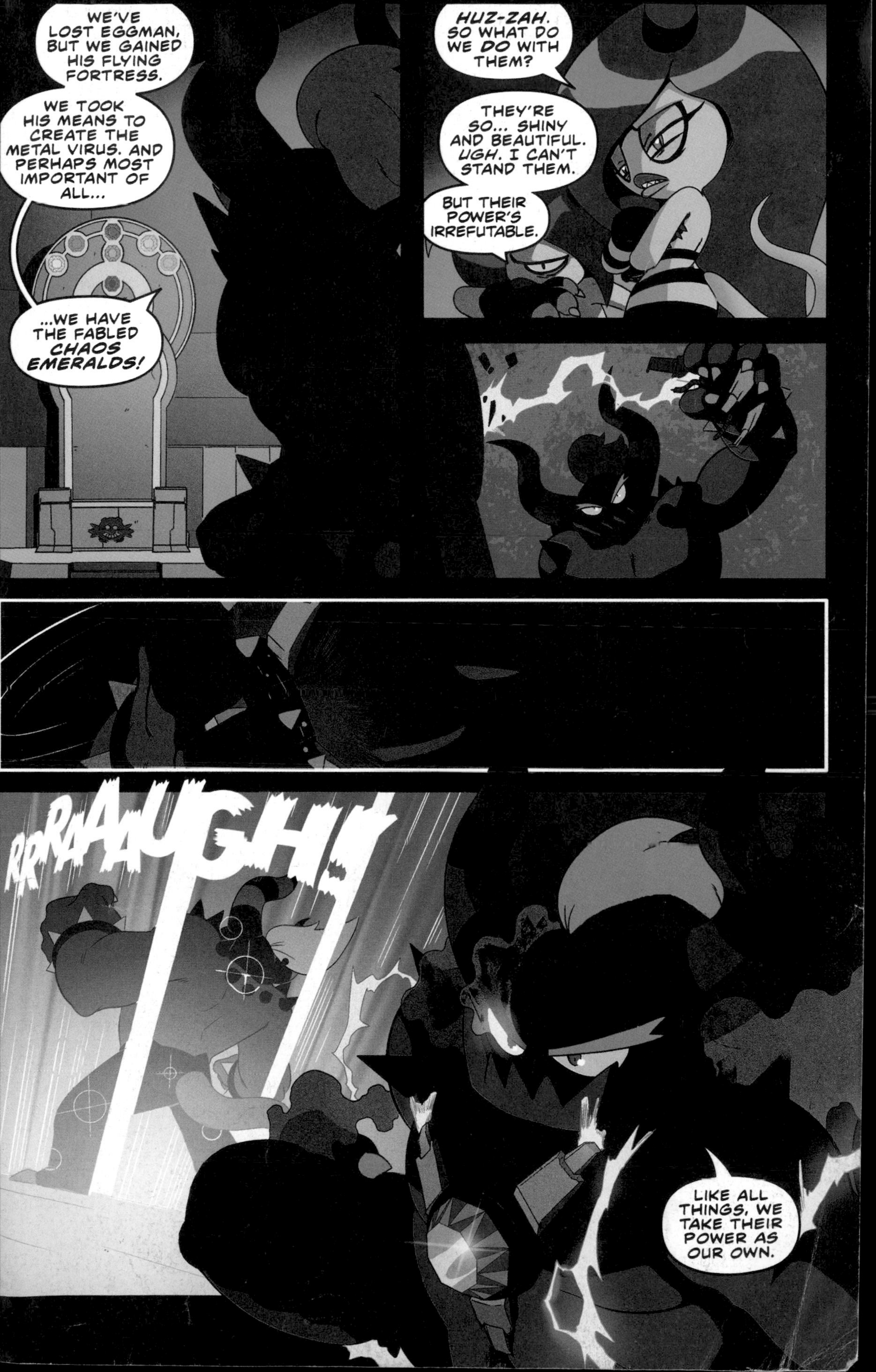
WE'VE LOST EGGMAN, BUT WE GAINED HIS FLYING FORTRESS.
WE TOOK HIS MEANS TO CREATE THE METAL VIRUS. AND PERHAPS MOST IMPORTANT OF ALL...
...WE HAVE THE FABLED CHAOS EMERALDS!
HUZ-ZAH. SO WHAT DO WE DO WITH THEM?
THEY'RE SO... SHINY AND BEAUTIFUL. UGH. I CAN'T STAND THEM.
BUT THEIR POWER'S IRREFUTABLE.
RRRAAAUGH!!
LIKE ALL THINGS, WE TAKE THEIR POWER AS OUR OWN.

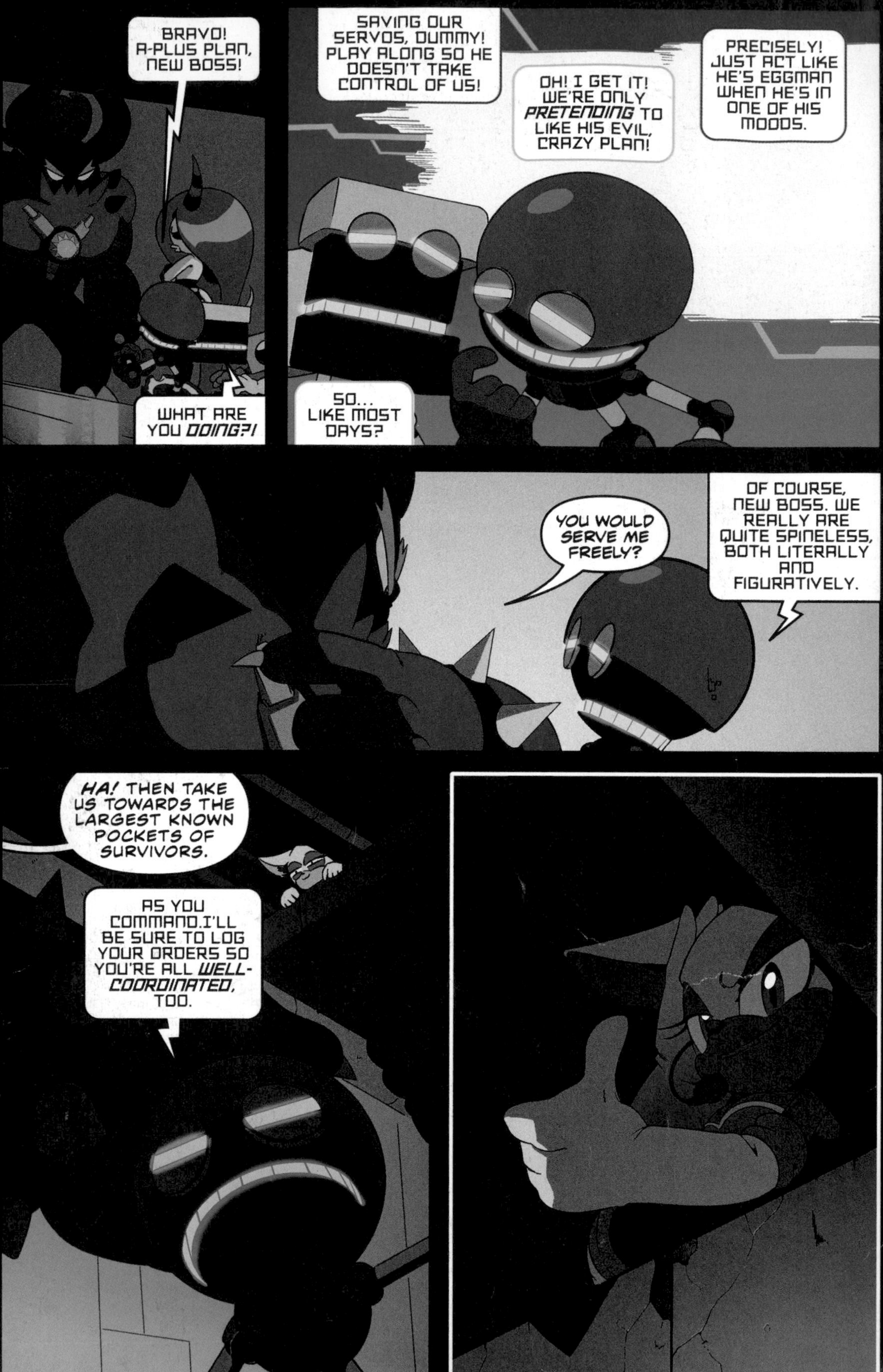
BRAVO! A-PLUS PLAN, NEW BOSS!
WHAT ARE YOU *DOING?!*
SAVING OUR SERVOS, DUMMY! PLAY ALONG SO HE DOESN'T TAKE CONTROL OF US!
OH! I GET IT! WE'RE ONLY *PRETENDING* TO LIKE HIS EVIL, CRAZY PLAN!
PRECISELY! JUST ACT LIKE HE'S EGGMAN WHEN HE'S IN ONE OF HIS MOODS.
SO... LIKE MOST DAYS?
YOU WOULD SERVE ME FREELY?
OF COURSE, NEW BOSS. WE REALLY ARE QUITE SPINELESS, BOTH LITERALLY AND FIGURATIVELY.
HA! THEN TAKE US TOWARDS THE LARGEST KNOWN POCKETS OF SURVIVORS.
AS YOU COMMAND. I'LL BE SURE TO LOG YOUR ORDERS SO YOU'RE ALL *WELL-COORDINATED,* TOO.

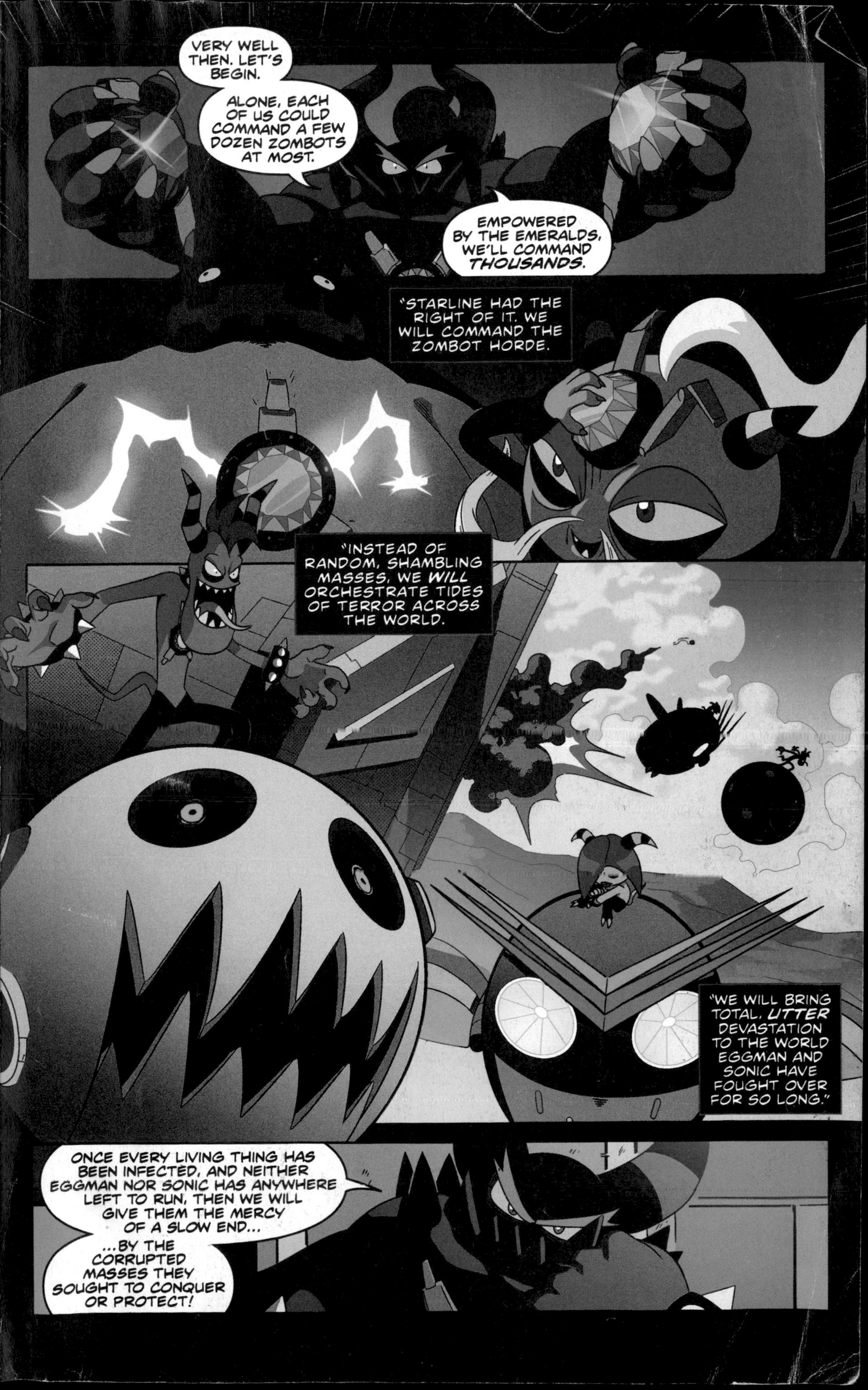
VERY WELL THEN. LET'S BEGIN.
ALONE, EACH OF US COULD COMMAND A FEW DOZEN ZOMBOTS AT MOST.
EMPOWERED BY THE EMERALDS, WE'LL COMMAND *THOUSANDS*.
"STARLINE HAD THE RIGHT OF IT. WE WILL COMMAND THE ZOMBOT HORDE.
"INSTEAD OF RANDOM, SHAMBLING MASSES, WE *WILL* ORCHESTRATE TIDES OF TERROR ACROSS THE WORLD.
"WE WILL BRING TOTAL, *UTTER* DEVASTATION TO THE WORLD EGGMAN AND SONIC HAVE FOUGHT OVER FOR SO LONG."
ONCE EVERY LIVING THING HAS BEEN INFECTED, AND NEITHER EGGMAN NOR SONIC HAS ANYWHERE LEFT TO RUN, THEN WE WILL GIVE THEM THE MERCY OF A SLOW END...
...BY THE CORRUPTED MASSES THEY SOUGHT TO CONQUER OR PROTECT!

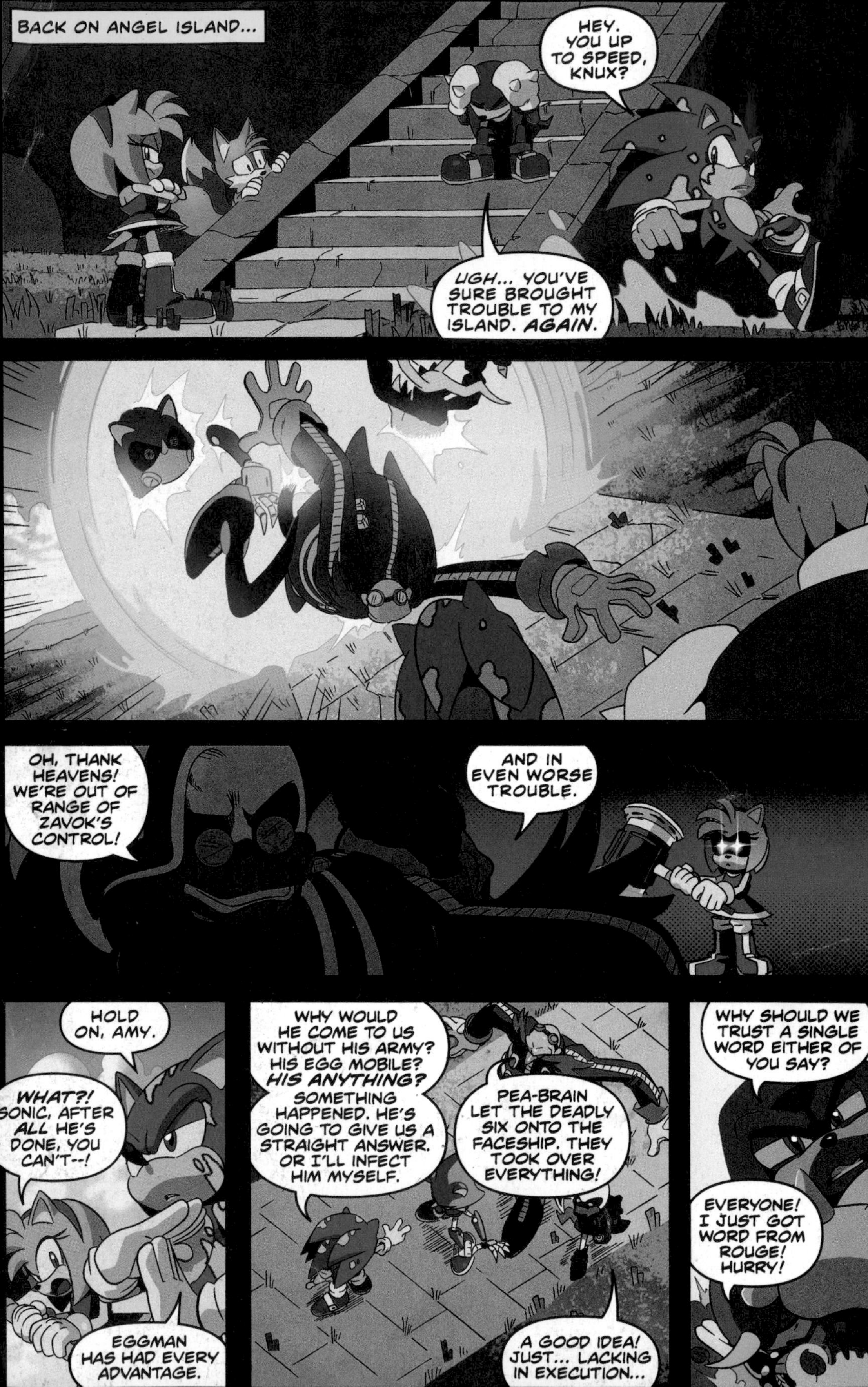
BACK ON ANGEL ISLAND...
HEY. YOU UP TO SPEED, KNUX?
UGH... YOU'VE SURE BROUGHT TROUBLE TO MY ISLAND. AGAIN.
OH, THANK HEAVENS! WE'RE OUT OF RANGE OF ZAVOK'S CONTROL!
AND IN EVEN WORSE TROUBLE.
HOLD ON, AMY.
WHAT?! SONIC, AFTER ALL HE'S DONE, YOU CAN'T--!
EGGMAN HAS HAD EVERY ADVANTAGE.
WHY WOULD HE COME TO US WITHOUT HIS ARMY? HIS EGG MOBILE? HIS ANYTHING?
SOMETHING HAPPENED. HE'S GOING TO GIVE US A STRAIGHT ANSWER. OR I'LL INFECT HIM MYSELF.
PEA-BRAIN LET THE DEADLY SIX ONTO THE FACESHIP. THEY TOOK OVER EVERYTHING!
A GOOD IDEA! JUST... LACKING IN EXECUTION...
WHY SHOULD WE TRUST A SINGLE WORD EITHER OF YOU SAY?
EVERYONE! I JUST GOT WORD FROM ROUGE! HURRY!

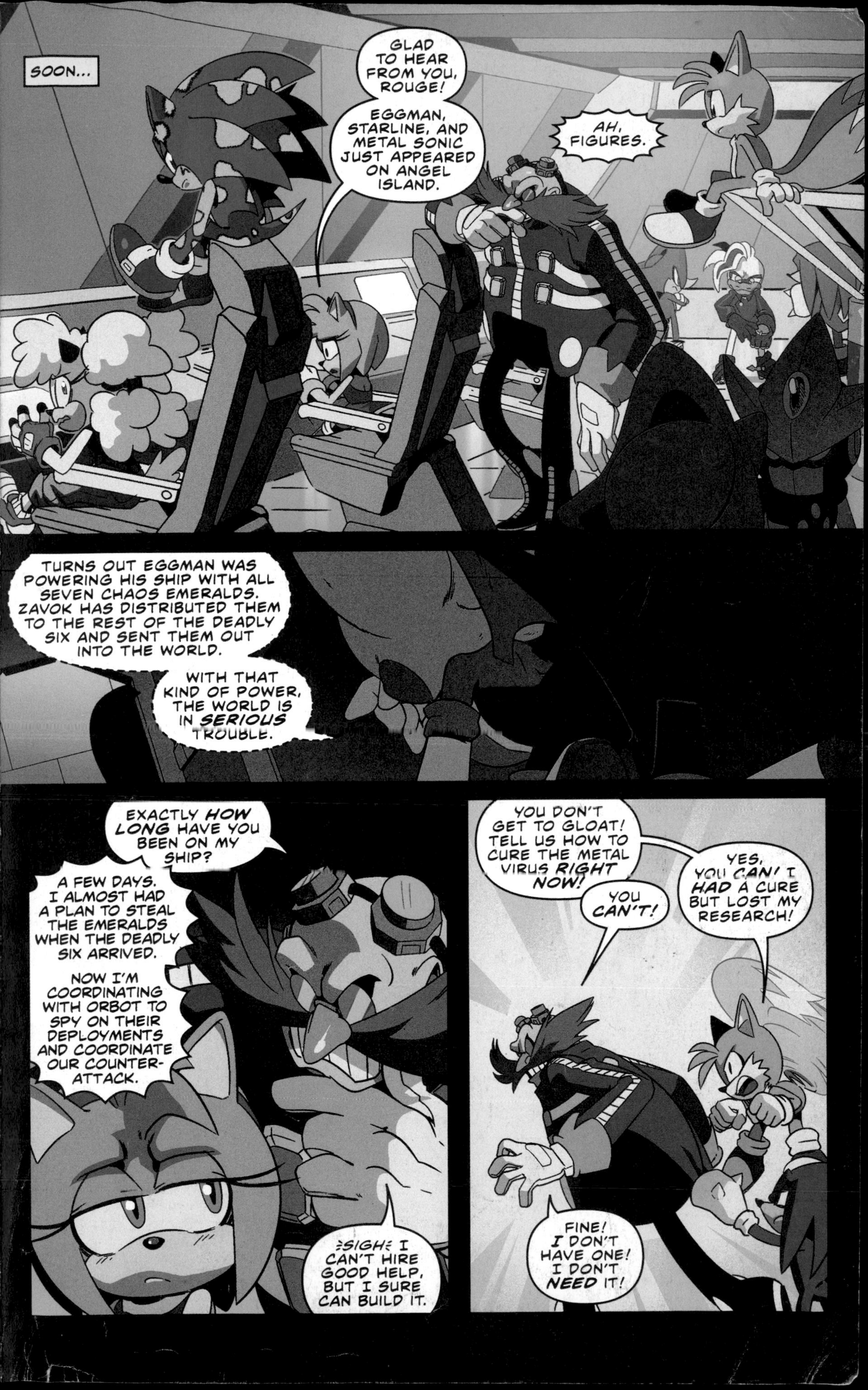
SOON...
GLAD TO HEAR FROM YOU, ROUGE!
EGGMAN, STARLINE, AND METAL SONIC JUST APPEARED ON ANGEL ISLAND.
AH, FIGURES.
TURNS OUT EGGMAN WAS POWERING HIS SHIP WITH ALL SEVEN CHAOS EMERALDS. ZAVOK HAS DISTRIBUTED THEM TO THE REST OF THE DEADLY SIX AND SENT THEM OUT INTO THE WORLD.
WITH THAT KIND OF POWER, THE WORLD IS IN *SERIOUS* TROUBLE.
EXACTLY *HOW LONG* HAVE YOU BEEN ON MY SHIP?
A FEW DAYS. I ALMOST HAD A PLAN TO STEAL THE EMERALDS WHEN THE DEADLY SIX ARRIVED.
NOW I'M COORDINATING WITH ORBOT TO SPY ON THEIR DEPLOYMENTS AND COORDINATE OUR COUNTER-ATTACK.
SIGH I CAN'T HIRE GOOD HELP, BUT I SURE CAN BUILD IT.
YOU DON'T GET TO GLOAT! TELL US HOW TO CURE THE METAL VIRUS *RIGHT NOW!*
YOU *CAN'T!*
YES, YOU *CAN!* I *HAD* A CURE BUT LOST MY RESEARCH!
FINE! *I* DON'T HAVE ONE! I DON'T *NEED* IT!

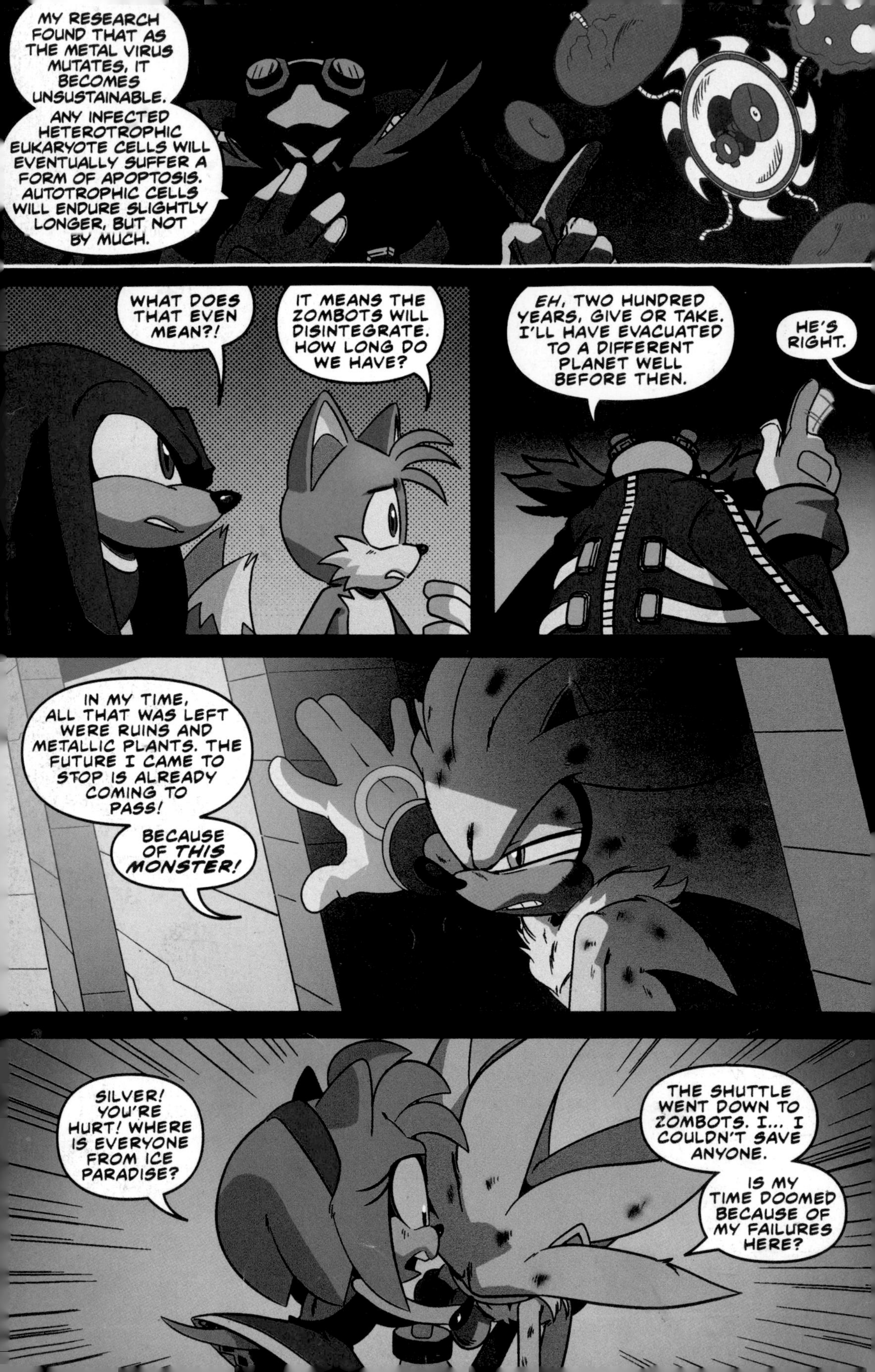
MY RESEARCH FOUND THAT AS THE METAL VIRUS MUTATES, IT BECOMES UNSUSTAINABLE.
ANY INFECTED HETEROTROPHIC EUKARYOTE CELLS WILL EVENTUALLY SUFFER A FORM OF APOPTOSIS. AUTOTROPHIC CELLS WILL ENDURE SLIGHTLY LONGER, BUT NOT BY MUCH.
WHAT DOES THAT EVEN MEAN?!
IT MEANS THE ZOMBOTS WILL DISINTEGRATE. HOW LONG DO WE HAVE?
EH, TWO HUNDRED YEARS, GIVE OR TAKE. I'LL HAVE EVACUATED TO A DIFFERENT PLANET WELL BEFORE THEN.
HE'S RIGHT.
IN MY TIME, ALL THAT WAS LEFT WERE RUINS AND METALLIC PLANTS. THE FUTURE I CAME TO STOP IS ALREADY COMING TO PASS!
BECAUSE OF THIS MONSTER!
SILVER! YOU'RE HURT! WHERE IS EVERYONE FROM ICE PARADISE?
THE SHUTTLE WENT DOWN TO ZOMBOTS. I... I COULDN'T SAVE ANYONE.
IS MY TIME DOOMED BECAUSE OF MY FAILURES HERE?

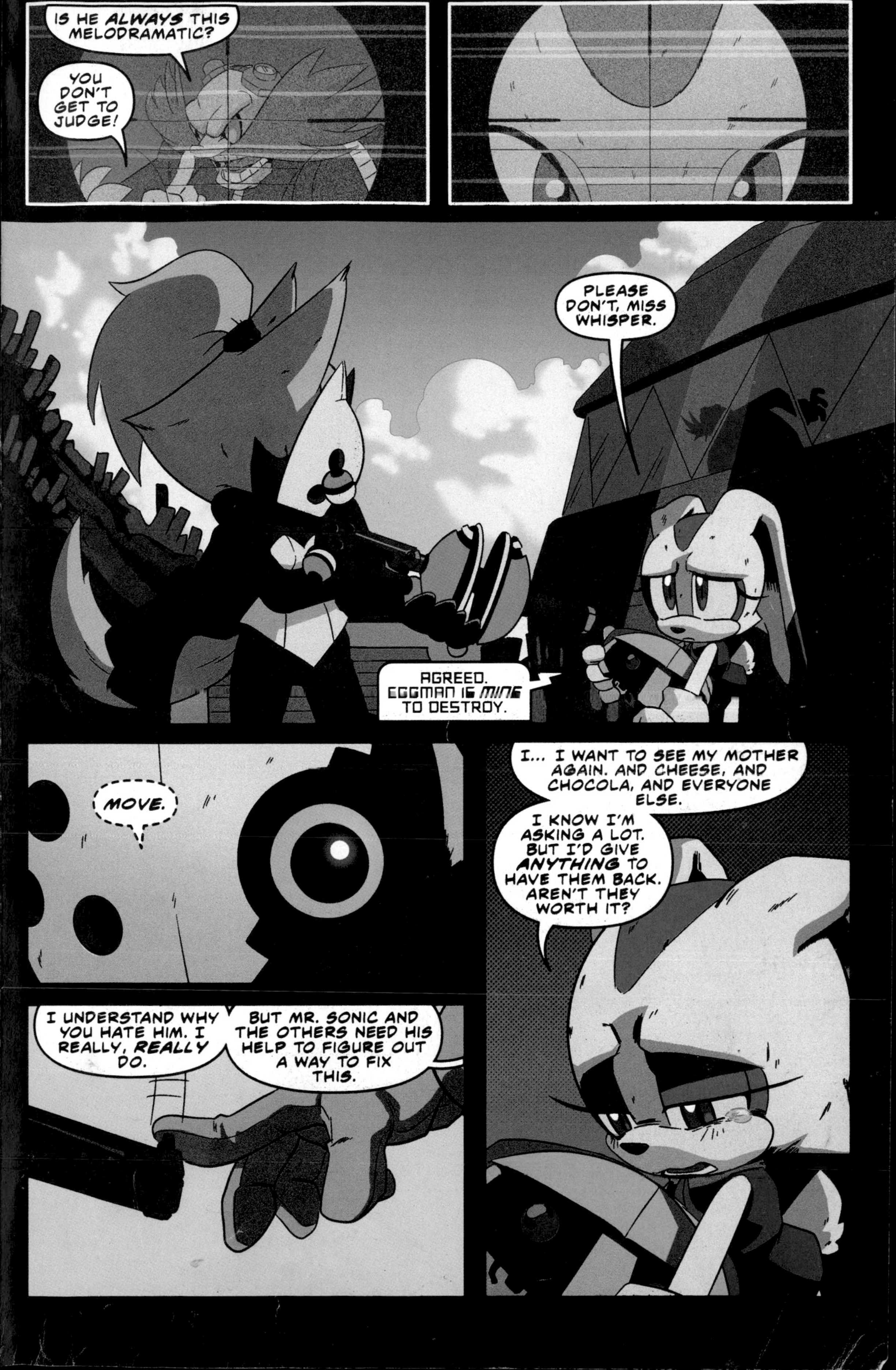
IS HE *ALWAYS* THIS MELODRAMATIC?
YOU DON'T GET TO JUDGE!
PLEASE DON'T, MISS WHISPER.
AGREED. EGGMAN IS *MINE* TO DESTROY.
MOVE.
I... I WANT TO SEE MY MOTHER AGAIN. AND CHEESE, AND CHOCOLA, AND EVERYONE ELSE.
I KNOW I'M ASKING A LOT. BUT I'D GIVE *ANYTHING* TO HAVE THEM BACK. AREN'T THEY WORTH IT?
I UNDERSTAND WHY YOU HATE HIM. I REALLY, *REALLY* DO.
BUT MR. SONIC AND THE OTHERS NEED HIS HELP TO FIGURE OUT A WAY TO FIX THIS.

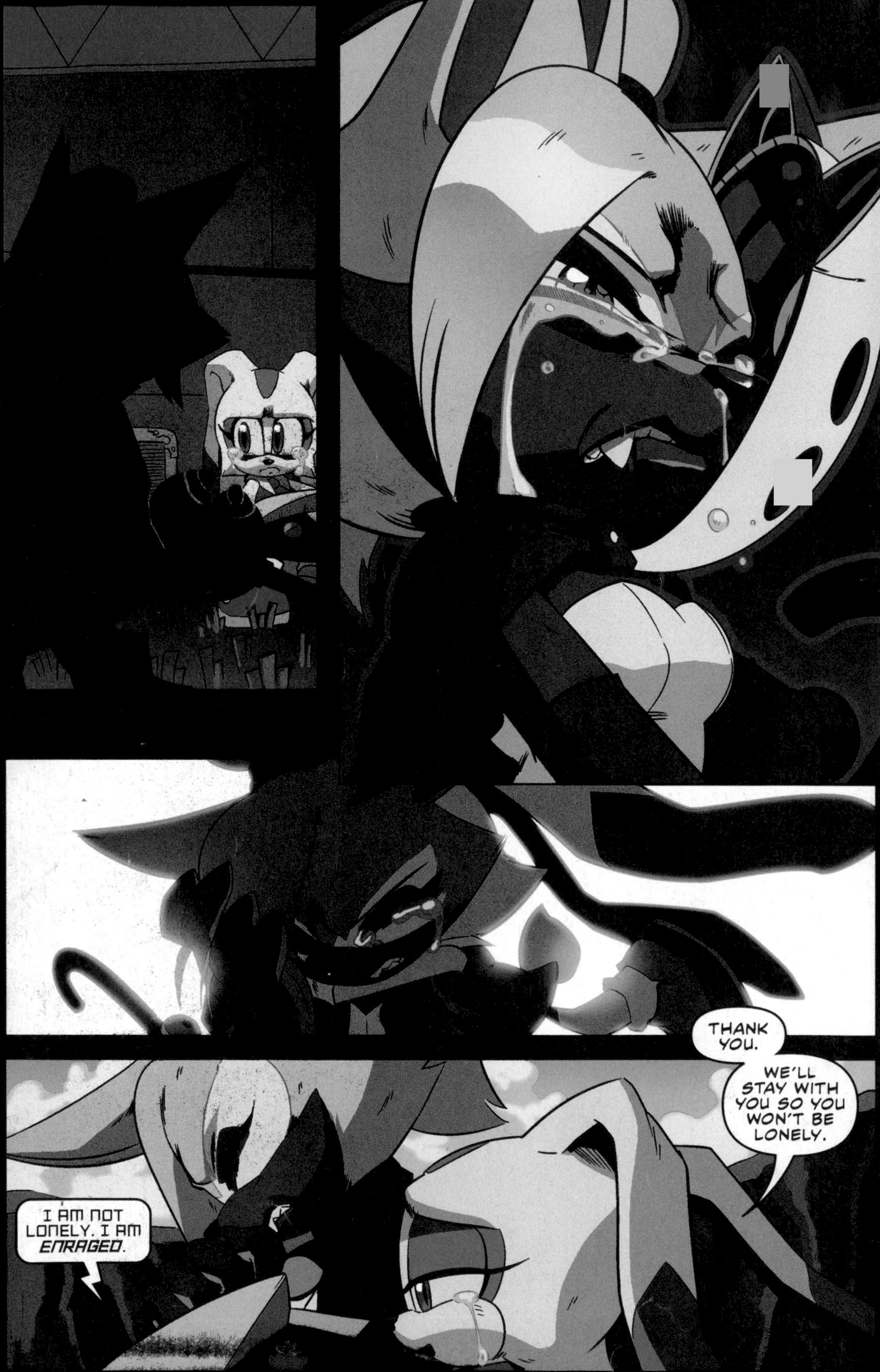
THANK YOU.
WE'LL STAY WITH YOU SO YOU WON'T BE LONELY.
I AM NOT LONELY. I AM *ENRAGED*.

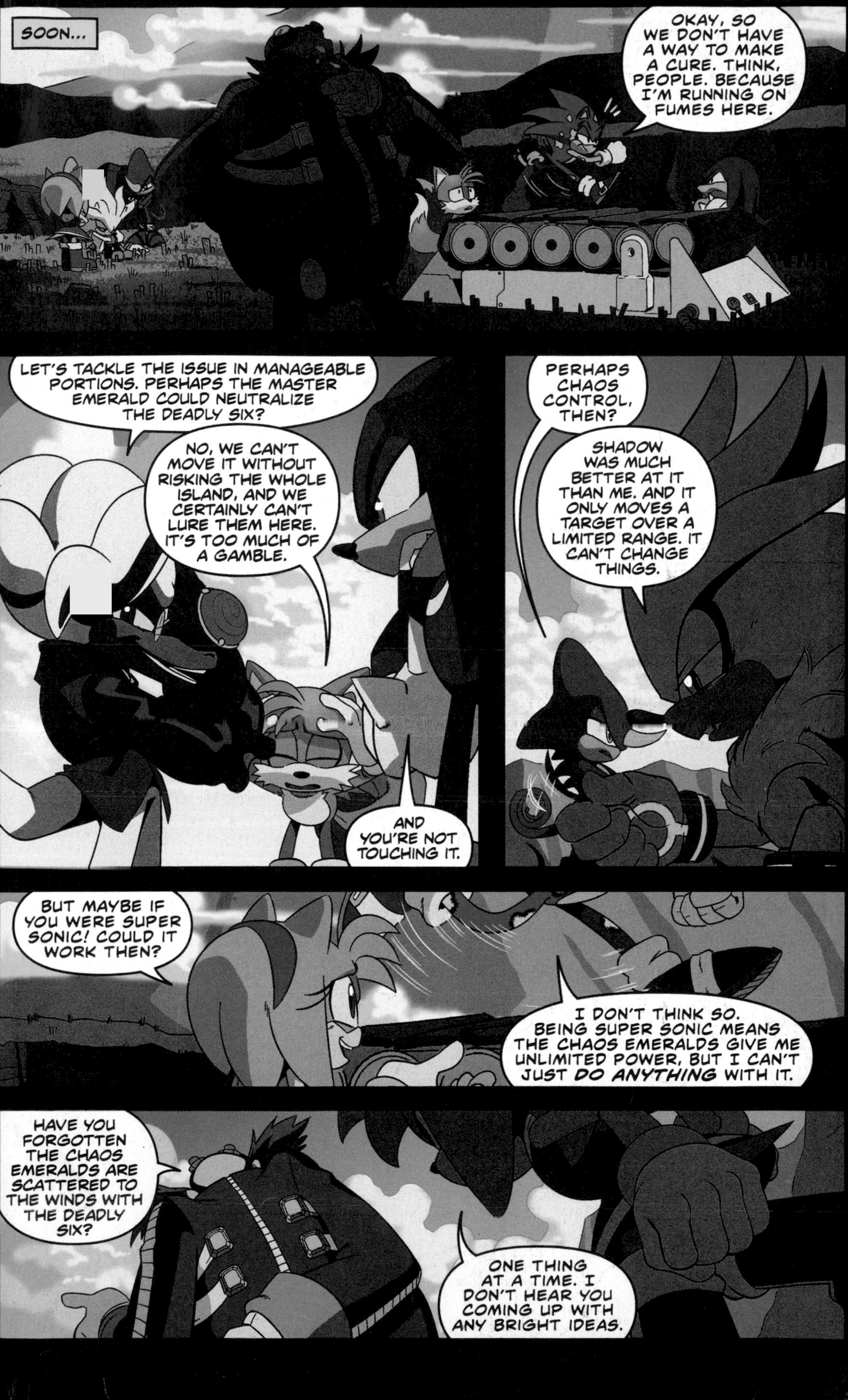
SOON...
OKAY, SO WE DON'T HAVE A WAY TO MAKE A CURE. THINK, PEOPLE. BECAUSE I'M RUNNING ON FUMES HERE.
LET'S TACKLE THE ISSUE IN MANAGEABLE PORTIONS. PERHAPS THE MASTER EMERALD COULD NEUTRALIZE THE DEADLY SIX?
NO, WE CAN'T MOVE IT WITHOUT RISKING THE WHOLE ISLAND, AND WE CERTAINLY CAN'T LURE THEM HERE. IT'S TOO MUCH OF A GAMBLE.
AND YOU'RE NOT TOUCHING IT.
PERHAPS CHAOS CONTROL, THEN?
SHADOW WAS MUCH BETTER AT IT THAN ME. AND IT ONLY MOVES A TARGET OVER A LIMITED RANGE. IT CAN'T CHANGE THINGS.
BUT MAYBE IF YOU WERE SUPER SONIC! COULD IT WORK THEN?
I DON'T THINK SO. BEING SUPER SONIC MEANS THE CHAOS EMERALDS GIVE ME UNLIMITED POWER, BUT I CAN'T JUST *DO ANYTHING* WITH IT.
HAVE YOU FORGOTTEN THE CHAOS EMERALDS ARE SCATTERED TO THE WINDS WITH THE DEADLY SIX?
ONE THING AT A TIME. I DON'T HEAR YOU COMING UP WITH ANY BRIGHT IDEAS.

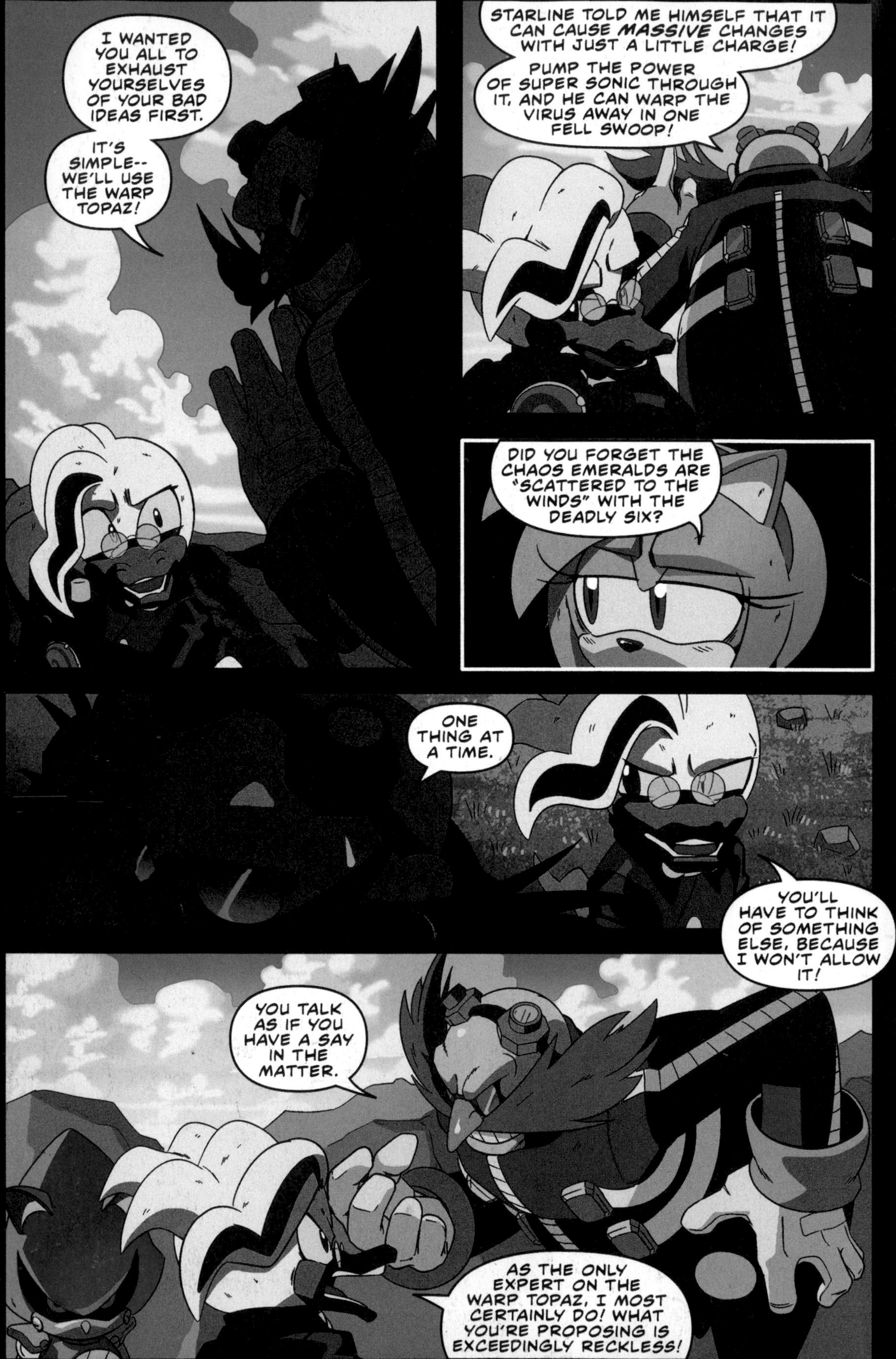
I WANTED YOU ALL TO EXHAUST YOURSELVES OF YOUR BAD IDEAS FIRST.
IT'S SIMPLE-- WE'LL USE THE WARP TOPAZ!
STARLINE TOLD ME HIMSELF THAT IT CAN CAUSE MASSIVE CHANGES WITH JUST A LITTLE CHARGE!
PUMP THE POWER OF SUPER SONIC THROUGH IT, AND HE CAN WARP THE VIRUS AWAY IN ONE FELL SWOOP!
DID YOU FORGET THE CHAOS EMERALDS ARE "SCATTERED TO THE WINDS" WITH THE DEADLY SIX?
ONE THING AT A TIME.
YOU'LL HAVE TO THINK OF SOMETHING ELSE, BECAUSE I WON'T ALLOW IT!
YOU TALK AS IF YOU HAVE A SAY IN THE MATTER.
AS THE ONLY EXPERT ON THE WARP TOPAZ, I MOST CERTAINLY DO! WHAT YOU'RE PROPOSING IS EXCEEDINGLY RECKLESS!

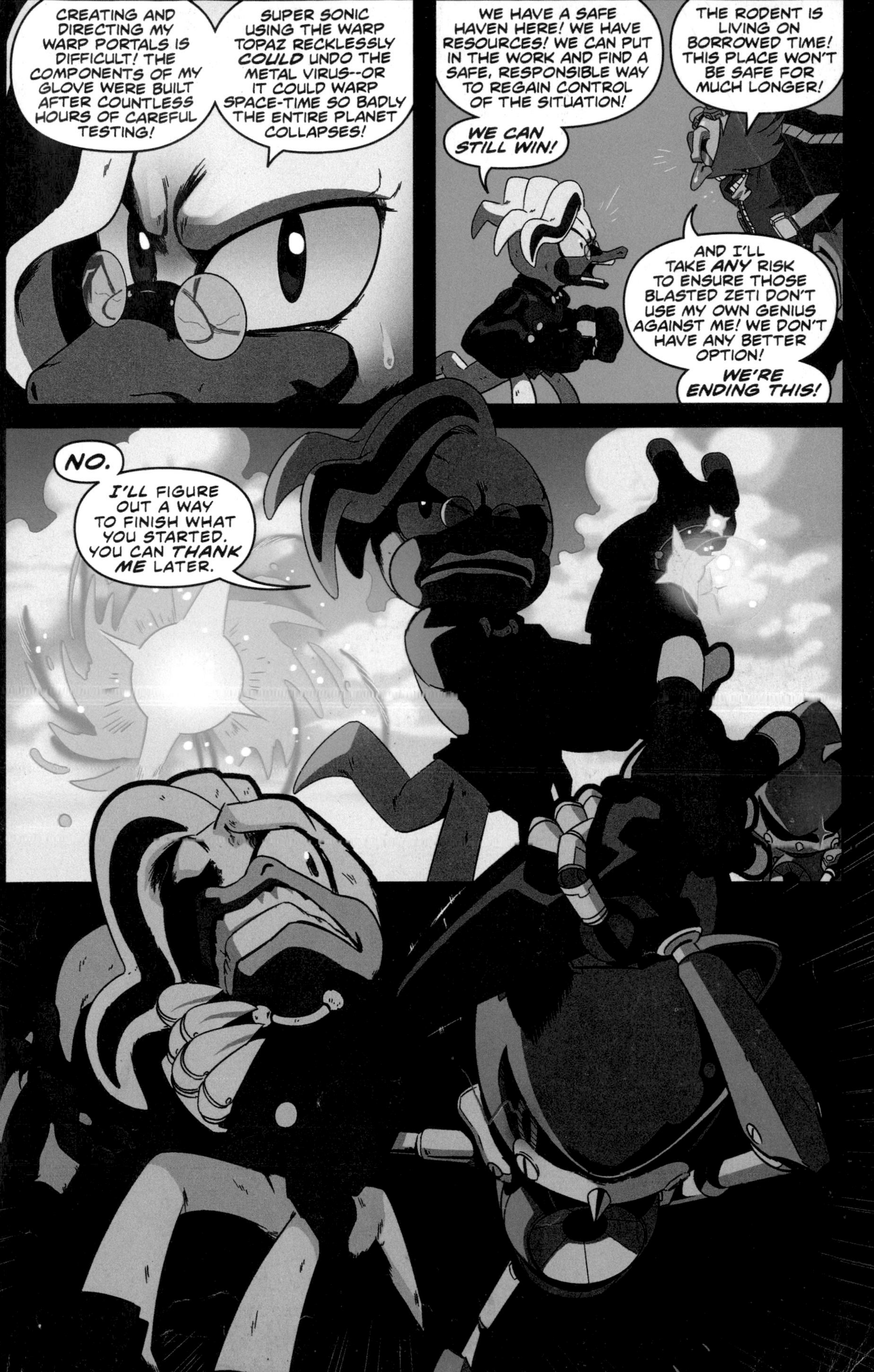

CREATING AND DIRECTING MY WARP PORTALS IS DIFFICULT! THE COMPONENTS OF MY GLOVE WERE BUILT AFTER COUNTLESS HOURS OF CAREFUL TESTING!
SUPER SONIC USING THE WARP TOPAZ RECKLESSLY COULD UNDO THE METAL VIRUS--OR IT COULD WARP SPACE-TIME SO BADLY THE ENTIRE PLANET COLLAPSES!
WE HAVE A SAFE HAVEN HERE! WE HAVE RESOURCES! WE CAN PUT IN THE WORK AND FIND A SAFE, RESPONSIBLE WAY TO REGAIN CONTROL OF THE SITUATION!
WE CAN STILL WIN!
THE RODENT IS LIVING ON BORROWED TIME! THIS PLACE WON'T BE SAFE FOR MUCH LONGER!
AND I'LL TAKE ANY RISK TO ENSURE THOSE BLASTED ZETI DON'T USE MY OWN GENIUS AGAINST ME! WE DON'T HAVE ANY BETTER OPTION!
WE'RE ENDING THIS!
NO.
I'LL FIGURE OUT A WAY TO FINISH WHAT YOU STARTED. YOU CAN THANK ME LATER.

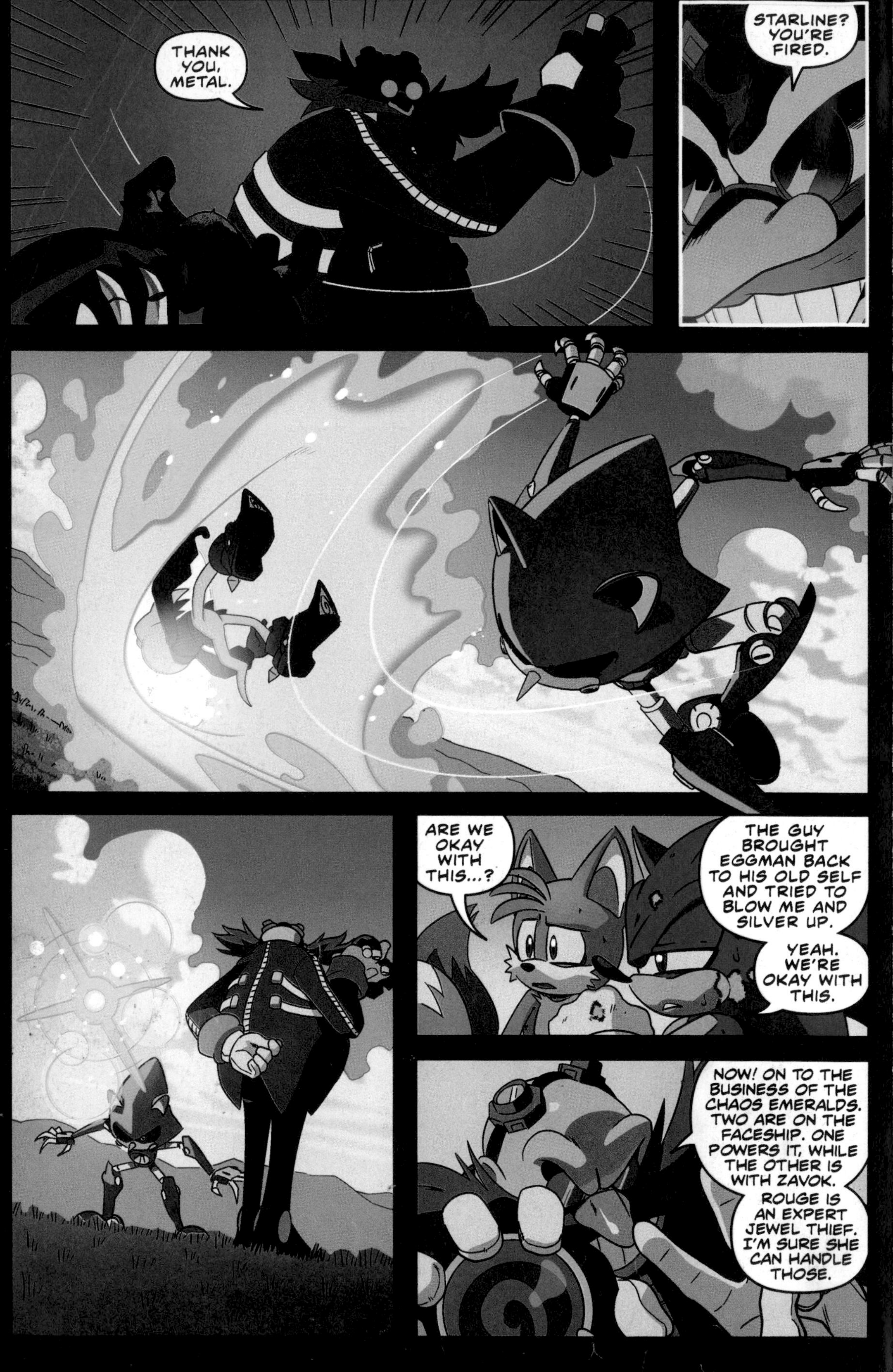
THANK YOU, METAL.
STARLINE? YOU'RE FIRED.
ARE WE OKAY WITH THIS...?
THE GUY BROUGHT EGGMAN BACK TO HIS OLD SELF AND TRIED TO BLOW ME AND SILVER UP.
YEAH. WE'RE OKAY WITH THIS.
NOW! ON TO THE BUSINESS OF THE CHAOS EMERALDS. TWO ARE ON THE FACESHIP. ONE POWERS IT, WHILE THE OTHER IS WITH ZAVOK.
ROUGE IS AN EXPERT JEWEL THIEF. I'M SURE SHE CAN HANDLE THOSE.

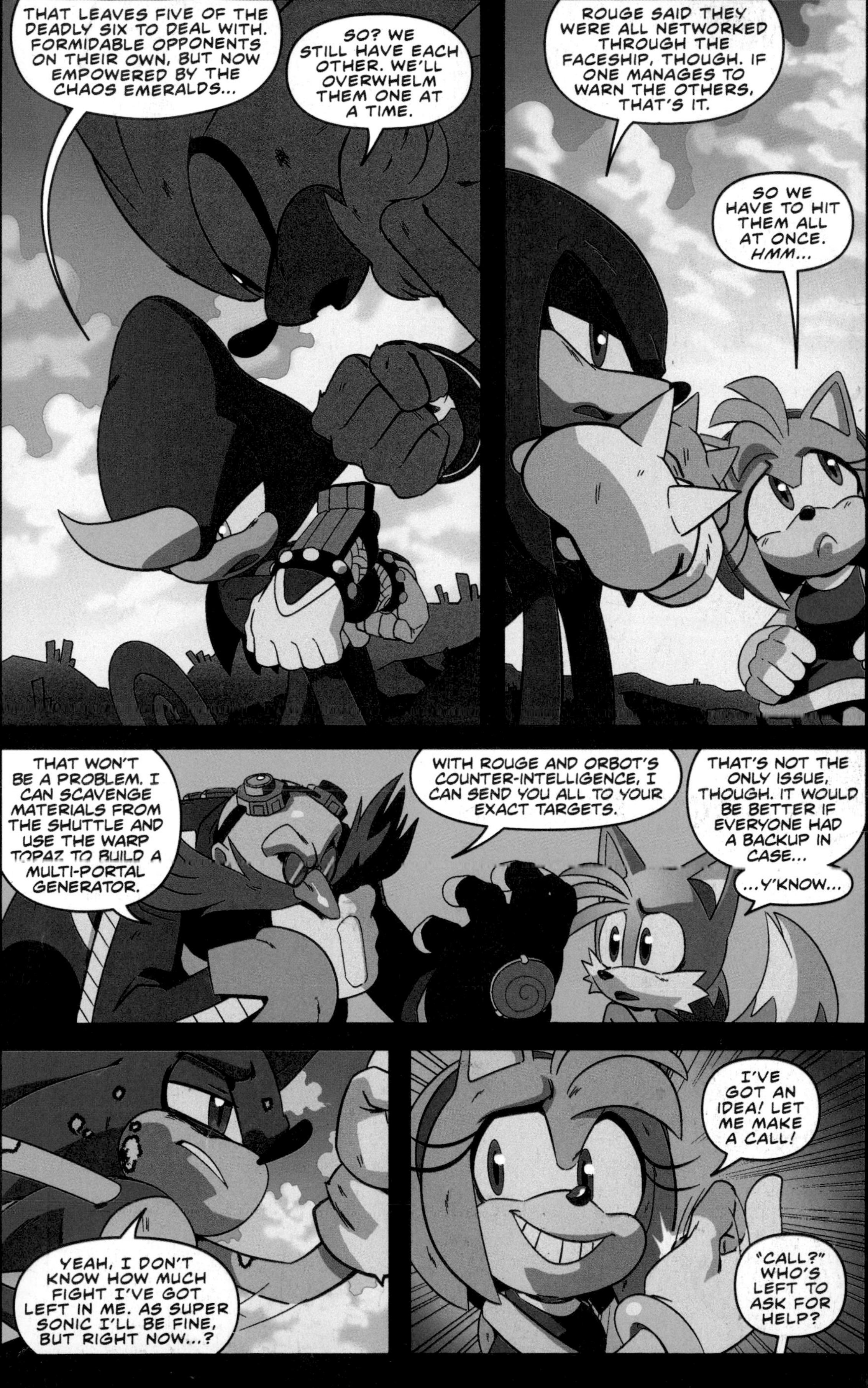
THAT LEAVES FIVE OF THE DEADLY SIX TO DEAL WITH. FORMIDABLE OPPONENTS ON THEIR OWN, BUT NOW EMPOWERED BY THE CHAOS EMERALDS...
SO? WE STILL HAVE EACH OTHER. WE'LL OVERWHELM THEM ONE AT A TIME.
ROUGE SAID THEY WERE ALL NETWORKED THROUGH THE FACESHIP, THOUGH. IF ONE MANAGES TO WARN THE OTHERS, THAT'S IT.
SO WE HAVE TO HIT THEM ALL AT ONCE. *HMM...*
THAT WON'T BE A PROBLEM. I CAN SCAVENGE MATERIALS FROM THE SHUTTLE AND USE THE WARP TOPAZ TO BUILD A MULTI-PORTAL GENERATOR.
WITH ROUGE AND ORBOT'S COUNTER-INTELLIGENCE, I CAN SEND YOU ALL TO YOUR EXACT TARGETS.
THAT'S NOT THE ONLY ISSUE, THOUGH. IT WOULD BE BETTER IF EVERYONE HAD A BACKUP IN CASE...
...Y'KNOW...
YEAH, I DON'T KNOW HOW MUCH FIGHT I'VE GOT LEFT IN ME. AS SUPER SONIC I'LL BE FINE, BUT RIGHT NOW...?
I'VE GOT AN IDEA! LET ME MAKE A CALL!
"CALL?" WHO'S LEFT TO ASK FOR HELP?

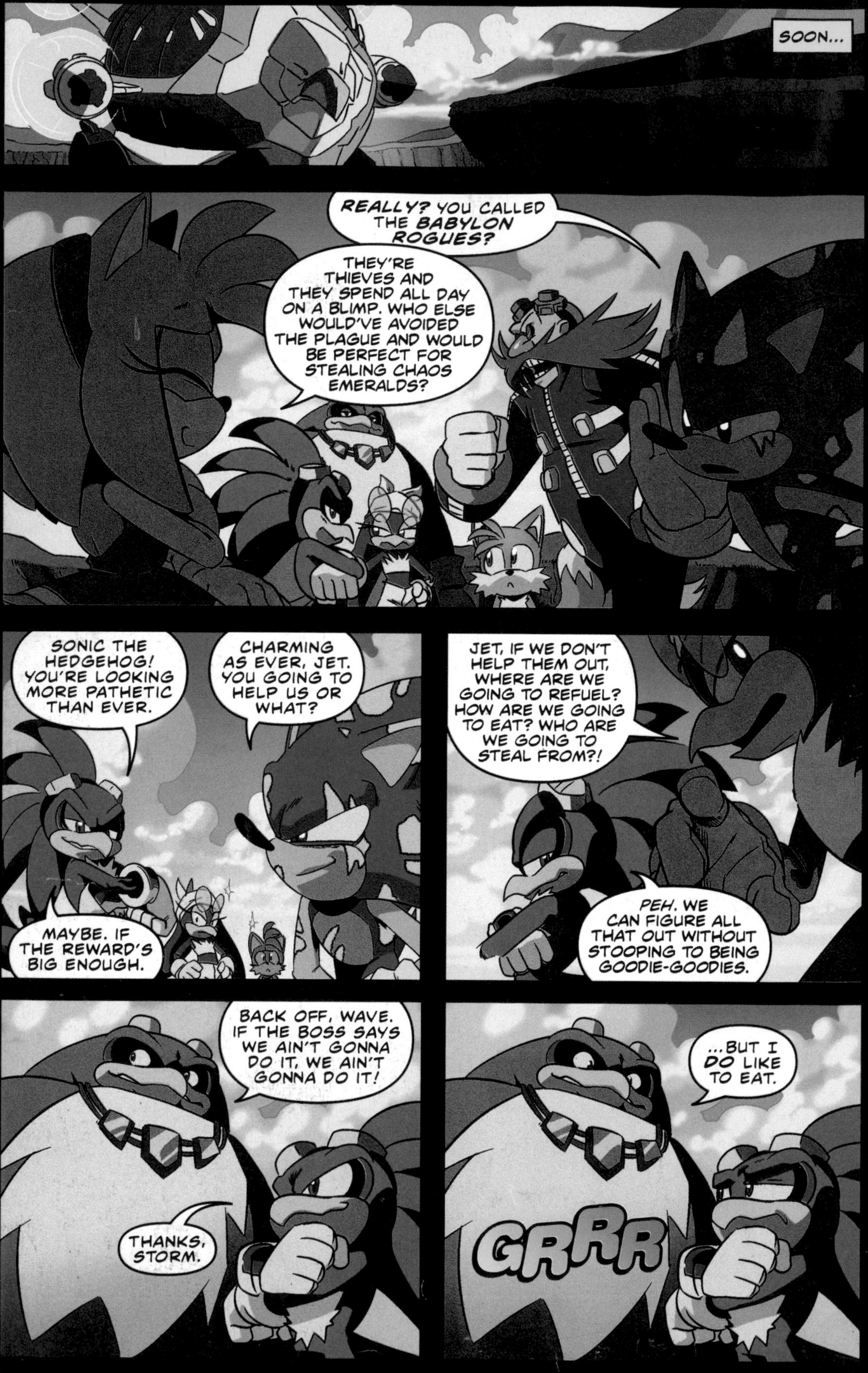
SOON...
REALLY? YOU CALLED THE BABYLON ROGUES?
THEY'RE THIEVES AND THEY SPEND ALL DAY ON A BLIMP. WHO ELSE WOULD'VE AVOIDED THE PLAGUE AND WOULD BE PERFECT FOR STEALING CHAOS EMERALDS?
SONIC THE HEDGEHOG! YOU'RE LOOKING MORE PATHETIC THAN EVER.
CHARMING AS EVER, JET. YOU GOING TO HELP US OR WHAT?
MAYBE. IF THE REWARD'S BIG ENOUGH.
JET, IF WE DON'T HELP THEM OUT, WHERE ARE WE GOING TO REFUEL? HOW ARE WE GOING TO EAT? WHO ARE WE GOING TO STEAL FROM?!
PEH. WE CAN FIGURE ALL THAT OUT WITHOUT STOOPING TO BEING GOODIE-GOODIES.
BACK OFF, WAVE. IF THE BOSS SAYS WE AIN'T GONNA DO IT, WE AIN'T GONNA DO IT!
THANKS, STORM.
...BUT I DO LIKE TO EAT.
GRRR

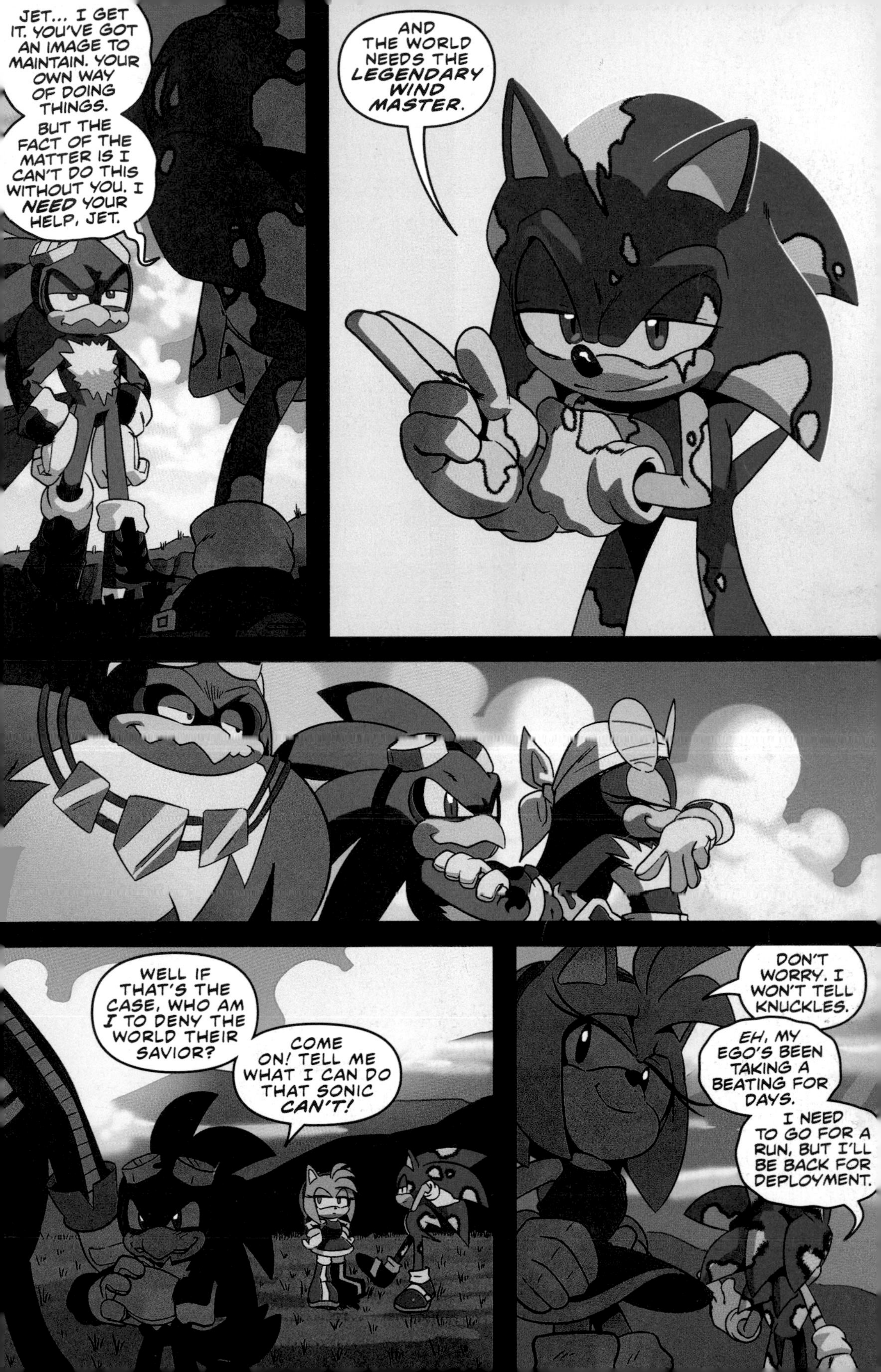

JET... I GET IT. YOU'VE GOT AN IMAGE TO MAINTAIN. YOUR OWN WAY OF DOING THINGS.
BUT THE FACT OF THE MATTER IS I CAN'T DO THIS WITHOUT YOU. I *NEED* YOUR HELP, JET.
AND THE WORLD NEEDS THE *LEGENDARY WIND MASTER*.
WELL IF THAT'S THE CASE, WHO AM *I* TO DENY THE WORLD THEIR SAVIOR?
COME ON! TELL ME WHAT I CAN DO THAT SONIC *CAN'T!*
DON'T WORRY. I WON'T TELL KNUCKLES.
EH, MY EGO'S BEEN TAKING A BEATING FOR DAYS.
I NEED TO GO FOR A RUN, BUT I'LL BE BACK FOR DEPLOYMENT.

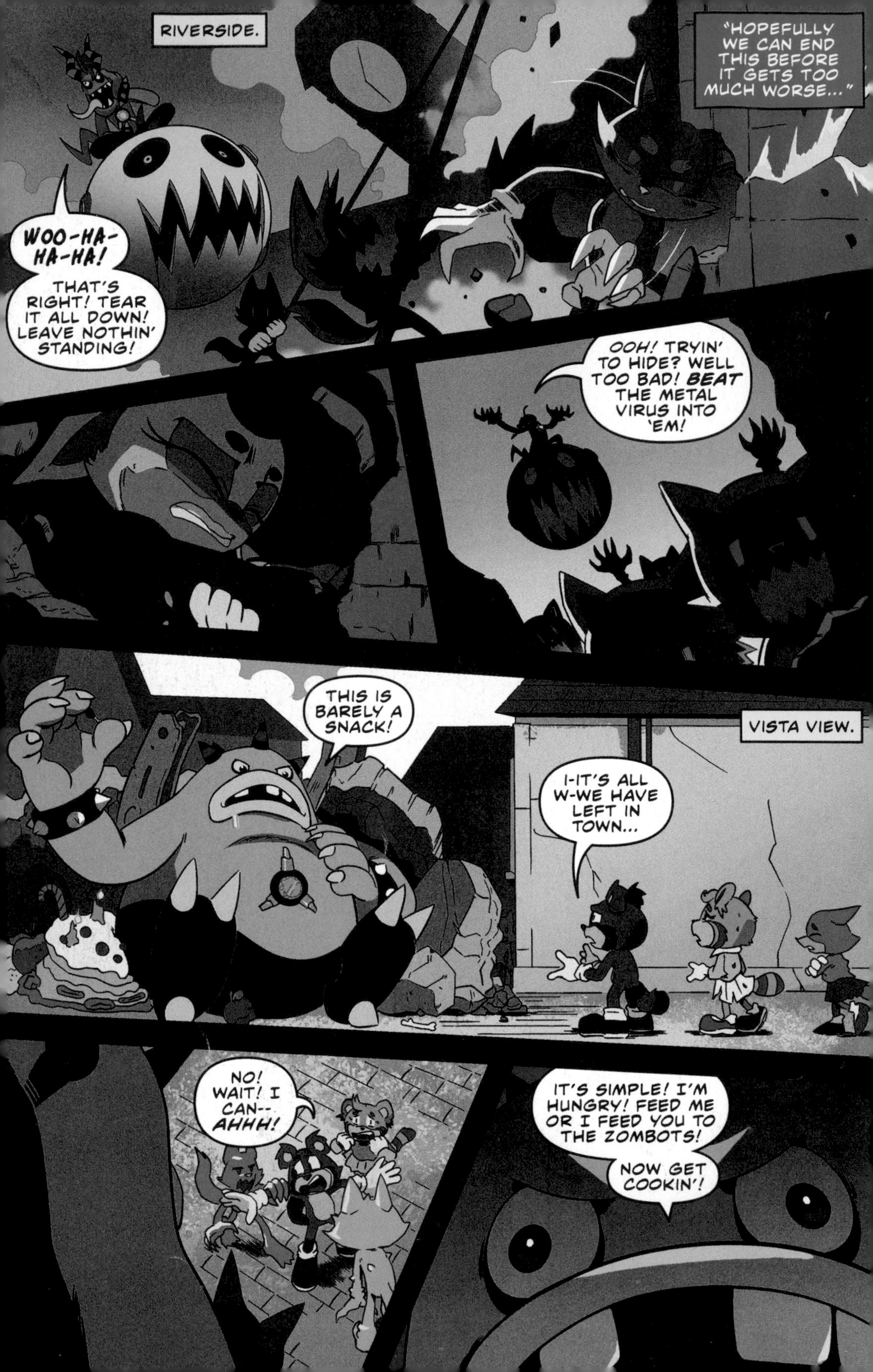
RIVERSIDE.
"HOPEFULLY WE CAN END THIS BEFORE IT GETS TOO MUCH WORSE..."
WOO-HA-HA-HA! THAT'S RIGHT! TEAR IT ALL DOWN! LEAVE NOTHIN' STANDING!
OOH! TRYIN' TO HIDE? WELL TOO BAD! BEAT THE METAL VIRUS INTO 'EM!
THIS IS BARELY A SNACK!
VISTA VIEW.
I-IT'S ALL W-WE HAVE LEFT IN TOWN...
NO! WAIT! I CAN-- AHHH!
IT'S SIMPLE! I'M HUNGRY! FEED ME OR I FEED YOU TO THE ZOMBOTS!
NOW GET COOKIN'!

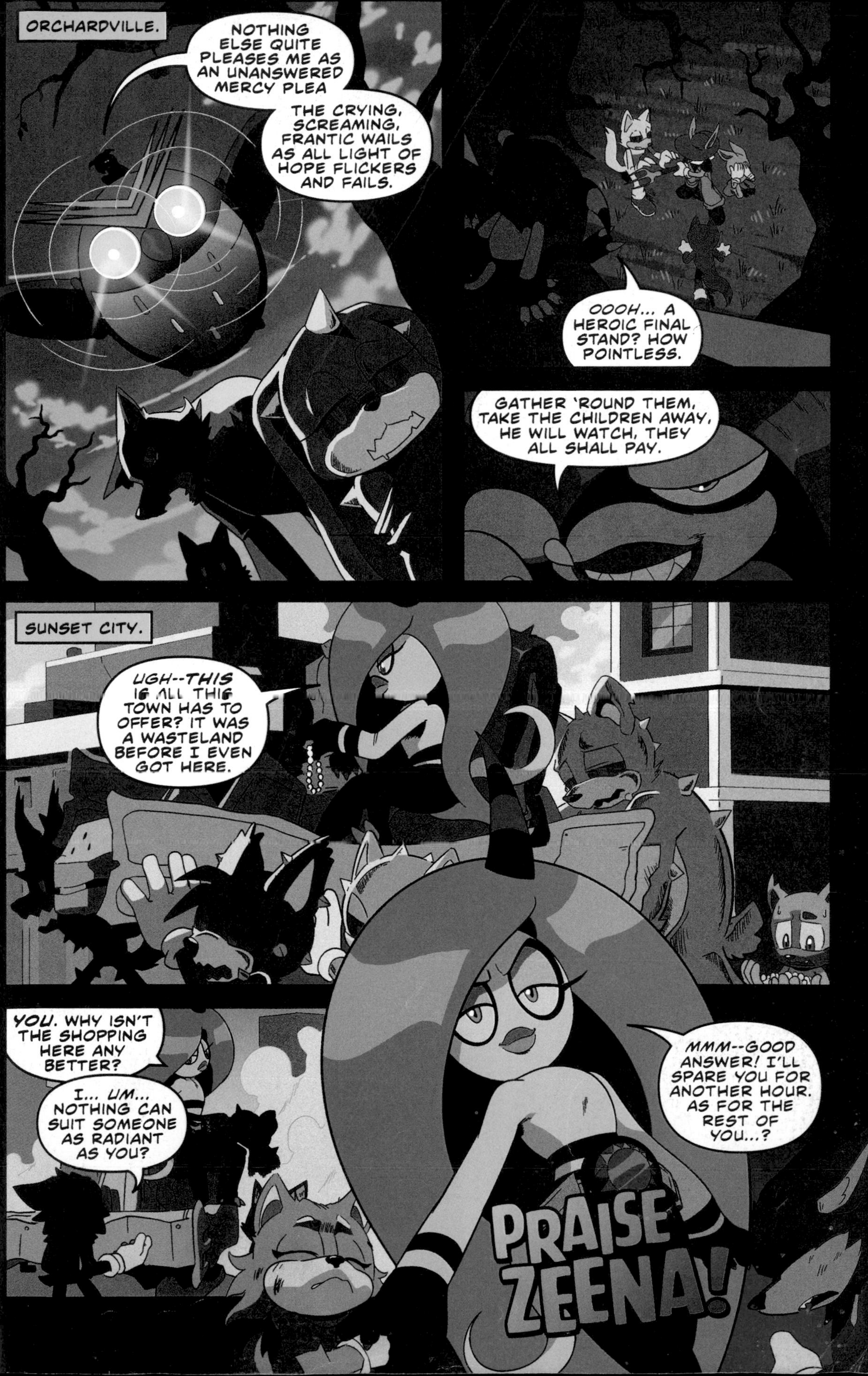
ORCHARDVILLE.
NOTHING ELSE QUITE PLEASES ME AS AN UNANSWERED MERCY PLEA
THE CRYING, SCREAMING, FRANTIC WAILS AS ALL LIGHT OF HOPE FLICKERS AND FAILS.
OOOH... A HEROIC FINAL STAND? HOW POINTLESS.
GATHER 'ROUND THEM, TAKE THE CHILDREN AWAY, HE WILL WATCH, THEY ALL SHALL PAY.
SUNSET CITY.
UGH--THIS IS ALL THIS TOWN HAS TO OFFER? IT WAS A WASTELAND BEFORE I EVEN GOT HERE.
YOU. WHY ISN'T THE SHOPPING HERE ANY BETTER?
I... UM... NOTHING CAN SUIT SOMEONE AS RADIANT AS YOU?
MMM--GOOD ANSWER! I'LL SPARE YOU FOR ANOTHER HOUR. AS FOR THE REST OF YOU...?
PRAISE ZEENA!

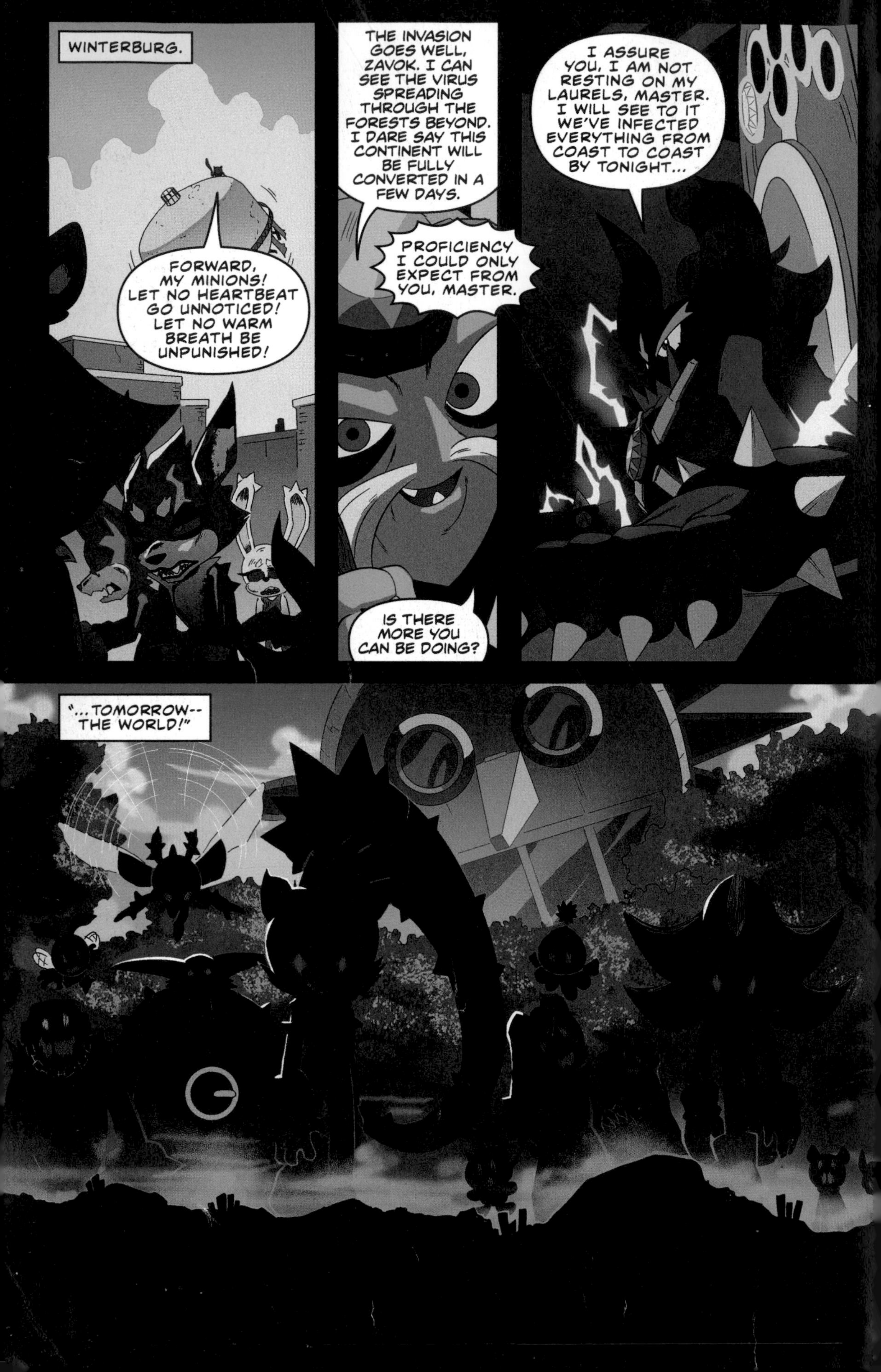
WINTERBURG.
FORWARD, MY MINIONS! LET NO HEARTBEAT GO UNNOTICED! LET NO WARM BREATH BE UNPUNISHED!
THE INVASION GOES WELL, ZAVOK. I CAN SEE THE VIRUS SPREADING THROUGH THE FORESTS BEYOND. I DARE SAY THIS CONTINENT WILL BE FULLY CONVERTED IN A FEW DAYS.
PROFICIENCY I COULD ONLY EXPECT FROM YOU, MASTER.
IS THERE MORE YOU CAN BE DOING?
I ASSURE YOU, I AM NOT RESTING ON MY LAURELS, MASTER. I WILL SEE TO IT WE'VE INFECTED EVERYTHING FROM COAST TO COAST BY TONIGHT...
"...TOMORROW--THE WORLD!"

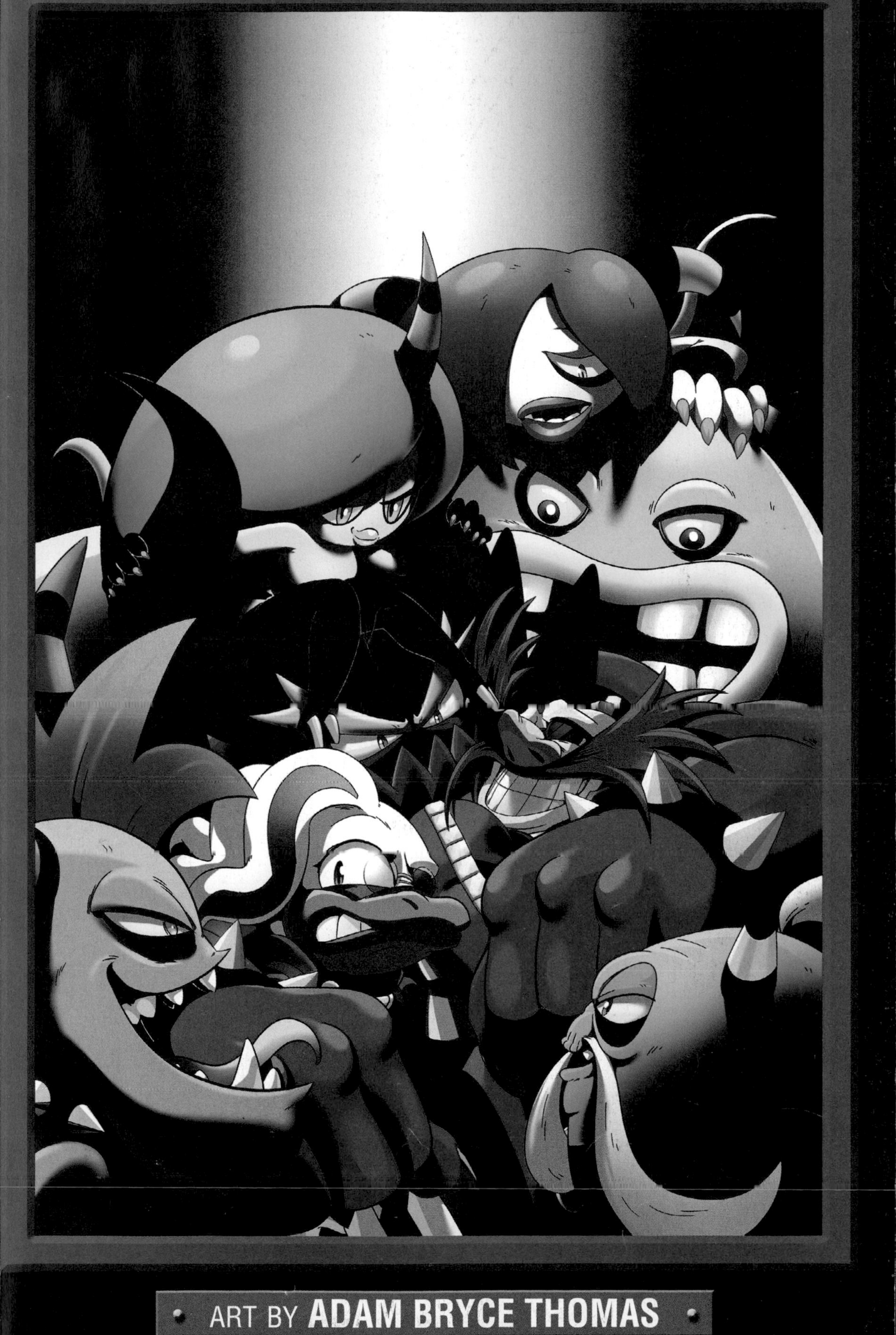

ART BY **ADAM BRYCE THOMAS**

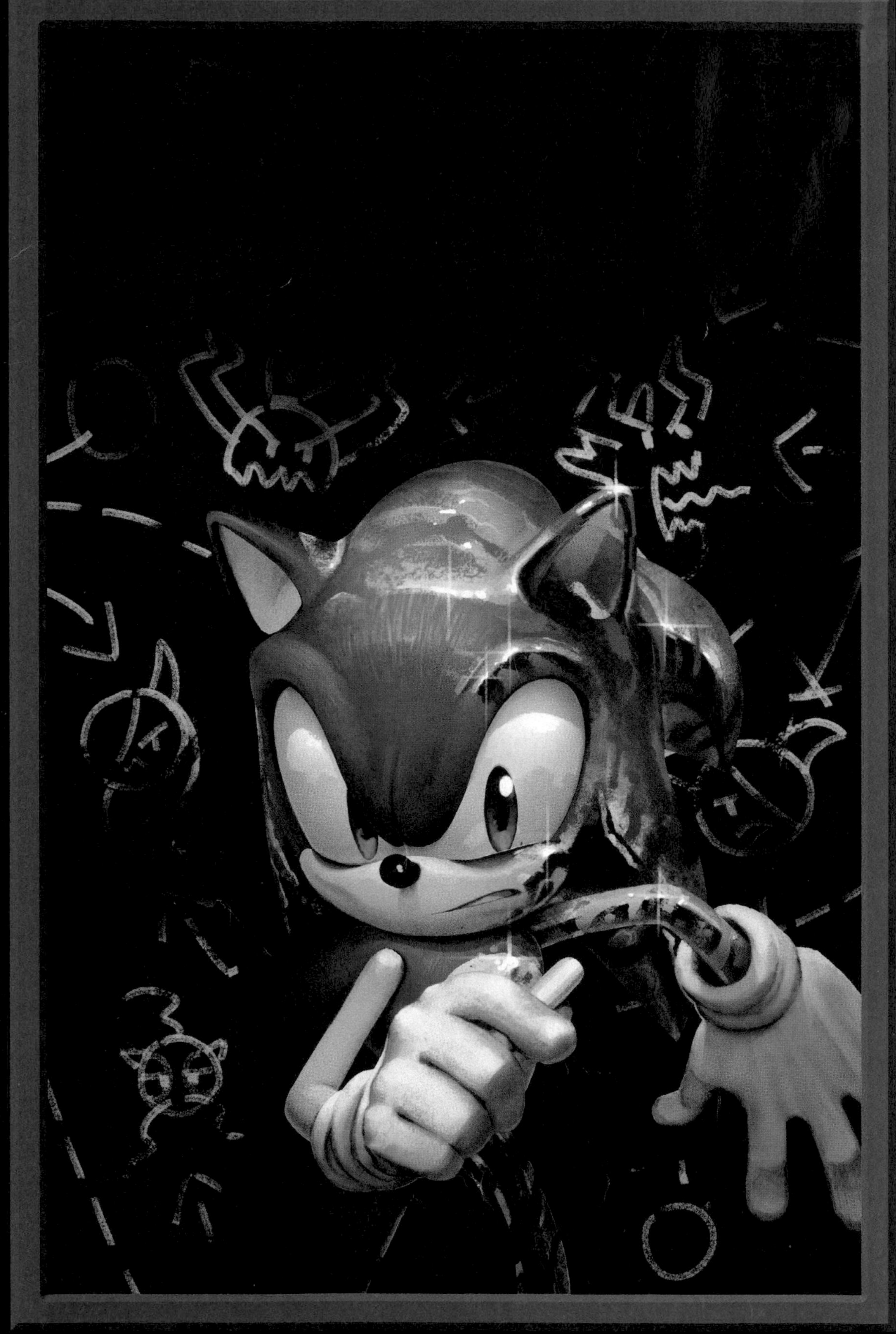

ART BY **EVAN STANLEY**

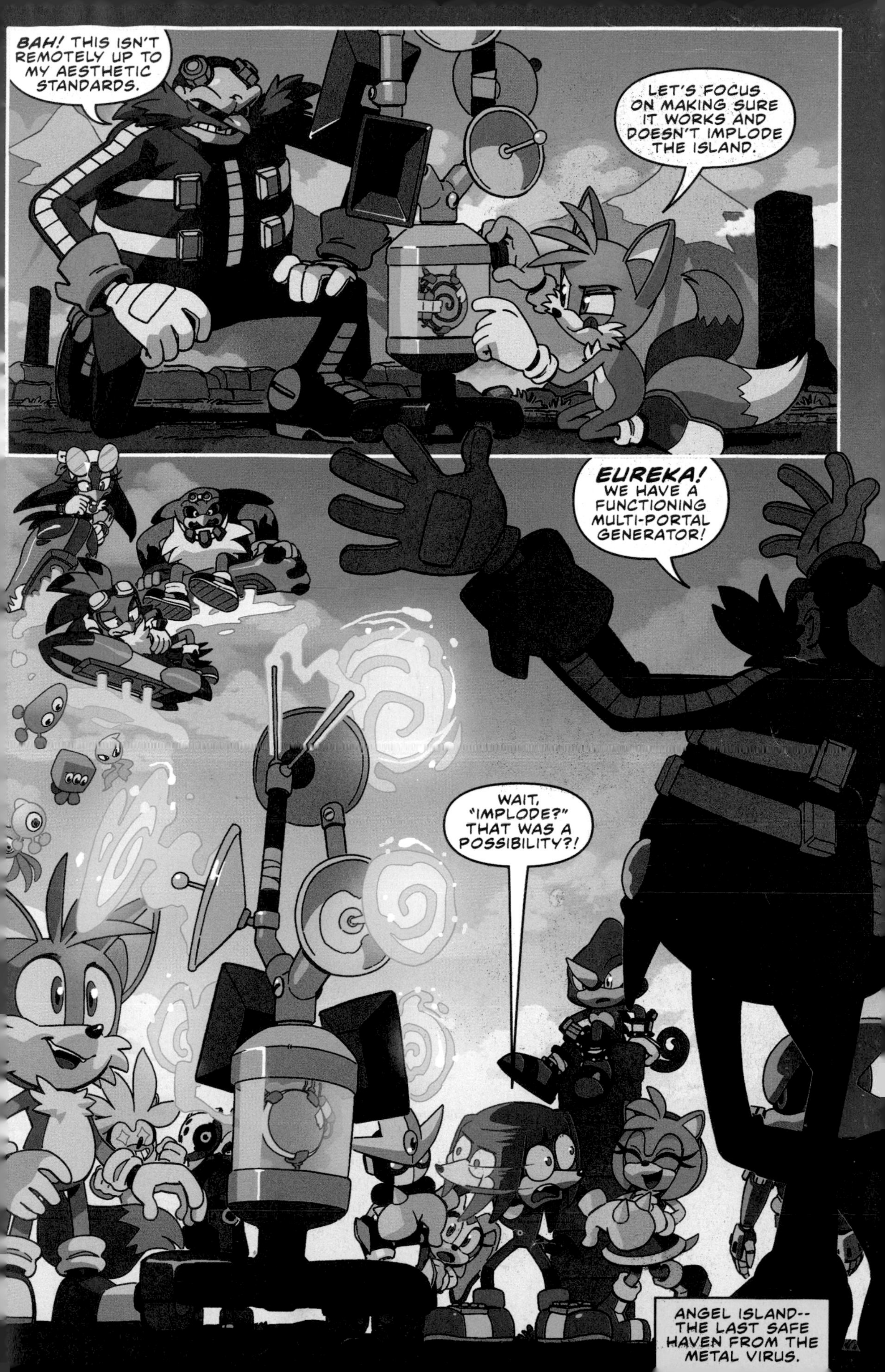

BAH! THIS ISN'T REMOTELY UP TO MY AESTHETIC STANDARDS.
LET'S FOCUS ON MAKING SURE IT WORKS AND DOESN'T IMPLODE THE ISLAND.
ANGEL ISLAND-- THE LAST SAFE HAVEN FROM THE METAL VIRUS.
EUREKA! WE HAVE A FUNCTIONING MULTI-PORTAL GENERATOR!
WAIT, "IMPLODE?" THAT WAS A POSSIBILITY?!

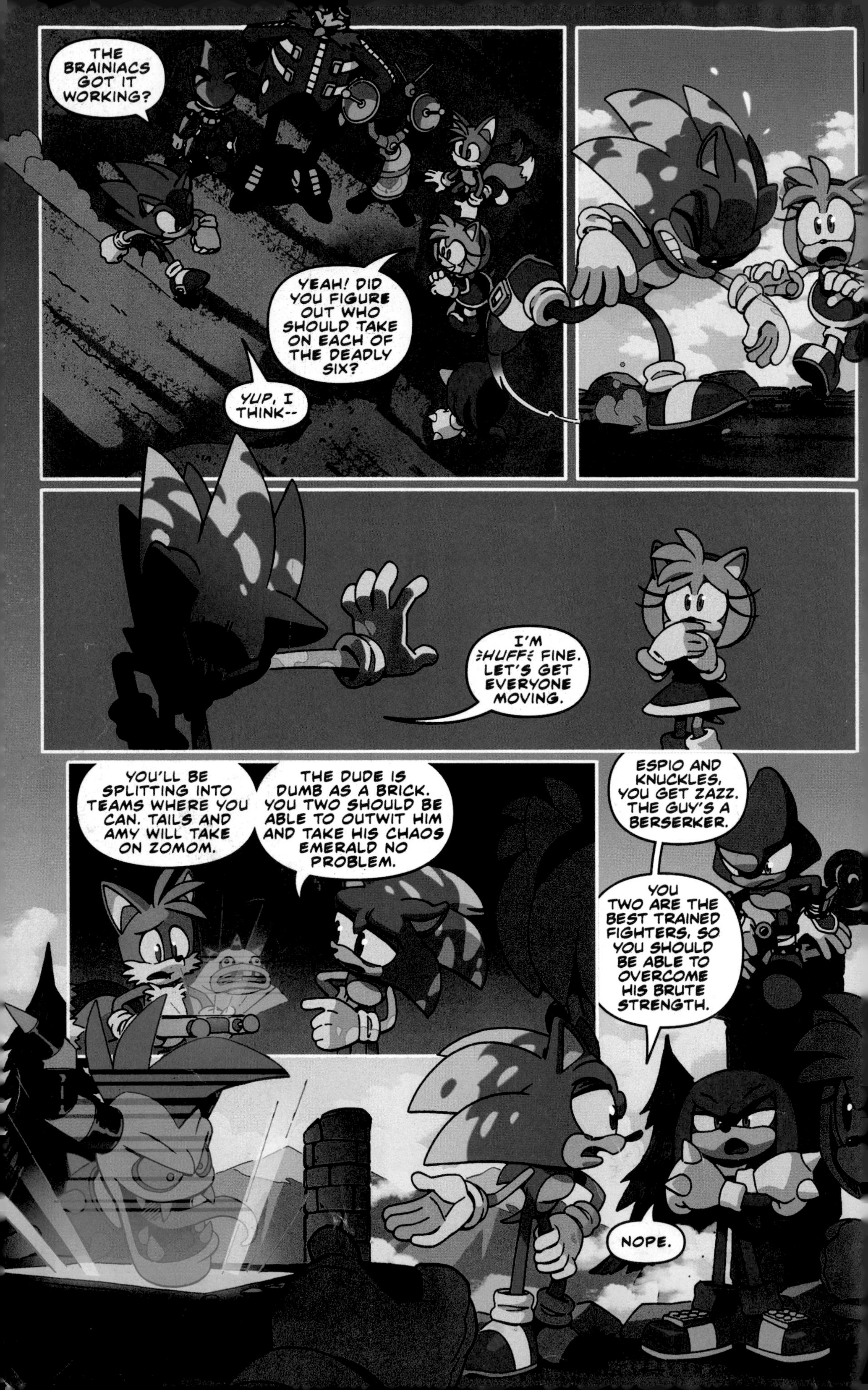

THE BRAINIACS GOT IT WORKING?
YEAH! DID YOU FIGURE OUT WHO SHOULD TAKE ON EACH OF THE DEADLY SIX?
YUP, I THINK--
I'M *HUFF* FINE. LET'S GET EVERYONE MOVING.
YOU'LL BE SPLITTING INTO TEAMS WHERE YOU CAN. TAILS AND AMY WILL TAKE ON ZOMOM.
THE DUDE IS DUMB AS A BRICK. YOU TWO SHOULD BE ABLE TO OUTWIT HIM AND TAKE HIS CHAOS EMERALD NO PROBLEM.
ESPIO AND KNUCKLES, YOU GET ZAZZ. THE GUY'S A BERSERKER.
YOU TWO ARE THE BEST TRAINED FIGHTERS, SO YOU SHOULD BE ABLE TO OVERCOME HIS BRUTE STRENGTH.
NOPE.

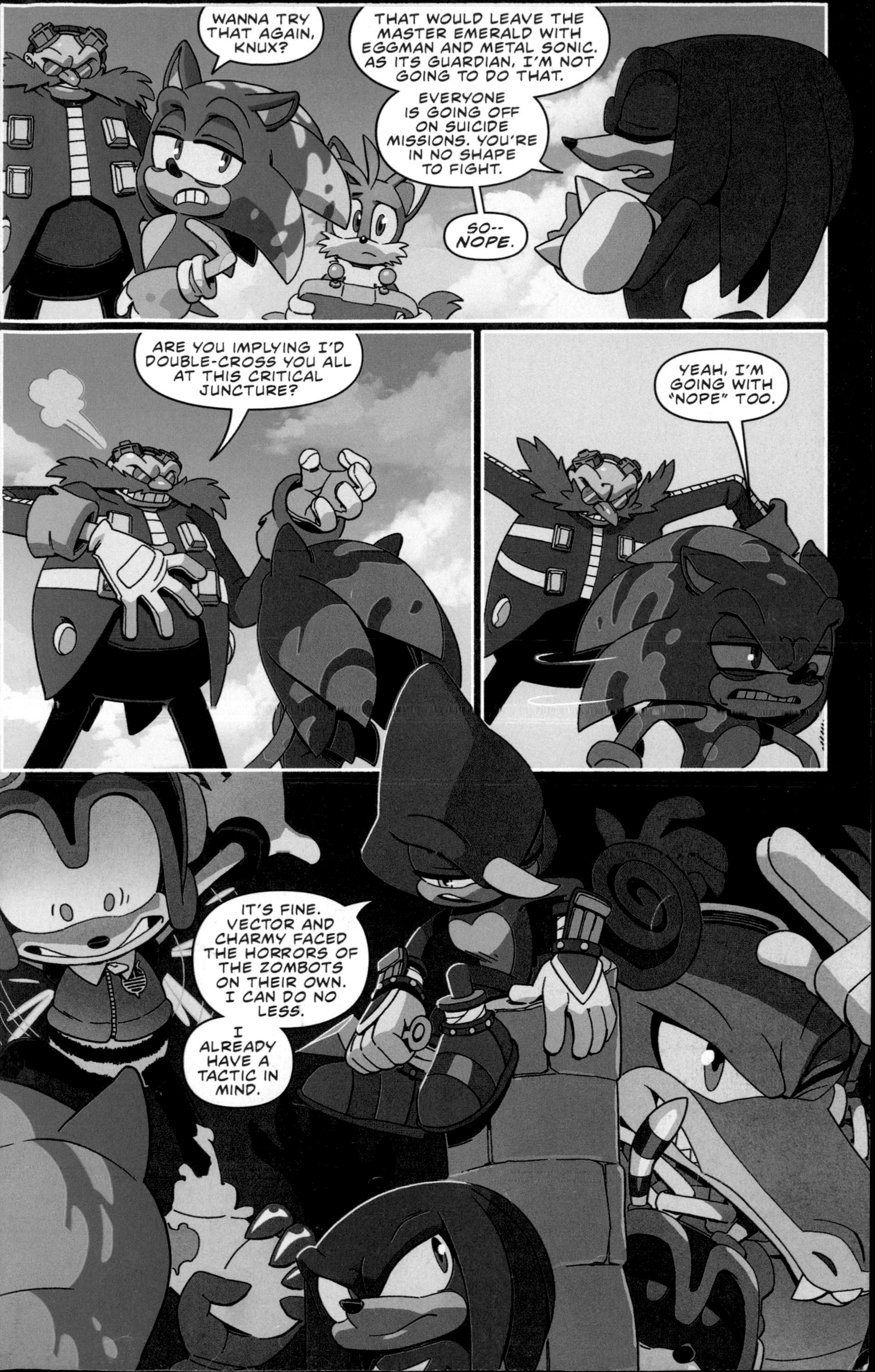
WANNA TRY THAT AGAIN, KNUX?
THAT WOULD LEAVE THE MASTER EMERALD WITH EGGMAN AND METAL SONIC. AS ITS GUARDIAN, I'M NOT GOING TO DO THAT.
EVERYONE IS GOING OFF ON SUICIDE MISSIONS. YOU'RE IN NO SHAPE TO FIGHT.
SO-- NOPE.
ARE YOU IMPLYING I'D DOUBLE-CROSS YOU ALL AT THIS CRITICAL JUNCTURE?
YEAH, I'M GOING WITH "NOPE" TOO.
IT'S FINE. VECTOR AND CHARMY FACED THE HORRORS OF THE ZOMBOTS ON THEIR OWN. I CAN DO NO LESS.
I ALREADY HAVE A TACTIC IN MIND.

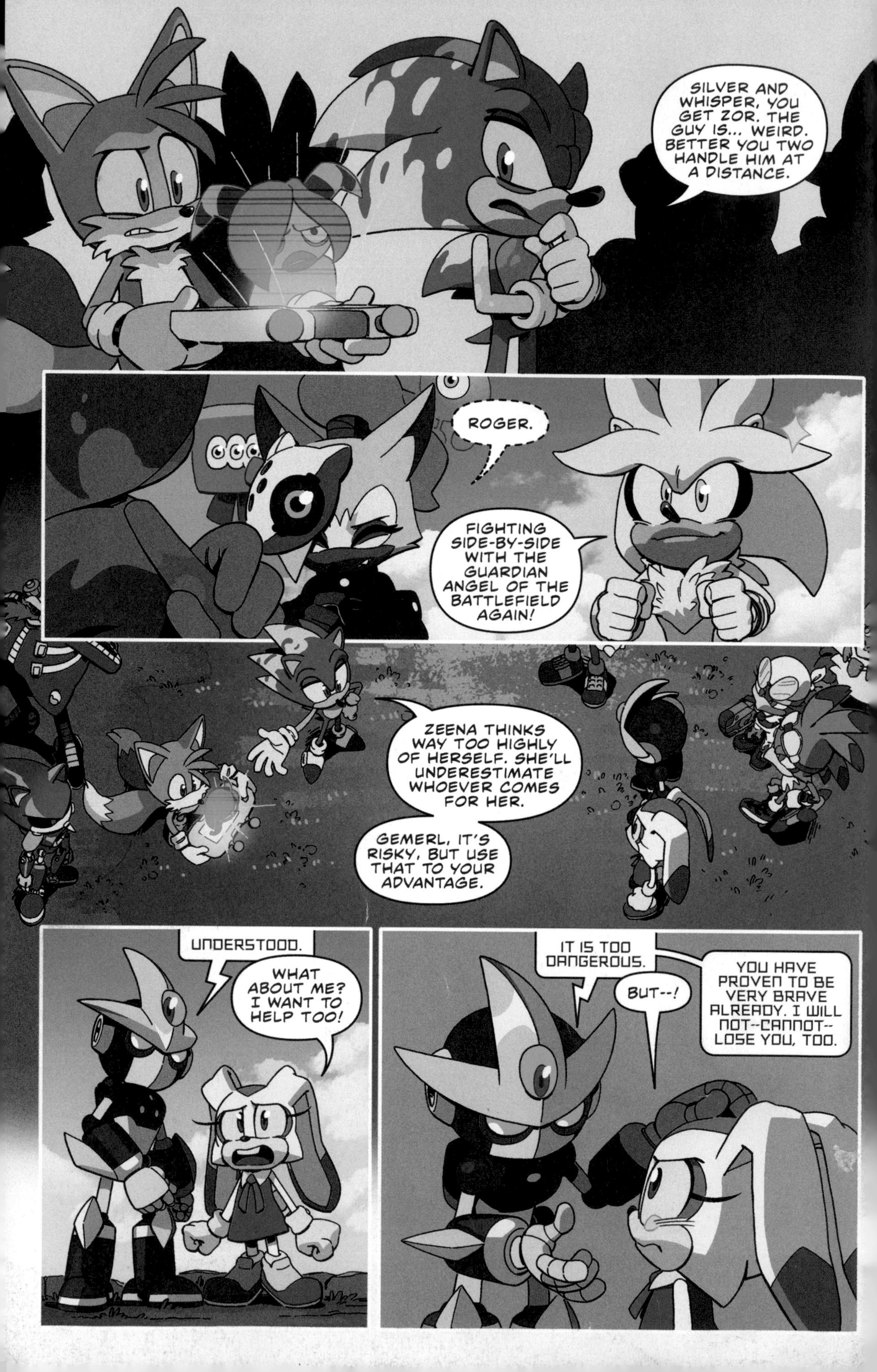
SILVER AND WHISPER, YOU GET ZOR. THE GUY IS... WEIRD. BETTER YOU TWO HANDLE HIM AT A DISTANCE.
ROGER.
FIGHTING SIDE-BY-SIDE WITH THE GUARDIAN ANGEL OF THE BATTLEFIELD AGAIN!
ZEENA THINKS WAY TOO HIGHLY OF HERSELF. SHE'LL UNDERESTIMATE WHOEVER COMES FOR HER.
GEMERL, IT'S RISKY, BUT USE THAT TO YOUR ADVANTAGE.
UNDERSTOOD.
WHAT ABOUT ME? I WANT TO HELP TOO!
IT IS TOO DANGEROUS.
BUT--!
YOU HAVE PROVEN TO BE VERY BRAVE ALREADY. I WILL NOT--CANNOT--LOSE YOU, TOO.

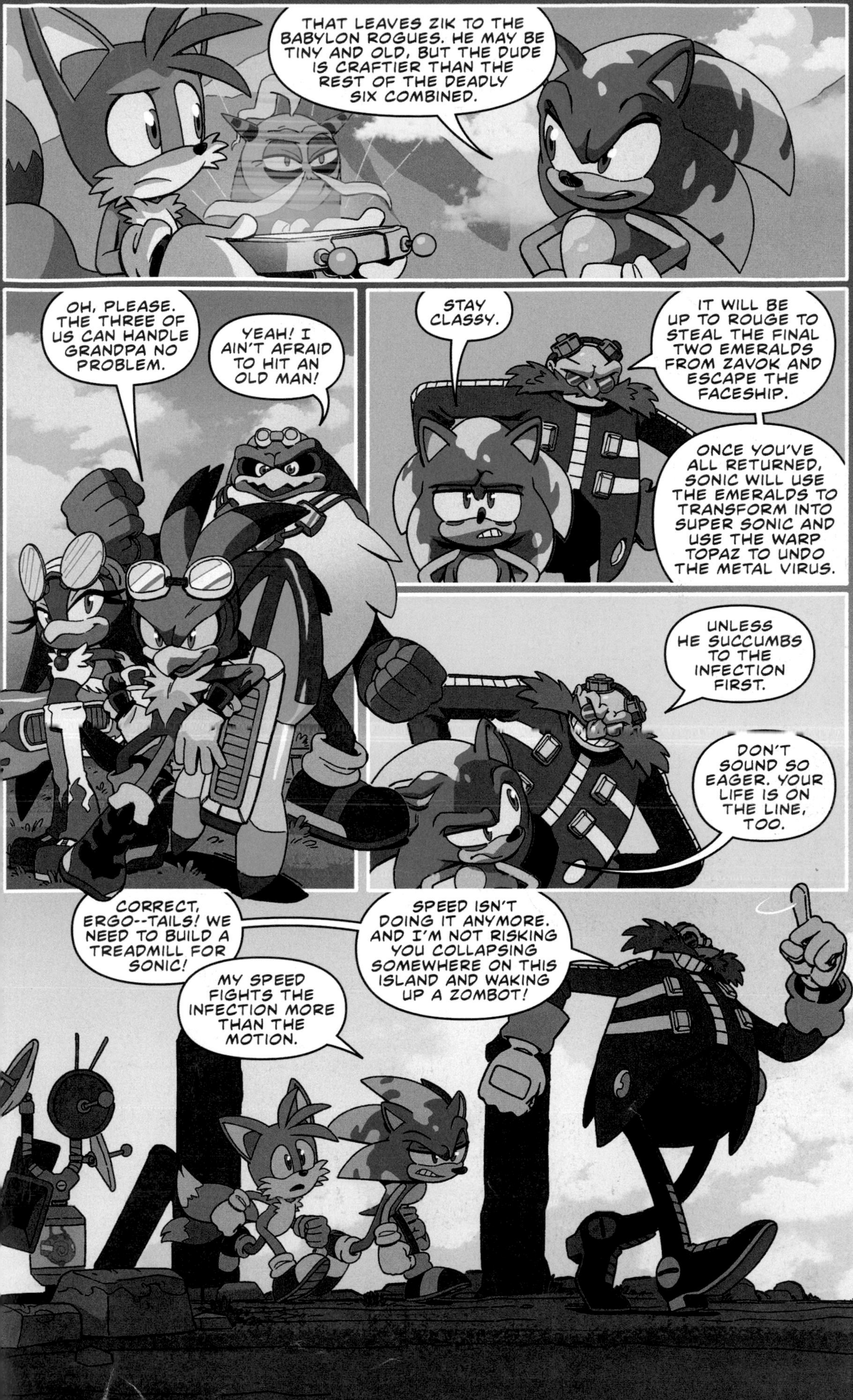
THAT LEAVES ZIK TO THE BABYLON ROGUES. HE MAY BE TINY AND OLD, BUT THE DUDE IS CRAFTIER THAN THE REST OF THE DEADLY SIX COMBINED.
OH, PLEASE. THE THREE OF US CAN HANDLE GRANDPA NO PROBLEM.
YEAH! I AIN'T AFRAID TO HIT AN OLD MAN!
STAY CLASSY.
IT WILL BE UP TO ROUGE TO STEAL THE FINAL TWO EMERALDS FROM ZAVOK AND ESCAPE THE FACESHIP.
ONCE YOU'VE ALL RETURNED, SONIC WILL USE THE EMERALDS TO TRANSFORM INTO SUPER SONIC AND USE THE WARP TOPAZ TO UNDO THE METAL VIRUS.
UNLESS HE SUCCUMBS TO THE INFECTION FIRST.
DON'T SOUND SO EAGER. YOUR LIFE IS ON THE LINE, TOO.
CORRECT, ERGO--TAILS! WE NEED TO BUILD A TREADMILL FOR SONIC!
MY SPEED FIGHTS THE INFECTION MORE THAN THE MOTION.
SPEED ISN'T DOING IT ANYMORE. AND I'M NOT RISKING YOU COLLAPSING SOMEWHERE ON THIS ISLAND AND WAKING UP A ZOMBOT!

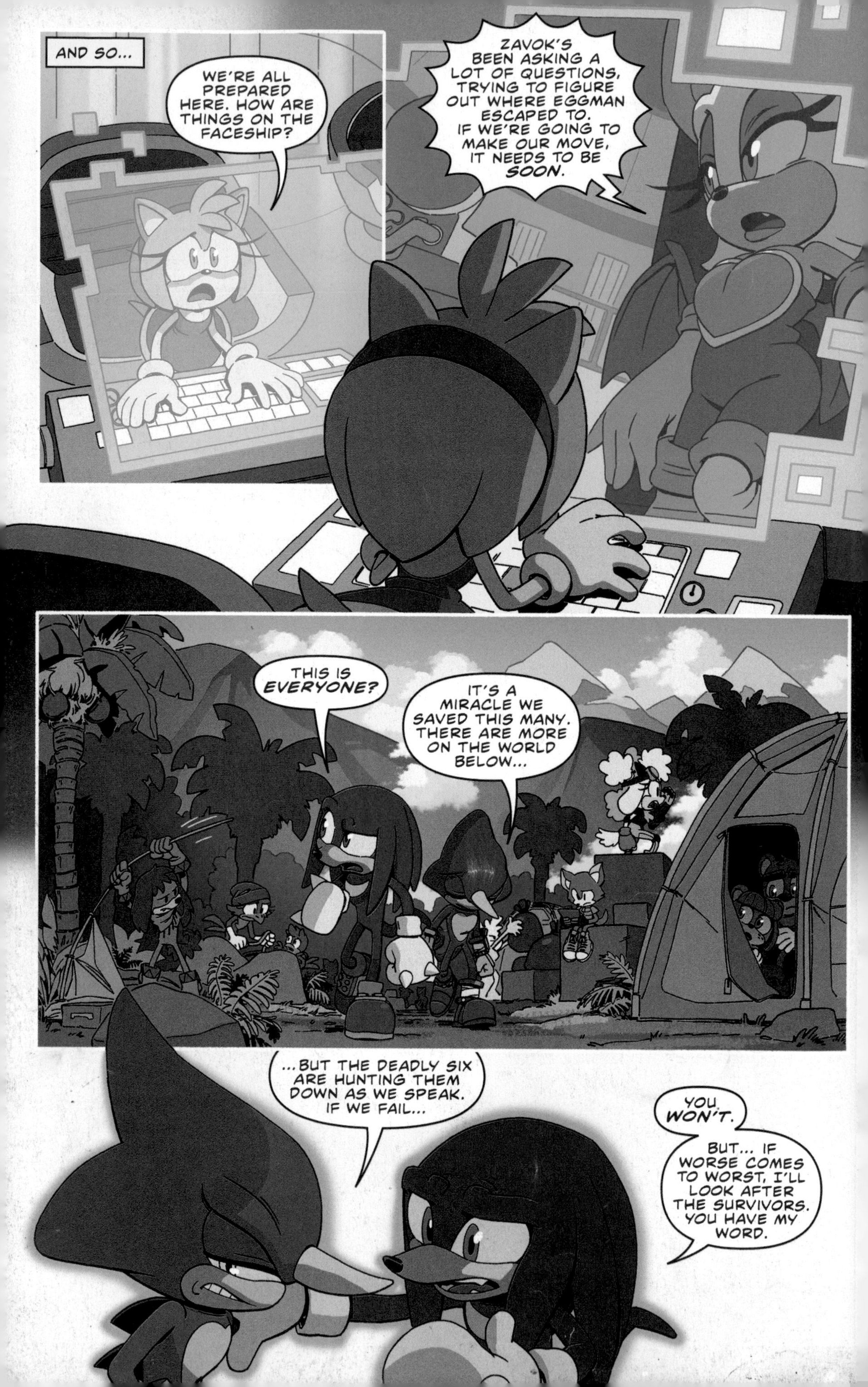
AND SO...
WE'RE ALL PREPARED HERE. HOW ARE THINGS ON THE FACESHIP?
ZAVOK'S BEEN ASKING A LOT OF QUESTIONS, TRYING TO FIGURE OUT WHERE EGGMAN ESCAPED TO. IF WE'RE GOING TO MAKE OUR MOVE, IT NEEDS TO BE SOON.
THIS IS EVERYONE?
IT'S A MIRACLE WE SAVED THIS MANY. THERE ARE MORE ON THE WORLD BELOW...
...BUT THE DEADLY SIX ARE HUNTING THEM DOWN AS WE SPEAK. IF WE FAIL...
YOU WON'T.
BUT... IF WORSE COMES TO WORST, I'LL LOOK AFTER THE SURVIVORS. YOU HAVE MY WORD.

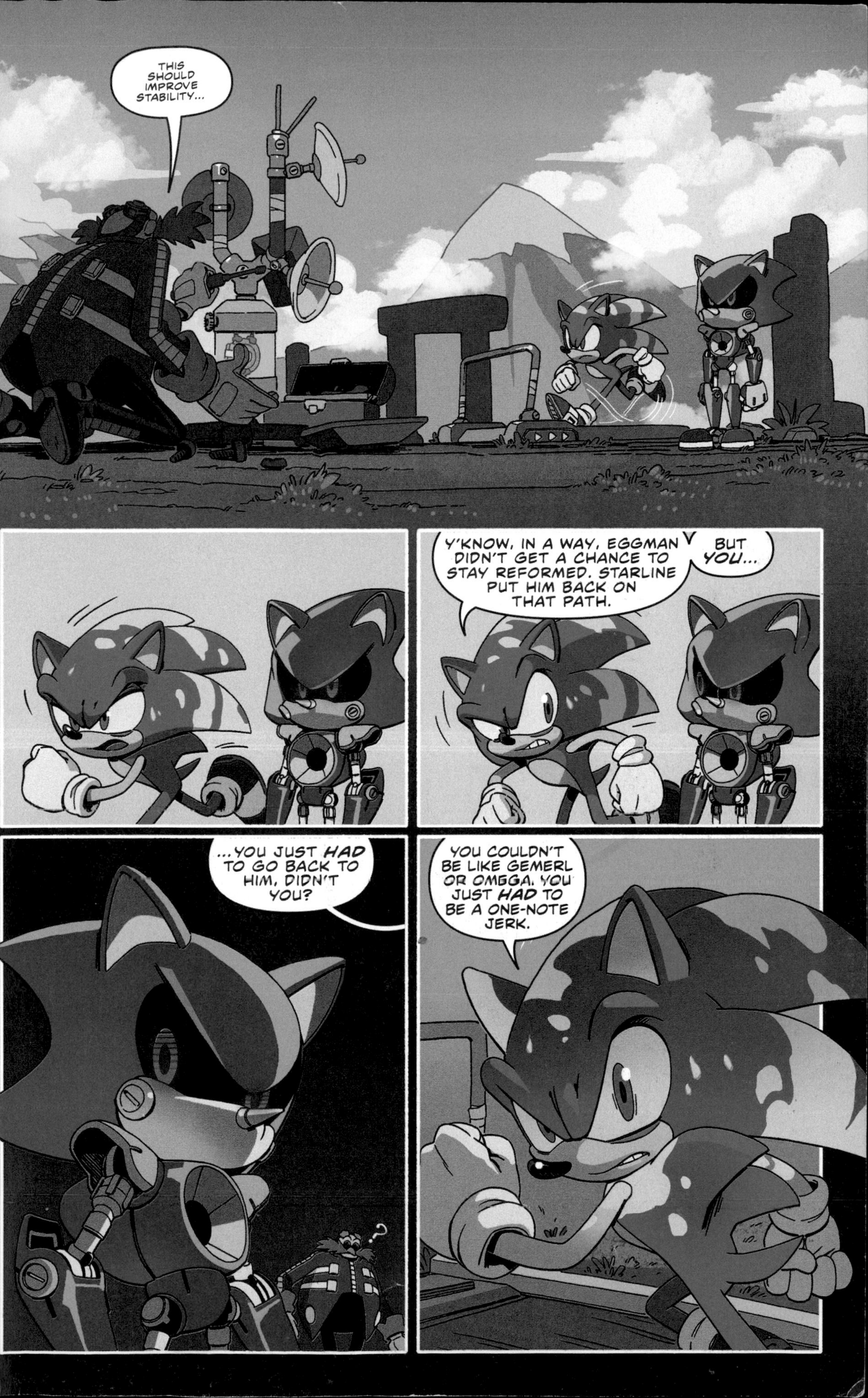
THIS SHOULD IMPROVE STABILITY...
Y'KNOW, IN A WAY, EGGMAN DIDN'T GET A CHANCE TO STAY REFORMED. STARLINE PUT HIM BACK ON THAT PATH.
BUT YOU...
...YOU JUST HAD TO GO BACK TO HIM, DIDN'T YOU?
YOU COULDN'T BE LIKE GEMERL OR OMEGA. YOU JUST HAD TO BE A ONE-NOTE JERK.

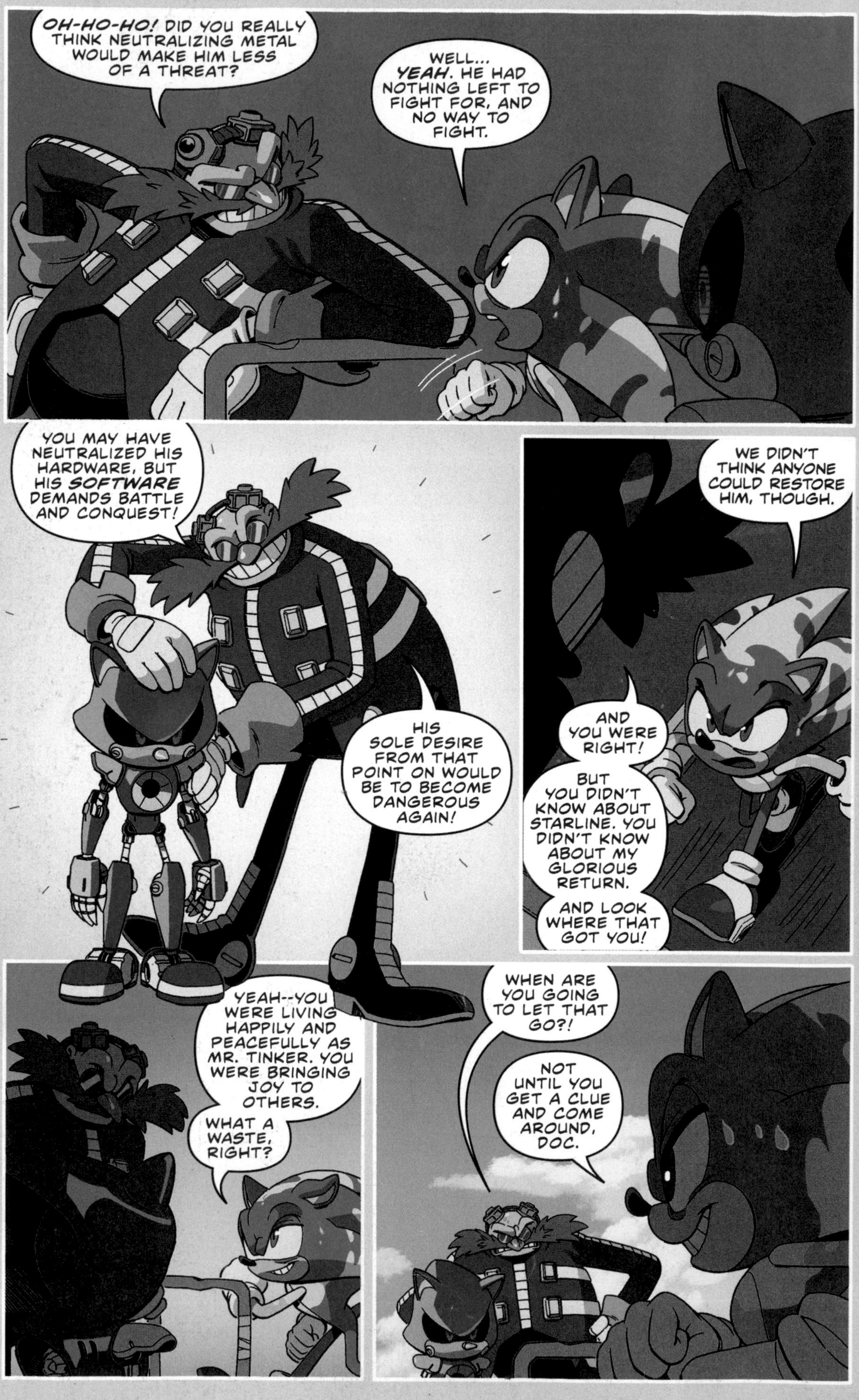
OH-HO-HO! DID YOU REALLY THINK NEUTRALIZING METAL WOULD MAKE HIM LESS OF A THREAT?
WELL... YEAH. HE HAD NOTHING LEFT TO FIGHT FOR, AND NO WAY TO FIGHT.
YOU MAY HAVE NEUTRALIZED HIS HARDWARE, BUT HIS SOFTWARE DEMANDS BATTLE AND CONQUEST!
HIS SOLE DESIRE FROM THAT POINT ON WOULD BE TO BECOME DANGEROUS AGAIN!
WE DIDN'T THINK ANYONE COULD RESTORE HIM, THOUGH.
AND YOU WERE RIGHT!
BUT YOU DIDN'T KNOW ABOUT STARLINE. YOU DIDN'T KNOW ABOUT MY GLORIOUS RETURN.
AND LOOK WHERE THAT GOT YOU!
YEAH--YOU WERE LIVING HAPPILY AND PEACEFULLY AS MR. TINKER. YOU WERE BRINGING JOY TO OTHERS.
WHAT A WASTE, RIGHT?
WHEN ARE YOU GOING TO LET THAT GO?!
NOT UNTIL YOU GET A CLUE AND COME AROUND, DOC.

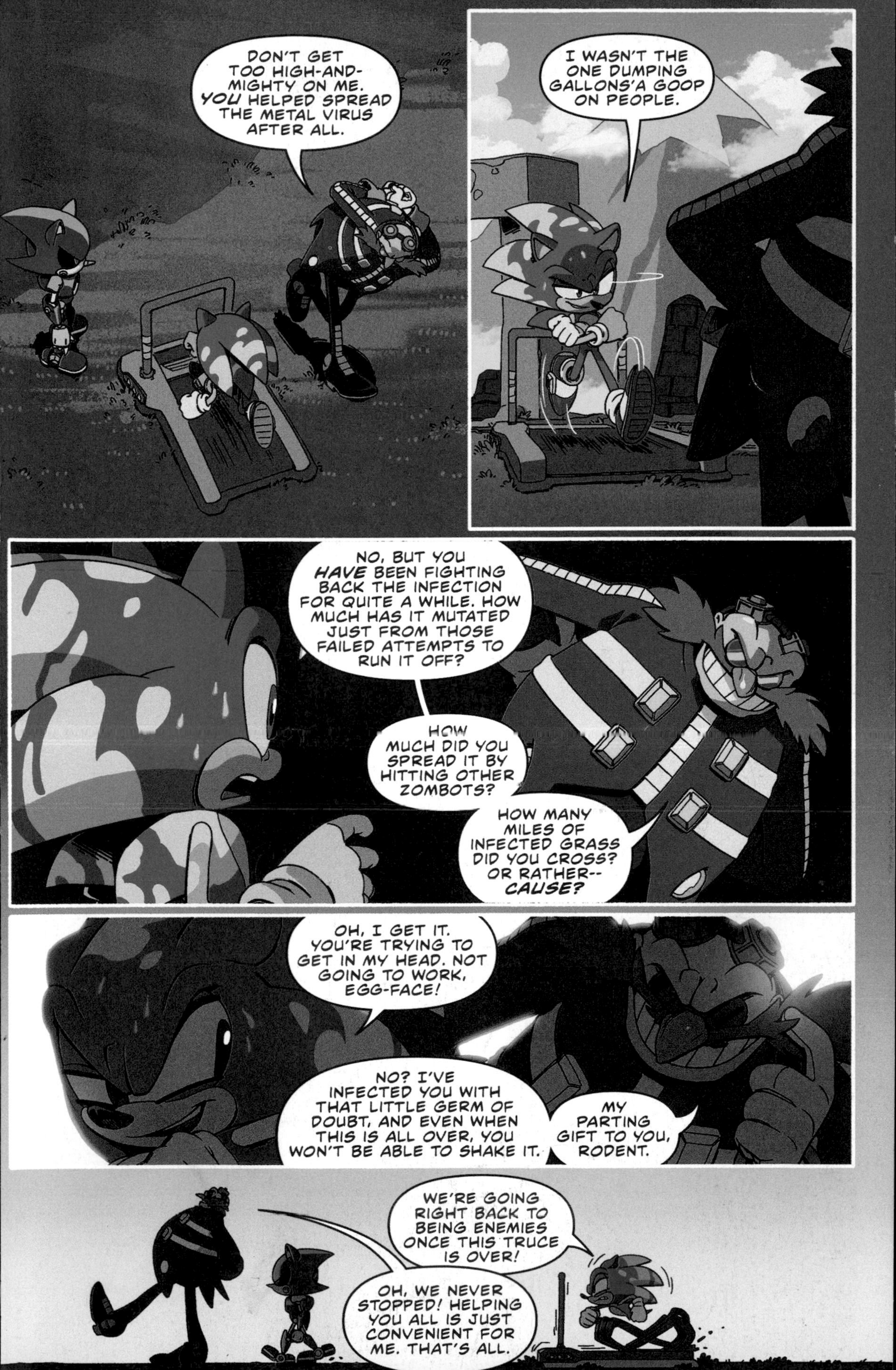
DON'T GET TOO HIGH-AND-MIGHTY ON ME. YOU HELPED SPREAD THE METAL VIRUS AFTER ALL.
I WASN'T THE ONE DUMPING GALLONS'A GOOP ON PEOPLE.
NO, BUT YOU HAVE BEEN FIGHTING BACK THE INFECTION FOR QUITE A WHILE. HOW MUCH HAS IT MUTATED JUST FROM THOSE FAILED ATTEMPTS TO RUN IT OFF?
HOW MUCH DID YOU SPREAD IT BY HITTING OTHER ZOMBOTS?
HOW MANY MILES OF INFECTED GRASS DID YOU CROSS? OR RATHER-- CAUSE?
OH, I GET IT. YOU'RE TRYING TO GET IN MY HEAD. NOT GOING TO WORK, EGG-FACE!
NO? I'VE INFECTED YOU WITH THAT LITTLE GERM OF DOUBT, AND EVEN WHEN THIS IS ALL OVER, YOU WON'T BE ABLE TO SHAKE IT.
MY PARTING GIFT TO YOU, RODENT.
WE'RE GOING RIGHT BACK TO BEING ENEMIES ONCE THIS TRUCE IS OVER!
OH, WE NEVER STOPPED! HELPING YOU ALL IS JUST CONVENIENT FOR ME. THAT'S ALL.

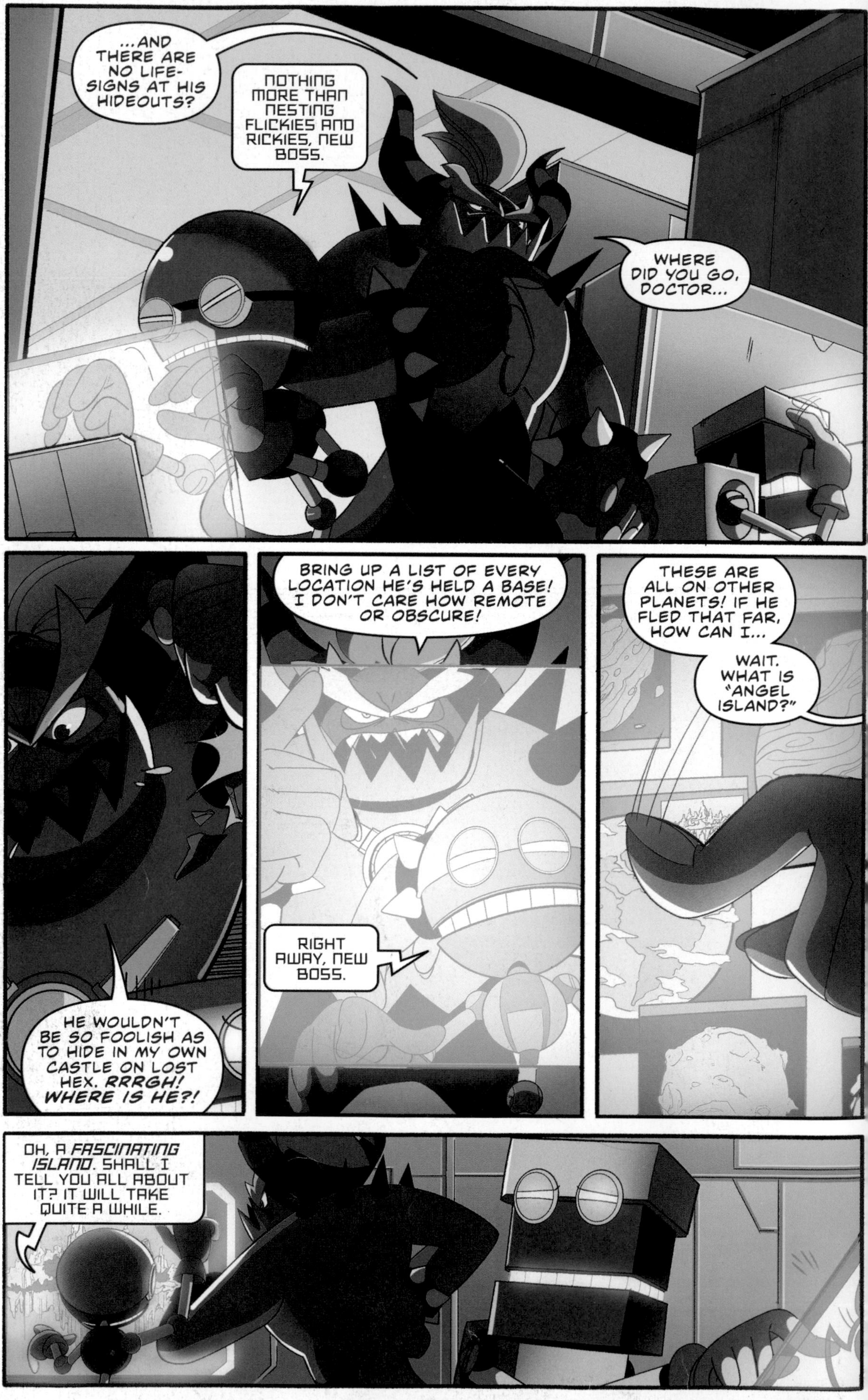
...AND THERE ARE NO LIFE-SIGNS AT HIS HIDEOUTS?
NOTHING MORE THAN NESTING FLICKIES AND RICKIES, NEW BOSS.
WHERE DID YOU GO, DOCTOR...
HE WOULDN'T BE SO FOOLISH AS TO HIDE IN MY OWN CASTLE ON LOST HEX. *RRRGH! WHERE IS HE?!*
BRING UP A LIST OF EVERY LOCATION HE'S HELD A BASE! I DON'T CARE HOW REMOTE OR OBSCURE!
RIGHT AWAY, NEW BOSS.
THESE ARE ALL ON OTHER PLANETS! IF HE FLED THAT FAR, HOW CAN I...
WAIT. WHAT IS "ANGEL ISLAND?"
OH, A *FASCINATING ISLAND*. SHALL I TELL YOU ALL ABOUT IT? IT WILL TAKE QUITE A WHILE.

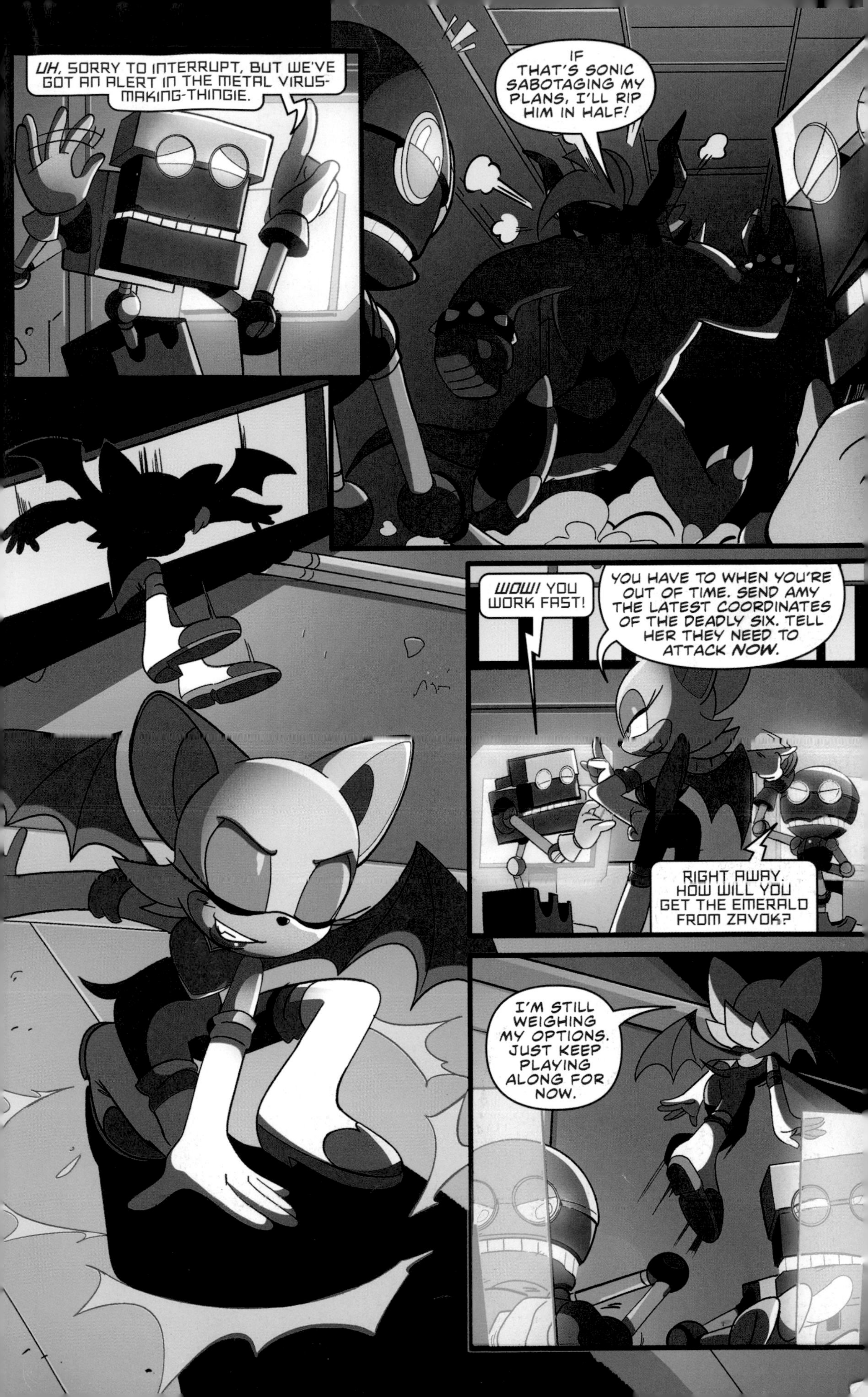
UH, SORRY TO INTERRUPT, BUT WE'VE GOT AN ALERT IN THE METAL VIRUS-MAKING-THINGIE.
IF THAT'S SONIC SABOTAGING MY PLANS, I'LL RIP HIM IN HALF!
WOW! YOU WORK FAST!
YOU HAVE TO WHEN YOU'RE OUT OF TIME. SEND AMY THE LATEST COORDINATES OF THE DEADLY SIX. TELL HER THEY NEED TO ATTACK NOW.
RIGHT AWAY. HOW WILL YOU GET THE EMERALD FROM ZAVOK?
I'M STILL WEIGHING MY OPTIONS. JUST KEEP PLAYING ALONG FOR NOW.

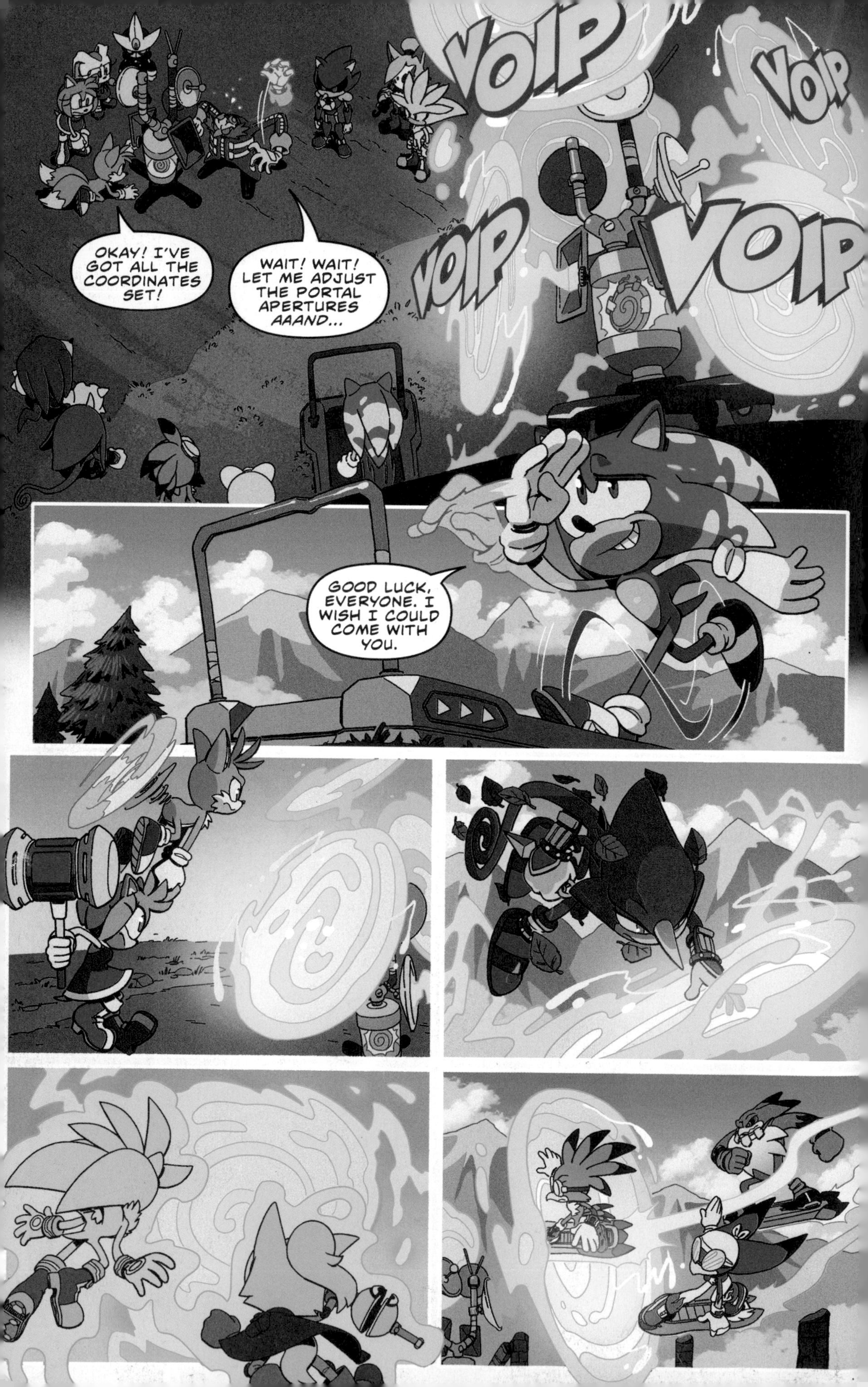
VOIP
VOIP
VOIP
VOIP
OKAY! I'VE GOT ALL THE COORDINATES SET!
WAIT! WAIT! LET ME ADJUST THE PORTAL APERTURES AAAND...
GOOD LUCK, EVERYONE. I WISH I COULD COME WITH YOU.

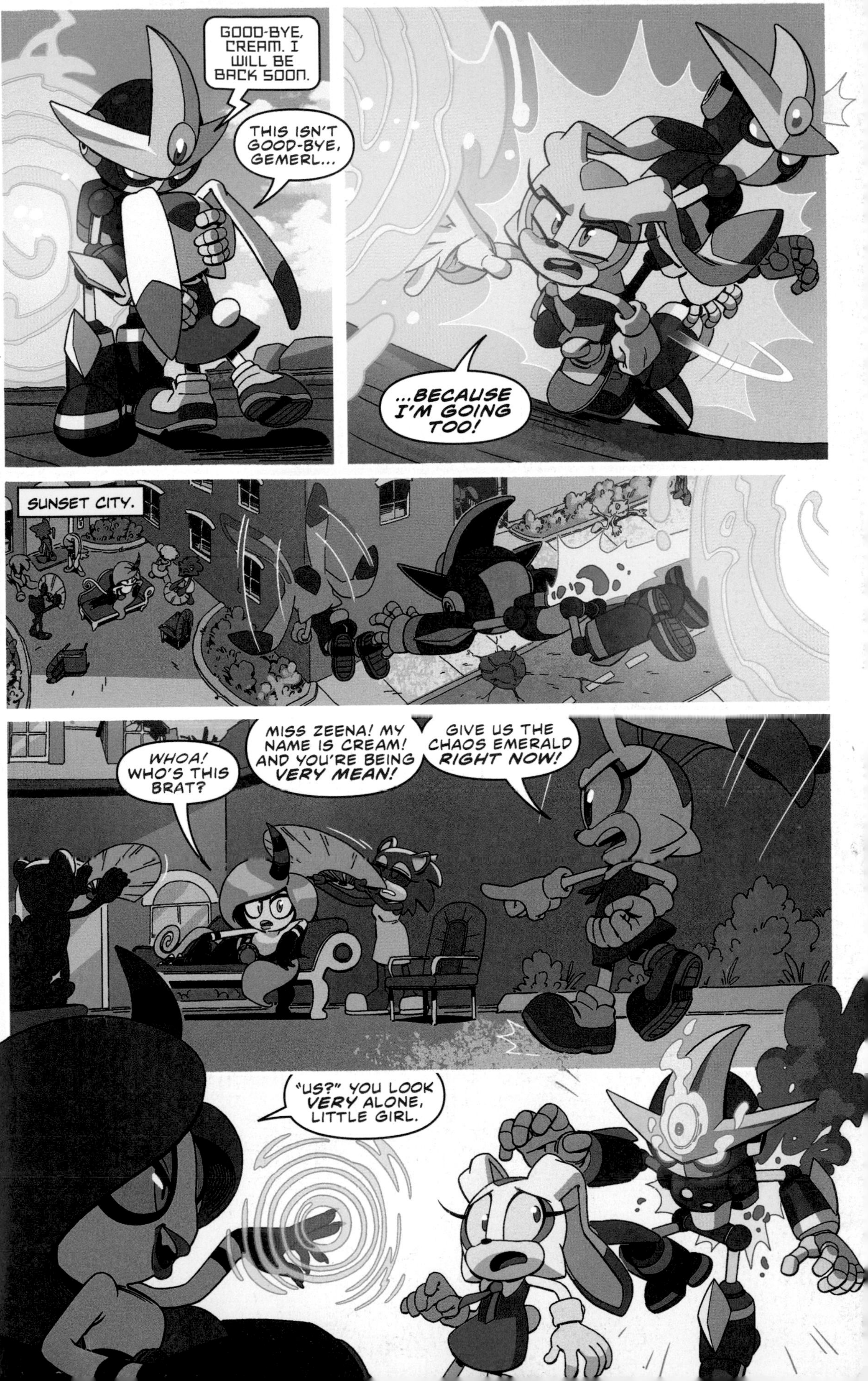
GOOD-BYE, CREAM. I WILL BE BACK SOON.
THIS ISN'T GOOD-BYE, GEMERL...
...BECAUSE I'M GOING TOO!
SUNSET CITY.
WHOA! WHO'S THIS BRAT?
MISS ZEENA! MY NAME IS CREAM! AND YOU'RE BEING VERY MEAN!
GIVE US THE CHAOS EMERALD RIGHT NOW!
"US?" YOU LOOK VERY ALONE, LITTLE GIRL.

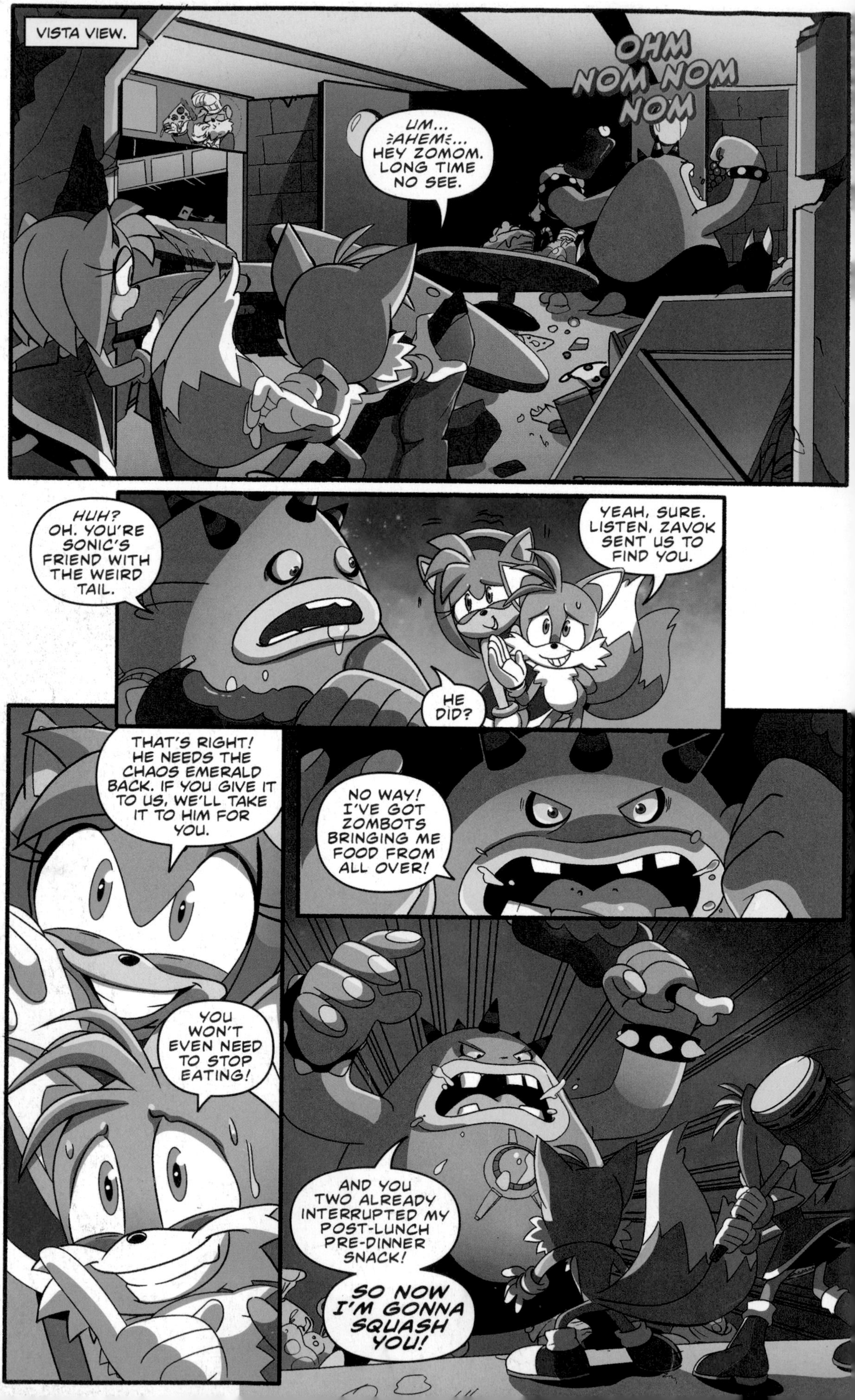
VISTA VIEW.
OHM NOM NOM NOM
UM... *AHEM*... HEY ZOMOM. LONG TIME NO SEE.
HUH? OH. YOU'RE SONIC'S FRIEND WITH THE WEIRD TAIL.
YEAH, SURE. LISTEN, ZAVOK SENT US TO FIND YOU.
HE DID?
THAT'S RIGHT! HE NEEDS THE CHAOS EMERALD BACK. IF YOU GIVE IT TO US, WE'LL TAKE IT TO HIM FOR YOU.
YOU WON'T EVEN NEED TO STOP EATING!
NO WAY! I'VE GOT ZOMBOTS BRINGING ME FOOD FROM ALL OVER!
AND YOU TWO ALREADY INTERRUPTED MY POST-LUNCH PRE-DINNER SNACK!
SO NOW I'M GONNA SQUASH YOU!

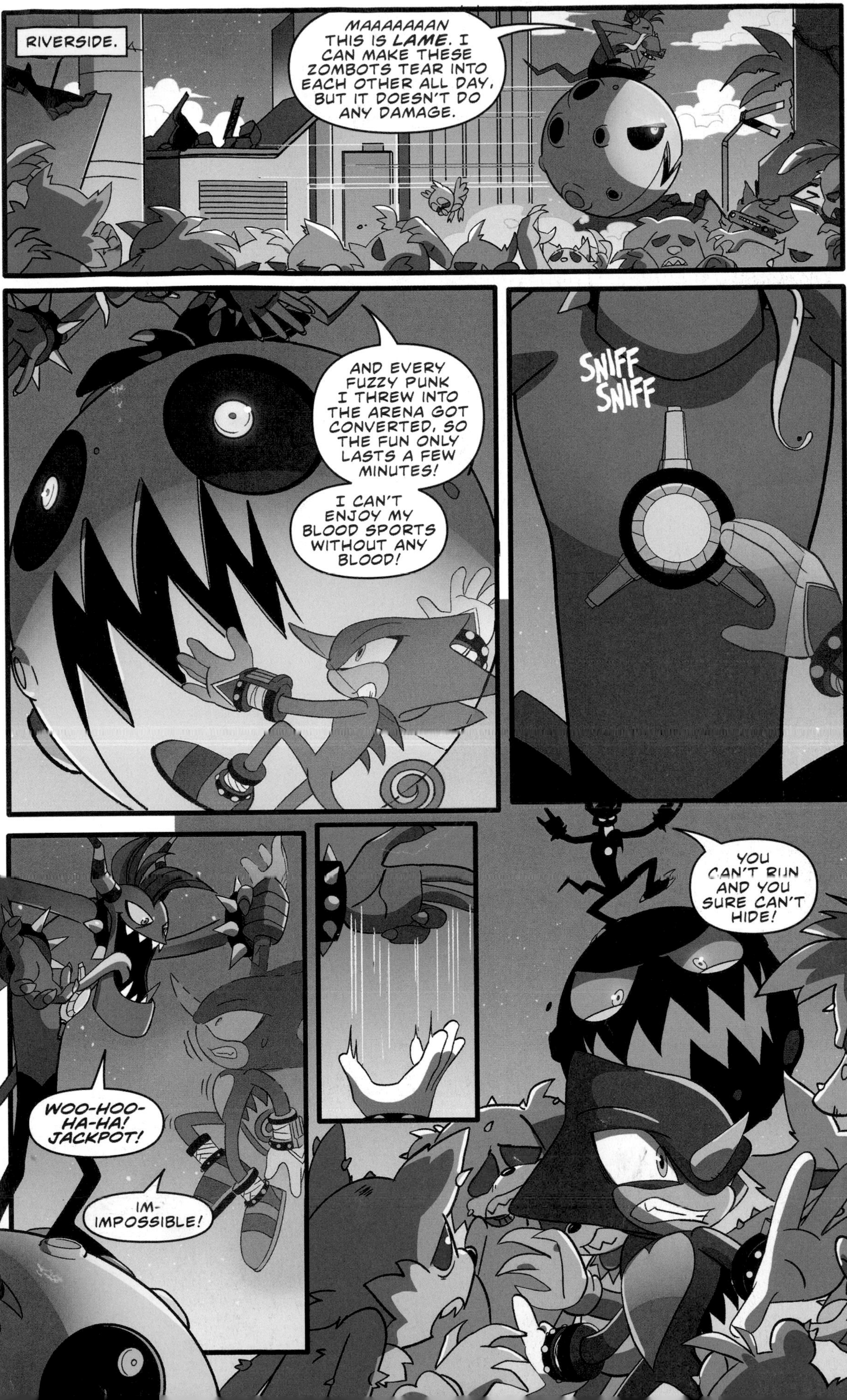
RIVERSIDE.
MAAAAAAAN THIS IS LAME. I CAN MAKE THESE ZOMBOTS TEAR INTO EACH OTHER ALL DAY, BUT IT DOESN'T DO ANY DAMAGE.
AND EVERY FUZZY PUNK I THREW INTO THE ARENA GOT CONVERTED, SO THE FUN ONLY LASTS A FEW MINUTES!
I CAN'T ENJOY MY BLOOD SPORTS WITHOUT ANY BLOOD!
SNIFF SNIFF
WOO-HOO-HA-HA! JACKPOT!
IM-IMPOSSIBLE!
YOU CAN'T RUN AND YOU SURE CAN'T HIDE!

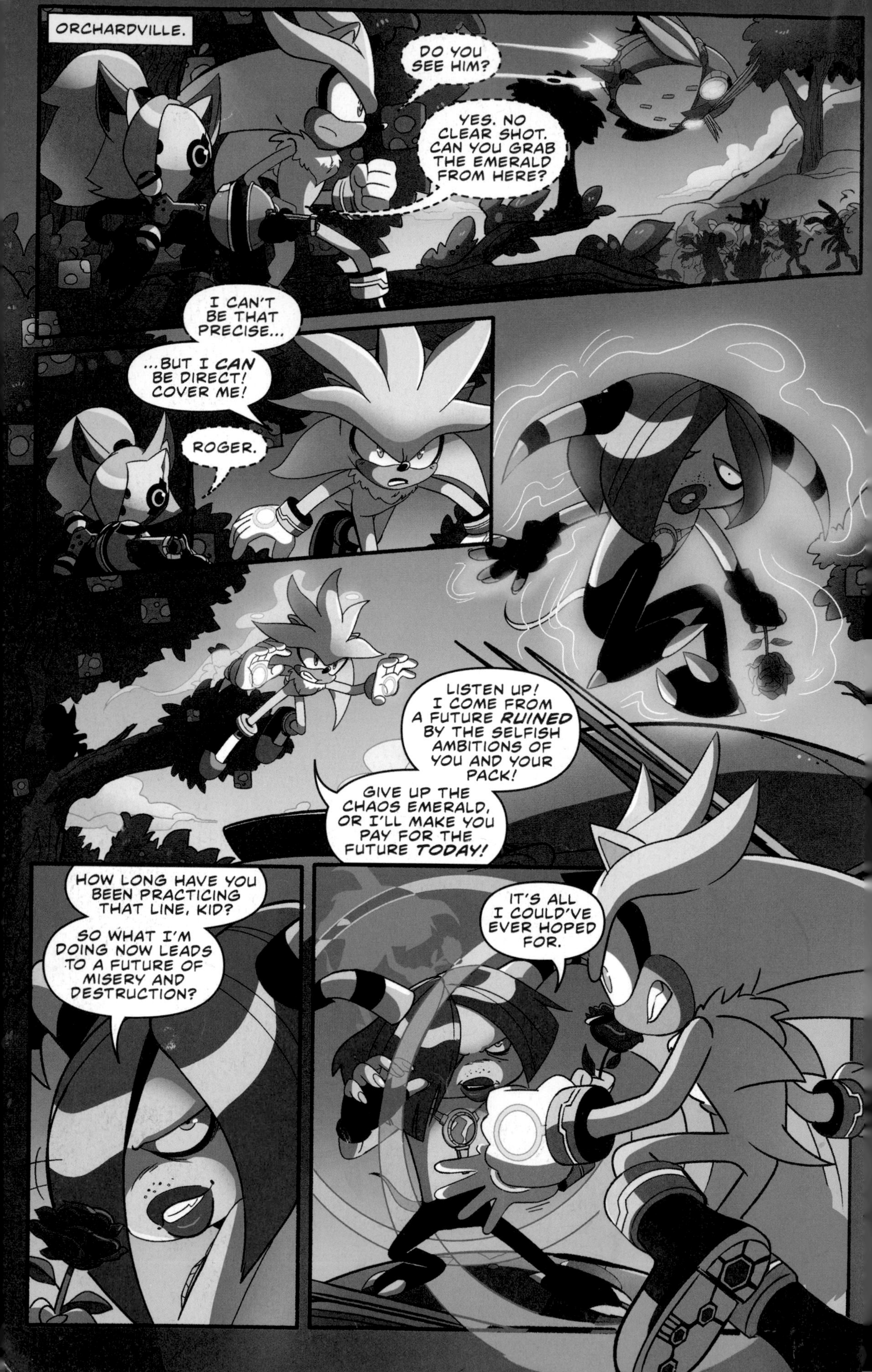
ORCHARDVILLE.
DO YOU SEE HIM?
YES. NO CLEAR SHOT. CAN YOU GRAB THE EMERALD FROM HERE?
I CAN'T BE THAT PRECISE...
...BUT I *CAN* BE DIRECT! COVER ME!
ROGER.
LISTEN UP! I COME FROM A FUTURE *RUINED* BY THE SELFISH AMBITIONS OF YOU AND YOUR PACK!
GIVE UP THE CHAOS EMERALD, OR I'LL MAKE YOU PAY FOR THE FUTURE *TODAY!*
HOW LONG HAVE YOU BEEN PRACTICING THAT LINE, KID?
SO WHAT I'M DOING NOW LEADS TO A FUTURE OF MISERY AND DESTRUCTION?
IT'S ALL I COULD'VE EVER HOPED FOR.

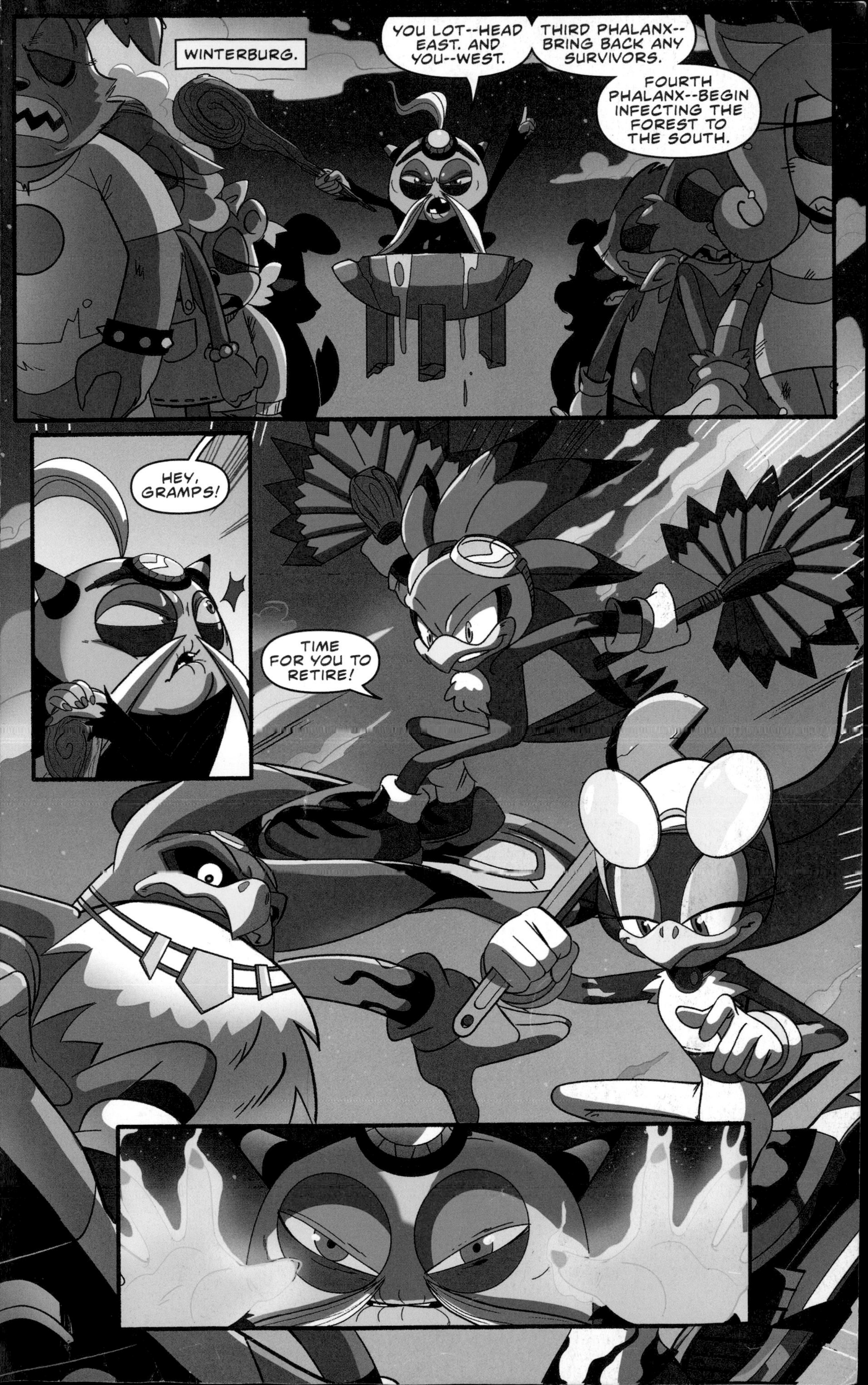
WINTERBURG.
YOU LOT--HEAD EAST. AND YOU--WEST.
THIRD PHALANX--BRING BACK ANY SURVIVORS.
FOURTH PHALANX--BEGIN INFECTING THE FOREST TO THE SOUTH.
HEY, GRAMPS!
TIME FOR YOU TO RETIRE!

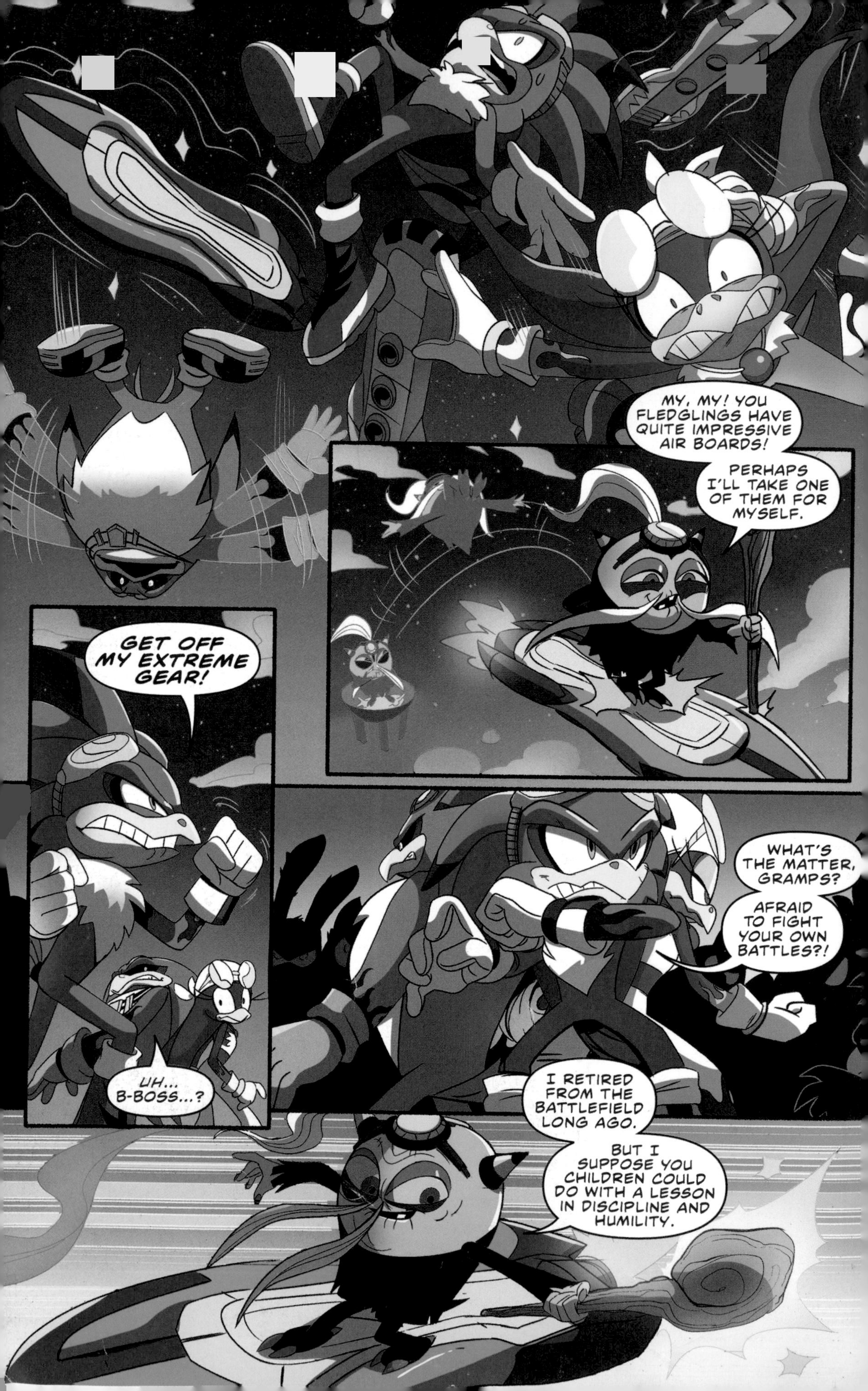

MY, MY! YOU FLEDGLINGS HAVE QUITE IMPRESSIVE AIR BOARDS!
PERHAPS I'LL TAKE ONE OF THEM FOR MYSELF.
GET OFF MY EXTREME GEAR!
UH... B-BOSS...?
WHAT'S THE MATTER, GRAMPS?
AFRAID TO FIGHT YOUR OWN BATTLES?!
I RETIRED FROM THE BATTLEFIELD LONG AGO.
BUT I SUPPOSE YOU CHILDREN COULD DO WITH A LESSON IN DISCIPLINE AND HUMILITY.

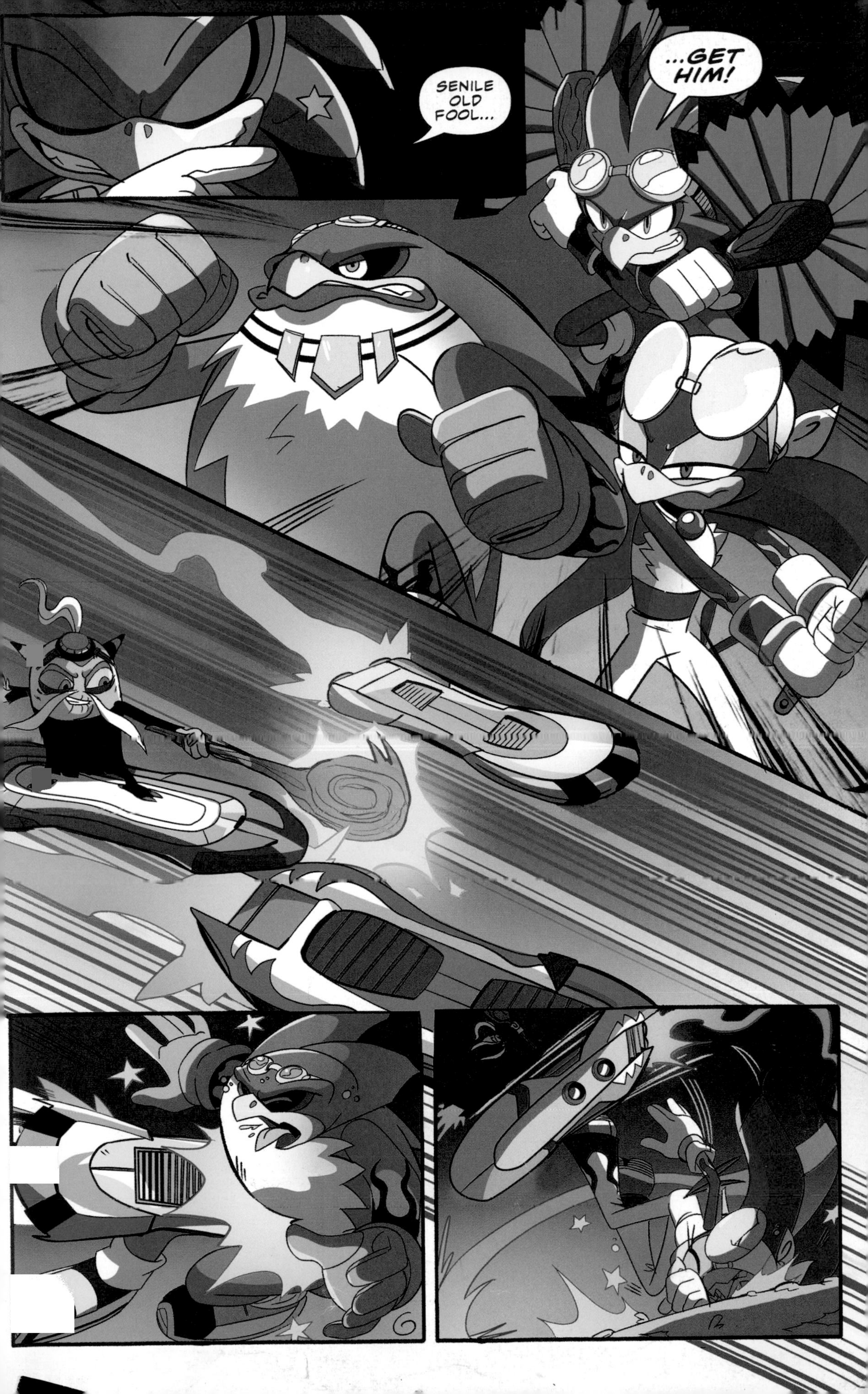
SENILE OLD FOOL...
...GET HIM!

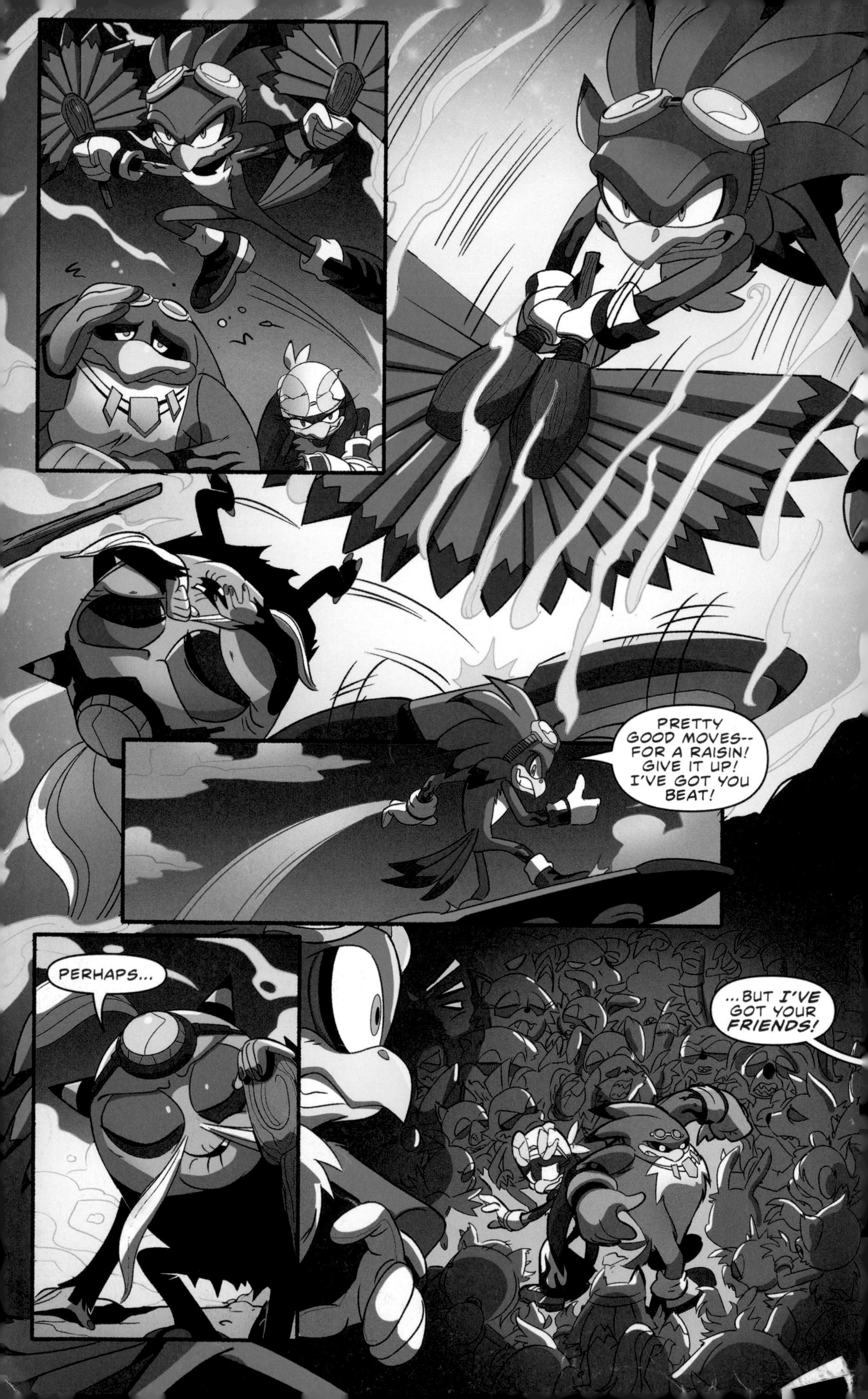
PRETTY GOOD MOVES-- FOR A RAISIN! GIVE IT UP! I'VE GOT YOU BEAT!
PERHAPS...
...BUT *I'VE* GOT YOUR *FRIENDS!*

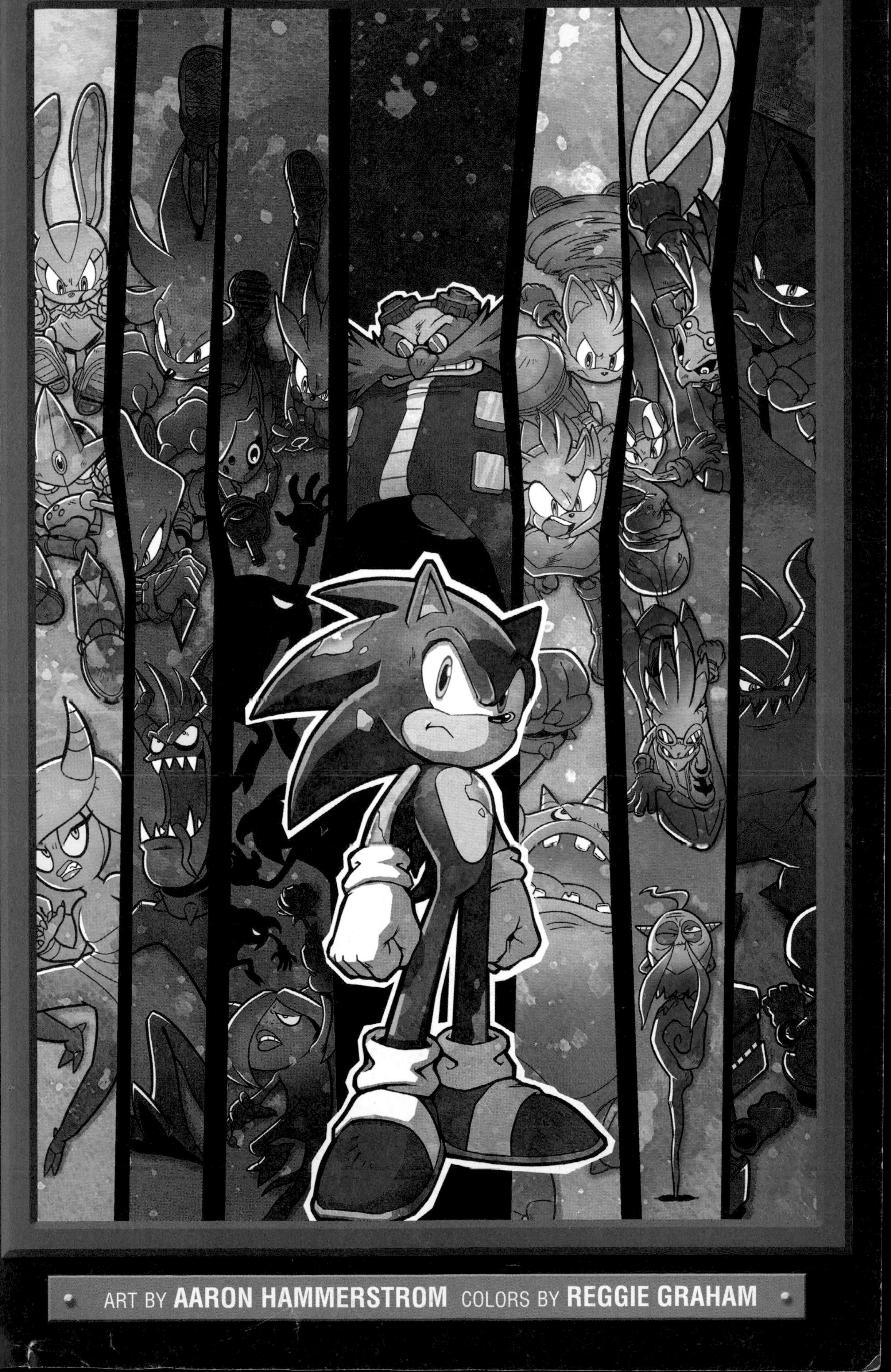

ART BY **AARON HAMMERSTROM** COLORS BY **REGGIE GRAHAM**

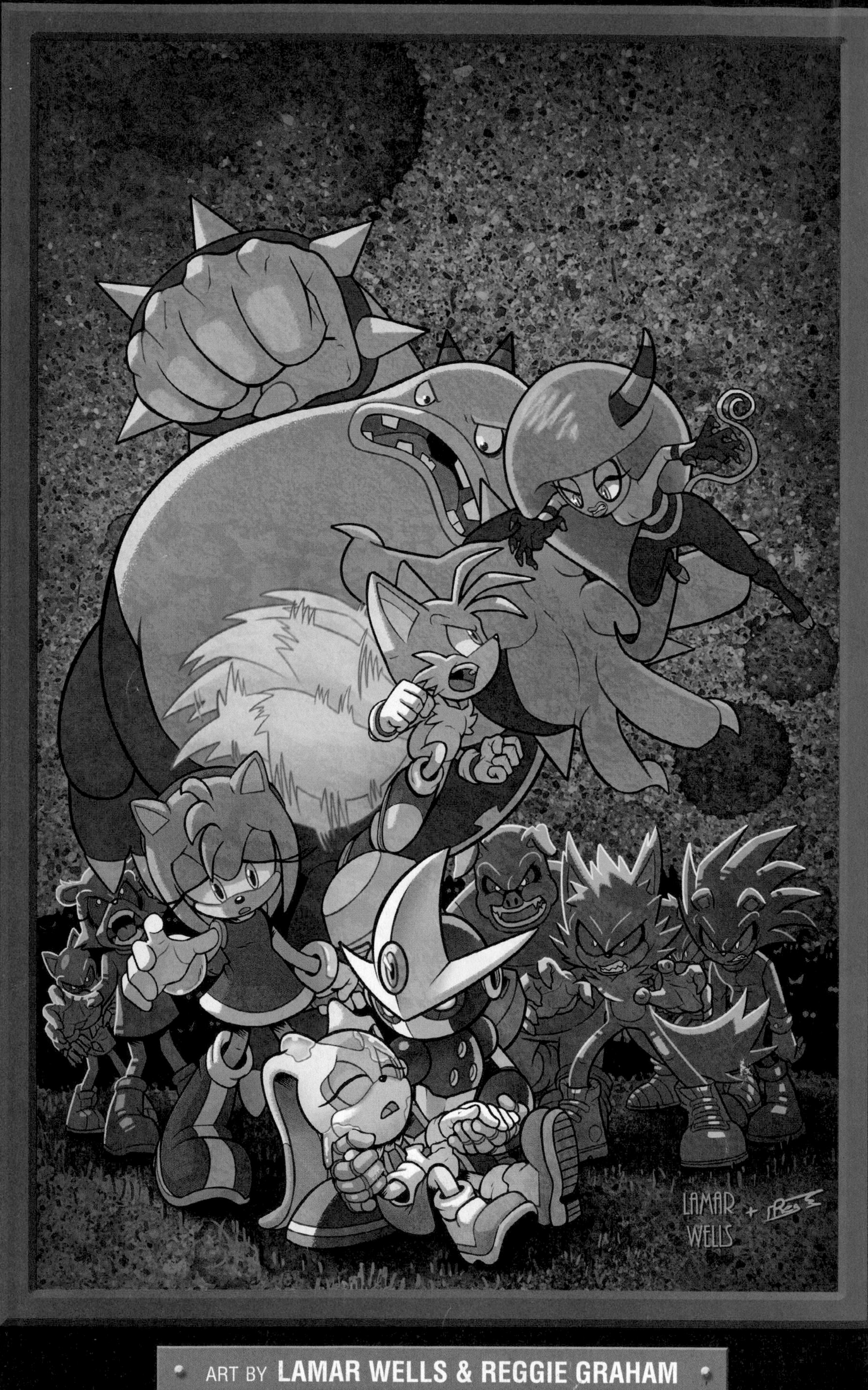
LAMAR
WELLS

ART BY **LAMAR WELLS & REGGIE GRAHAM**

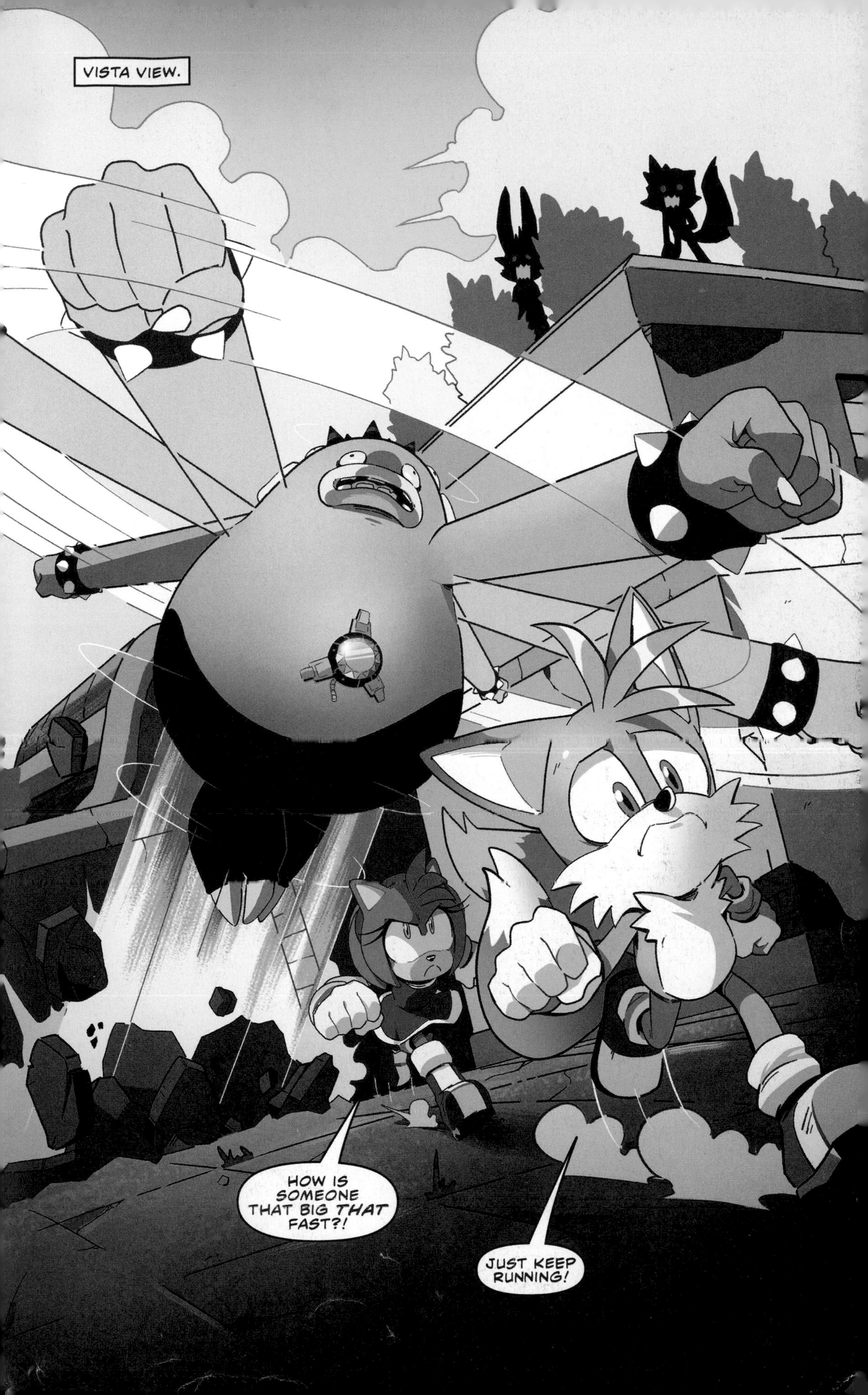
VISTA VIEW.
HOW IS SOMEONE THAT BIG *THAT* FAST?!
JUST KEEP RUNNING!

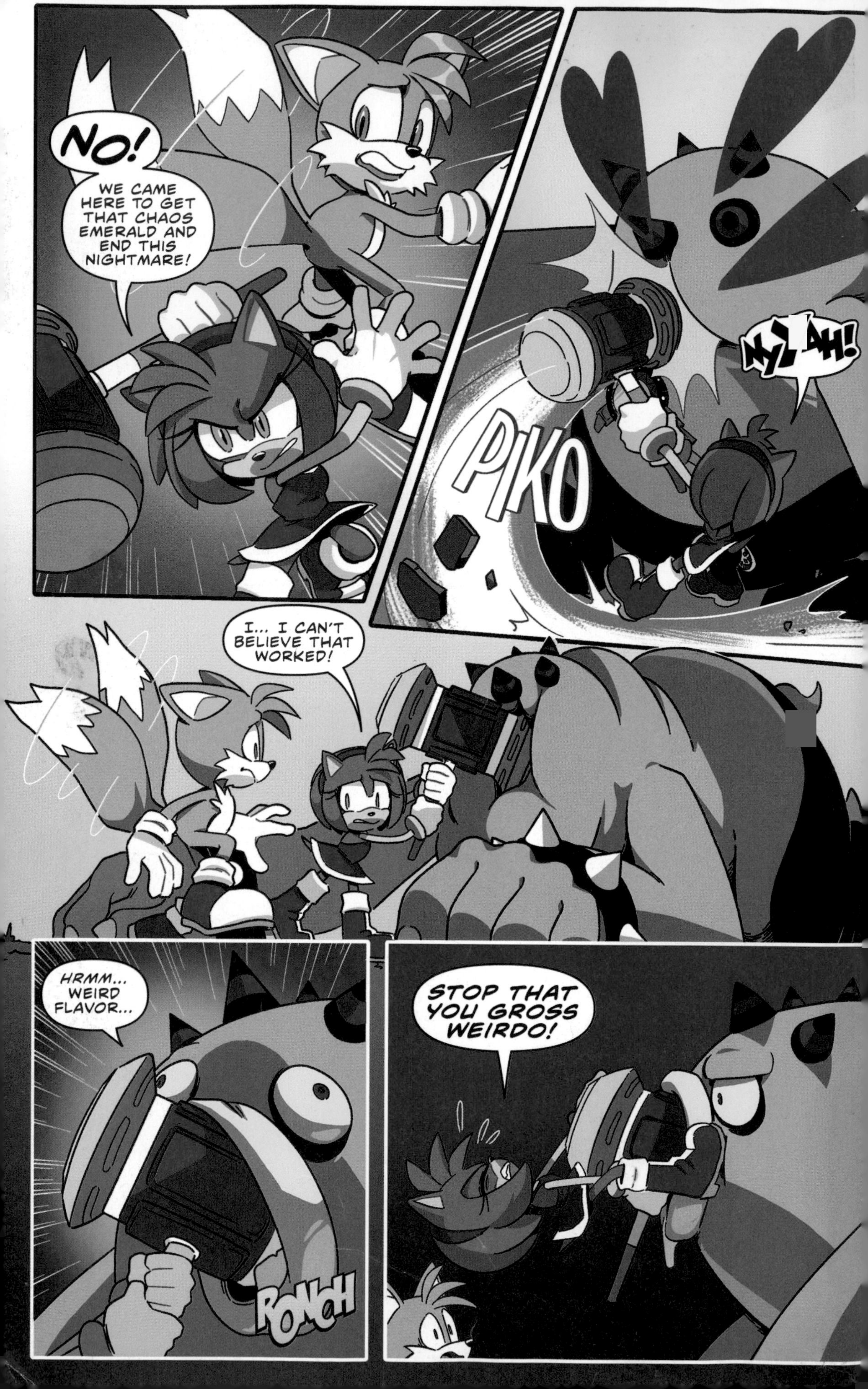
NO!
WE CAME HERE TO GET THAT CHAOS EMERALD AND END THIS NIGHTMARE!
NY[redacted]AH!
PIKO
I... I CAN'T BELIEVE THAT WORKED!
HRMM... WEIRD FLAVOR...
RONCH
STOP THAT YOU GROSS WEIRDO!

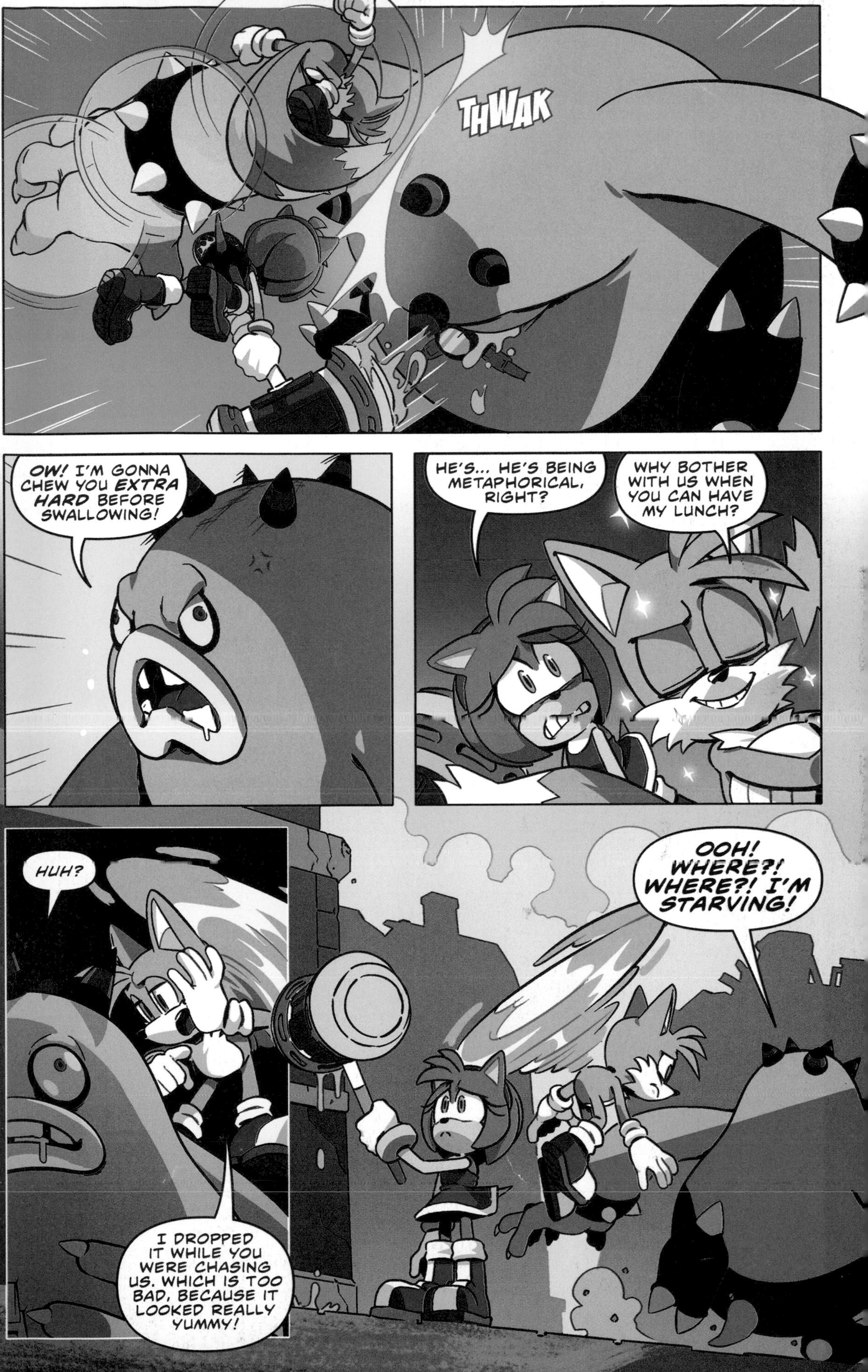
THWAK
OW! I'M GONNA CHEW YOU EXTRA HARD BEFORE SWALLOWING!
HE'S... HE'S BEING METAPHORICAL, RIGHT?
WHY BOTHER WITH US WHEN YOU CAN HAVE MY LUNCH?
HUH?
I DROPPED IT WHILE YOU WERE CHASING US. WHICH IS TOO BAD, BECAUSE IT LOOKED REALLY YUMMY!
OOH! WHERE?! WHERE?! I'M STARVING!

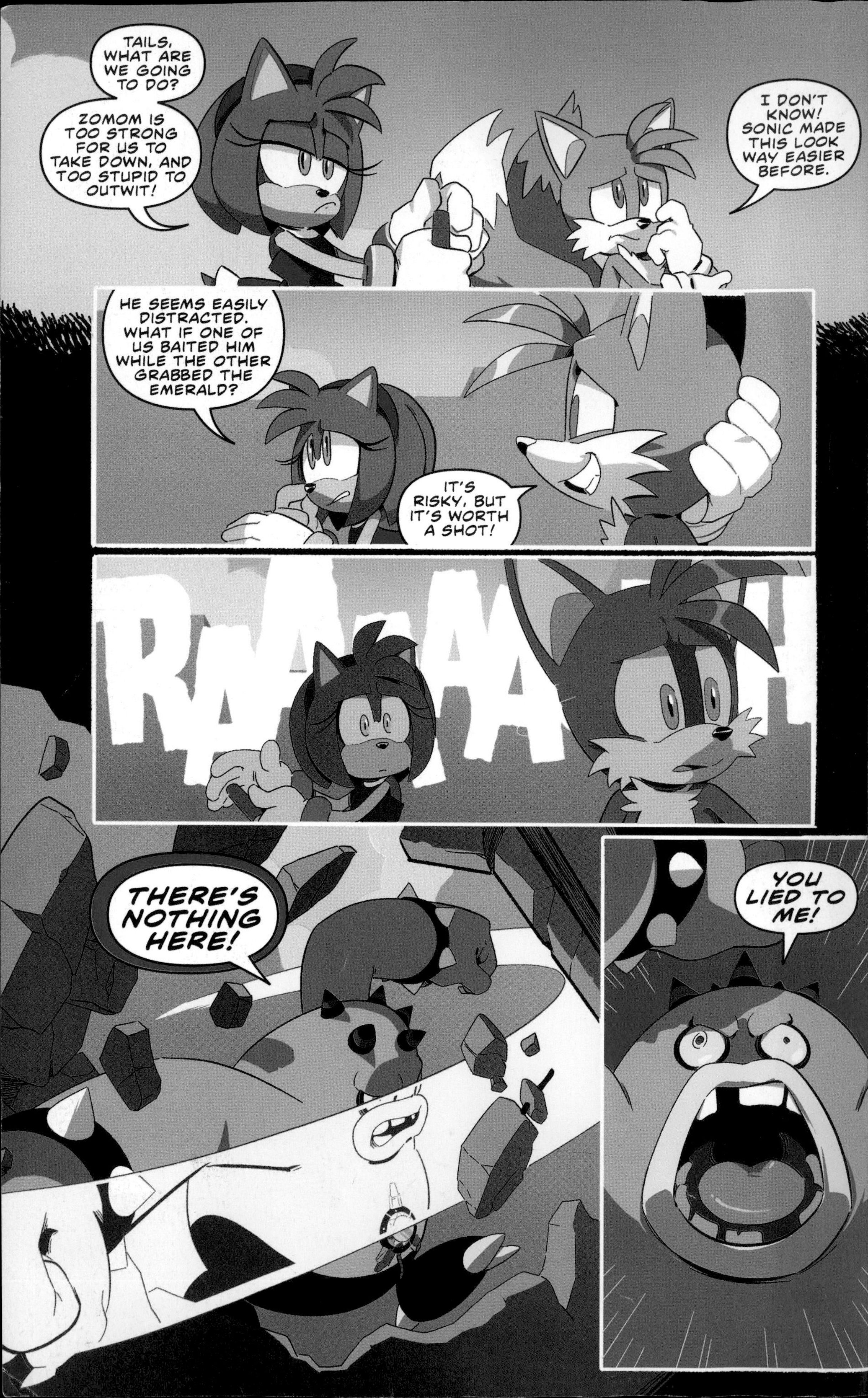
TAILS, WHAT ARE WE GOING TO DO?
ZOMOM IS TOO STRONG FOR US TO TAKE DOWN, AND TOO STUPID TO OUTWIT!
I DON'T KNOW! SONIC MADE THIS LOOK WAY EASIER BEFORE.
HE SEEMS EASILY DISTRACTED. WHAT IF ONE OF US BAITED HIM WHILE THE OTHER GRABBED THE EMERALD?
IT'S RISKY, BUT IT'S WORTH A SHOT!
RAAAAAH
THERE'S NOTHING HERE!
YOU LIED TO ME!

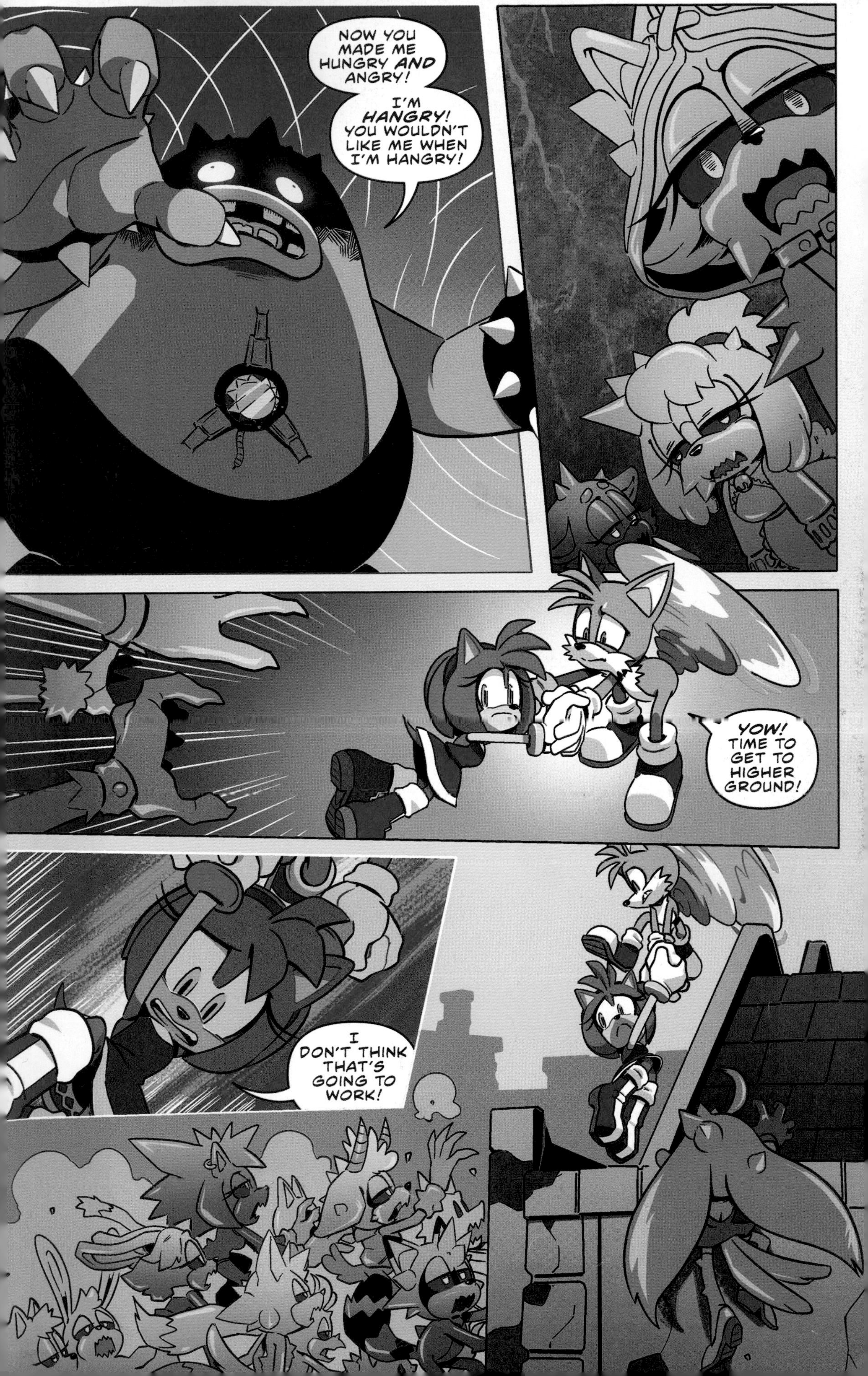
NOW YOU MADE ME HUNGRY AND ANGRY!
I'M HANGRY! YOU WOULDN'T LIKE ME WHEN I'M HANGRY!
YOW! TIME TO GET TO HIGHER GROUND!
I DON'T THINK THAT'S GOING TO WORK!

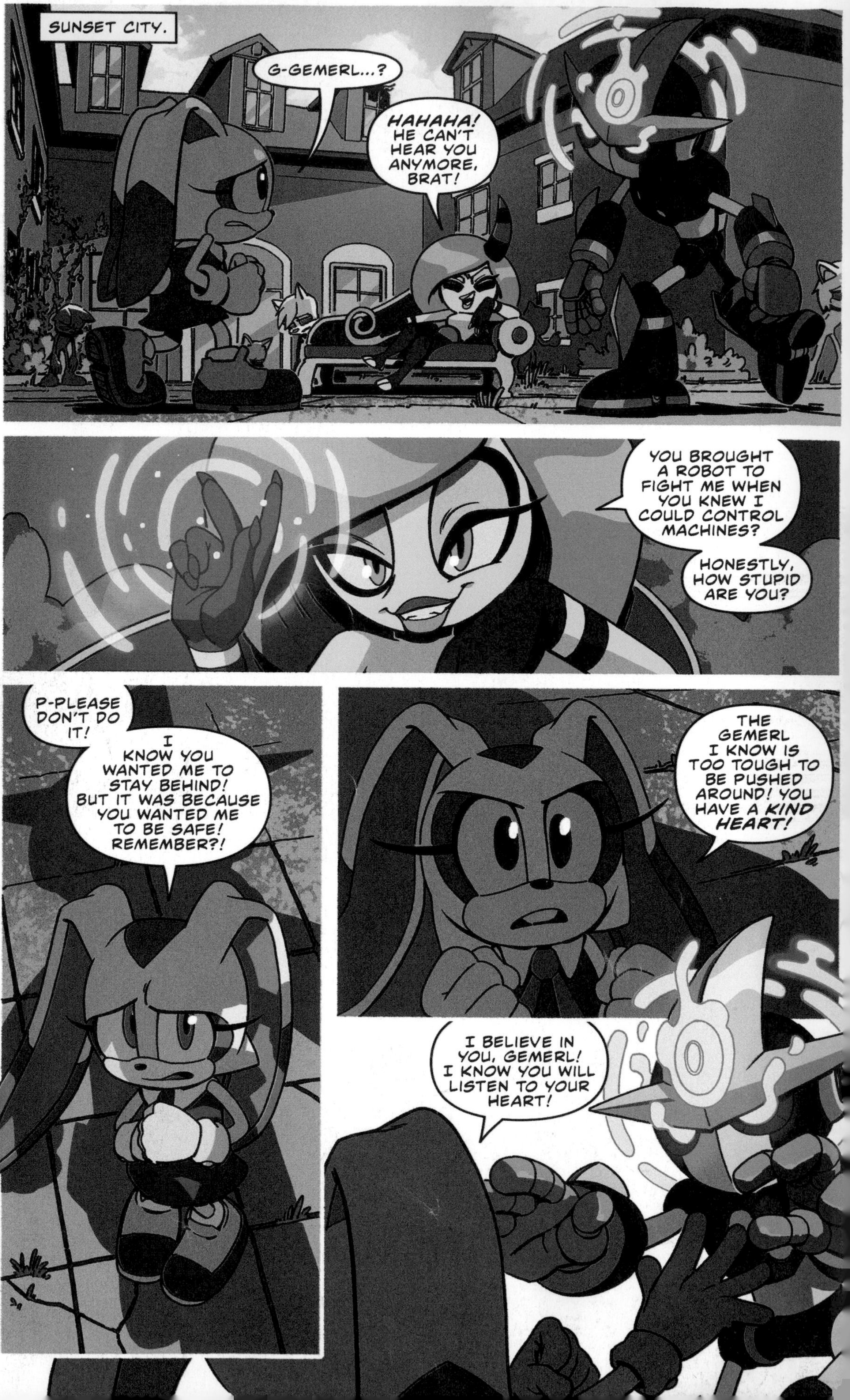

SUNSET CITY.
G-GEMERL...?
HAHAHA! HE CAN'T HEAR YOU ANYMORE, BRAT!
YOU BROUGHT A ROBOT TO FIGHT ME WHEN YOU KNEW I COULD CONTROL MACHINES?
HONESTLY, HOW STUPID ARE YOU?
P-PLEASE DON'T DO IT!
I KNOW YOU WANTED ME TO STAY BEHIND! BUT IT WAS BECAUSE YOU WANTED ME TO BE SAFE! REMEMBER?!
THE GEMERL I KNOW IS TOO TOUGH TO BE PUSHED AROUND! YOU HAVE A KIND HEART!
I BELIEVE IN YOU, GEMERL! I KNOW YOU WILL LISTEN TO YOUR HEART!

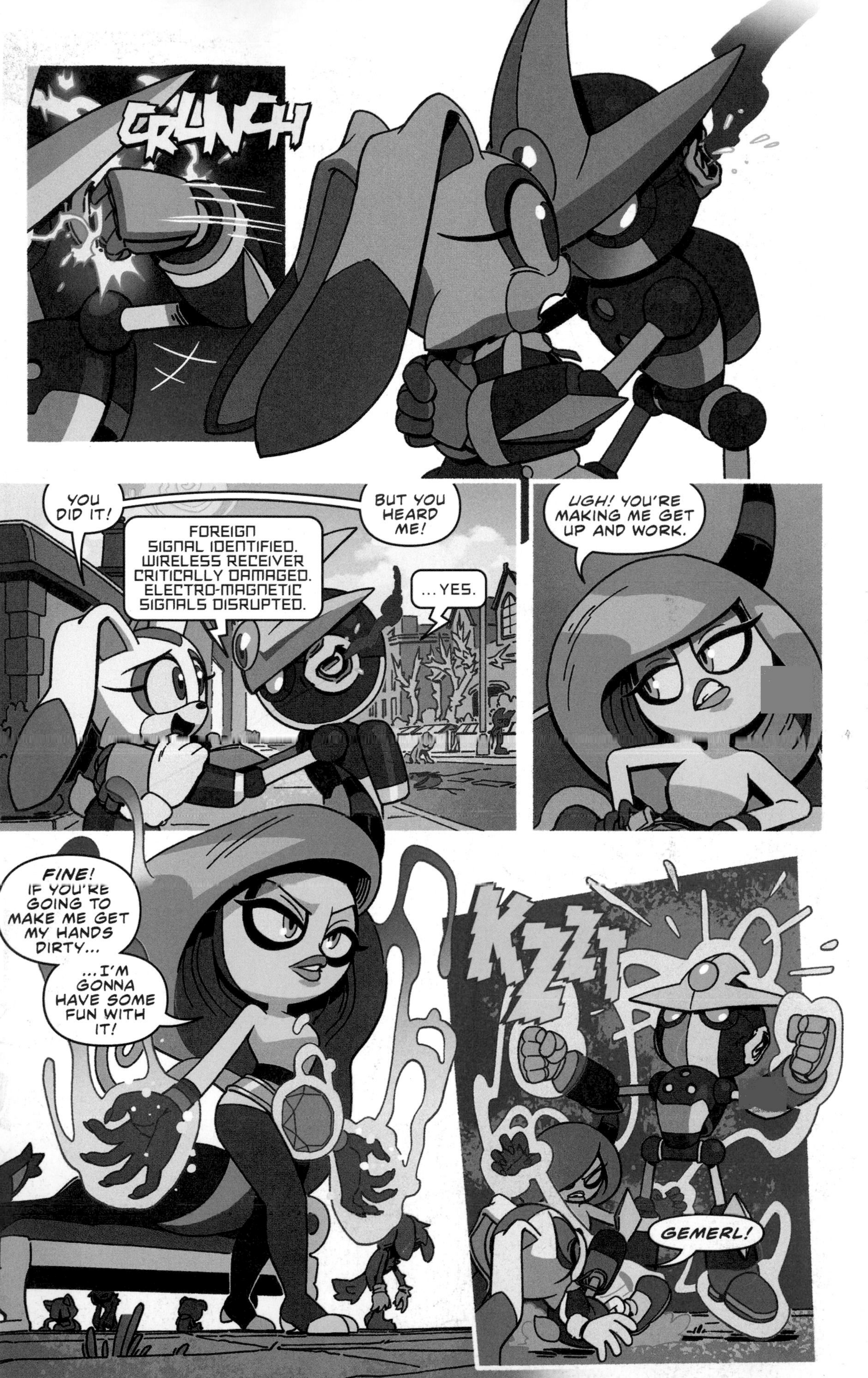
CRUNCH
YOU DID IT!
FOREIGN SIGNAL IDENTIFIED. WIRELESS RECEIVER CRITICALLY DAMAGED. ELECTRO-MAGNETIC SIGNALS DISRUPTED.
BUT YOU HEARD ME!
...YES.
UGH! YOU'RE MAKING ME GET UP AND WORK.
FINE! IF YOU'RE GOING TO MAKE ME GET MY HANDS DIRTY...
...I'M GONNA HAVE SOME FUN WITH IT!
KZZT
GEMERL!

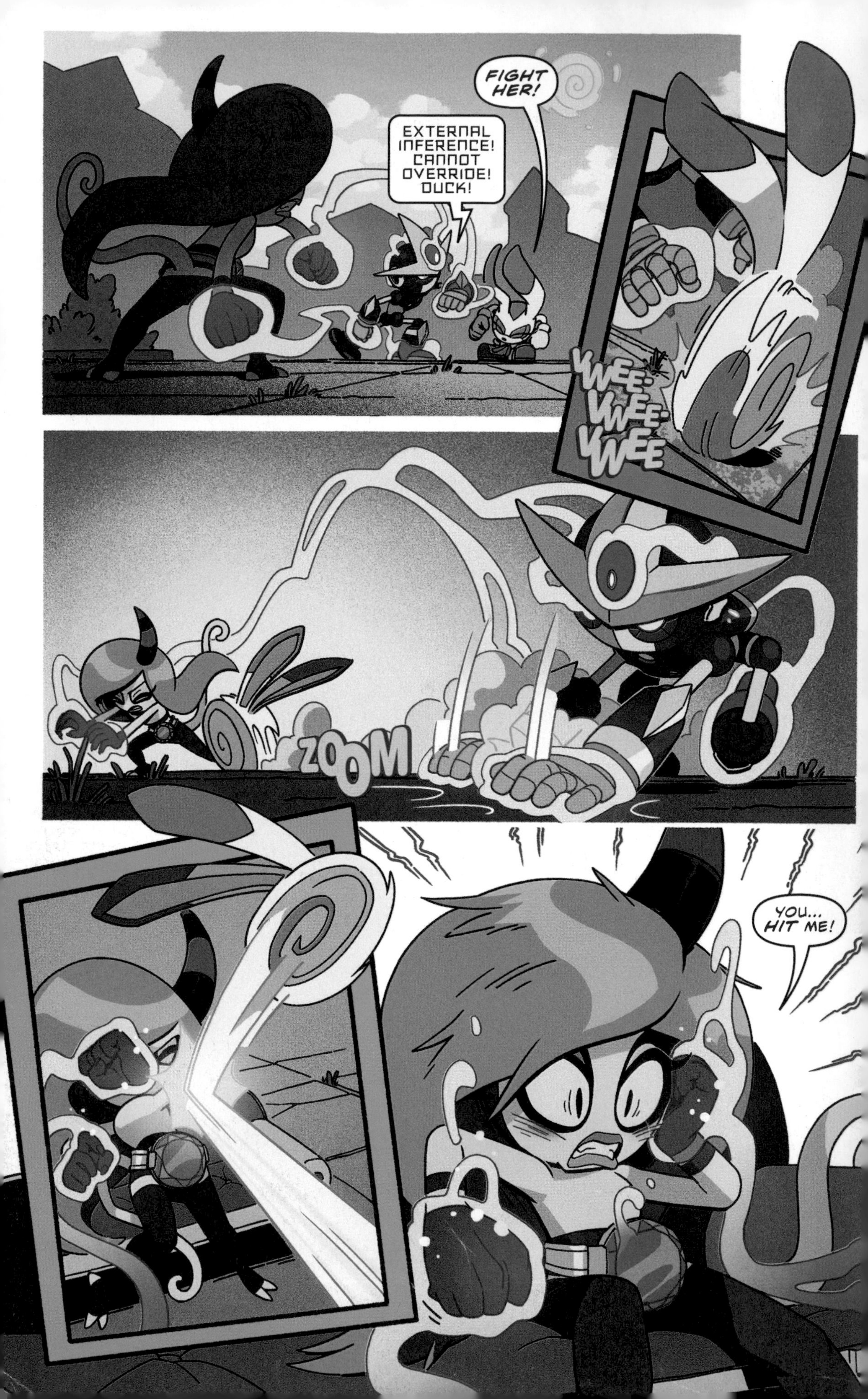
EXTERNAL INFERENCE! CANNOT OVERRIDE! DUCK!
FIGHT HER!
VWEE-VWEE-VWEE
ZOOM
YOU... HIT ME!

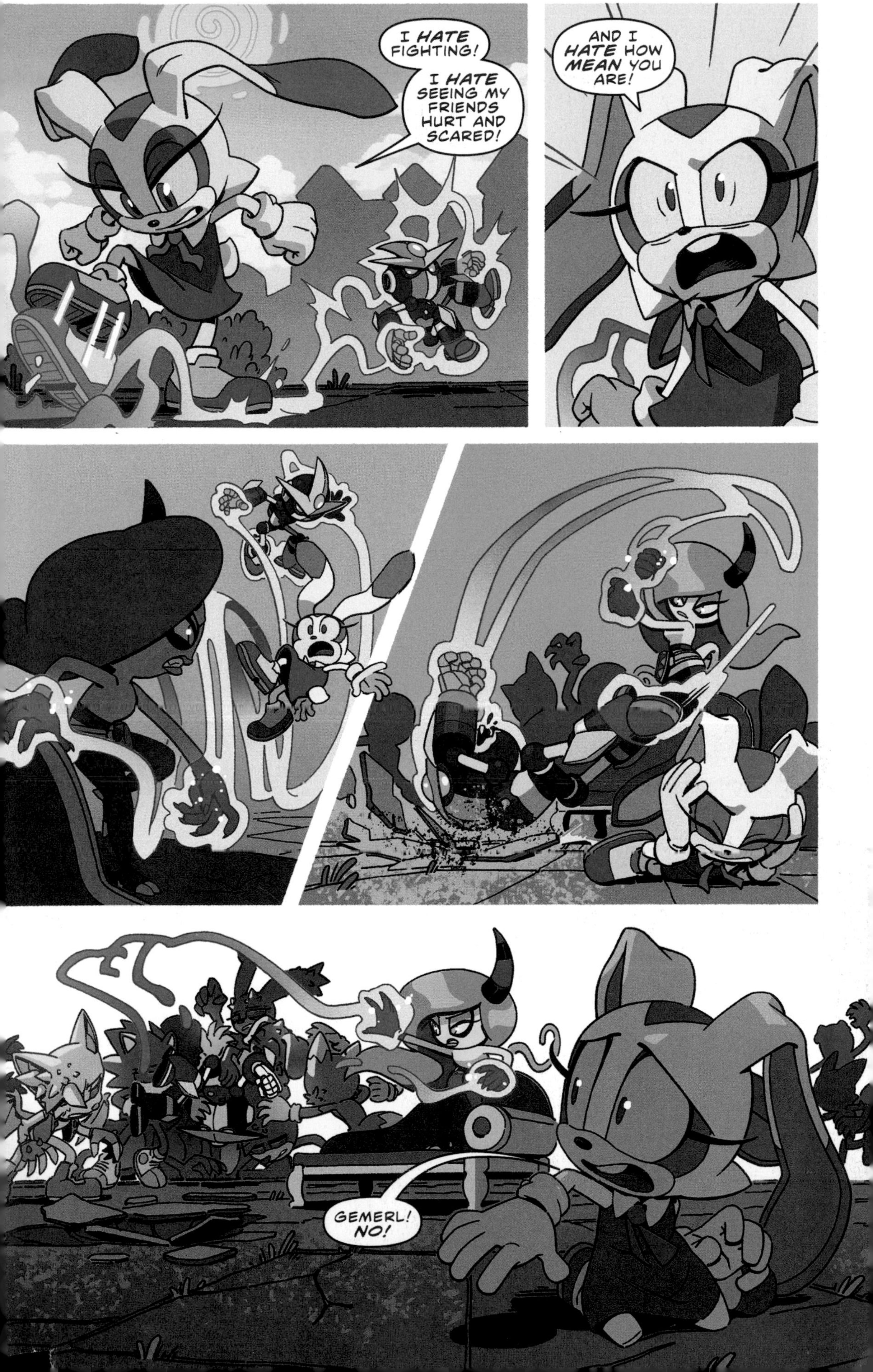
I HATE FIGHTING!
I HATE SEEING MY FRIENDS HURT AND SCARED!
AND I HATE HOW MEAN YOU ARE!
GEMERL! NO!

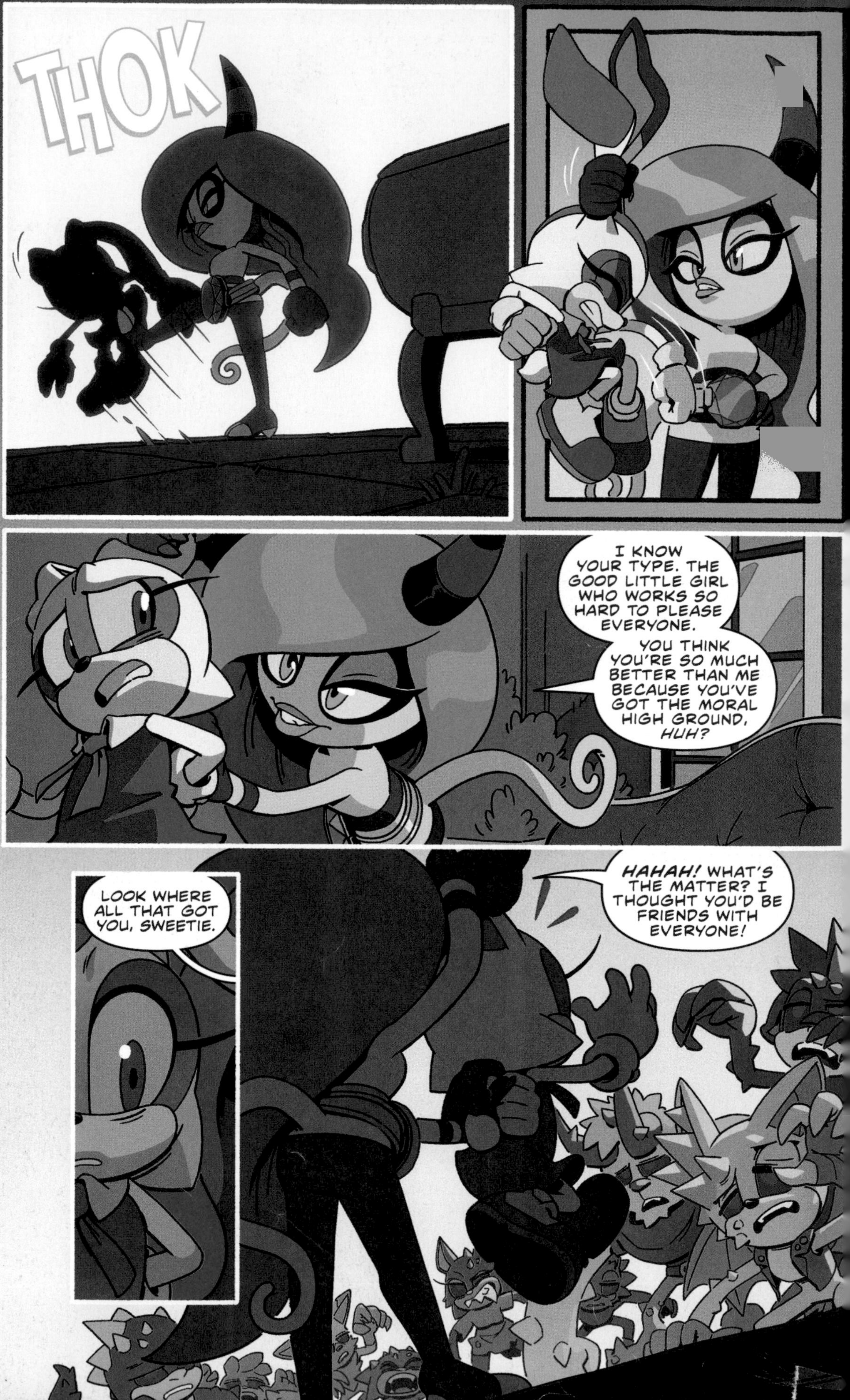
THOK
I KNOW YOUR TYPE. THE GOOD LITTLE GIRL WHO WORKS SO HARD TO PLEASE EVERYONE.
YOU THINK YOU'RE SO MUCH BETTER THAN ME BECAUSE YOU'VE GOT THE MORAL HIGH GROUND, *HUH?*
LOOK WHERE ALL THAT GOT YOU, SWEETIE.
HAHAH! WHAT'S THE MATTER? I THOUGHT YOU'D BE FRIENDS WITH EVERYONE!

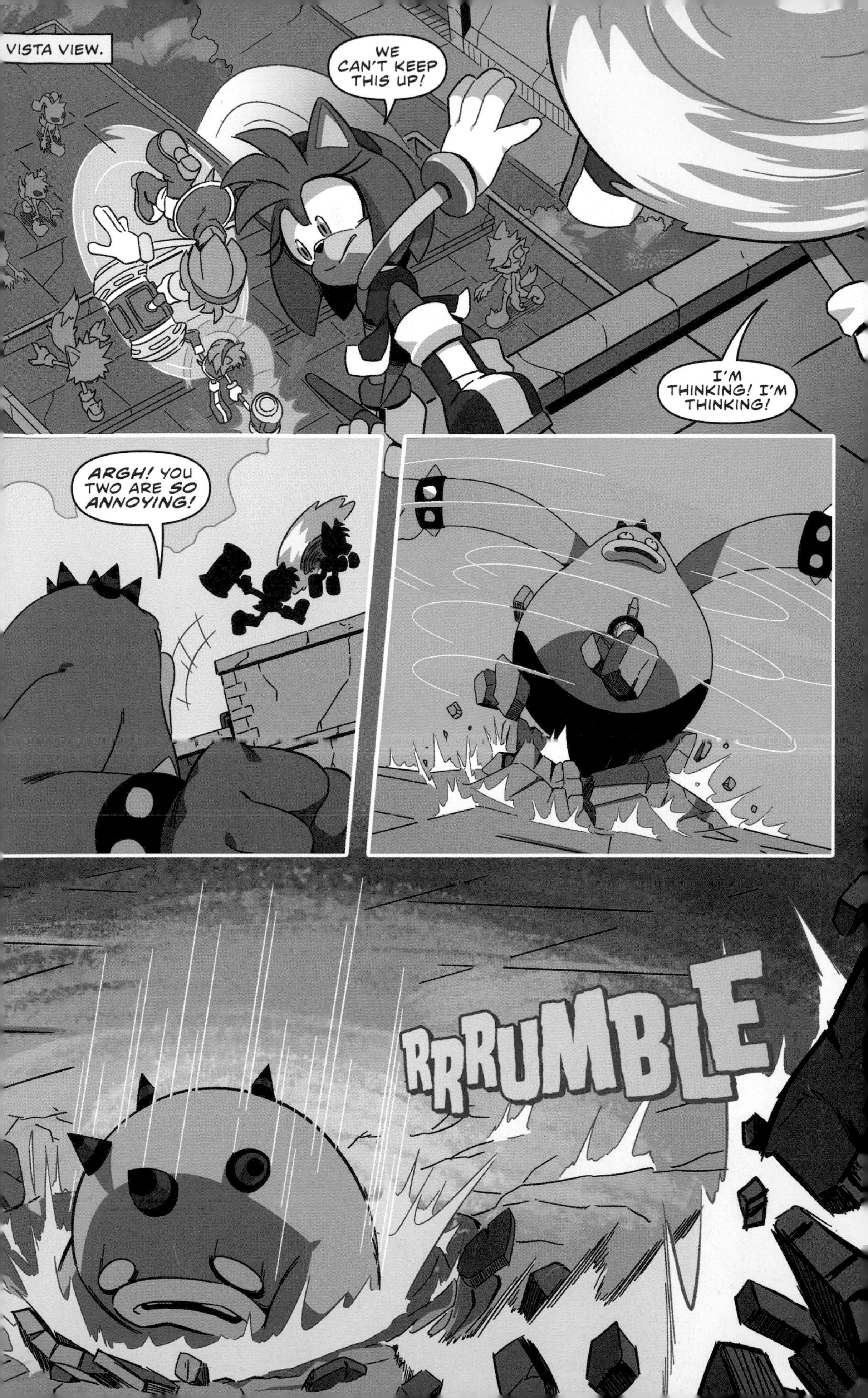
VISTA VIEW.
WE CAN'T KEEP THIS UP!
I'M THINKING! I'M THINKING!
ARGH! YOU TWO ARE SO ANNOYING!
RRRUMBLE

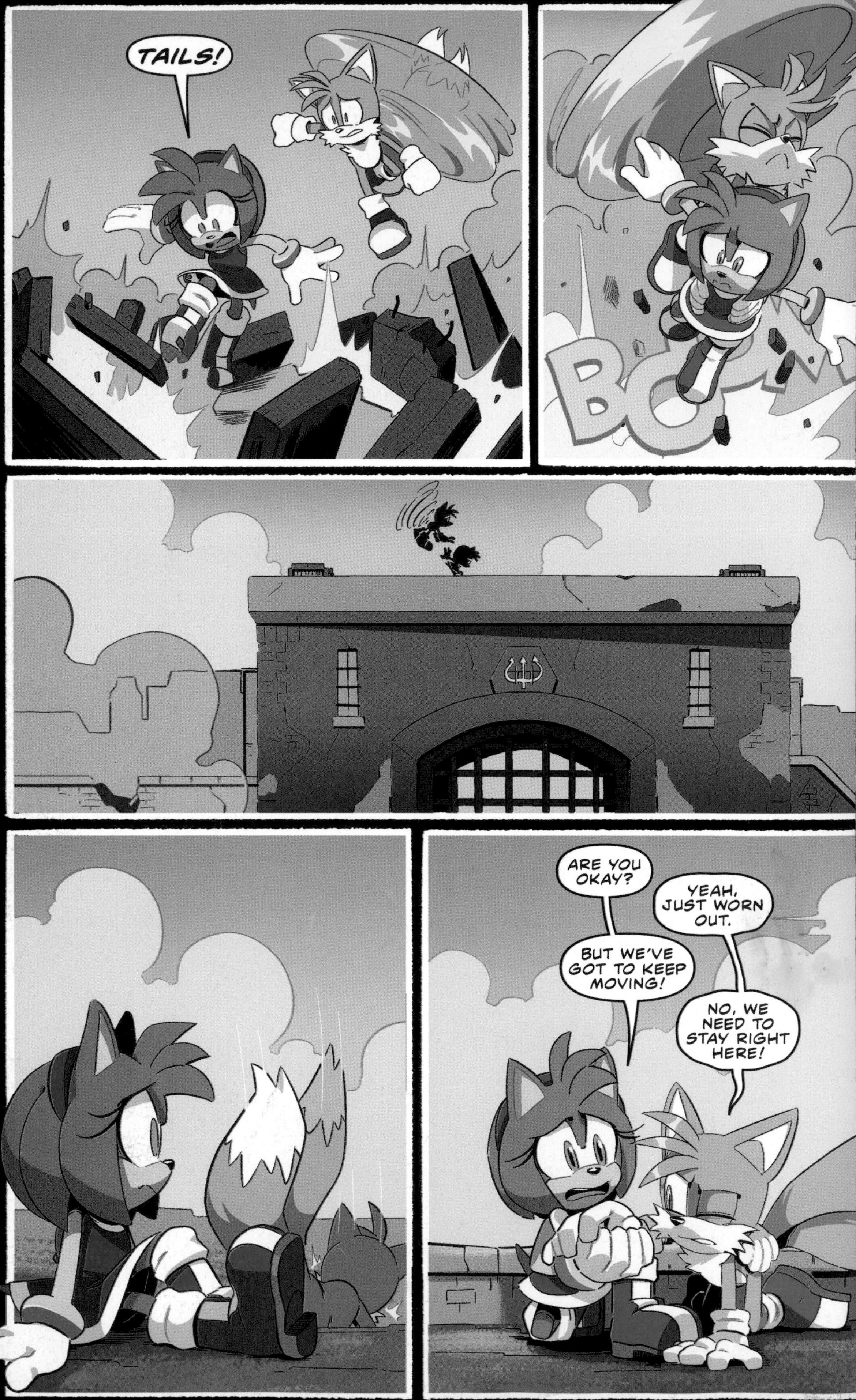
TAILS!
BO
ARE YOU OKAY?
YEAH, JUST WORN OUT.
BUT WE'VE GOT TO KEEP MOVING!
NO, WE NEED TO STAY RIGHT HERE!

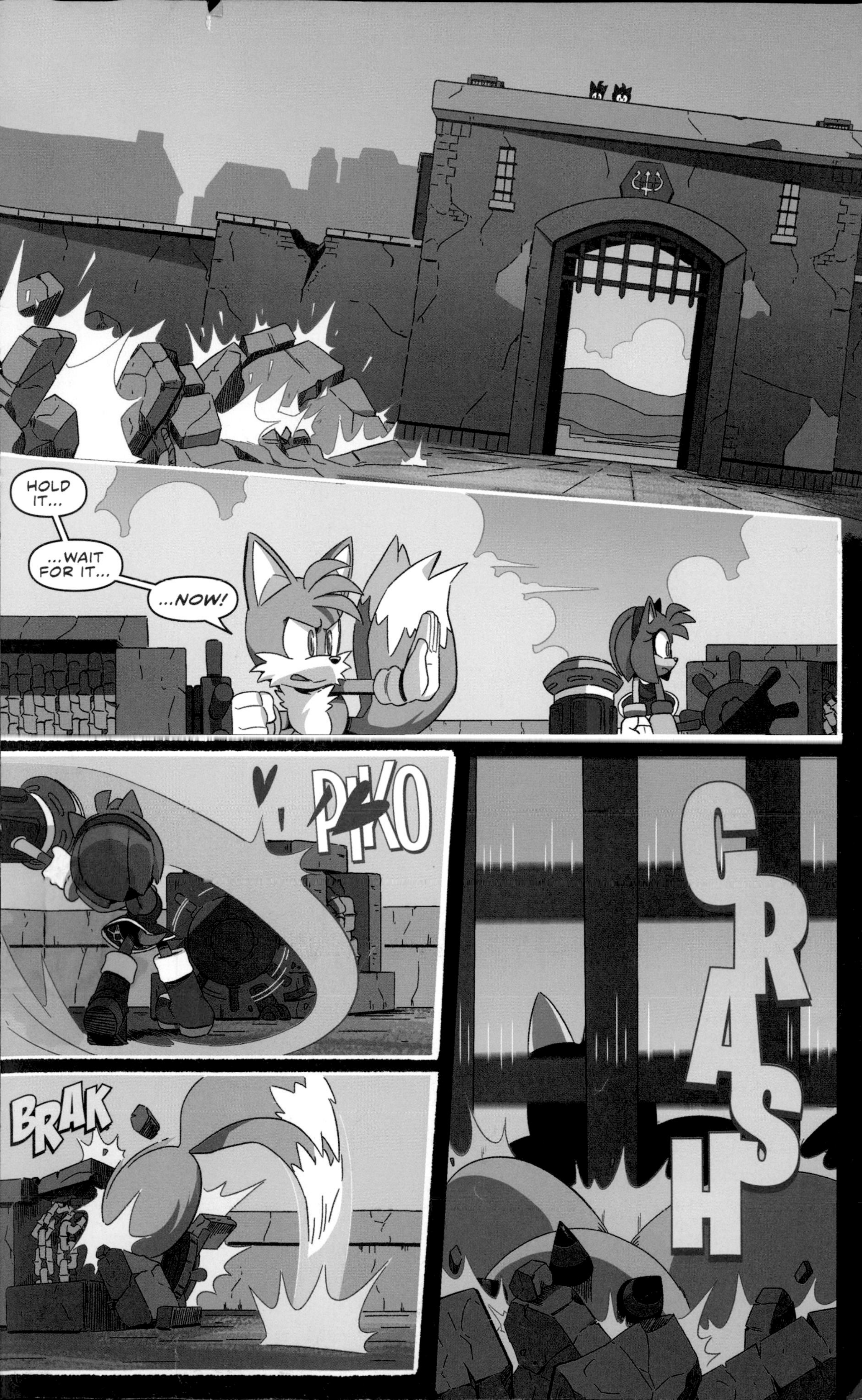
HOLD IT...
...WAIT FOR IT...
...NOW!
PIKO
BRAK
CRASH

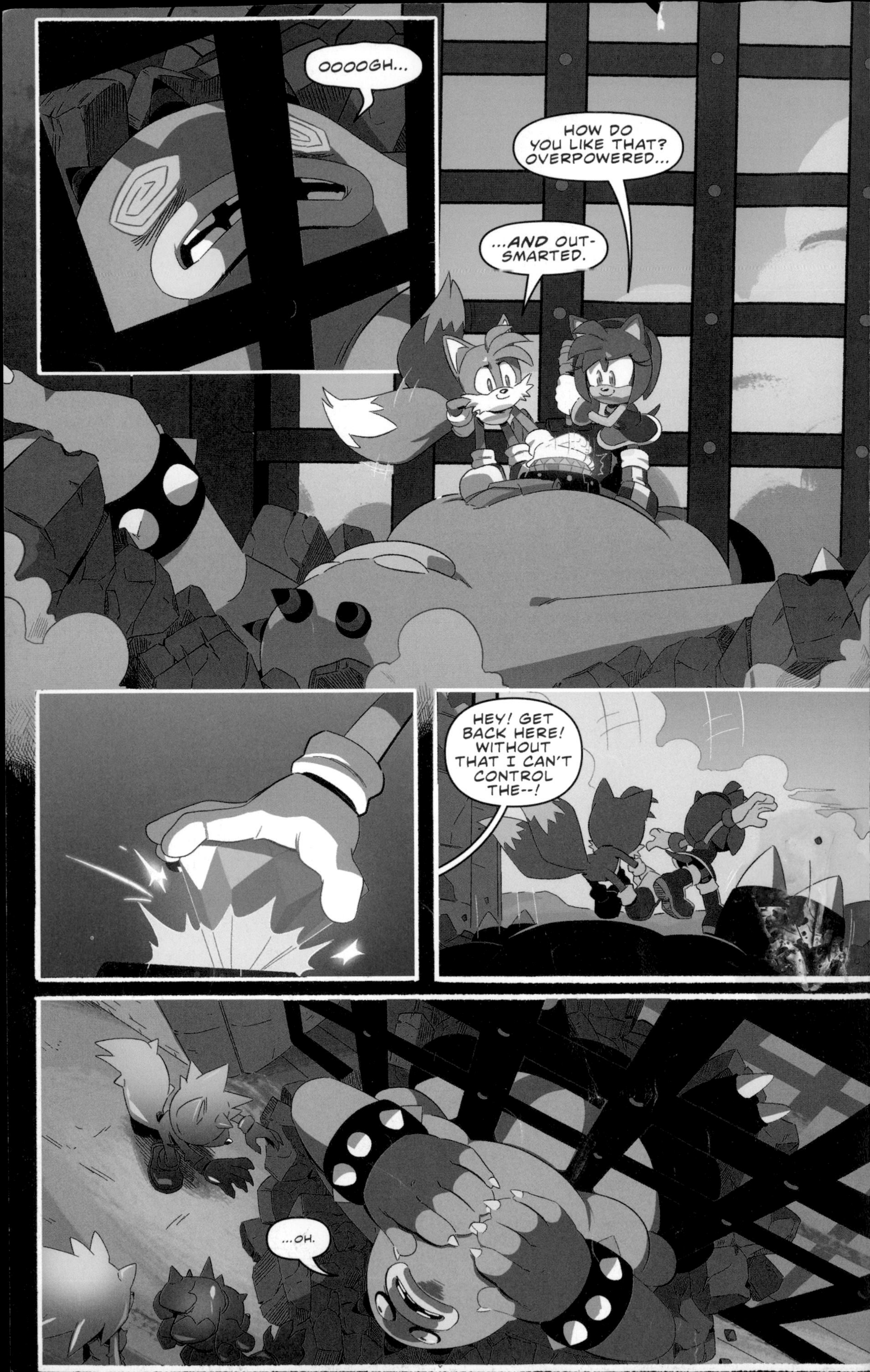
OOOOGH...
HOW DO YOU LIKE THAT? OVERPOWERED...
...**AND** OUT-SMARTED.
HEY! GET BACK HERE! WITHOUT THAT I CAN'T CONTROL THE--!
...OH.

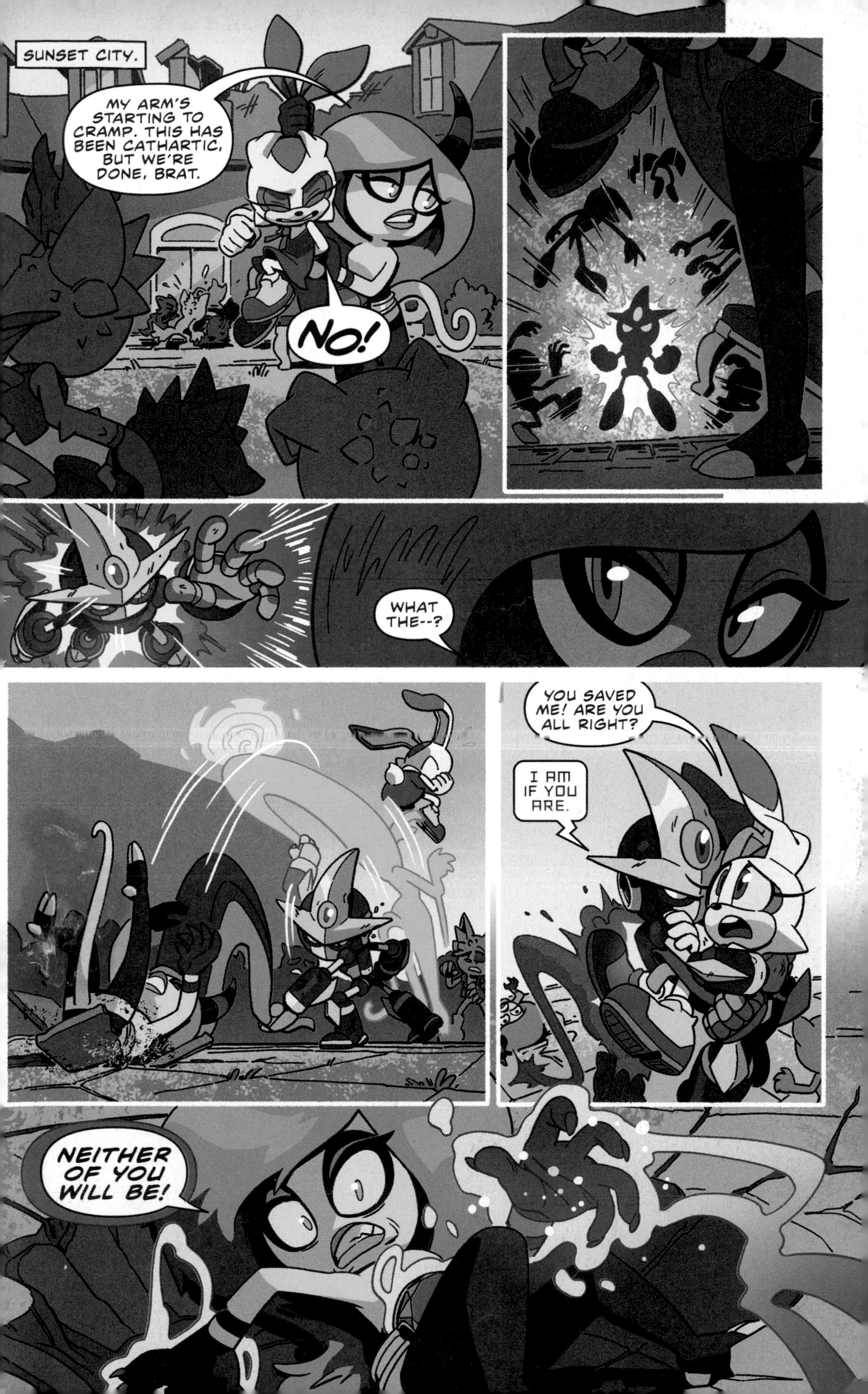
SUNSET CITY.
MY ARM'S STARTING TO CRAMP. THIS HAS BEEN CATHARTIC, BUT WE'RE DONE, BRAT.
NO!
WHAT THE--?
YOU SAVED ME! ARE YOU ALL RIGHT?
I AM IF YOU ARE.
NEITHER OF YOU WILL BE!

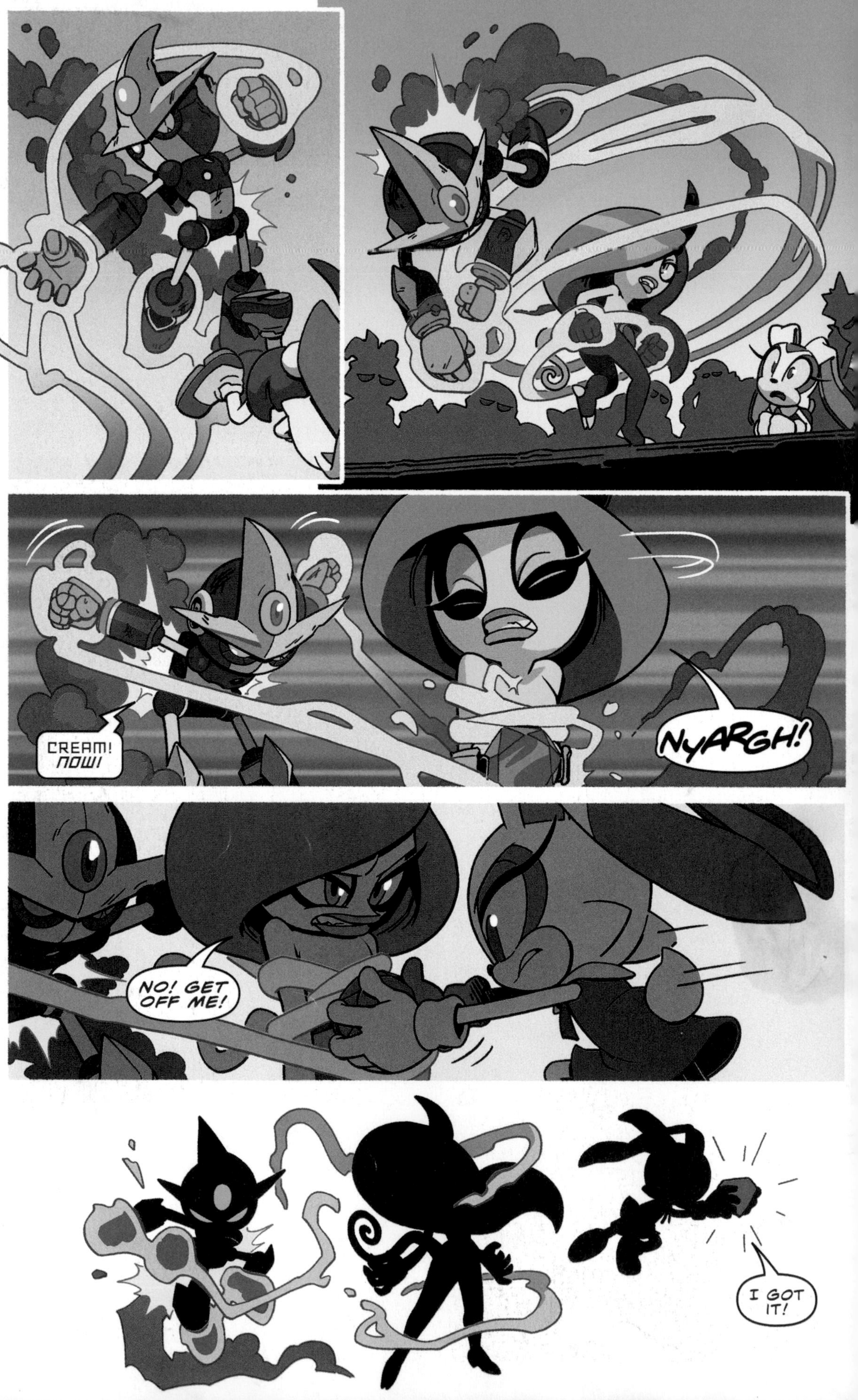
CREAM! NOW!
NYARGH!
NO! GET OFF ME!
I GOT IT!

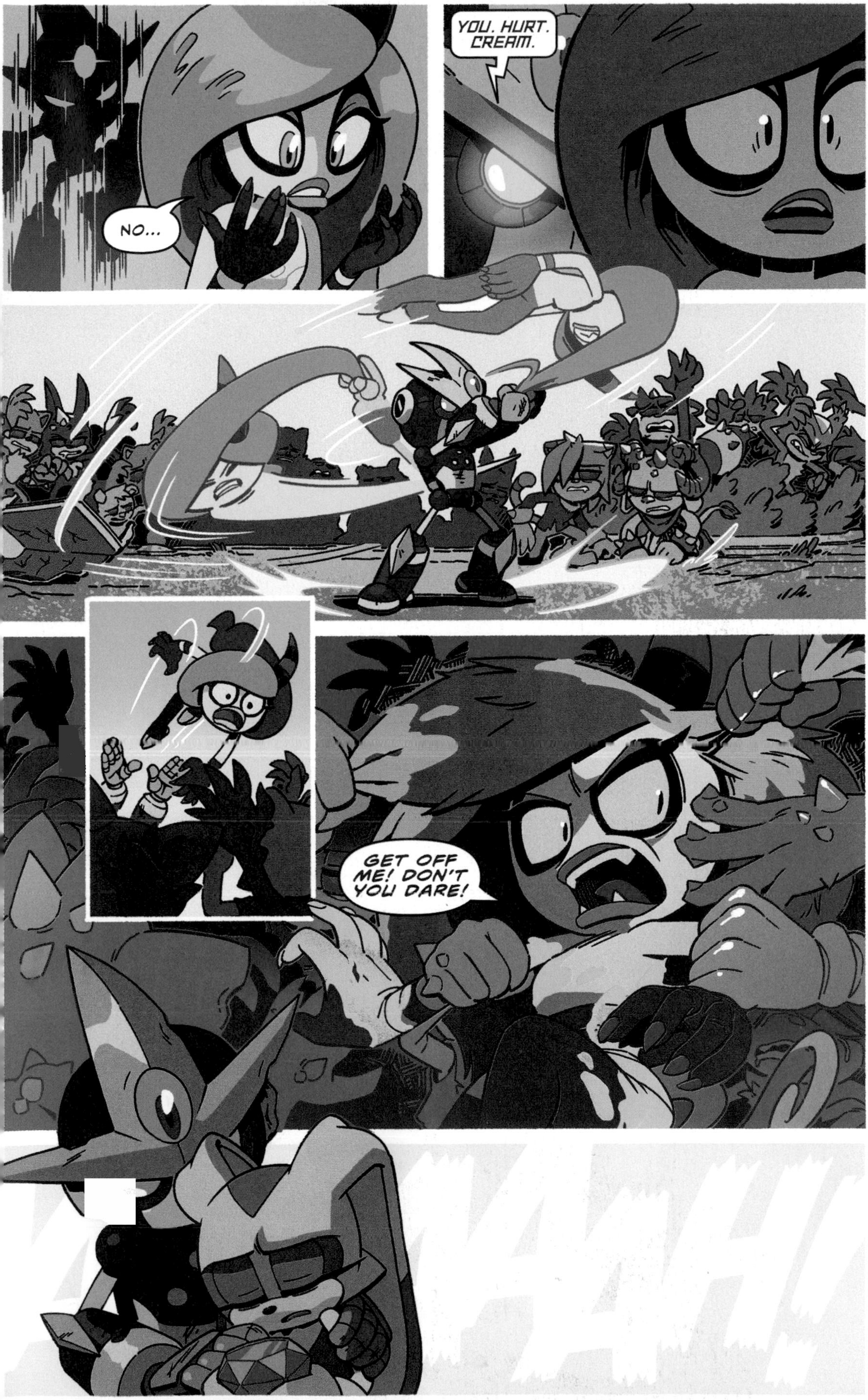
NO...
YOU. HURT. CREAM.
GET OFF ME! DON'T YOU DARE!

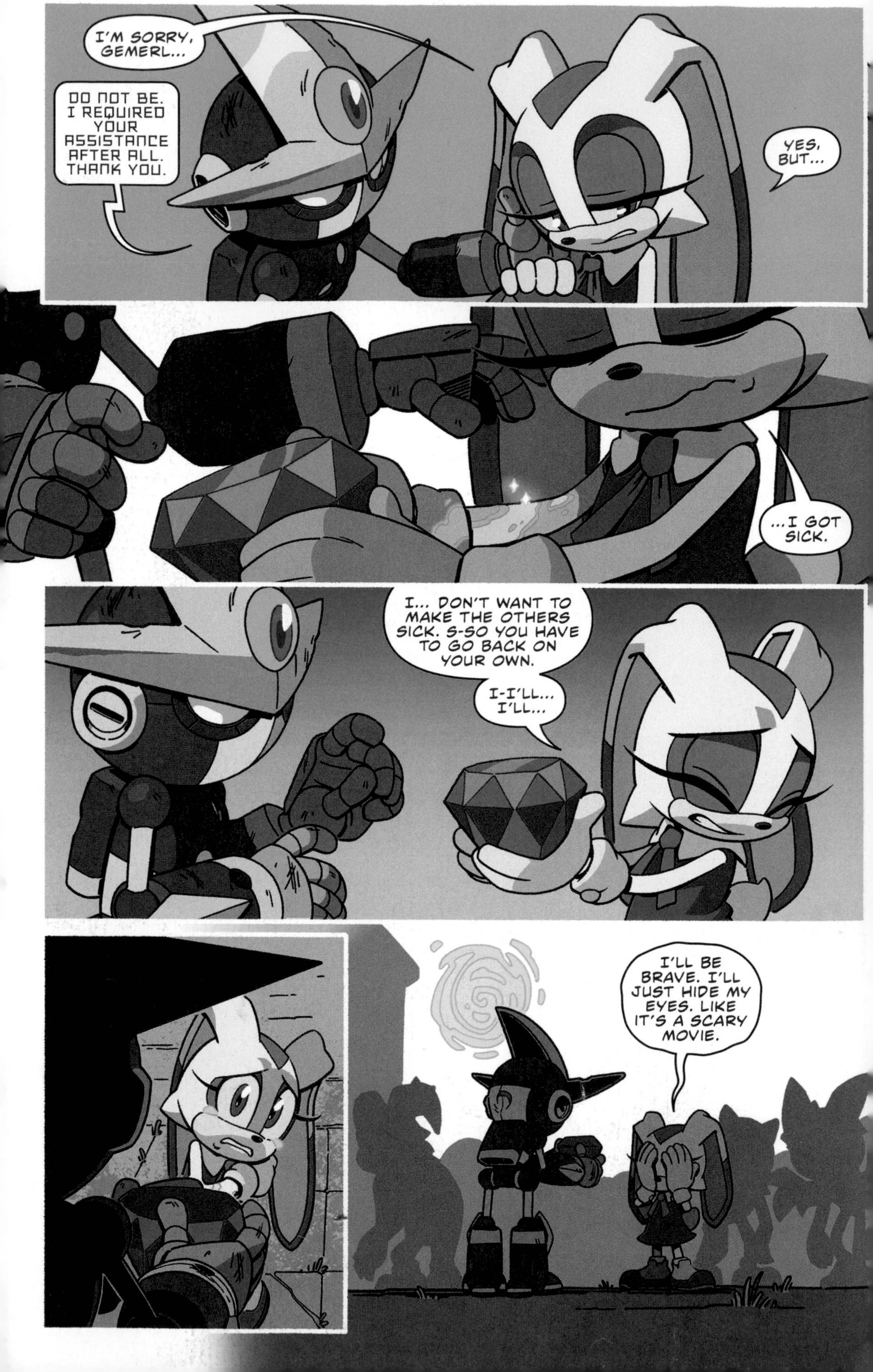
I'M SORRY, GEMERL...
DO NOT BE. I REQUIRED YOUR ASSISTANCE AFTER ALL. THANK YOU.
YES, BUT...
...I GOT SICK.
I... DON'T WANT TO MAKE THE OTHERS SICK. S-SO YOU HAVE TO GO BACK ON YOUR OWN.
I-I'LL... I'LL...
I'LL BE BRAVE. I'LL JUST HIDE MY EYES. LIKE IT'S A SCARY MOVIE.

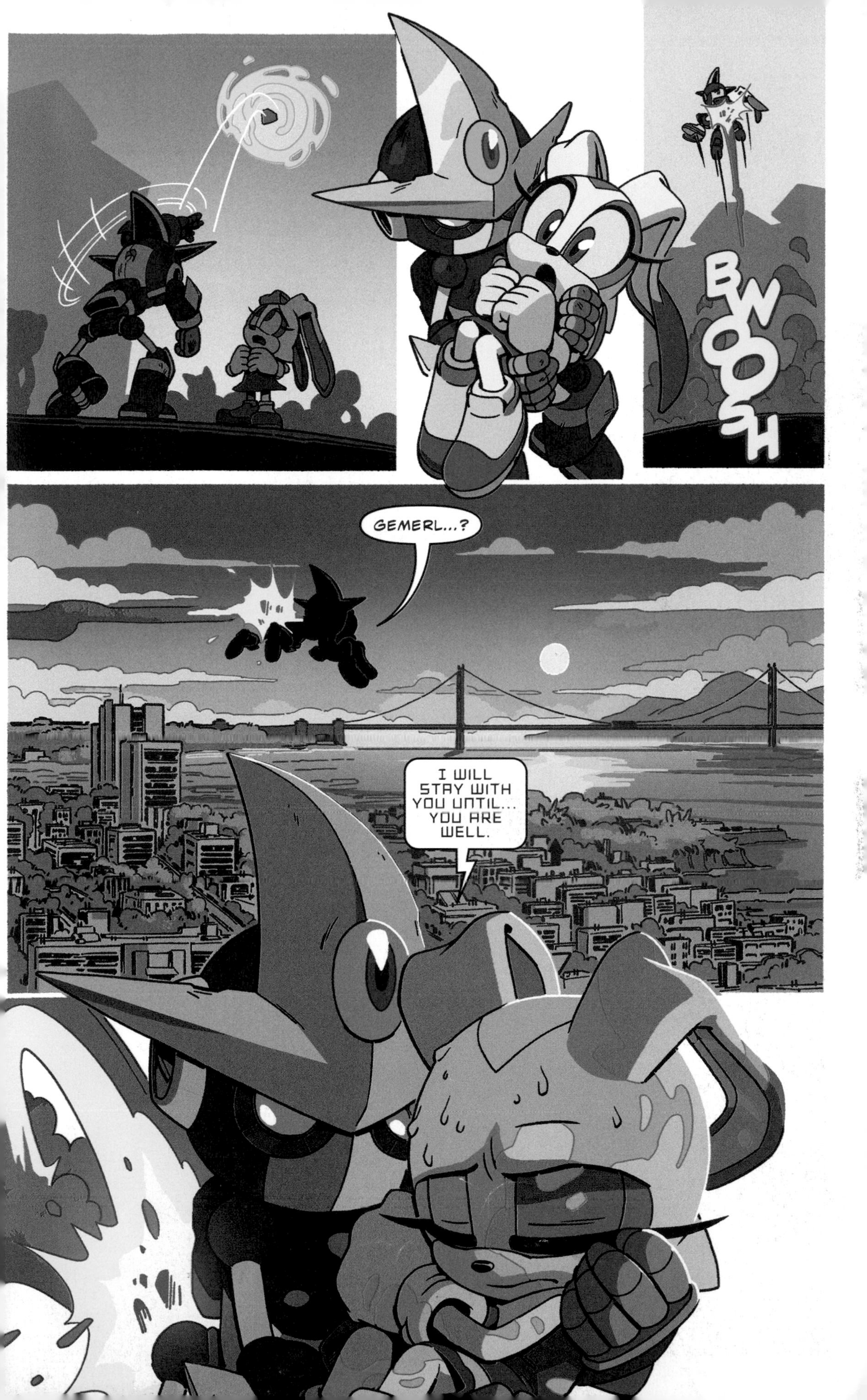
BWOOSH
GEMERL...?
I WILL STAY WITH YOU UNTIL... YOU ARE WELL.

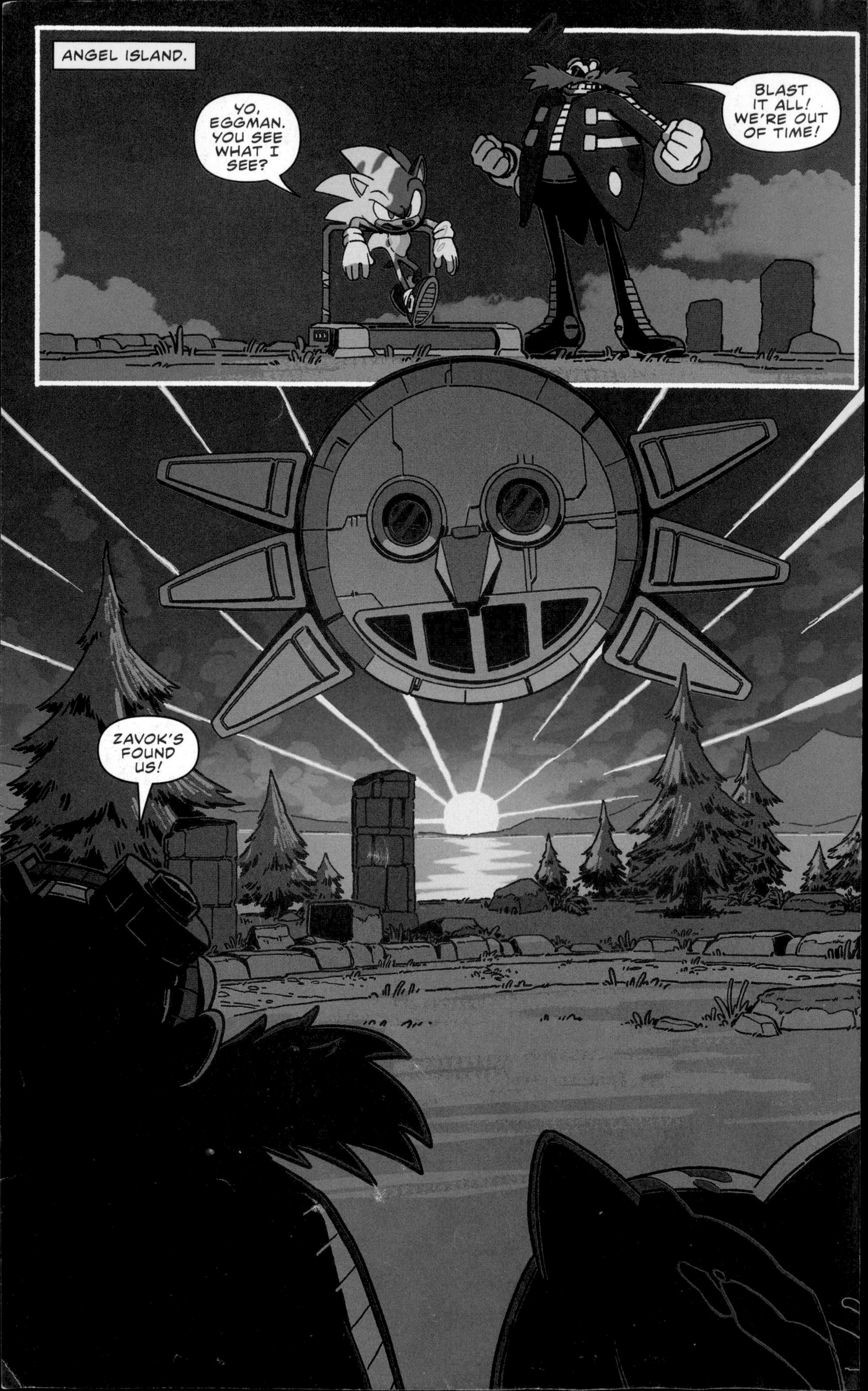
ANGEL ISLAND.
YO, EGGMAN. YOU SEE WHAT I SEE?
BLAST IT ALL! WE'RE OUT OF TIME!
ZAVOK'S FOUND US!

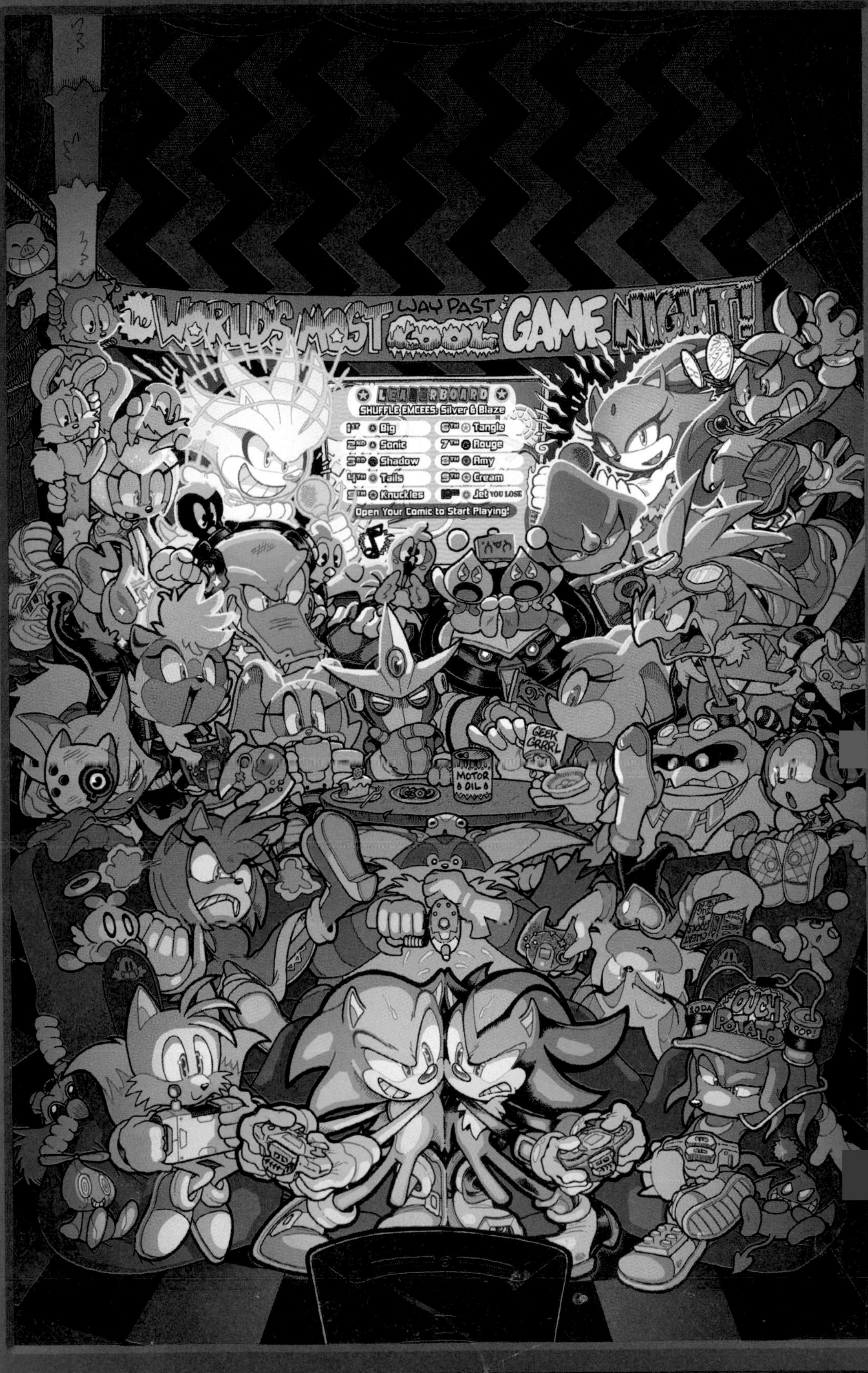
The WORLD'S MOST WAY PAST COOL GAME NIGHT!!
LEADERBOARD
SHUFFLE EMCEES: Silver & Blaze
1ST Big
2ND Sonic
3RD Shadow
4TH Tails
5TH Knuckles
6TH Tangle
7TH Rouge
8TH Amy
9TH Cream
10TH Jet YOU LOSE
Open Your Comic to Start Playing!
GEEK GRRRL
MOTOR OIL
OUCH POTATO
SODA
POP!

ART BY **JONATHAN GRAY** COLORS BY **REGGIE GRAHAM**

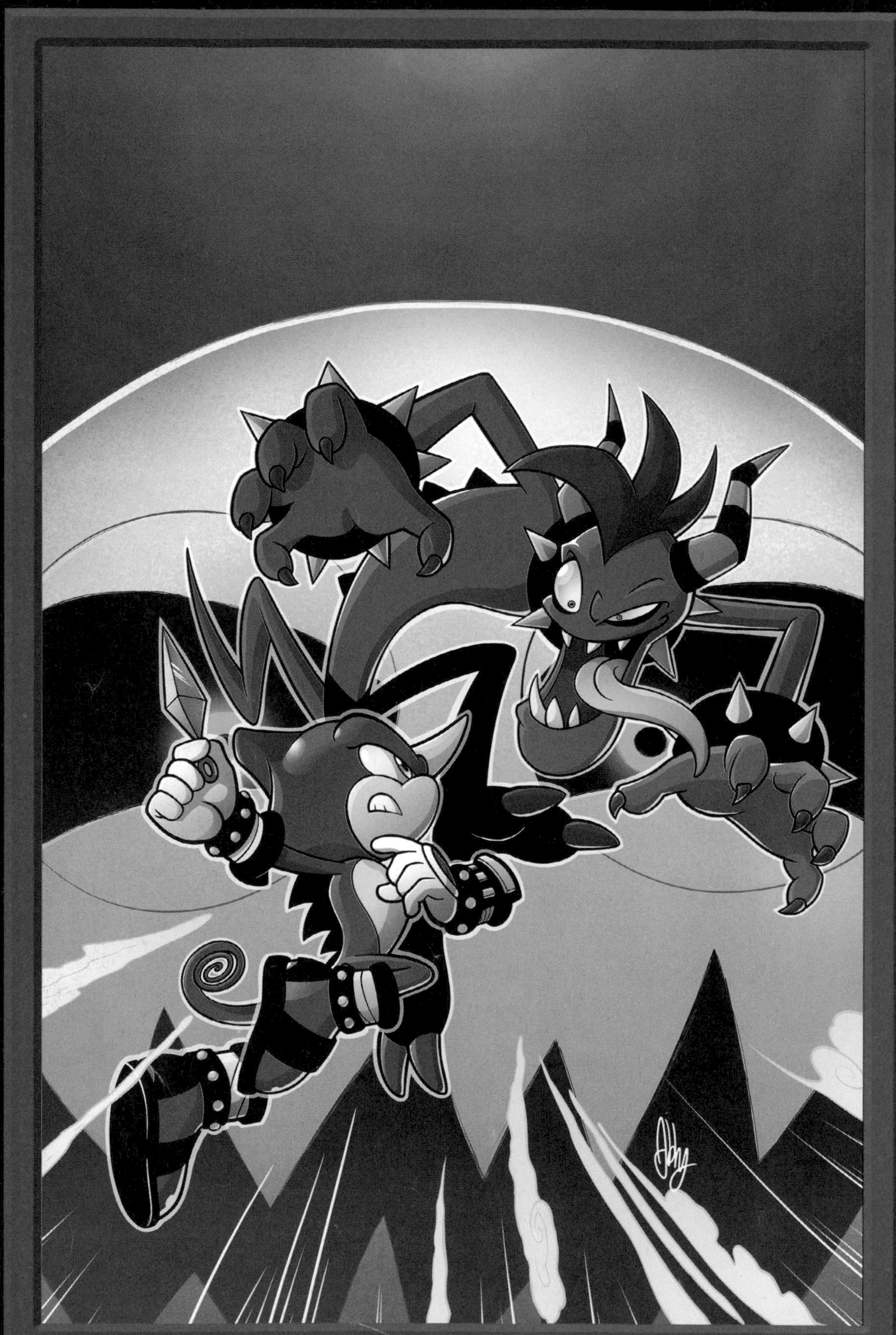

ART BY **ABBY BULMER**

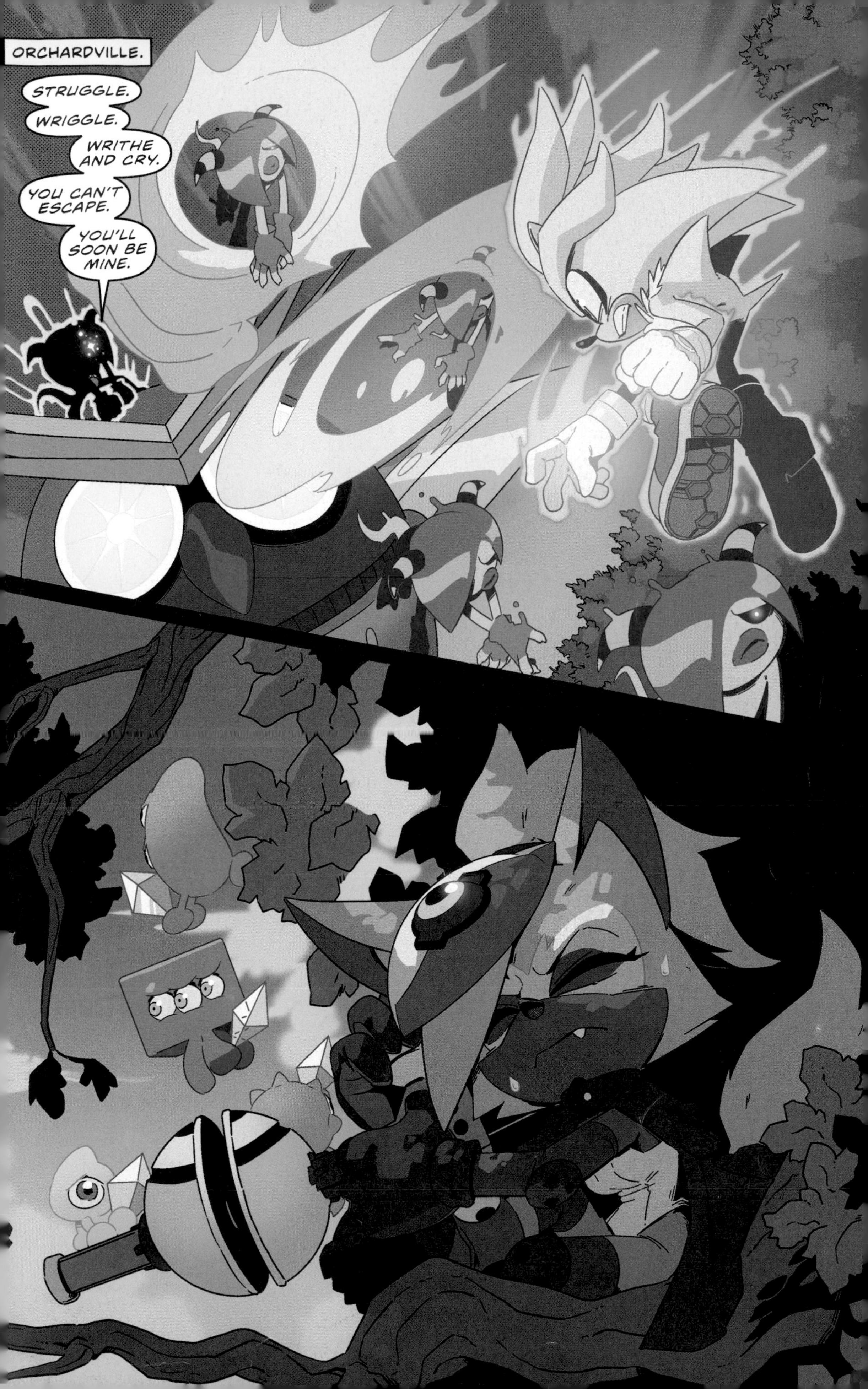
ORCHARDVILLE.
STRUGGLE.
WRIGGLE.
WRITHE AND CRY.
YOU CAN'T ESCAPE.
YOU'LL SOON BE MINE.

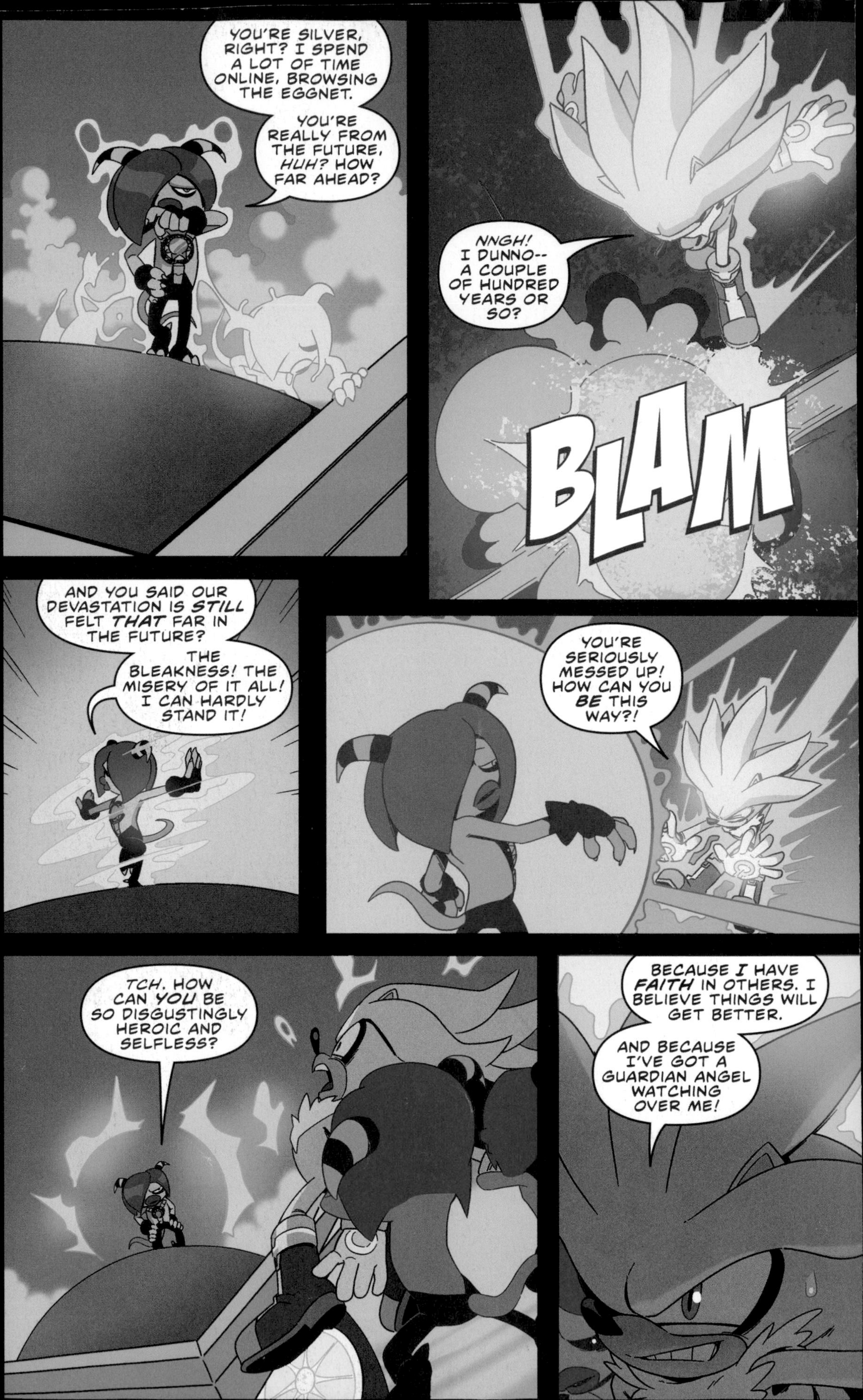
YOU'RE SILVER, RIGHT? I SPEND A LOT OF TIME ONLINE, BROWSING THE EGGNET.
YOU'RE REALLY FROM THE FUTURE, HUH? HOW FAR AHEAD?
NNGH! I DUNNO-- A COUPLE OF HUNDRED YEARS OR SO?
BLAM
AND YOU SAID OUR DEVASTATION IS STILL FELT THAT FAR IN THE FUTURE?
THE BLEAKNESS! THE MISERY OF IT ALL! I CAN HARDLY STAND IT!
YOU'RE SERIOUSLY MESSED UP! HOW CAN YOU BE THIS WAY?!
TCH. HOW CAN YOU BE SO DISGUSTINGLY HEROIC AND SELFLESS?
BECAUSE I HAVE FAITH IN OTHERS. I BELIEVE THINGS WILL GET BETTER.
AND BECAUSE I'VE GOT A GUARDIAN ANGEL WATCHING OVER ME!

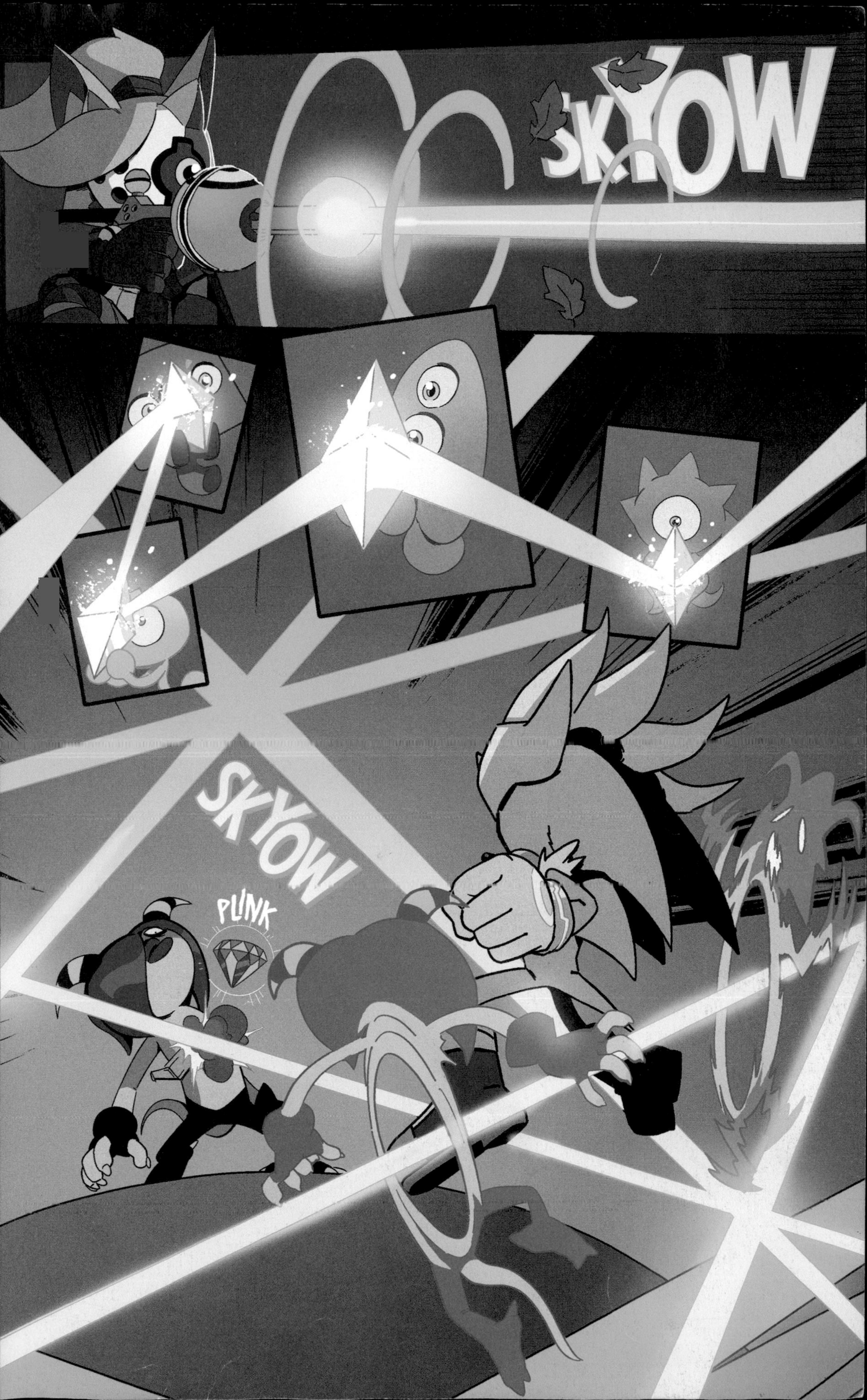
SKYOW
SKYOW
PLINK

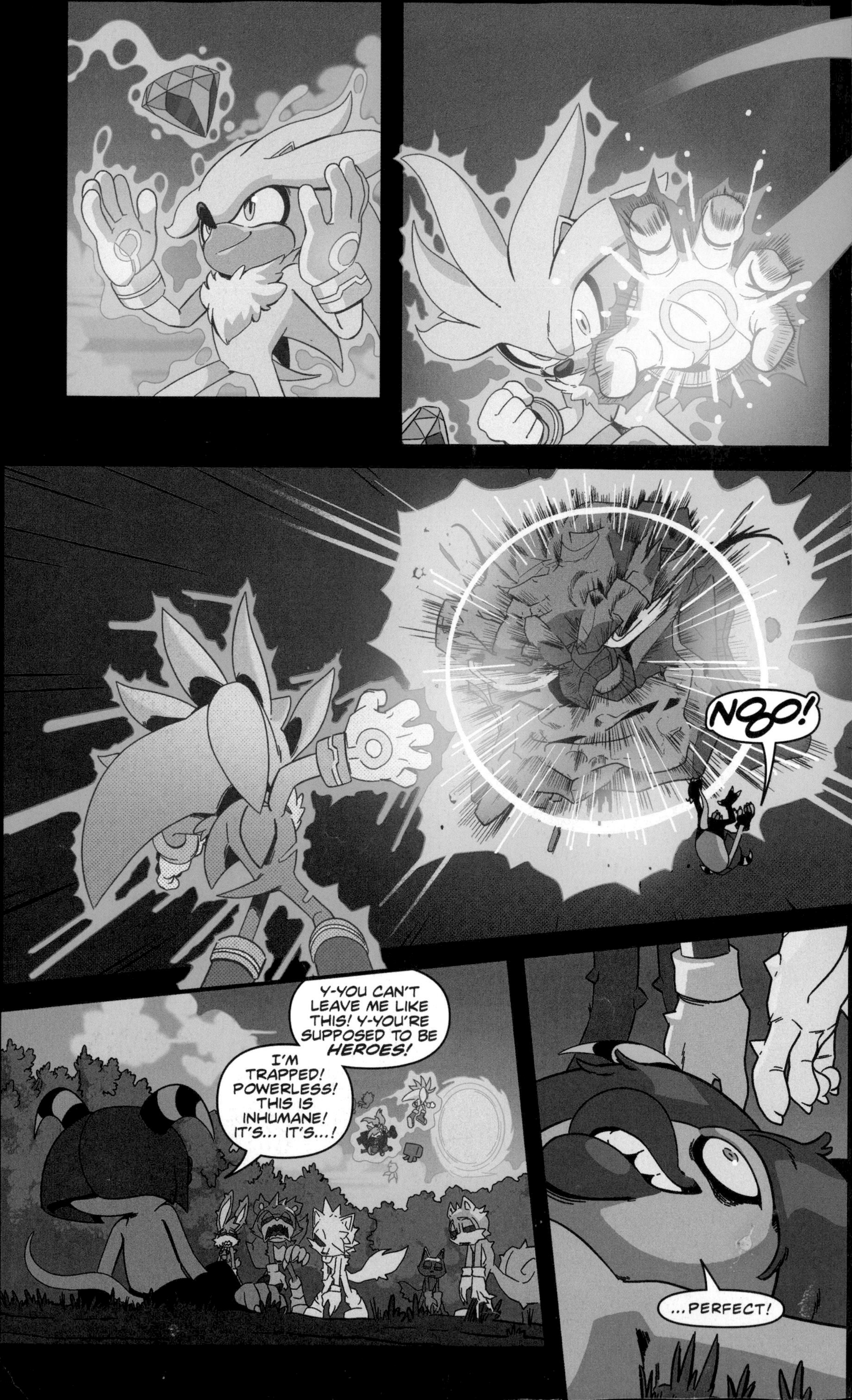
NOO!
Y-YOU CAN'T LEAVE ME LIKE THIS! Y-YOU'RE SUPPOSED TO BE HEROES!
I'M TRAPPED! POWERLESS! THIS IS INHUMANE! IT'S... IT'S...!
...PERFECT!

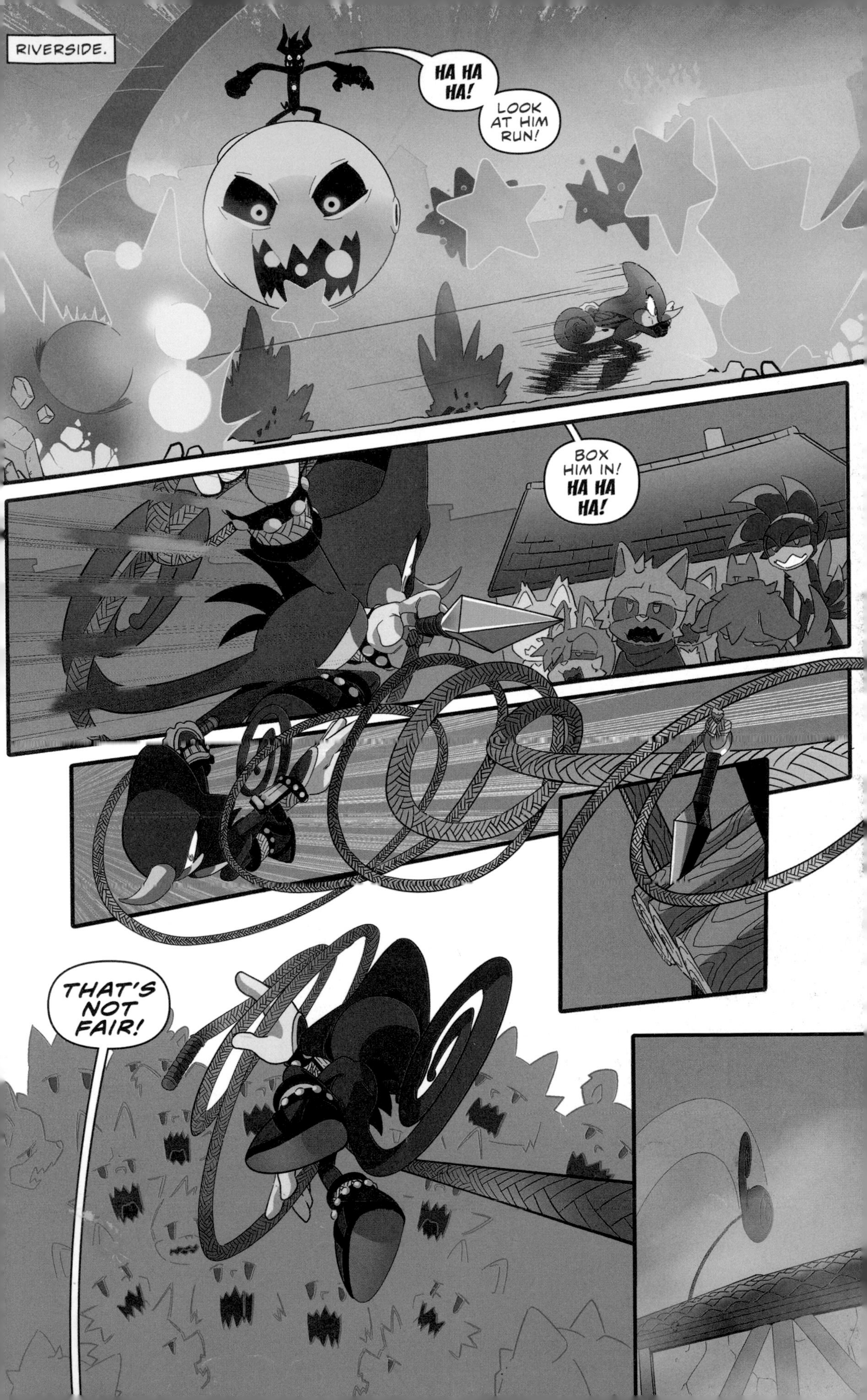
RIVERSIDE.
HA HA HA!
LOOK AT HIM RUN!
BOX HIM IN! HA HA HA!
THAT'S NOT FAIR!

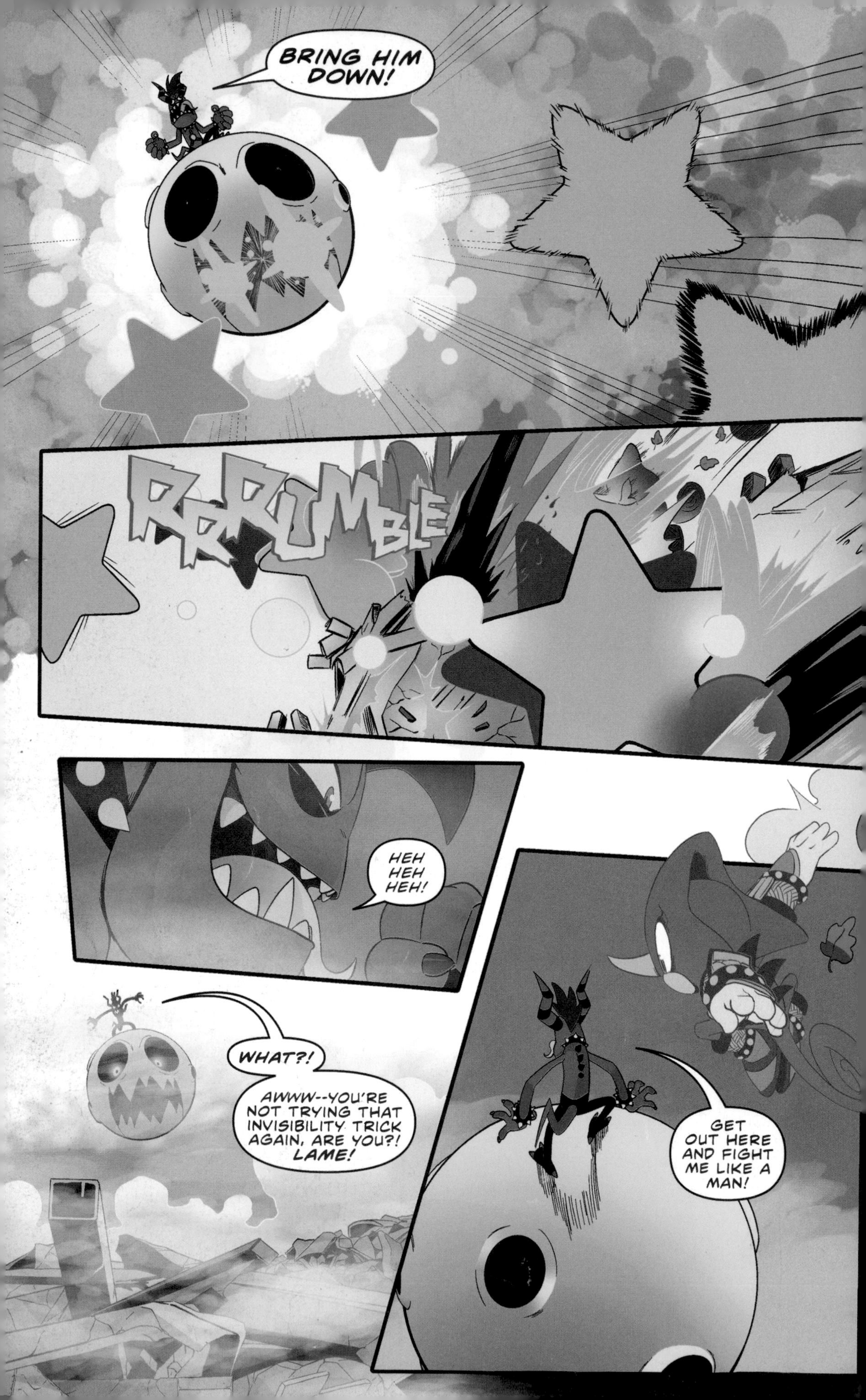
BRING HIM DOWN!
RRRUMBLE
HEH HEH HEH!
WHAT?!
AWWW--YOU'RE NOT TRYING THAT INVISIBILITY TRICK AGAIN, ARE YOU?! LAME!
GET OUT HERE AND FIGHT ME LIKE A MAN!

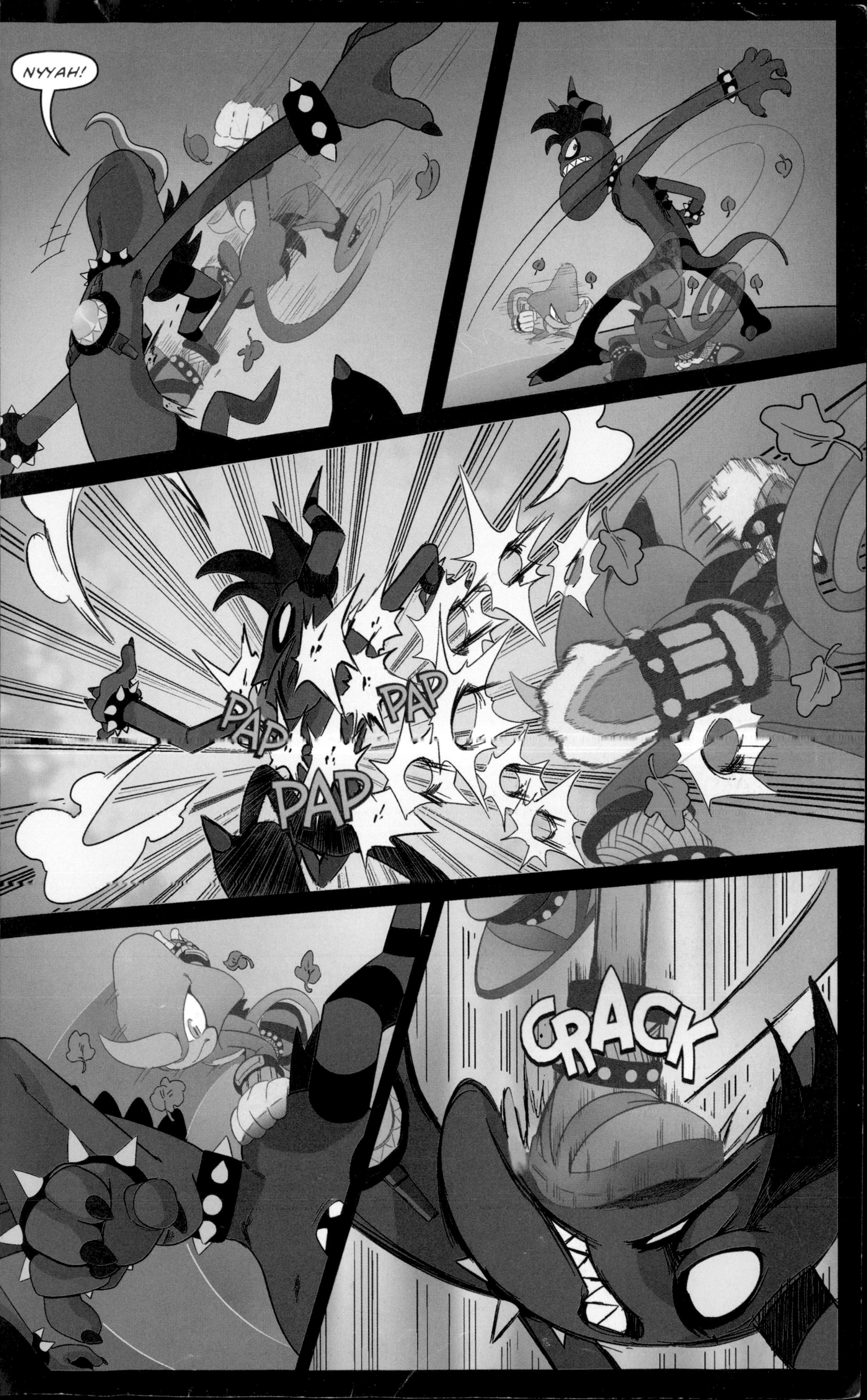
NYYAH!
PAP
PAP
PAP
CRACK

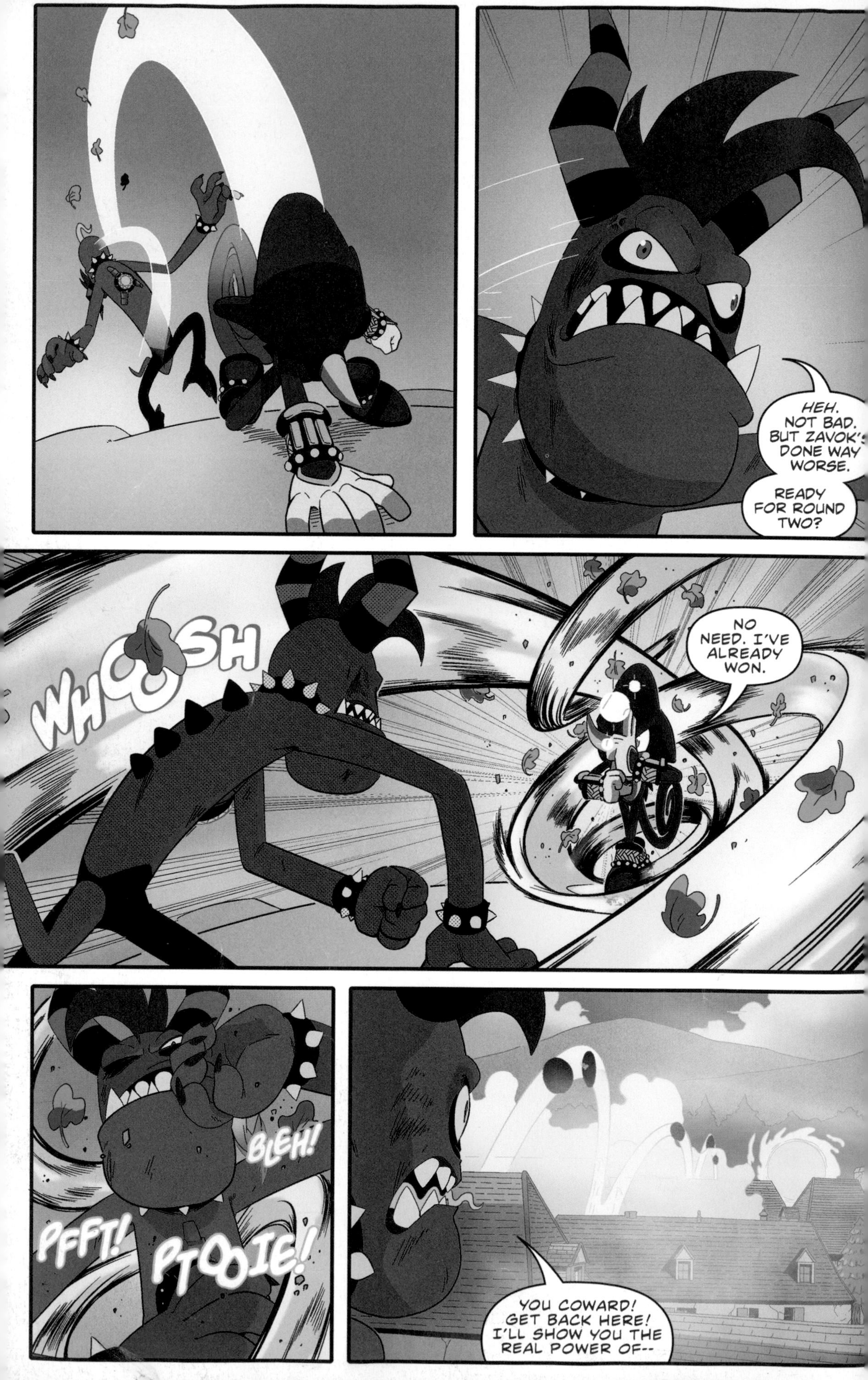
HEH. NOT BAD. BUT ZAVOK'S DONE WAY WORSE.
READY FOR ROUND TWO?
WHOOSH
NO NEED. I'VE ALREADY WON.
BLEH!
PFFT!
PTOOIE!
YOU COWARD! GET BACK HERE! I'LL SHOW YOU THE REAL POWER OF--

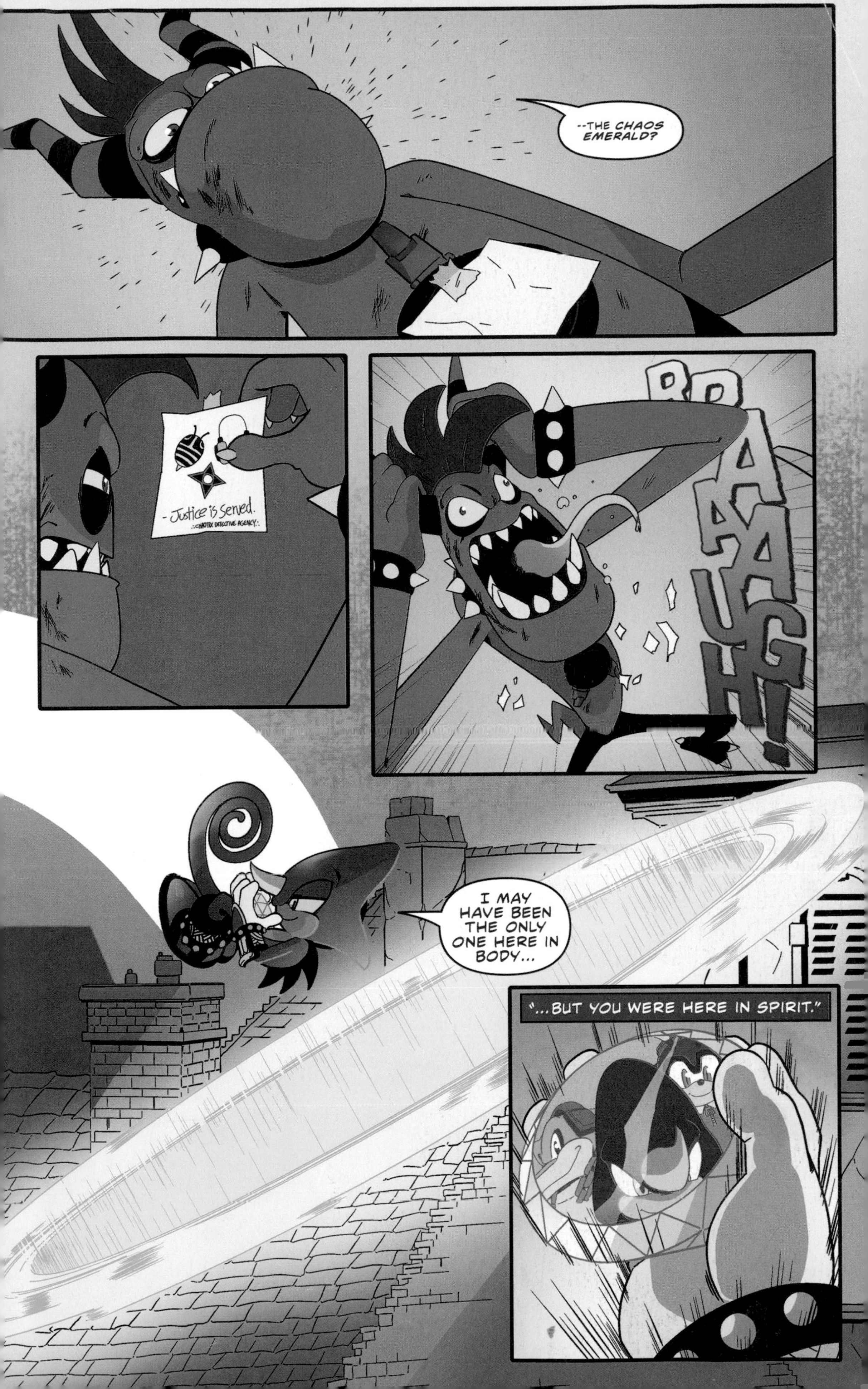
--THE CHAOS EMERALD?
- Justice is Served.
CHAOTIX DETECTIVE AGENCY
BRAAAAUGH!
I MAY HAVE BEEN THE ONLY ONE HERE IN BODY...
"...BUT YOU WERE HERE IN SPIRIT."

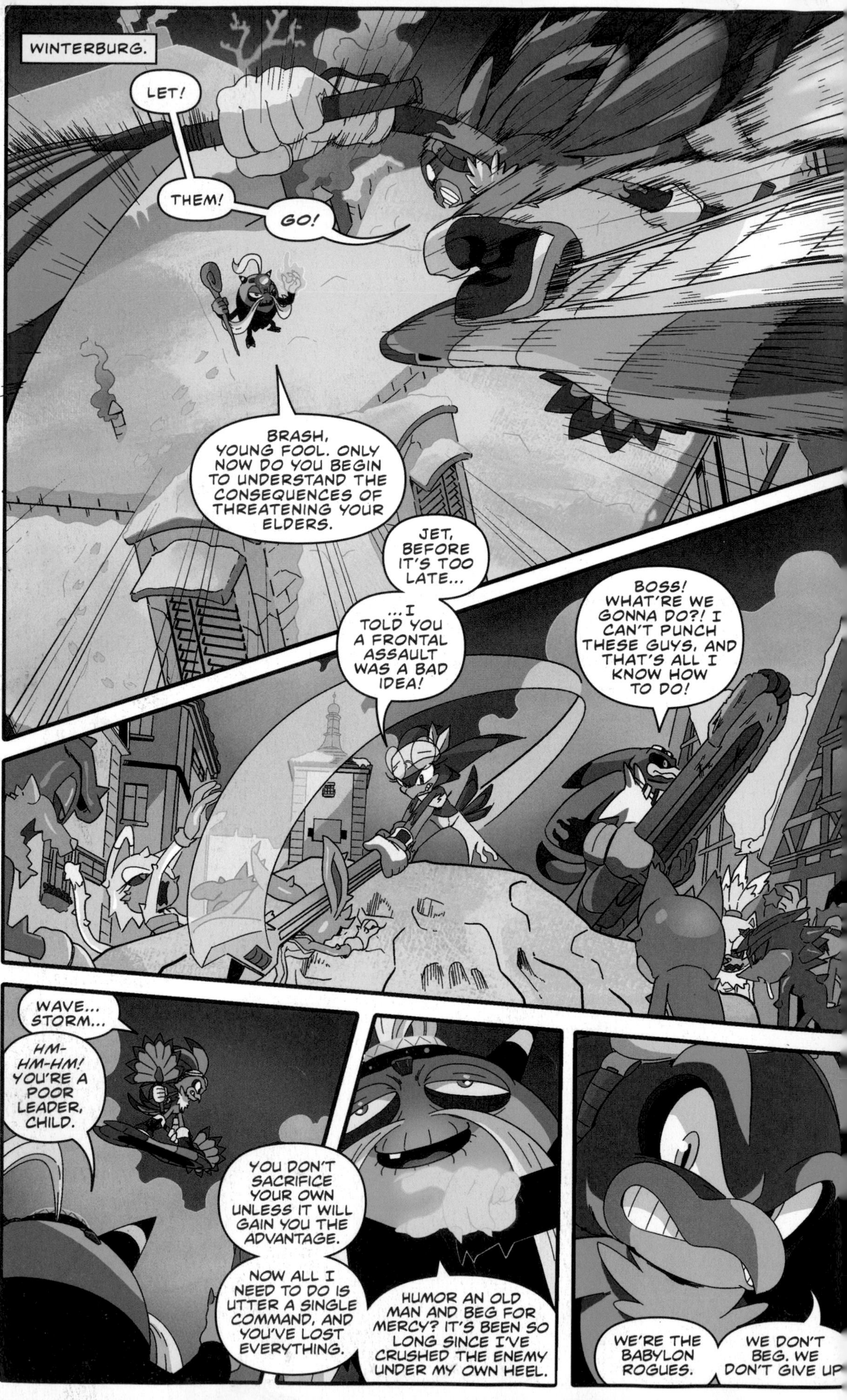
WINTERBURG.
LET!
THEM!
GO!
BRASH, YOUNG FOOL. ONLY NOW DO YOU BEGIN TO UNDERSTAND THE CONSEQUENCES OF THREATENING YOUR ELDERS.
JET, BEFORE IT'S TOO LATE...
...I TOLD YOU A FRONTAL ASSAULT WAS A BAD IDEA!
BOSS! WHAT'RE WE GONNA DO?! I CAN'T PUNCH THESE GUYS, AND THAT'S ALL I KNOW HOW TO DO!
WAVE... STORM...
HM-HM-HM! YOU'RE A POOR LEADER, CHILD.
YOU DON'T SACRIFICE YOUR OWN UNLESS IT WILL GAIN YOU THE ADVANTAGE.
NOW ALL I NEED TO DO IS UTTER A SINGLE COMMAND, AND YOU'VE LOST EVERYTHING.
HUMOR AN OLD MAN AND BEG FOR MERCY? IT'S BEEN SO LONG SINCE I'VE CRUSHED THE ENEMY UNDER MY OWN HEEL.
WE'RE THE BABYLON ROGUES.
WE DON'T BEG. WE DON'T GIVE UP

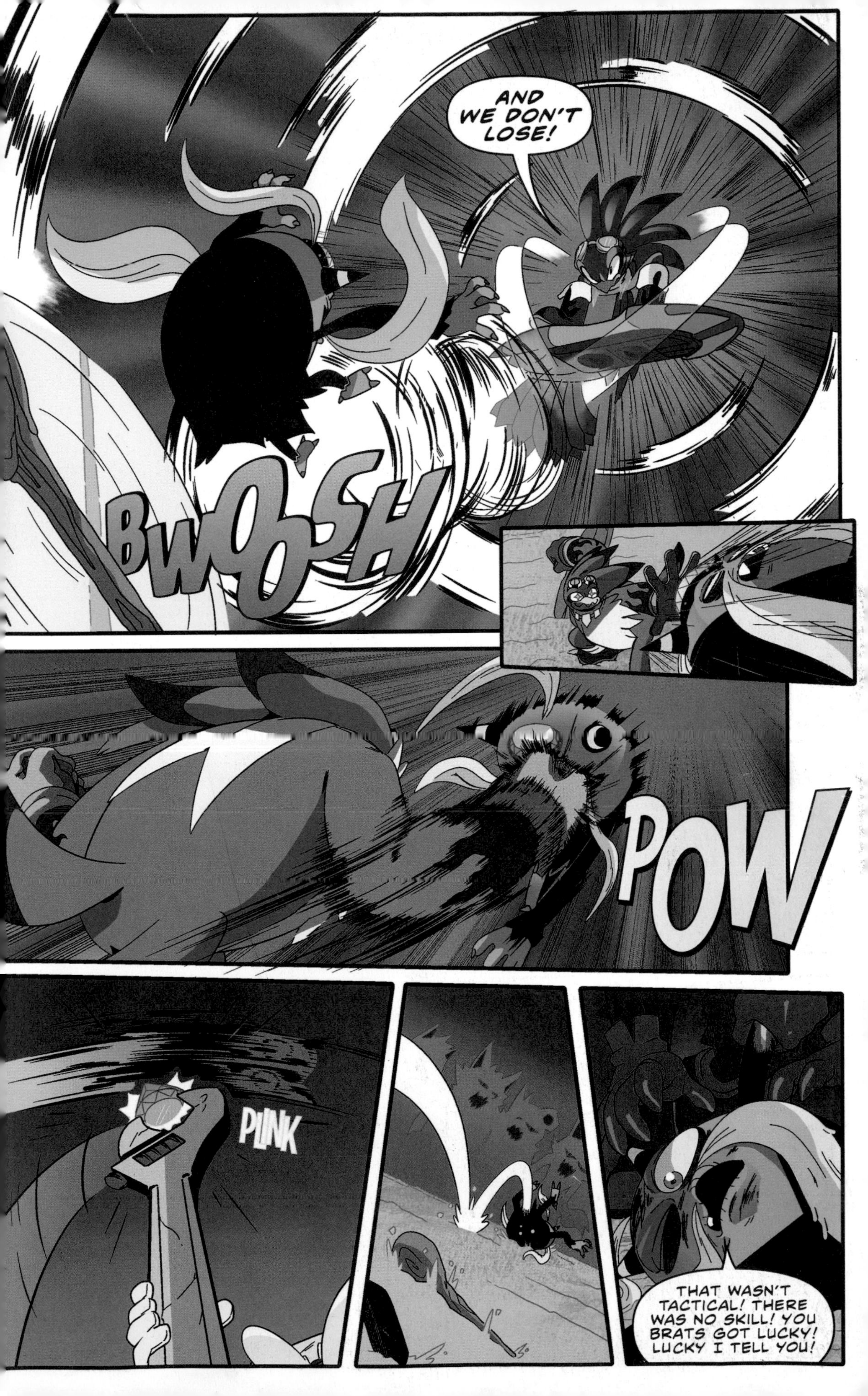
AND WE DON'T LOSE!
BWOOSH
POW
PLINK
THAT WASN'T TACTICAL! THERE WAS NO SKILL! YOU BRATS GOT LUCKY! LUCKY I TELL YOU!

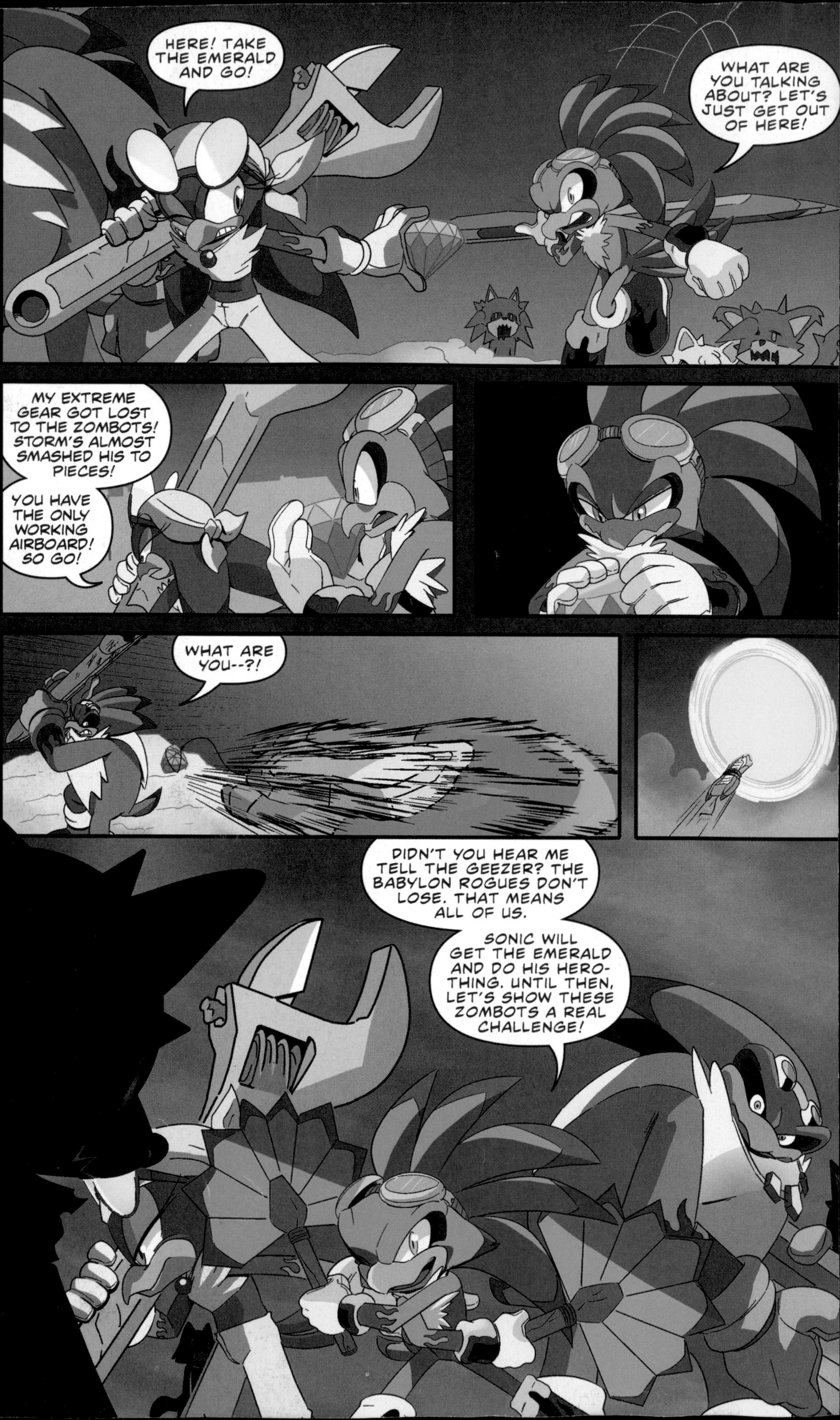
HERE! TAKE THE EMERALD AND GO!
WHAT ARE YOU TALKING ABOUT? LET'S JUST GET OUT OF HERE!
MY EXTREME GEAR GOT LOST TO THE ZOMBOTS! STORM'S ALMOST SMASHED HIS TO PIECES!
YOU HAVE THE ONLY WORKING AIRBOARD! SO GO!
WHAT ARE YOU--?!
DIDN'T YOU HEAR ME TELL THE GEEZER? THE BABYLON ROGUES DON'T LOSE. THAT MEANS ALL OF US.
SONIC WILL GET THE EMERALD AND DO HIS HERO-THING. UNTIL THEN, LET'S SHOW THESE ZOMBOTS A REAL CHALLENGE!

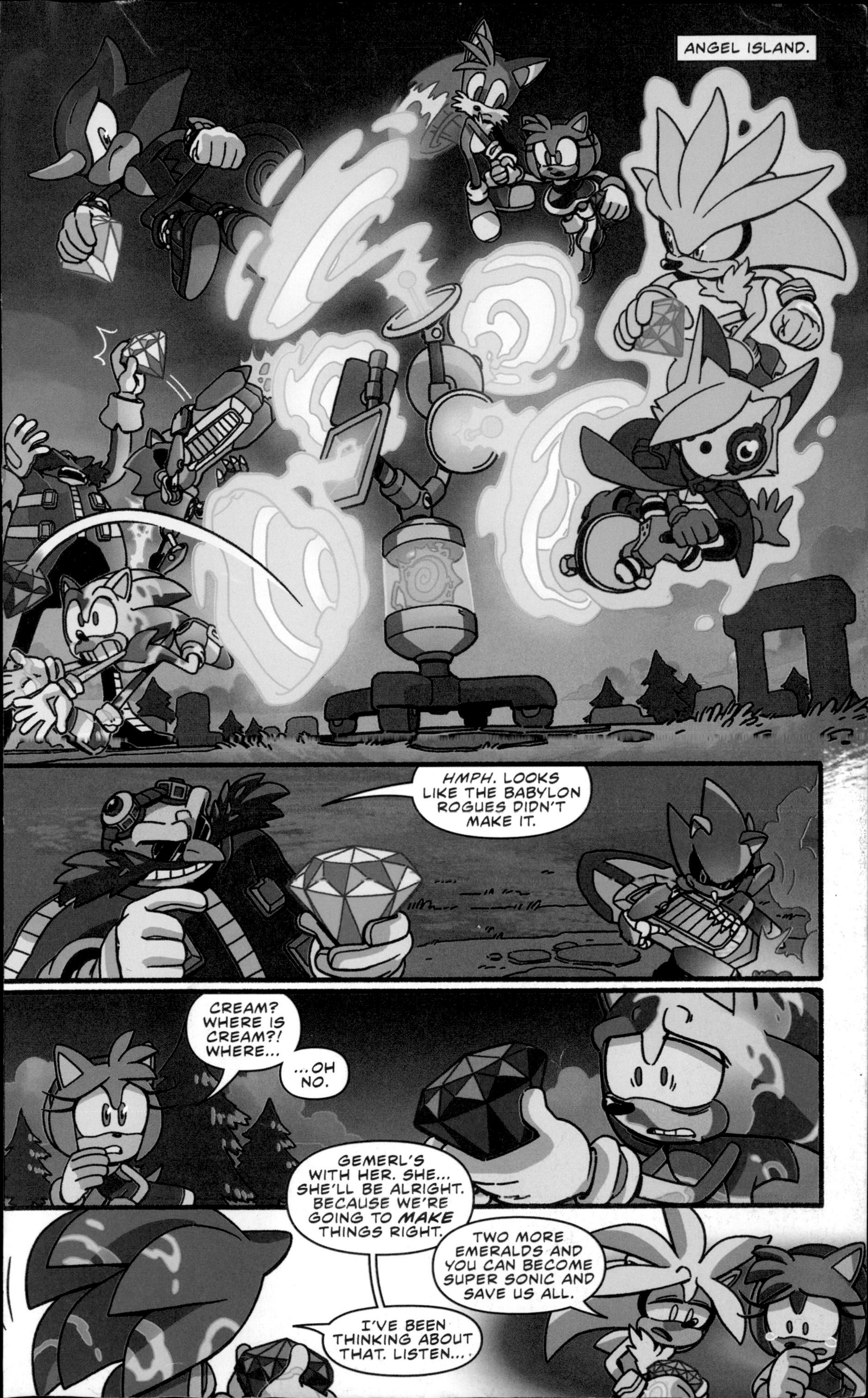

ANGEL ISLAND.
HMPH. LOOKS LIKE THE BABYLON ROGUES DIDN'T MAKE IT.
CREAM? WHERE IS CREAM?! WHERE...
...OH NO.
GEMERL'S WITH HER. SHE... SHE'LL BE ALRIGHT. BECAUSE WE'RE GOING TO MAKE THINGS RIGHT.
TWO MORE EMERALDS AND YOU CAN BECOME SUPER SONIC AND SAVE US ALL.
I'VE BEEN THINKING ABOUT THAT. LISTEN...

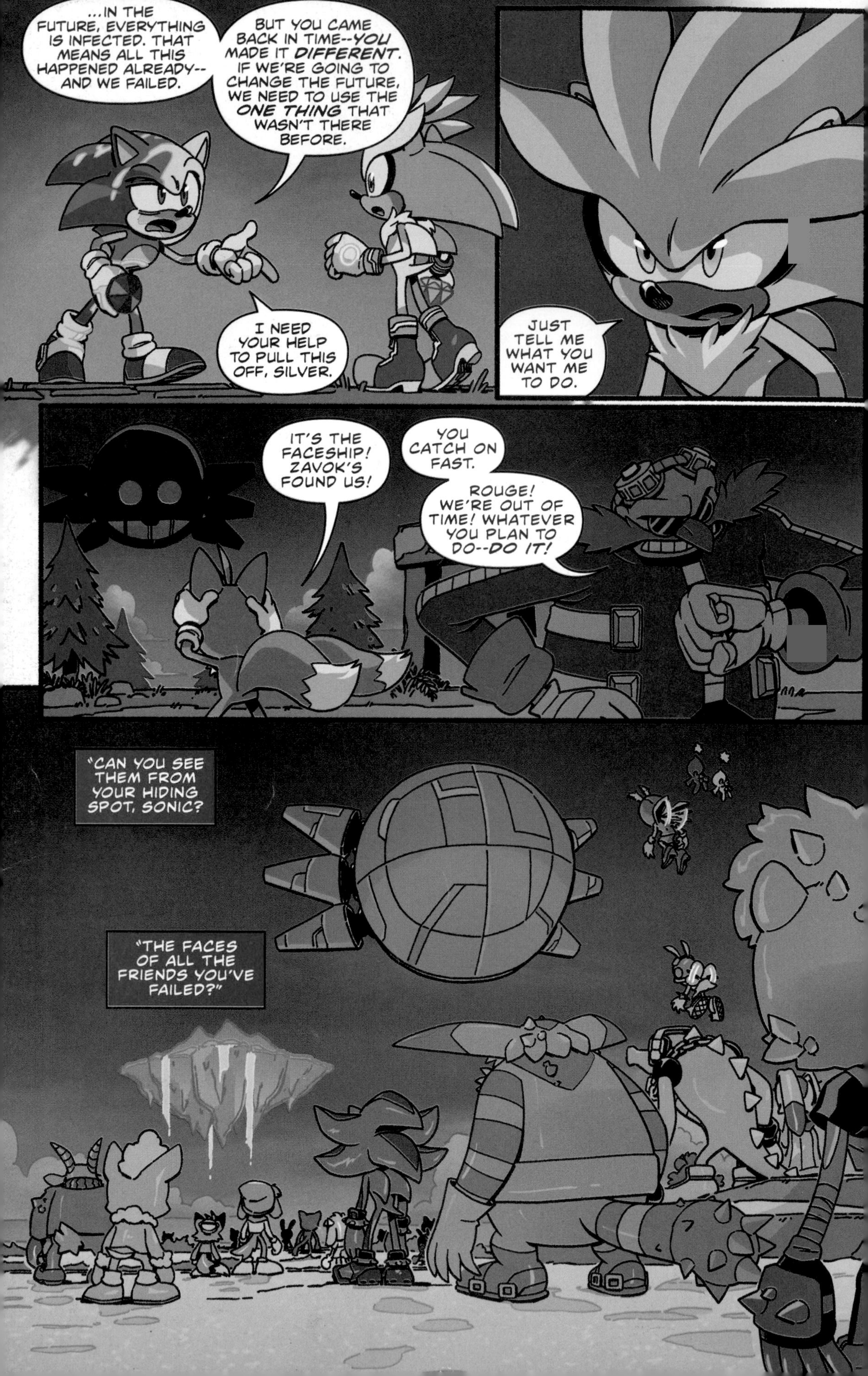
...IN THE FUTURE, EVERYTHING IS INFECTED. THAT MEANS ALL THIS HAPPENED ALREADY-- AND WE FAILED.
BUT YOU CAME BACK IN TIME--YOU MADE IT DIFFERENT. IF WE'RE GOING TO CHANGE THE FUTURE, WE NEED TO USE THE ONE THING THAT WASN'T THERE BEFORE.
I NEED YOUR HELP TO PULL THIS OFF, SILVER.
JUST TELL ME WHAT YOU WANT ME TO DO.
IT'S THE FACESHIP! ZAVOK'S FOUND US!
YOU CATCH ON FAST.
ROUGE! WE'RE OUT OF TIME! WHATEVER YOU PLAN TO DO--DO IT!
"CAN YOU SEE THEM FROM YOUR HIDING SPOT, SONIC?
"THE FACES OF ALL THE FRIENDS YOU'VE FAILED?"

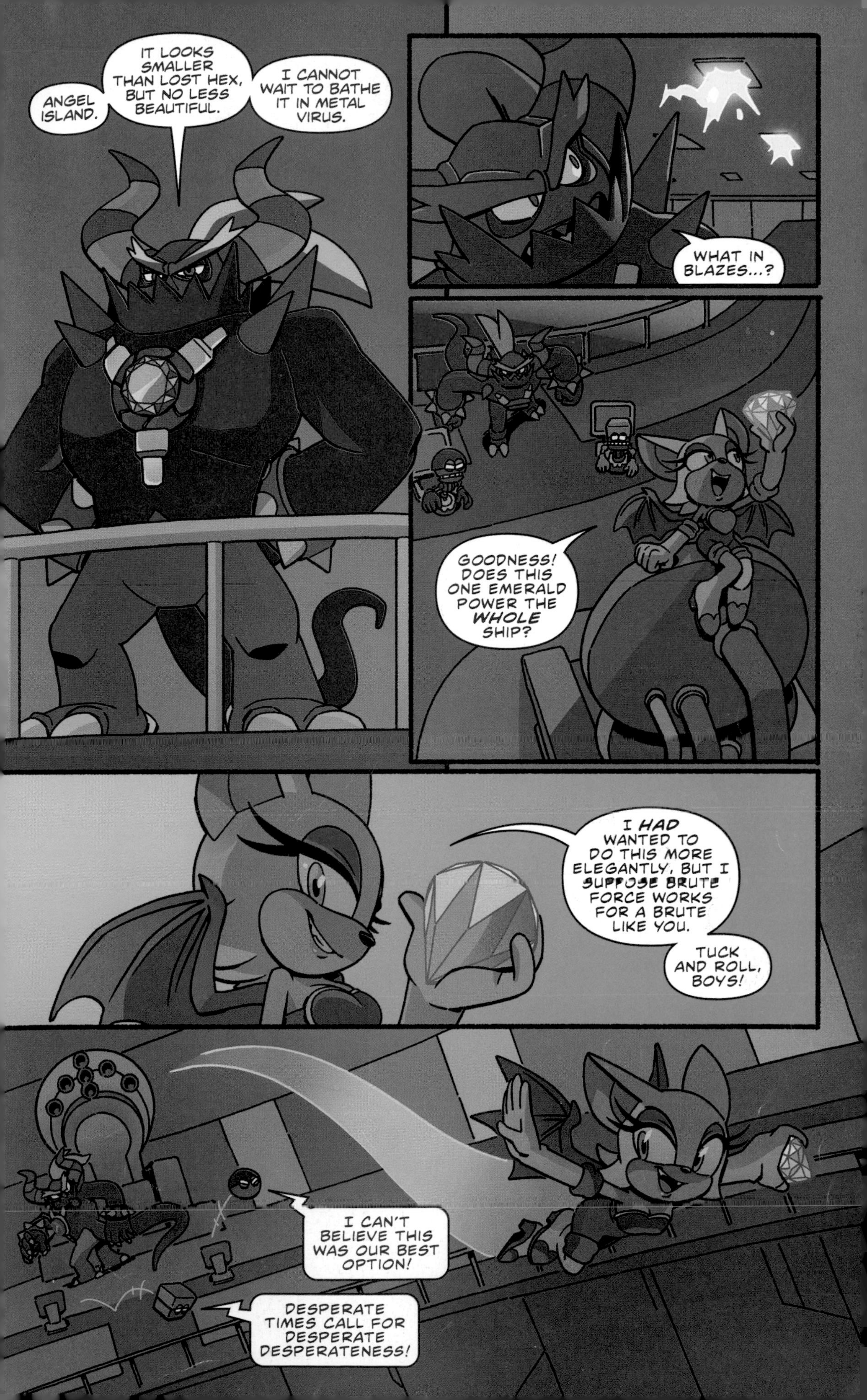
ANGEL ISLAND.
IT LOOKS SMALLER THAN LOST HEX, BUT NO LESS BEAUTIFUL.
I CANNOT WAIT TO BATHE IT IN METAL VIRUS.
WHAT IN BLAZES...?
GOODNESS! DOES THIS ONE EMERALD POWER THE *WHOLE* SHIP?
I *HAD* WANTED TO DO THIS MORE ELEGANTLY, BUT I SUPPOSE BRUTE FORCE WORKS FOR A BRUTE LIKE YOU.
TUCK AND ROLL, BOYS!
I CAN'T BELIEVE THIS WAS OUR BEST OPTION!
DESPERATE TIMES CALL FOR DESPERATE DESPERATENESS!

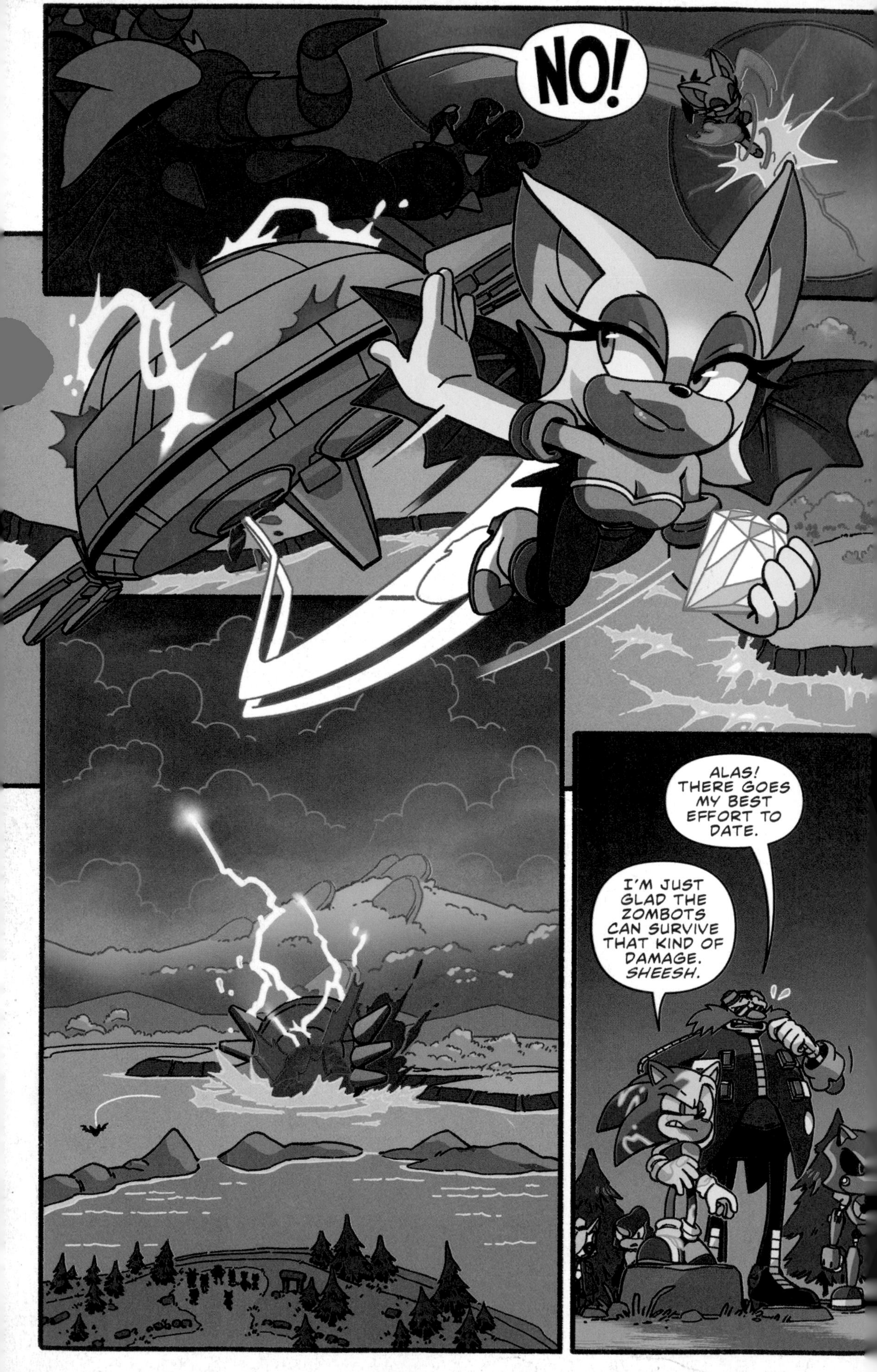
NO!
ALAS! THERE GOES MY BEST EFFORT TO DATE.
I'M JUST GLAD THE ZOMBOTS CAN SURVIVE THAT KIND OF DAMAGE. SHEESH.

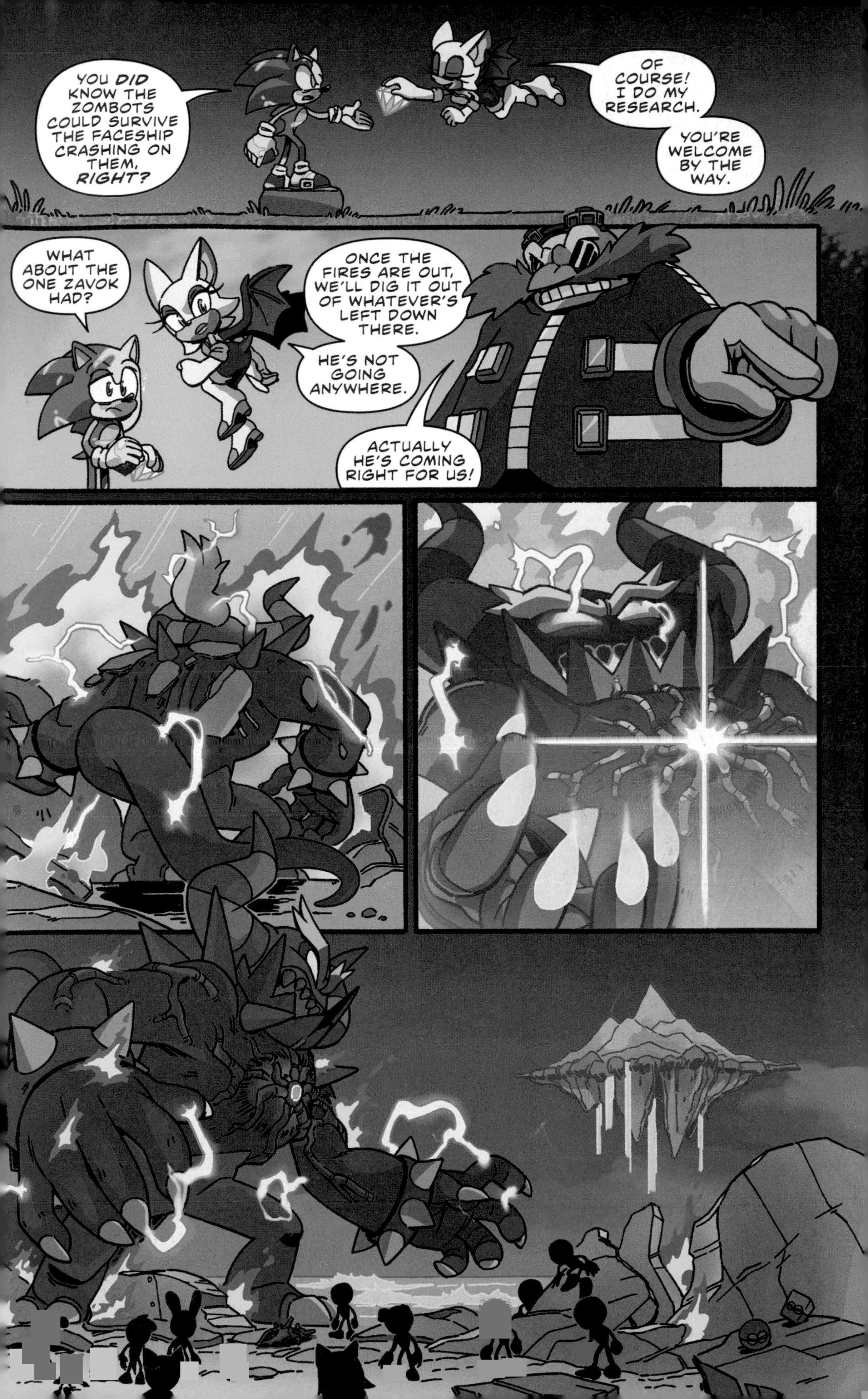
YOU *DID* KNOW THE ZOMBOTS COULD SURVIVE THE FACESHIP CRASHING ON THEM, *RIGHT?*
OF COURSE! I DO MY RESEARCH.
YOU'RE WELCOME BY THE WAY.
WHAT ABOUT THE ONE ZAVOK HAD?
ONCE THE FIRES ARE OUT, WE'LL DIG IT OUT OF WHATEVER'S LEFT DOWN THERE.
HE'S NOT GOING ANYWHERE.
ACTUALLY HE'S COMING RIGHT FOR US!

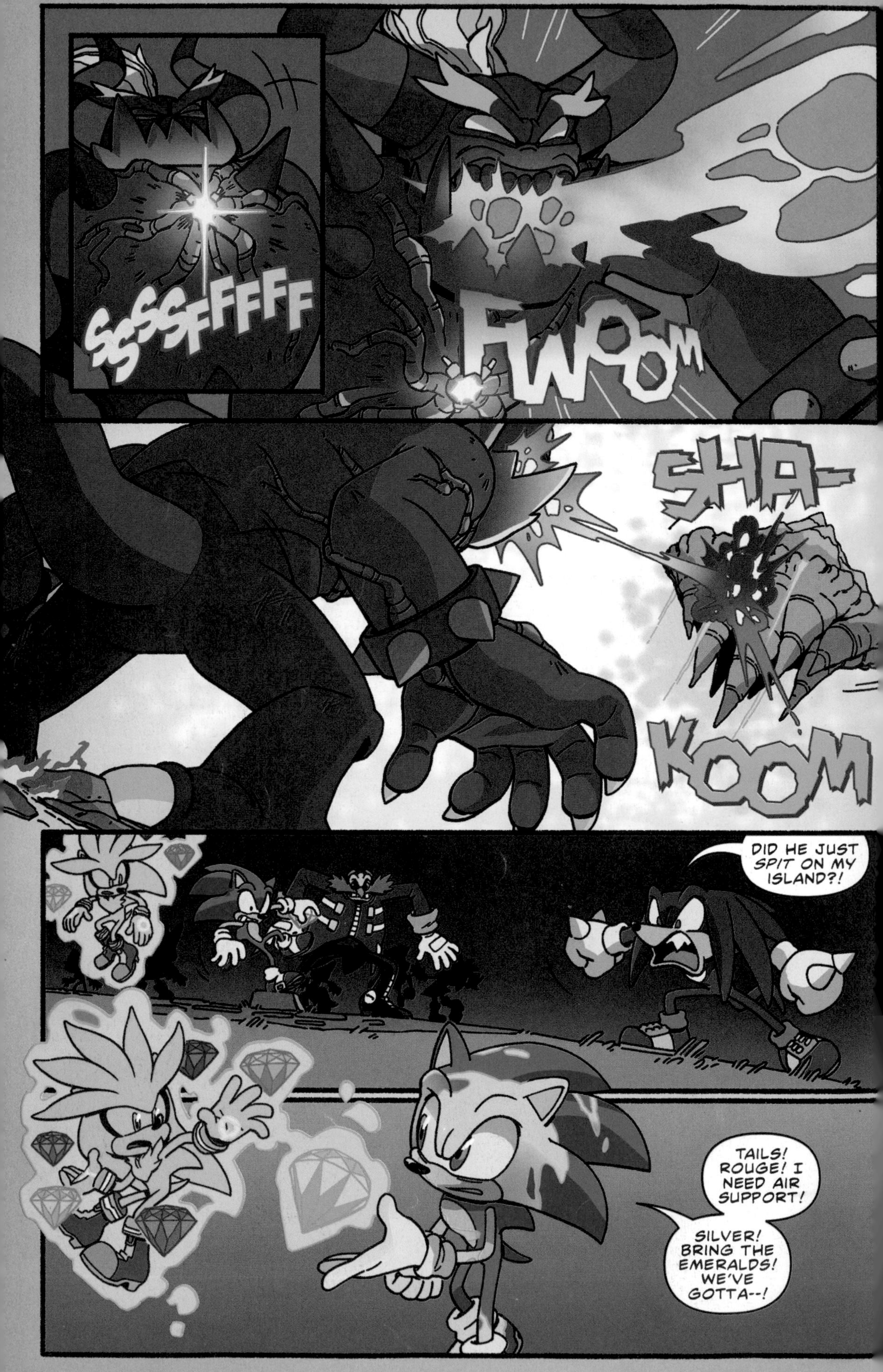
SSSSFFFFF
FWOOM
SHA-
KOOM
DID HE JUST SPIT ON MY ISLAND?!
TAILS! ROUGE! I NEED AIR SUPPORT!
SILVER! BRING THE EMERALDS! WE'VE GOTTA--!

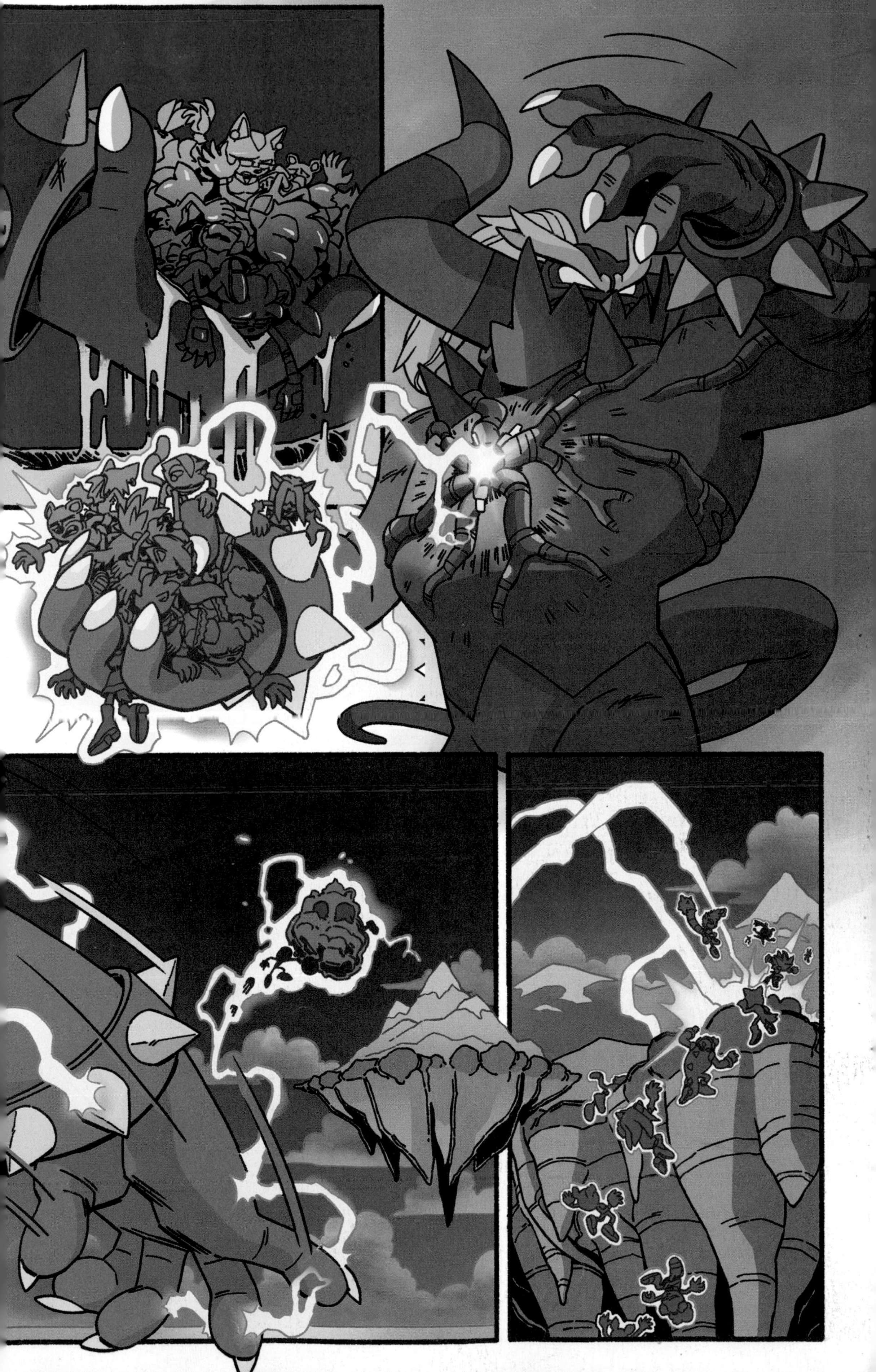

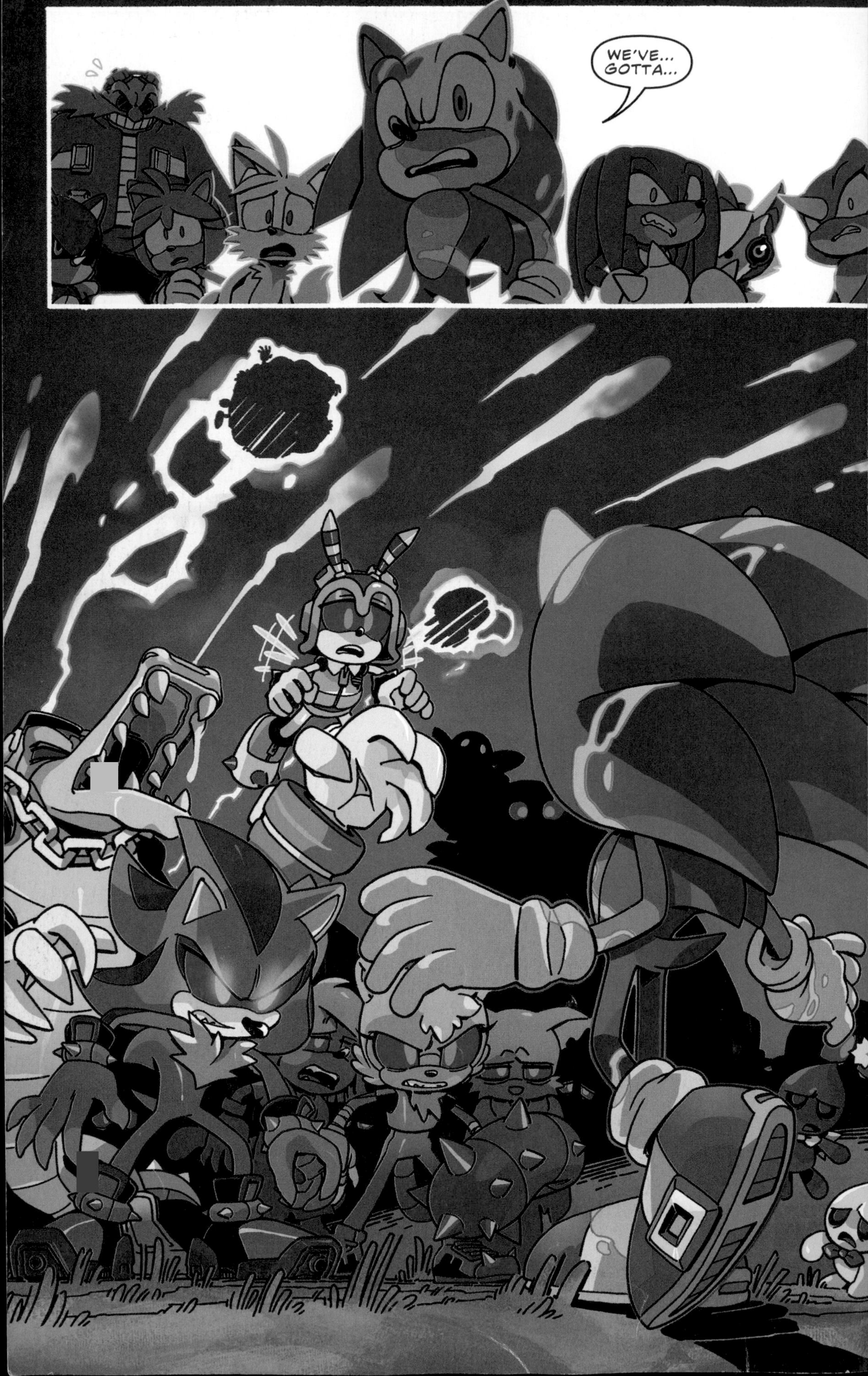
WE'VE... GOTTA...

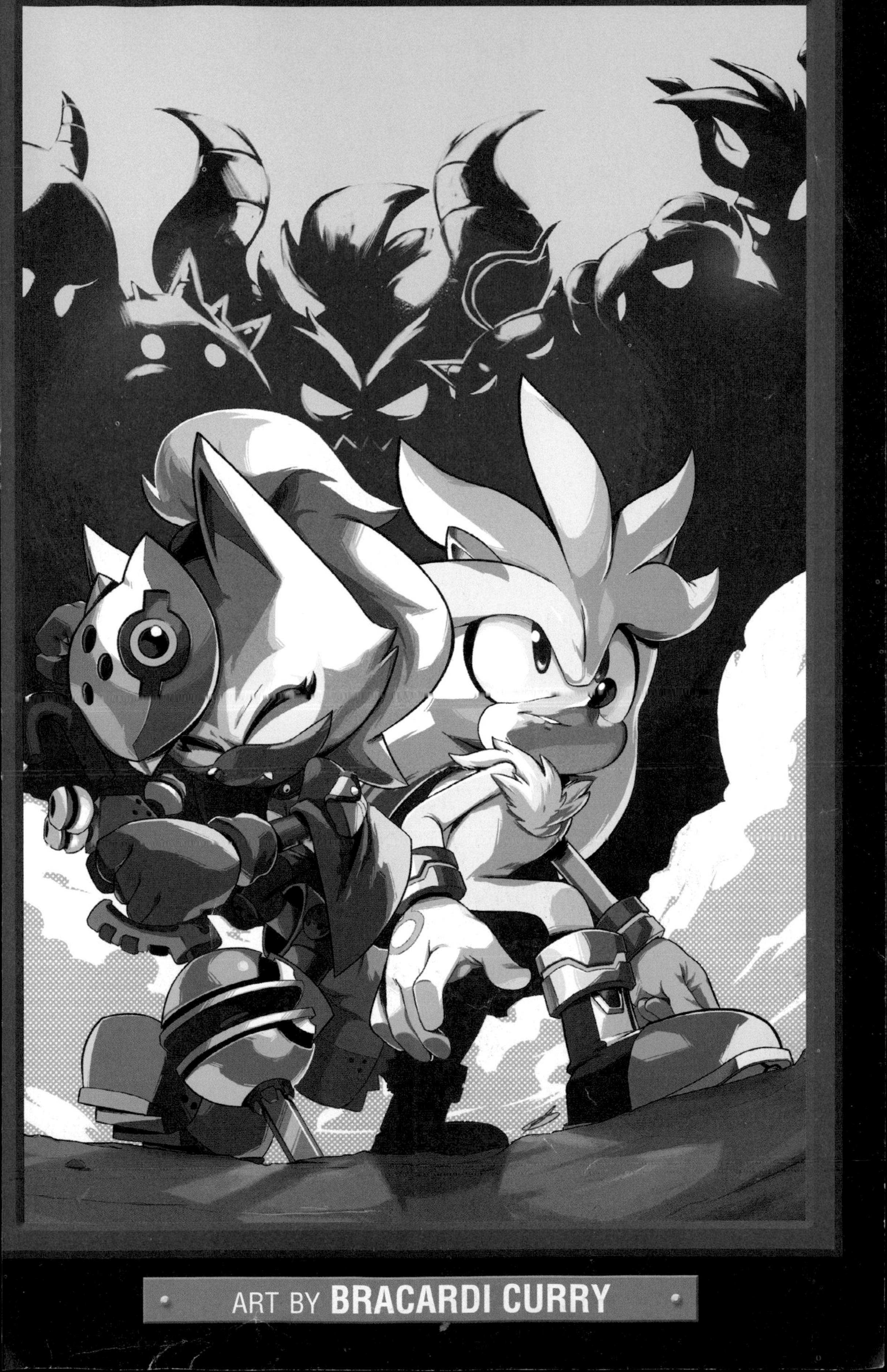

ART BY **BRACARDI CURRY**

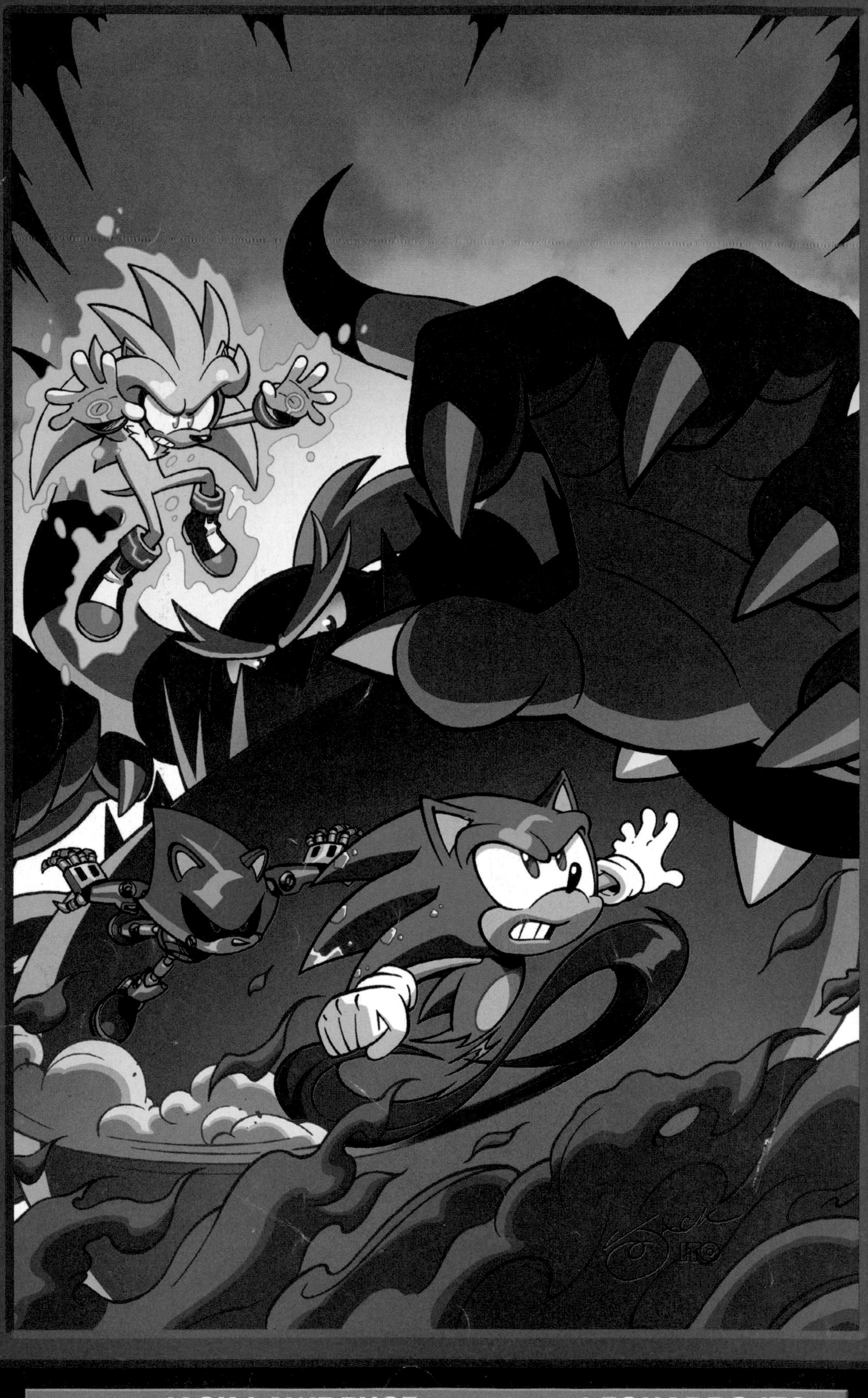

ART BY **JACK LAWRENCE** COLORS BY **LEONARDO ITO**

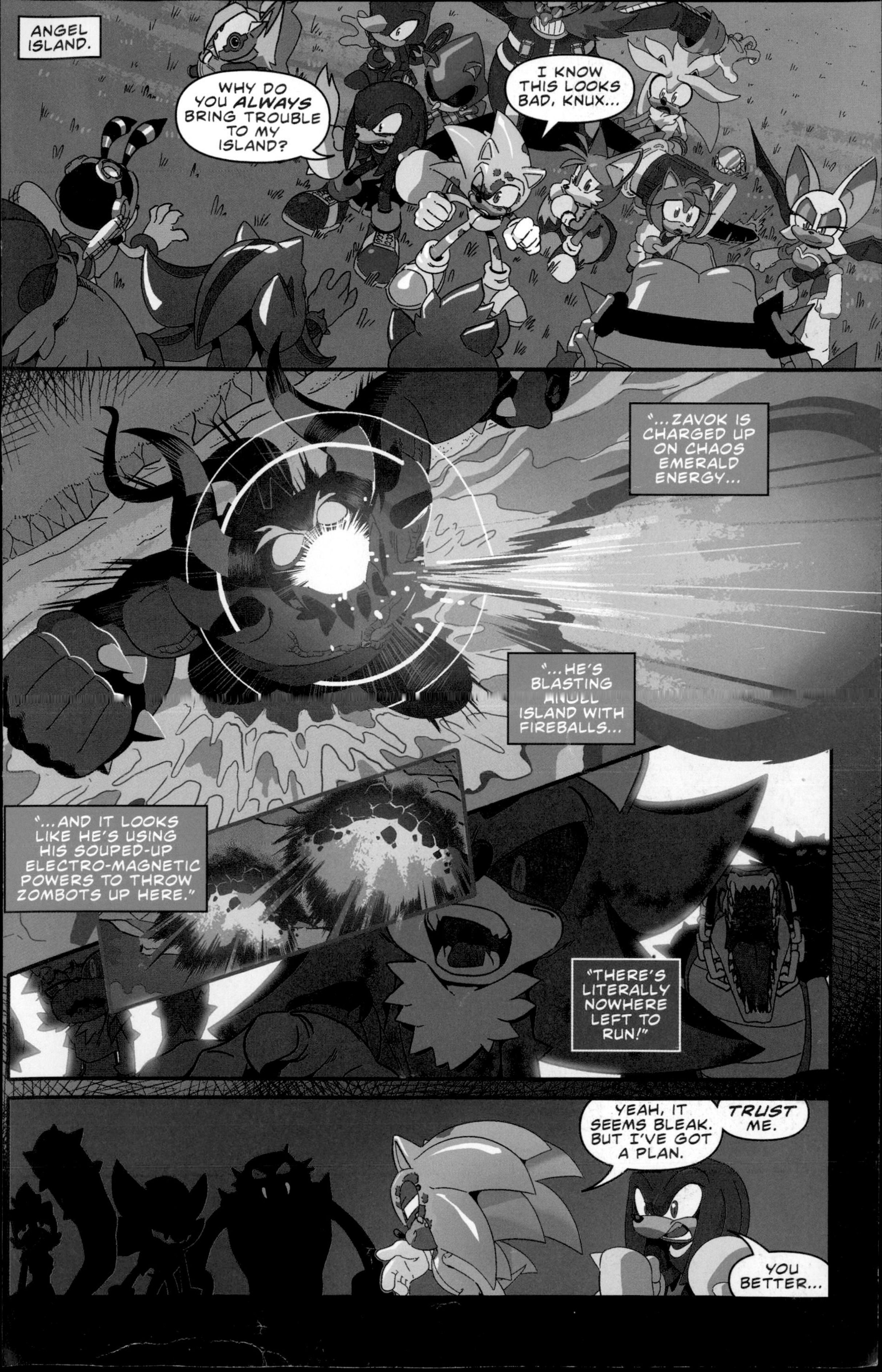
ANGEL ISLAND.
WHY DO YOU ALWAYS BRING TROUBLE TO MY ISLAND?
I KNOW THIS LOOKS BAD, KNUX...
"...ZAVOK IS CHARGED UP ON CHAOS EMERALD ENERGY...
"...HE'S BLASTING ANGEL ISLAND WITH FIREBALLS...
"...AND IT LOOKS LIKE HE'S USING HIS SOUPED-UP ELECTRO-MAGNETIC POWERS TO THROW ZOMBOTS UP HERE."
"THERE'S LITERALLY NOWHERE LEFT TO RUN!"
YEAH, IT SEEMS BLEAK. BUT I'VE GOT A PLAN.
TRUST ME.
YOU BETTER...

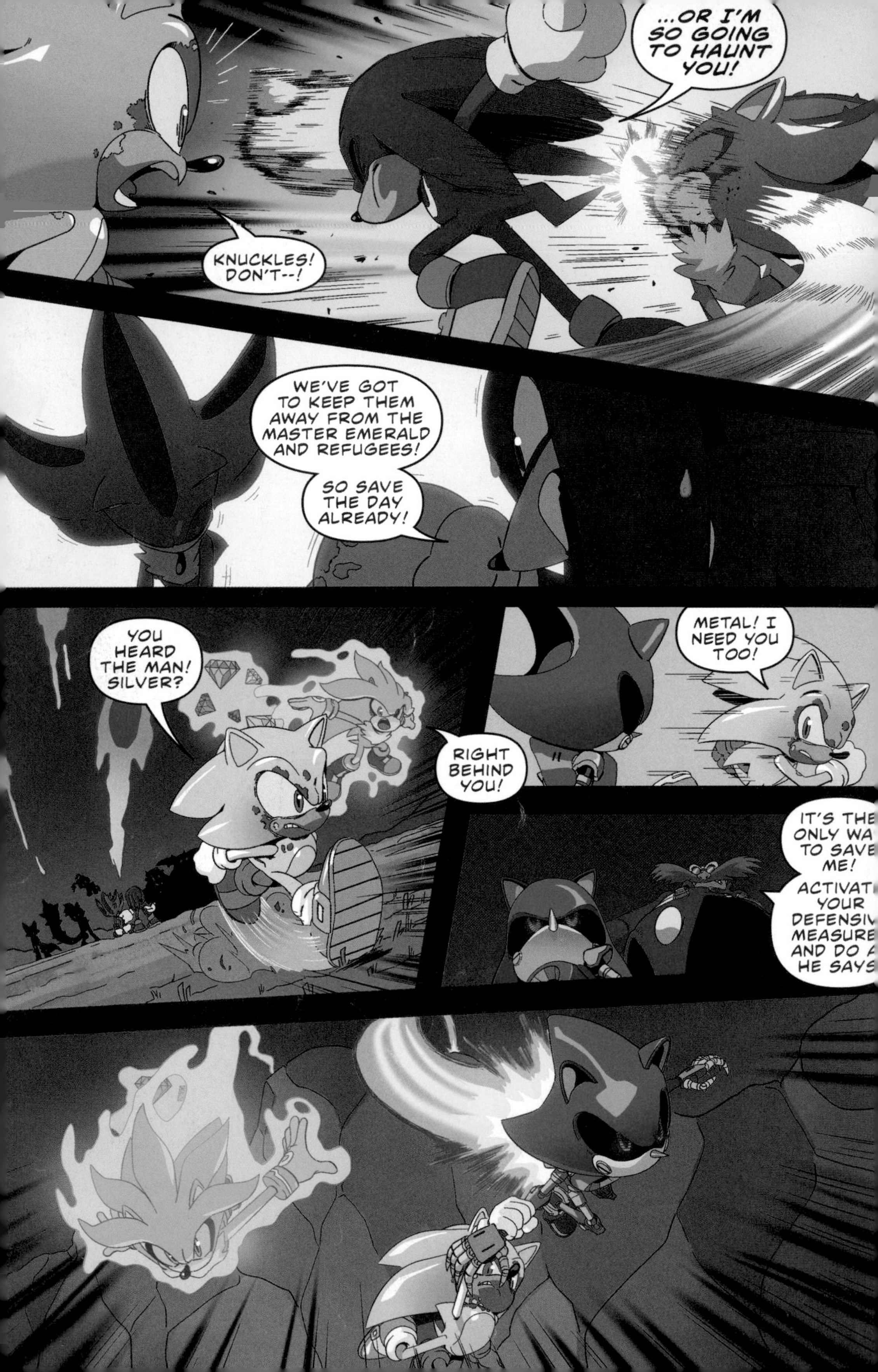

...OR I'M SO GOING TO HAUNT YOU!
KNUCKLES! DON'T--!
WE'VE GOT TO KEEP THEM AWAY FROM THE MASTER EMERALD AND REFUGEES!
SO SAVE THE DAY ALREADY!
YOU HEARD THE MAN! SILVER?
RIGHT BEHIND YOU!
METAL! I NEED YOU TOO!
IT'S THE ONLY WA TO SAVE ME!
ACTIVAT YOUR DEFENSIV MEASURE AND DO A HE SAYS

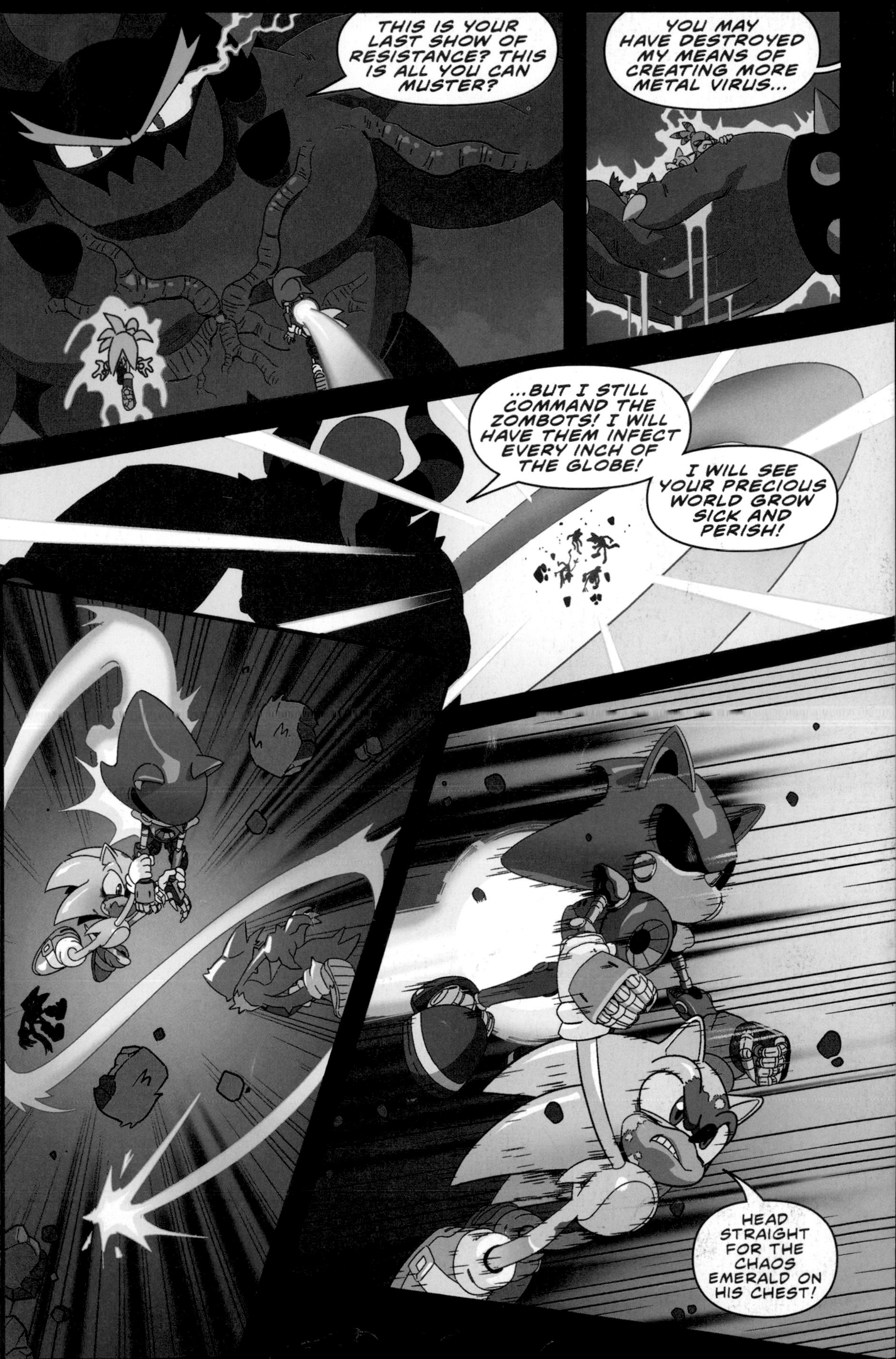
THIS IS YOUR LAST SHOW OF RESISTANCE? THIS IS ALL YOU CAN MUSTER?
YOU MAY HAVE DESTROYED MY MEANS OF CREATING MORE METAL VIRUS...
...BUT I STILL COMMAND THE ZOMBOTS! I WILL HAVE THEM INFECT EVERY INCH OF THE GLOBE!
I WILL SEE YOUR PRECIOUS WORLD GROW SICK AND PERISH!
HEAD STRAIGHT FOR THE CHAOS EMERALD ON HIS CHEST!

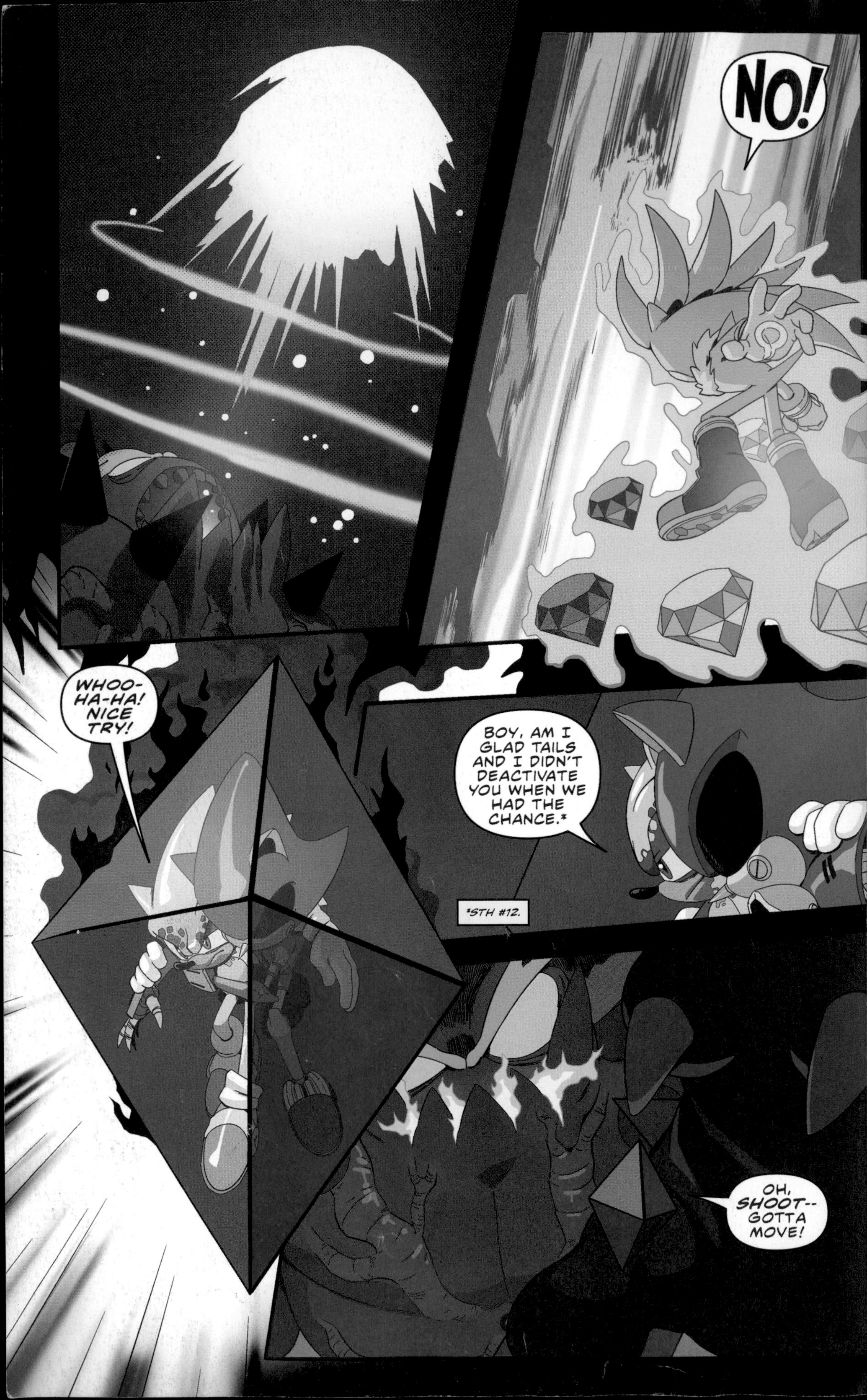
NO!
WHOO-HA-HA! NICE TRY!
BOY, AM I GLAD TAILS AND I DIDN'T DEACTIVATE YOU WHEN WE HAD THE CHANCE.*
*STH #12.
OH, SHOOT--GOTTA MOVE!

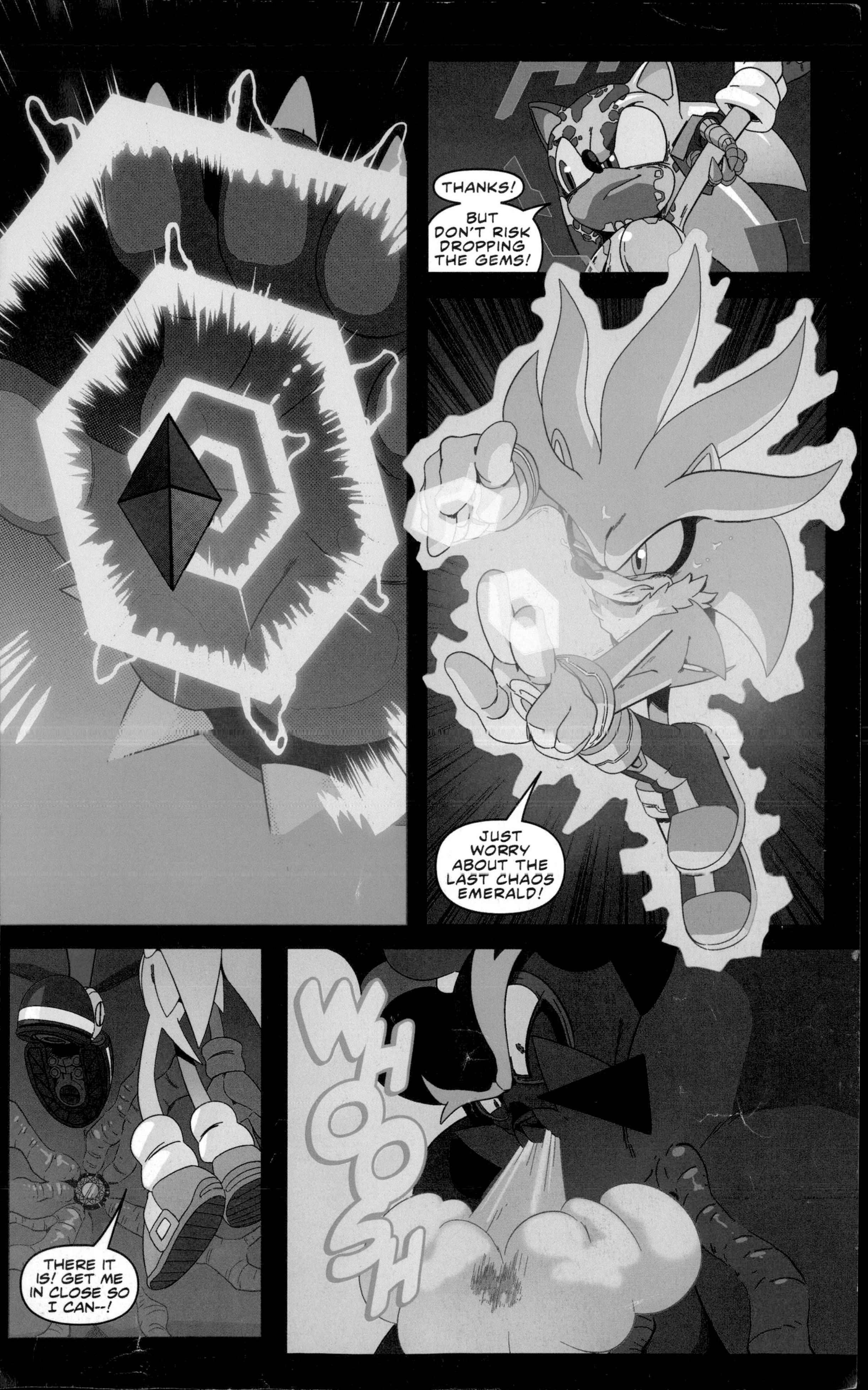
THANKS!
BUT DON'T RISK DROPPING THE GEMS!
JUST WORRY ABOUT THE LAST CHAOS EMERALD!
THERE IT IS! GET ME IN CLOSE SO I CAN--!
WHOOSH

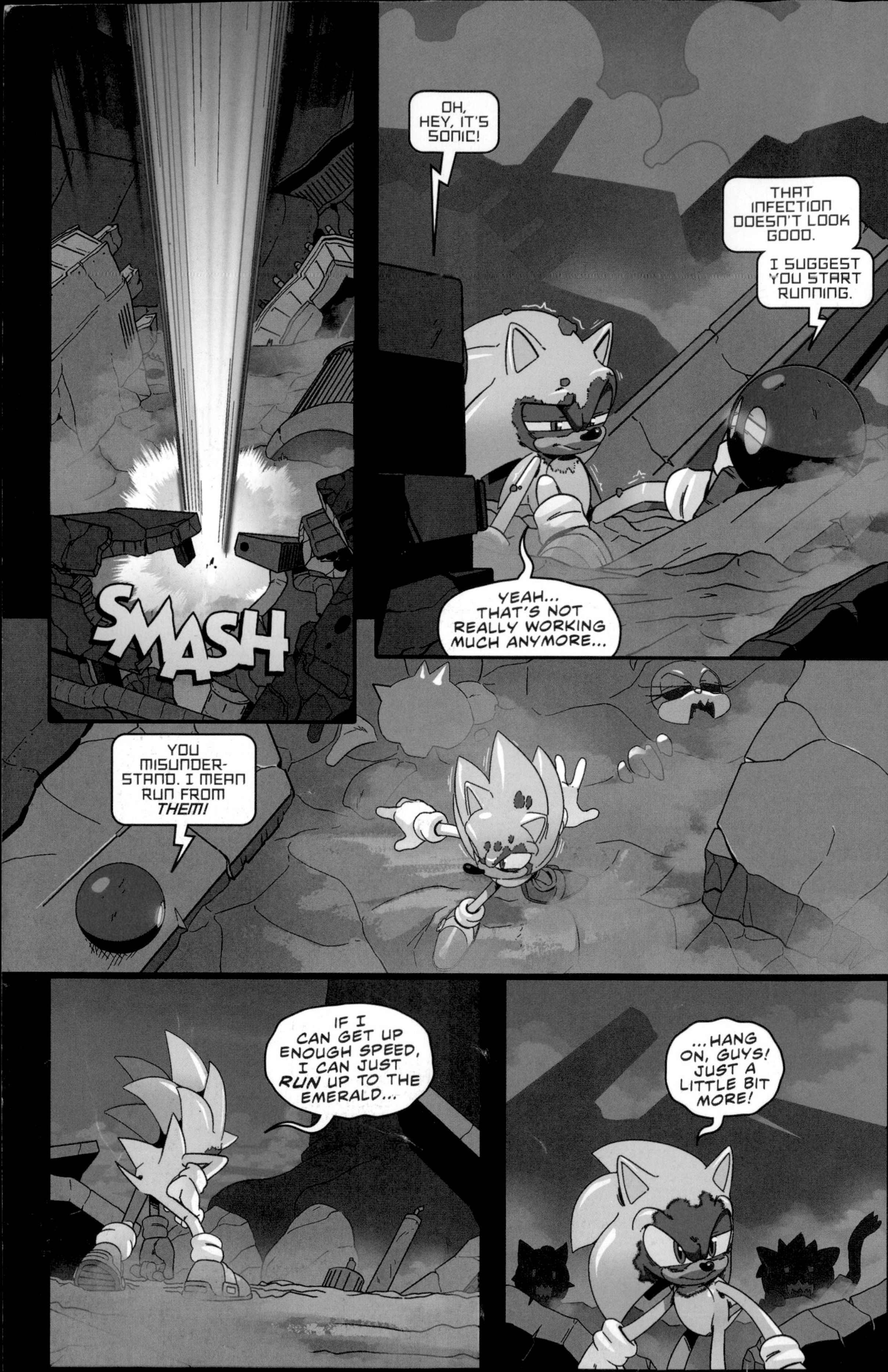
SMASH
OH, HEY, IT'S SONIC!
THAT INFECTION DOESN'T LOOK GOOD.
I SUGGEST YOU START RUNNING.
YEAH... THAT'S NOT REALLY WORKING MUCH ANYMORE...
YOU MISUNDER-STAND. I MEAN RUN FROM *THEM!*
IF I CAN GET UP ENOUGH SPEED, I CAN JUST *RUN* UP TO THE EMERALD...
...HANG ON, GUYS! JUST A LITTLE BIT MORE!

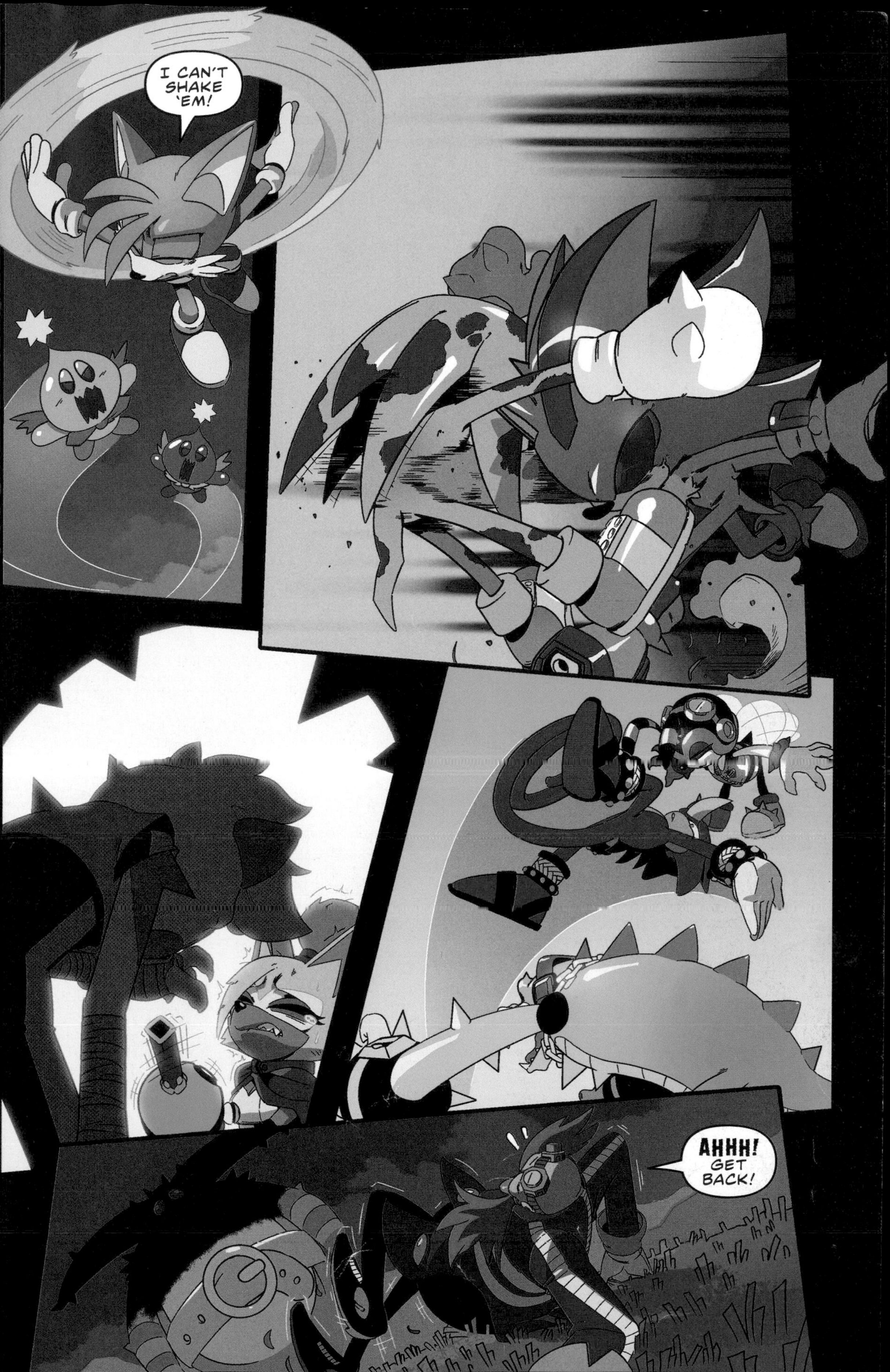
I CAN'T SHAKE 'EM!
AHHH! GET BACK!

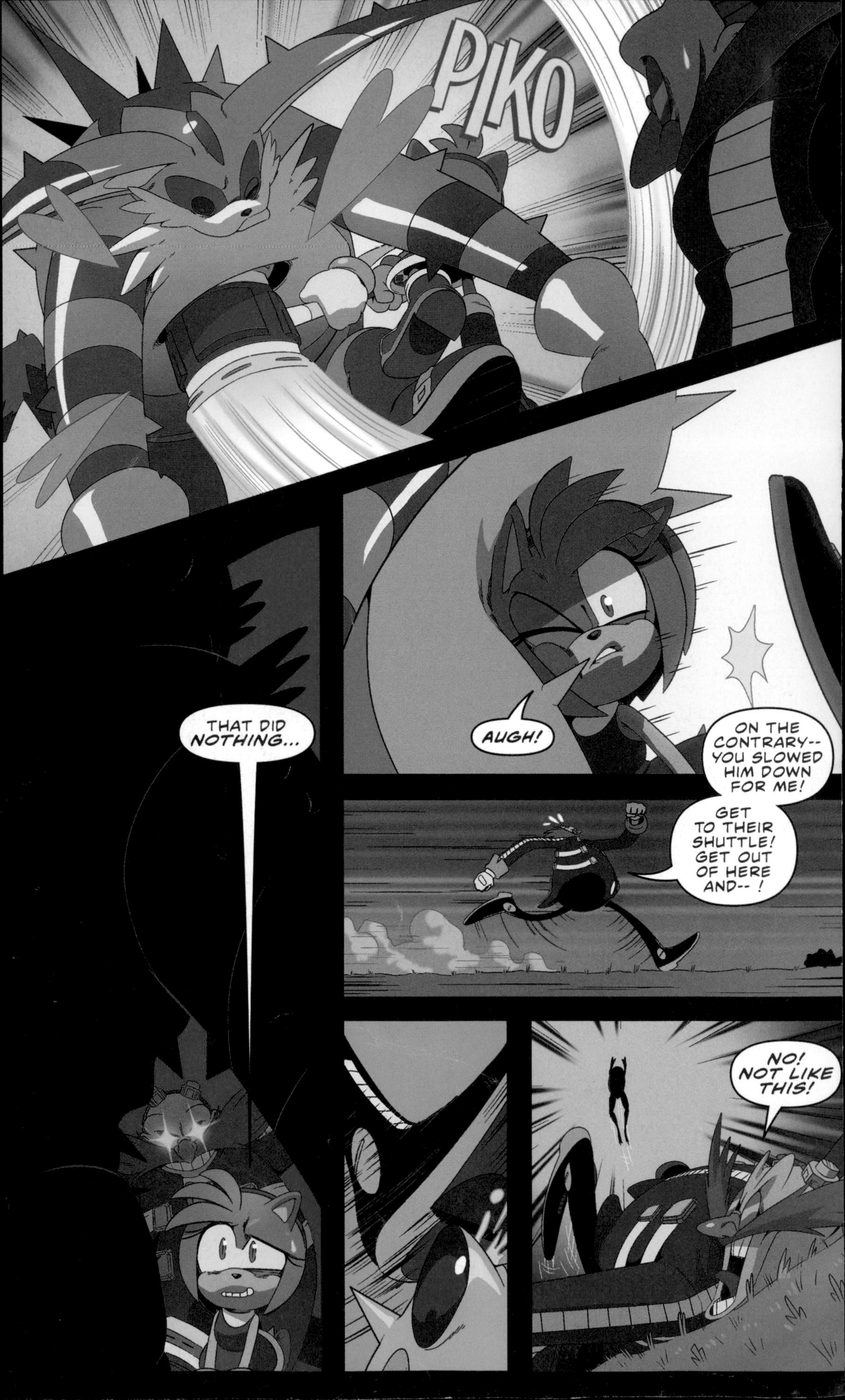
PIKO
AUGH!
ON THE CONTRARY-- YOU SLOWED HIM DOWN FOR ME!
THAT DID NOTHING...
GET TO THEIR SHUTTLE! GET OUT OF HERE AND-- !
NO! NOT LIKE THIS!

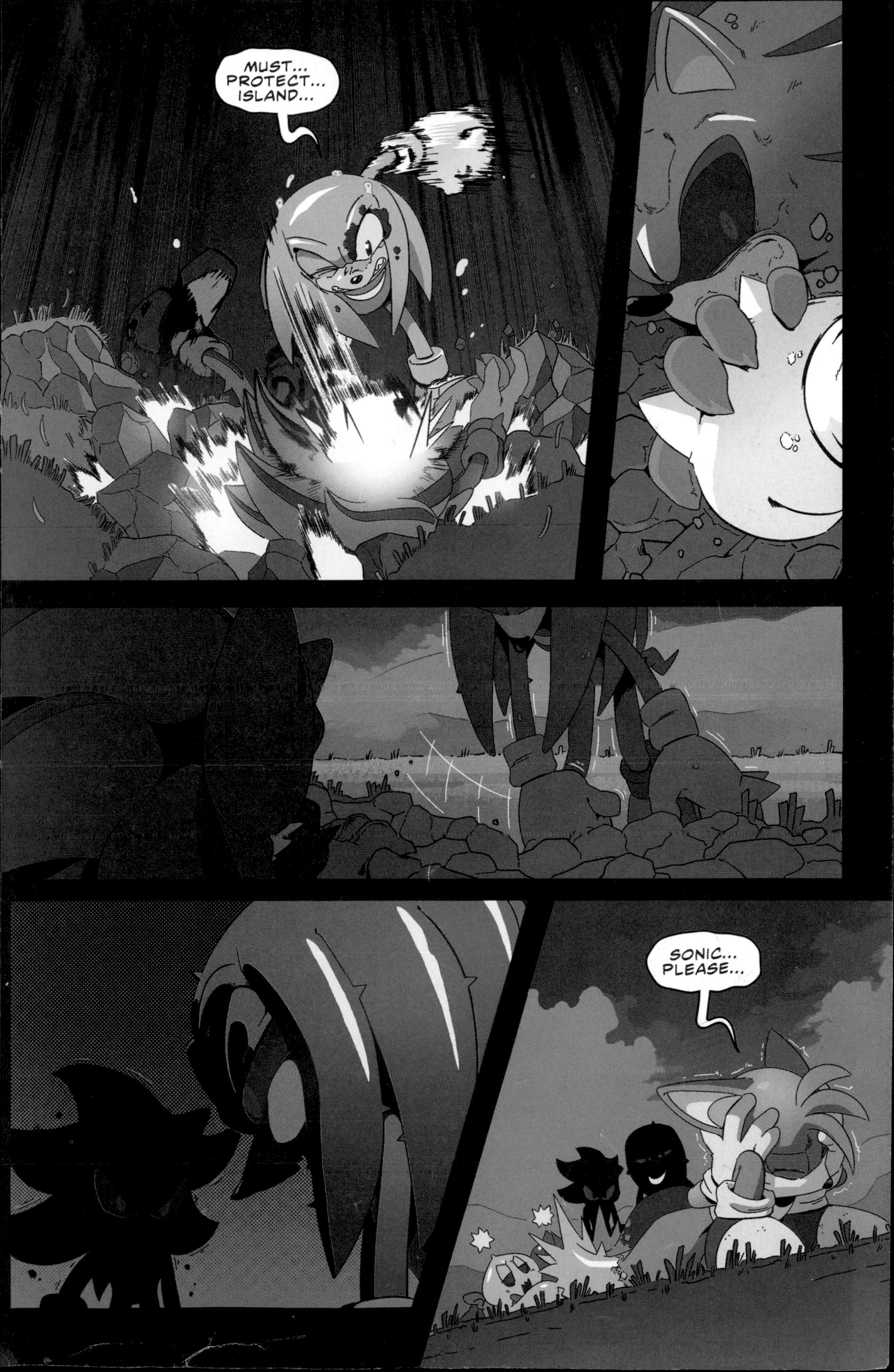
MUST... PROTECT... ISLAND...
SONIC... PLEASE...

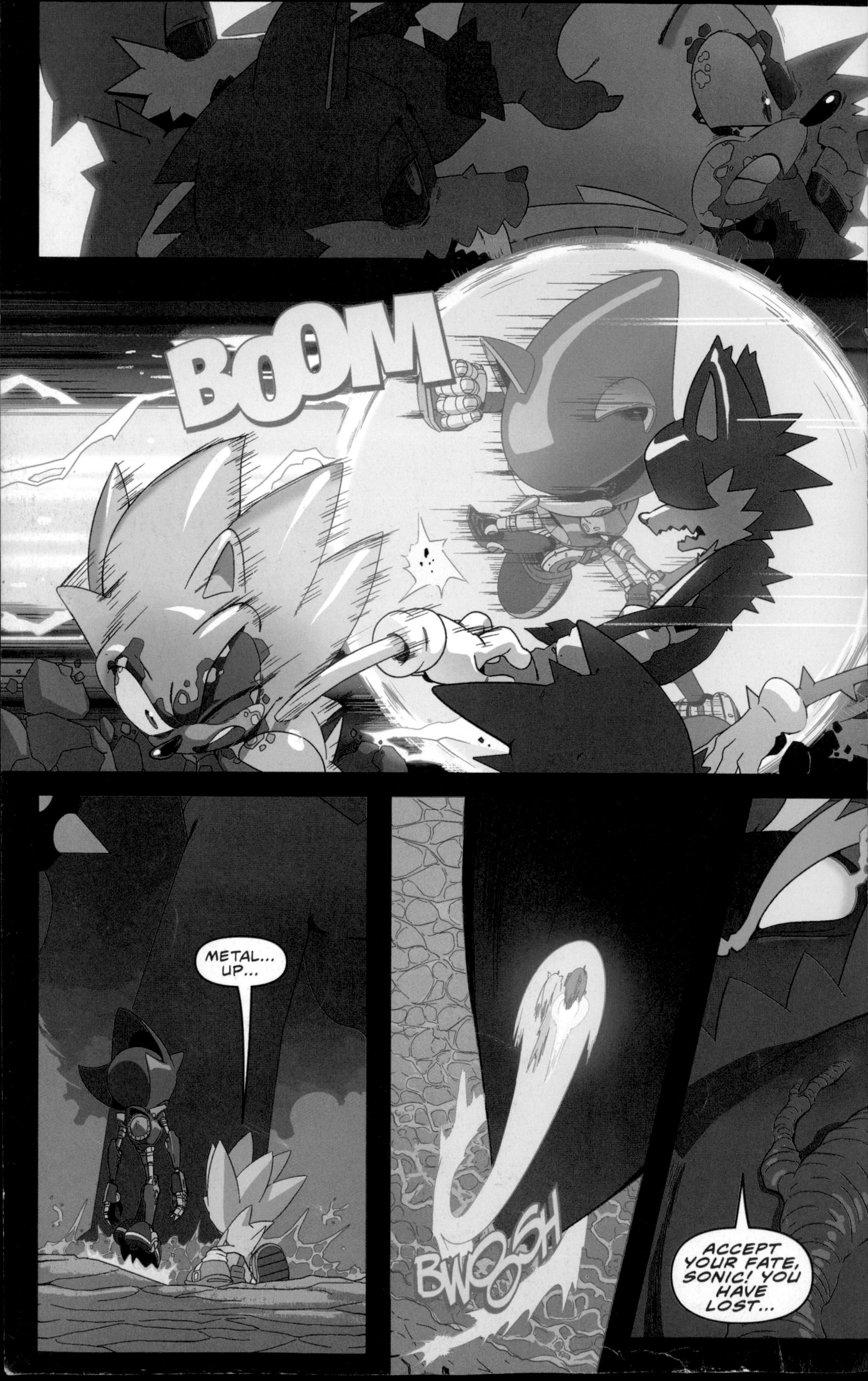
BOOM
METAL... UP...
BWOOSH
ACCEPT YOUR FATE, SONIC! YOU HAVE LOST...

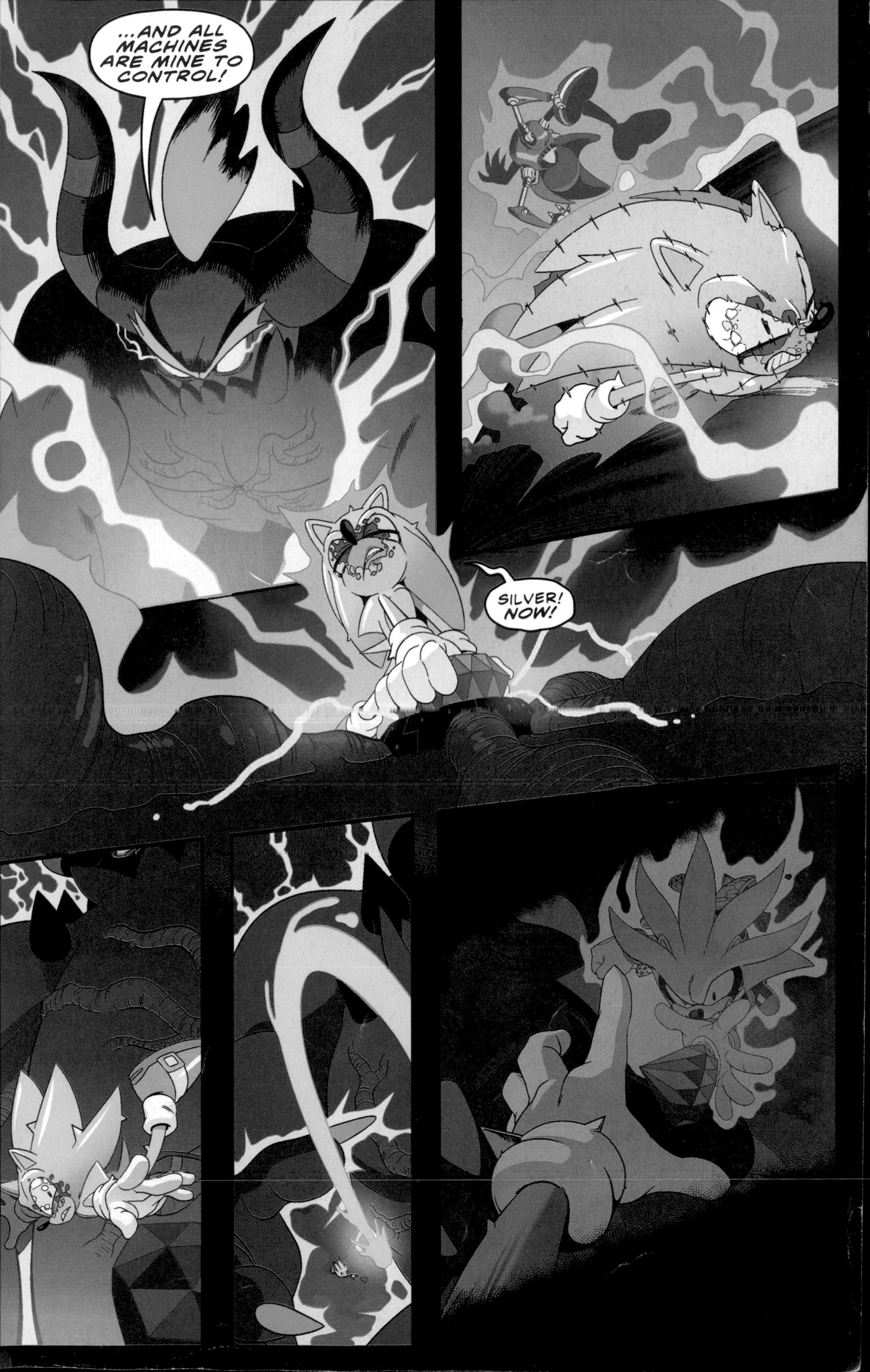
...AND ALL MACHINES ARE MINE TO CONTROL!
SILVER! NOW!

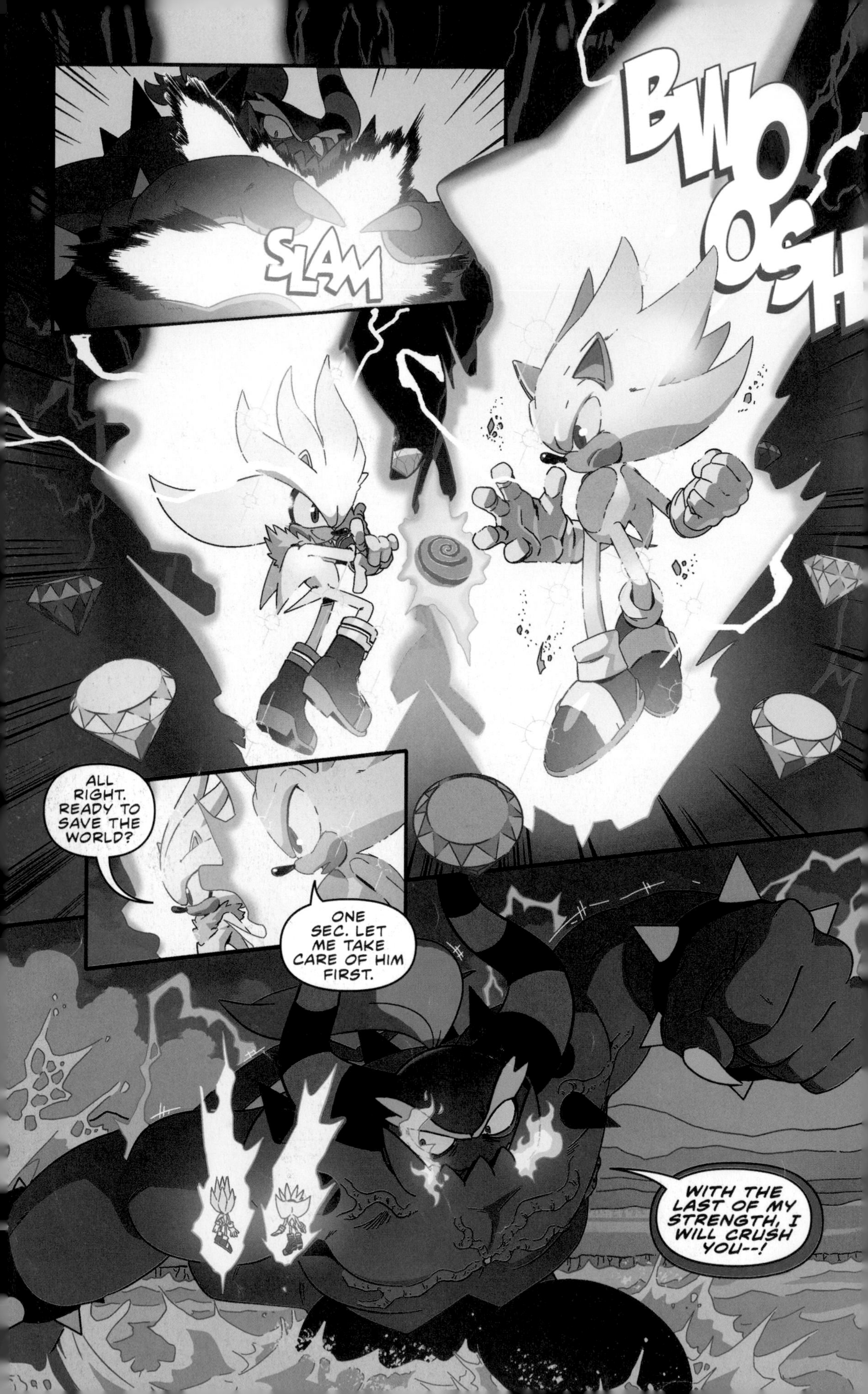
SLAM
BWOOSH
ALL RIGHT. READY TO SAVE THE WORLD?
ONE SEC. LET ME TAKE CARE OF HIM FIRST.
WITH THE LAST OF MY STRENGTH, I WILL CRUSH YOU--!

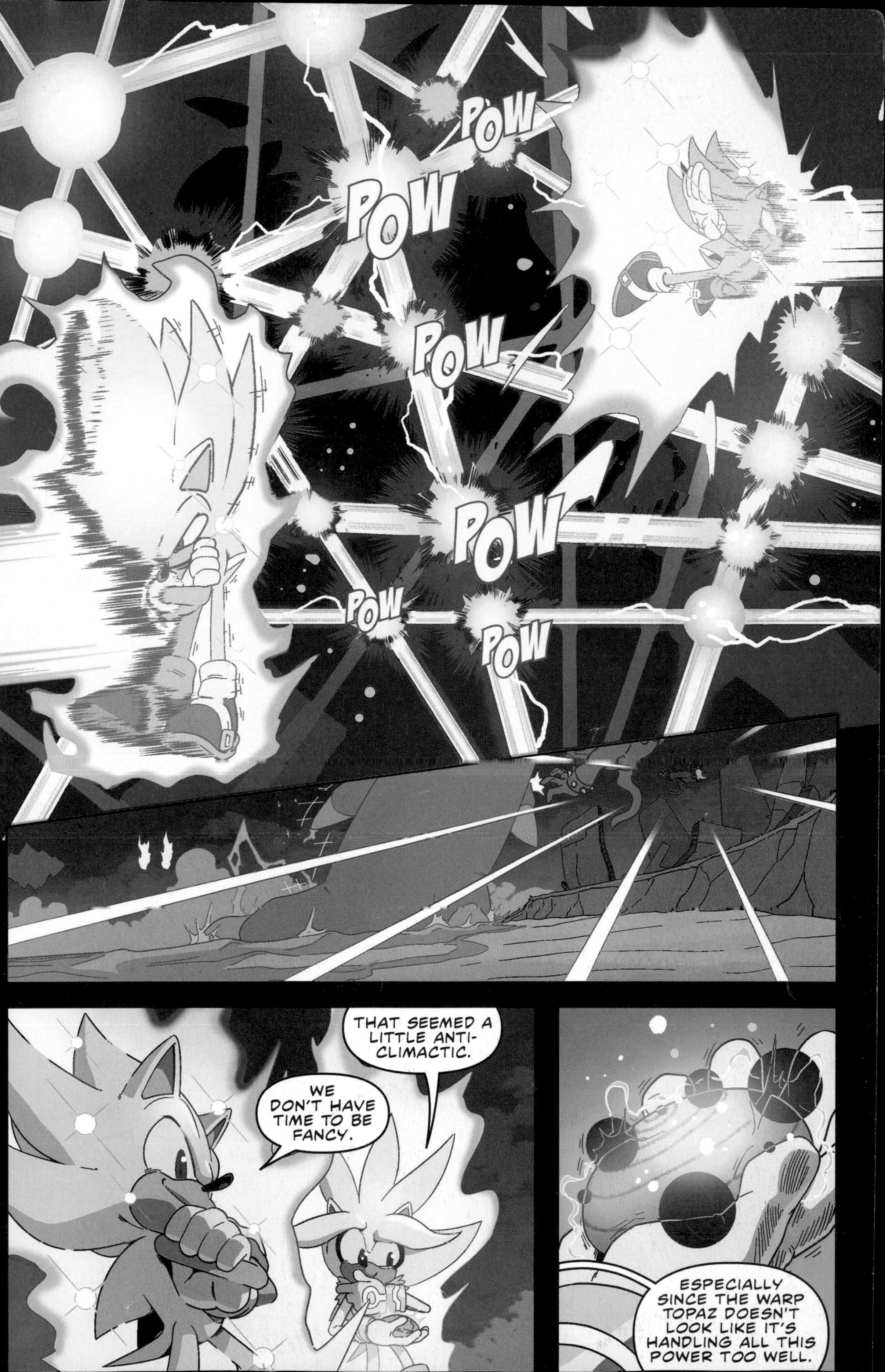
POW
POW
POW
POW
POW
POW
THAT SEEMED A LITTLE ANTI-CLIMACTIC.
WE DON'T HAVE TIME TO BE FANCY.
ESPECIALLY SINCE THE WARP TOPAZ DOESN'T LOOK LIKE IT'S HANDLING ALL THIS POWER TOO WELL.

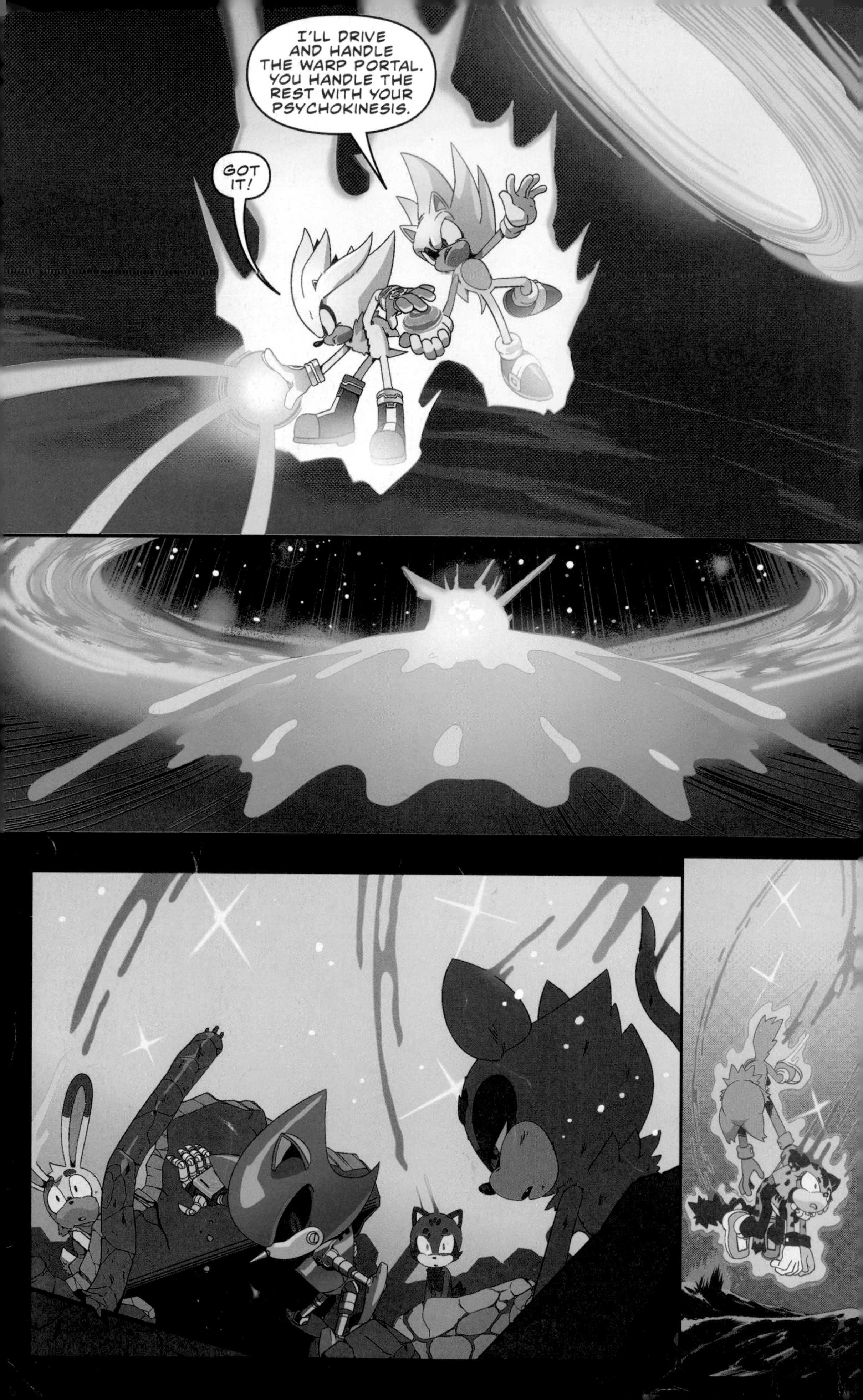
I'LL DRIVE AND HANDLE THE WARP PORTAL. YOU HANDLE THE REST WITH YOUR PSYCHOKINESIS.
GOT IT!

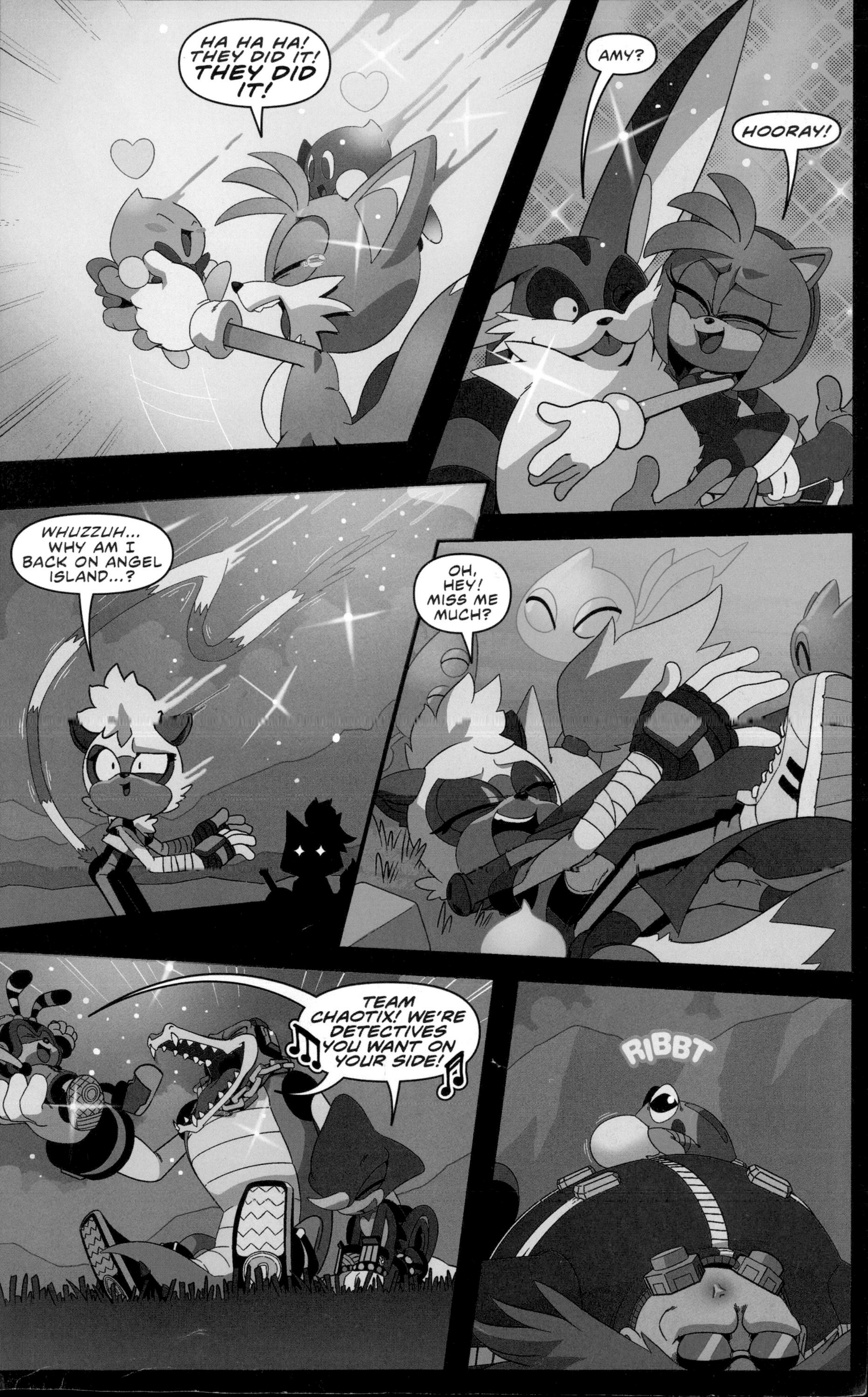
HA HA HA! THEY DID IT! THEY DID IT!
AMY?
HOORAY!
WHUZZUH... WHY AM I BACK ON ANGEL ISLAND...?
OH, HEY! MISS ME MUCH?
TEAM CHAOTIX! WE'RE DETECTIVES YOU WANT ON YOUR SIDE!
RIBBT

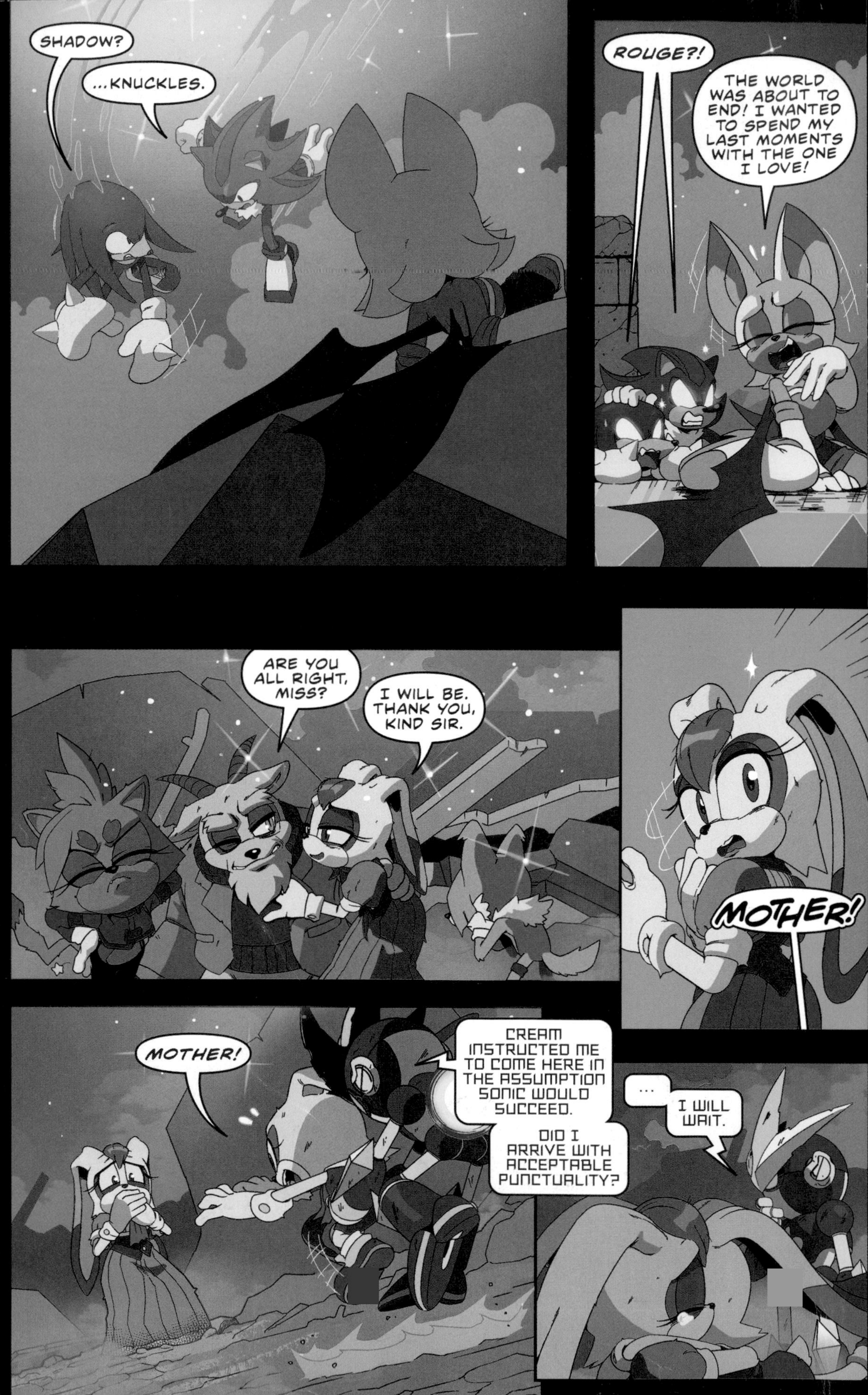
SHADOW?
...KNUCKLES.
ROUGE?!
THE WORLD WAS ABOUT TO END! I WANTED TO SPEND MY LAST MOMENTS WITH THE ONE I LOVE!
ARE YOU ALL RIGHT, MISS?
I WILL BE. THANK YOU, KIND SIR.
MOTHER!
MOTHER!
CREAM INSTRUCTED ME TO COME HERE IN THE ASSUMPTION SONIC WOULD SUCCEED.
DID I ARRIVE WITH ACCEPTABLE PUNCTUALITY?
...
I WILL WAIT.

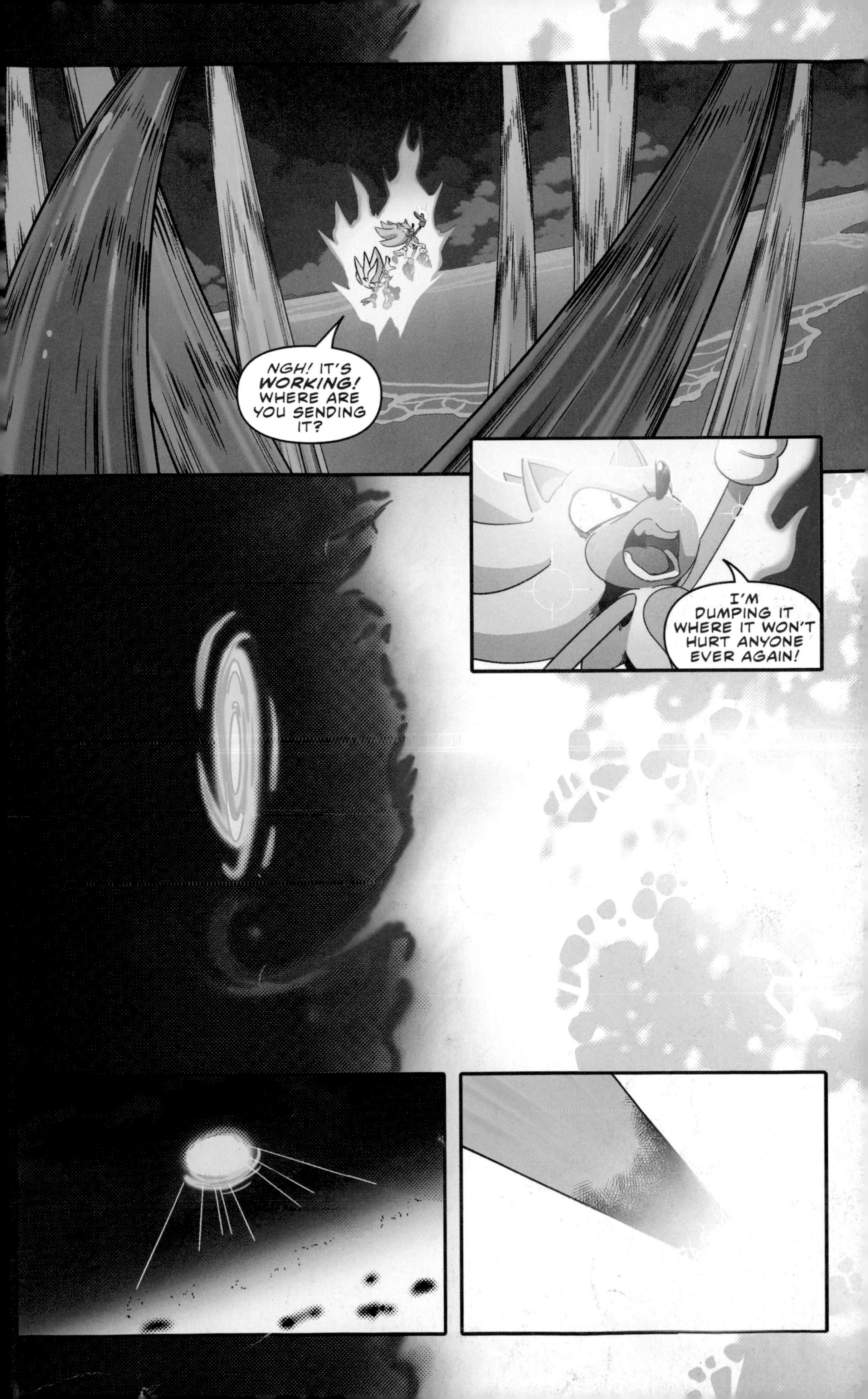
NGH! IT'S *WORKING!* WHERE ARE YOU SENDING IT?
I'M DUMPING IT WHERE IT WON'T HURT ANYONE EVER AGAIN!

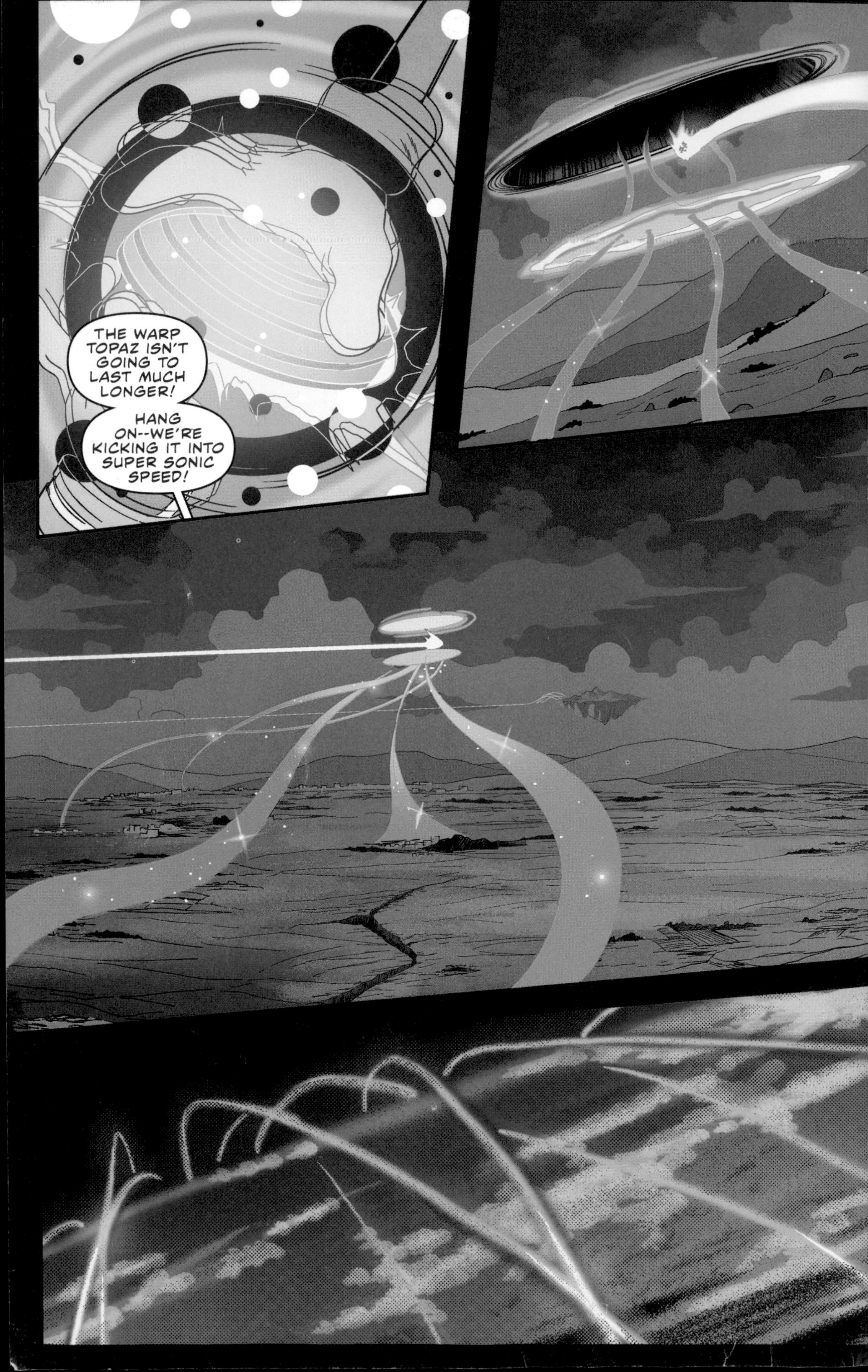
THE WARP TOPAZ ISN'T GOING TO LAST MUCH LONGER!
HANG ON--WE'RE KICKING IT INTO SUPER SONIC SPEED!

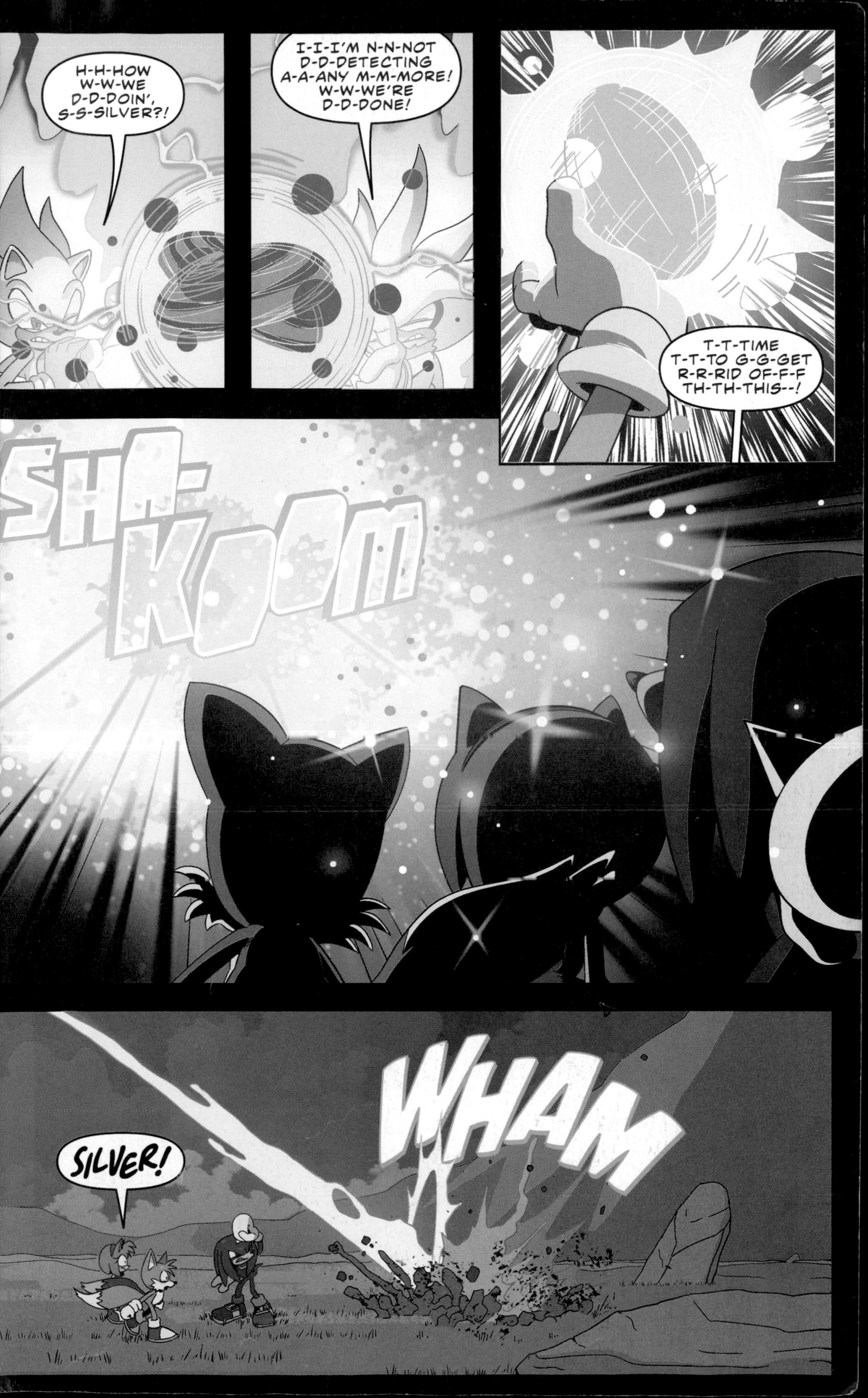
H-H-HOW W-W-WE D-D-DOIN', S-S-SILVER?!
I-I-I'M N-N-NOT D-D-DETECTING A-A-ANY M-M-MORE! W-W-WE'RE D-D-DONE!
T-T-TIME T-T-TO G-G-GET R-R-RID OF-F-F TH-TH-THIS--!
SHA-KOOM
WHAM
SILVER!

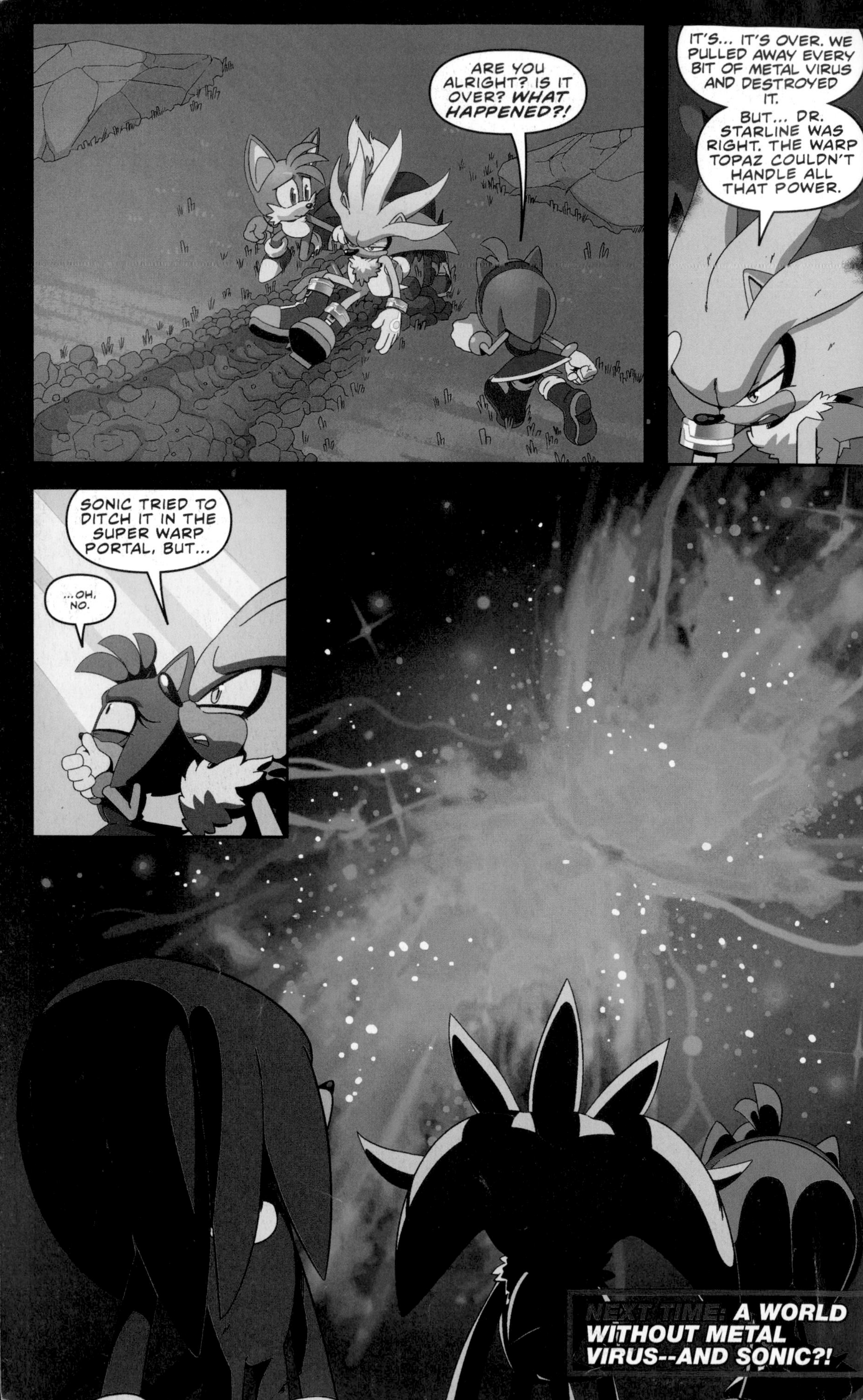
ARE YOU ALRIGHT? IS IT OVER? WHAT HAPPENED?!
IT'S... IT'S OVER. WE PULLED AWAY EVERY BIT OF METAL VIRUS AND DESTROYED IT.
BUT... DR. STARLINE WAS RIGHT. THE WARP TOPAZ COULDN'T HANDLE ALL THAT POWER.
SONIC TRIED TO DITCH IT IN THE SUPER WARP PORTAL, BUT...
...OH, NO.
NEXT TIME: A WORLD WITHOUT METAL VIRUS--AND SONIC?!

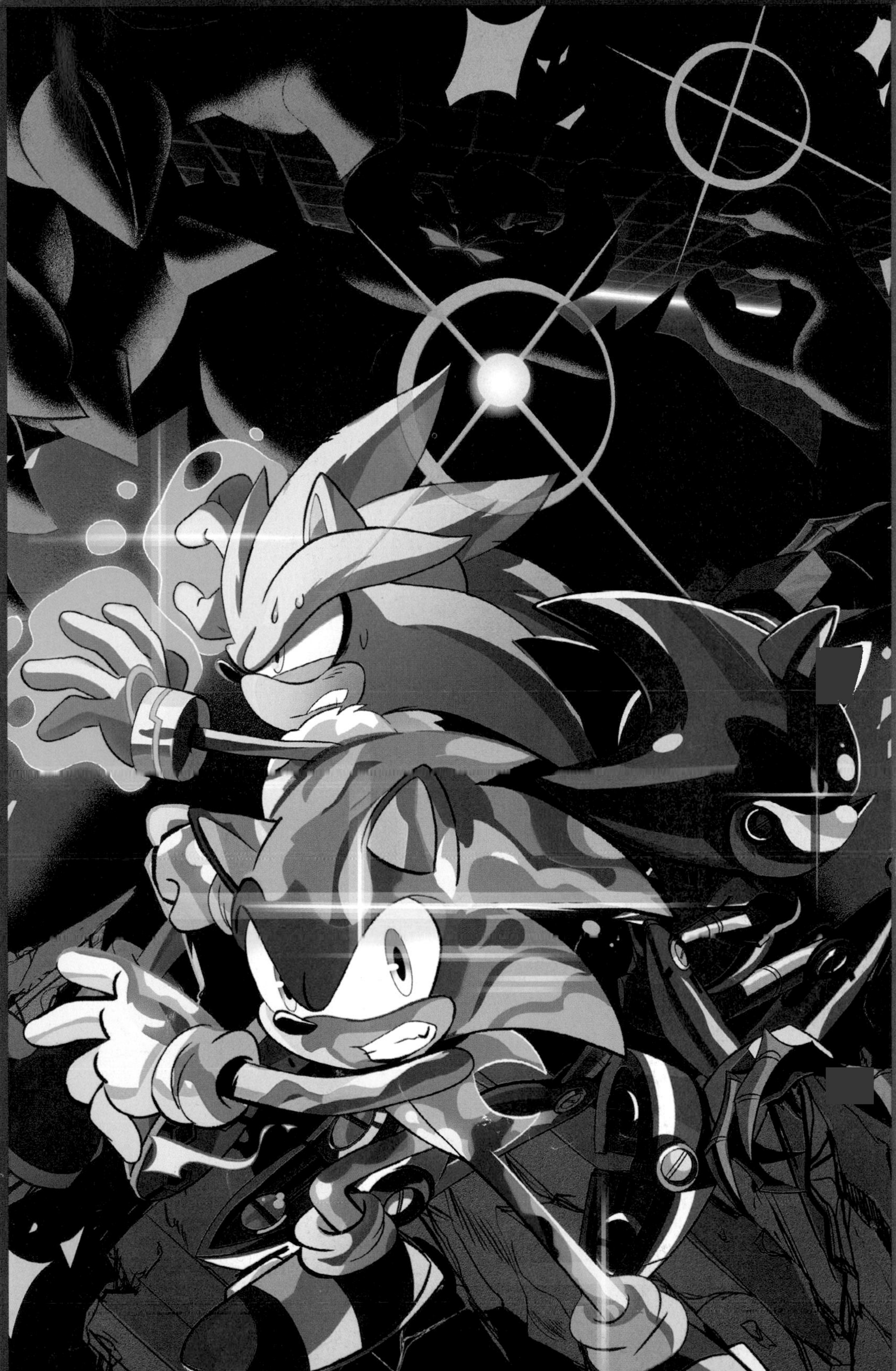

ART BY PRISCILLA TRAMONTANO

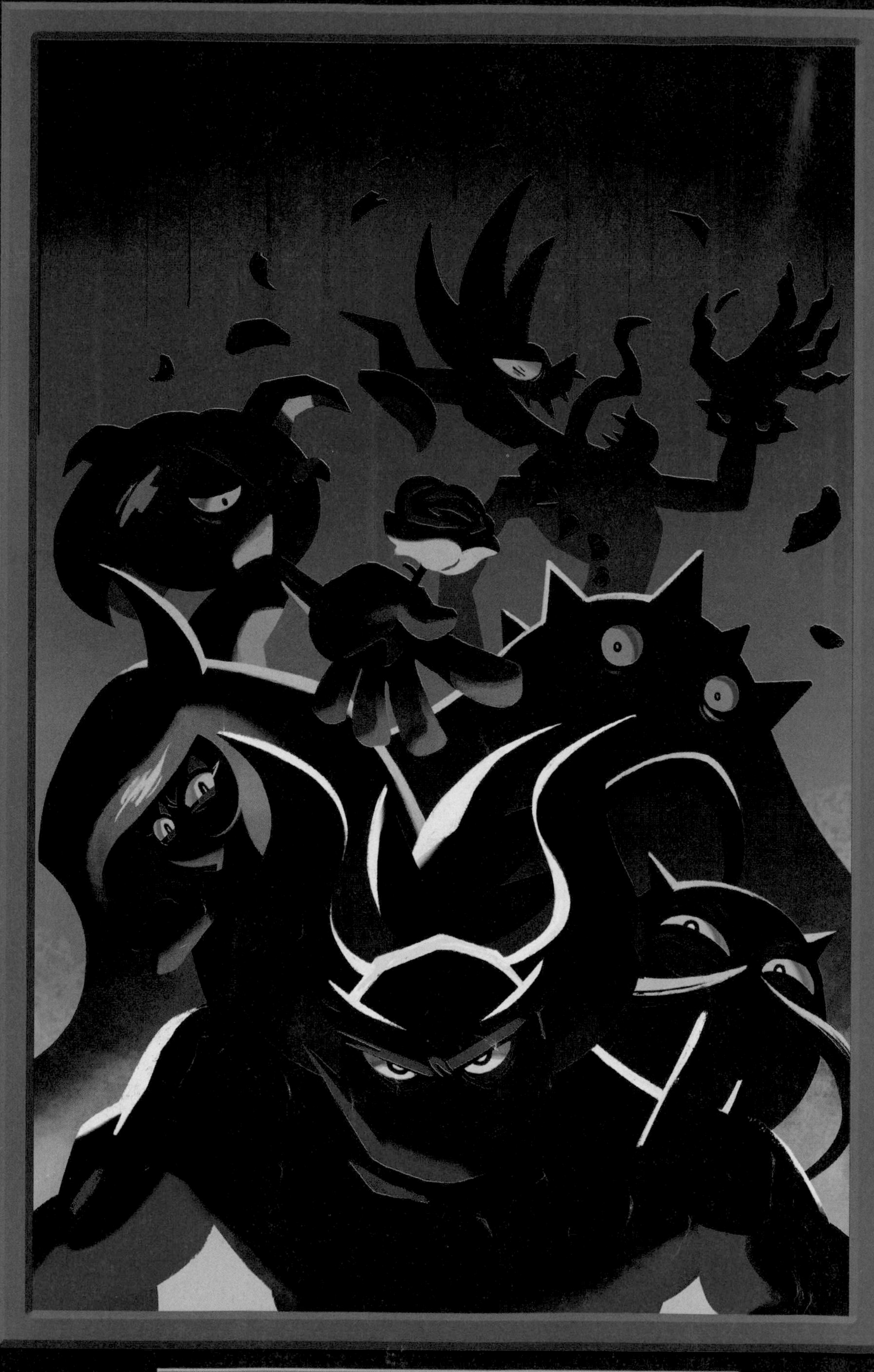

ART BY **NATHALIE FOURDRAINE**

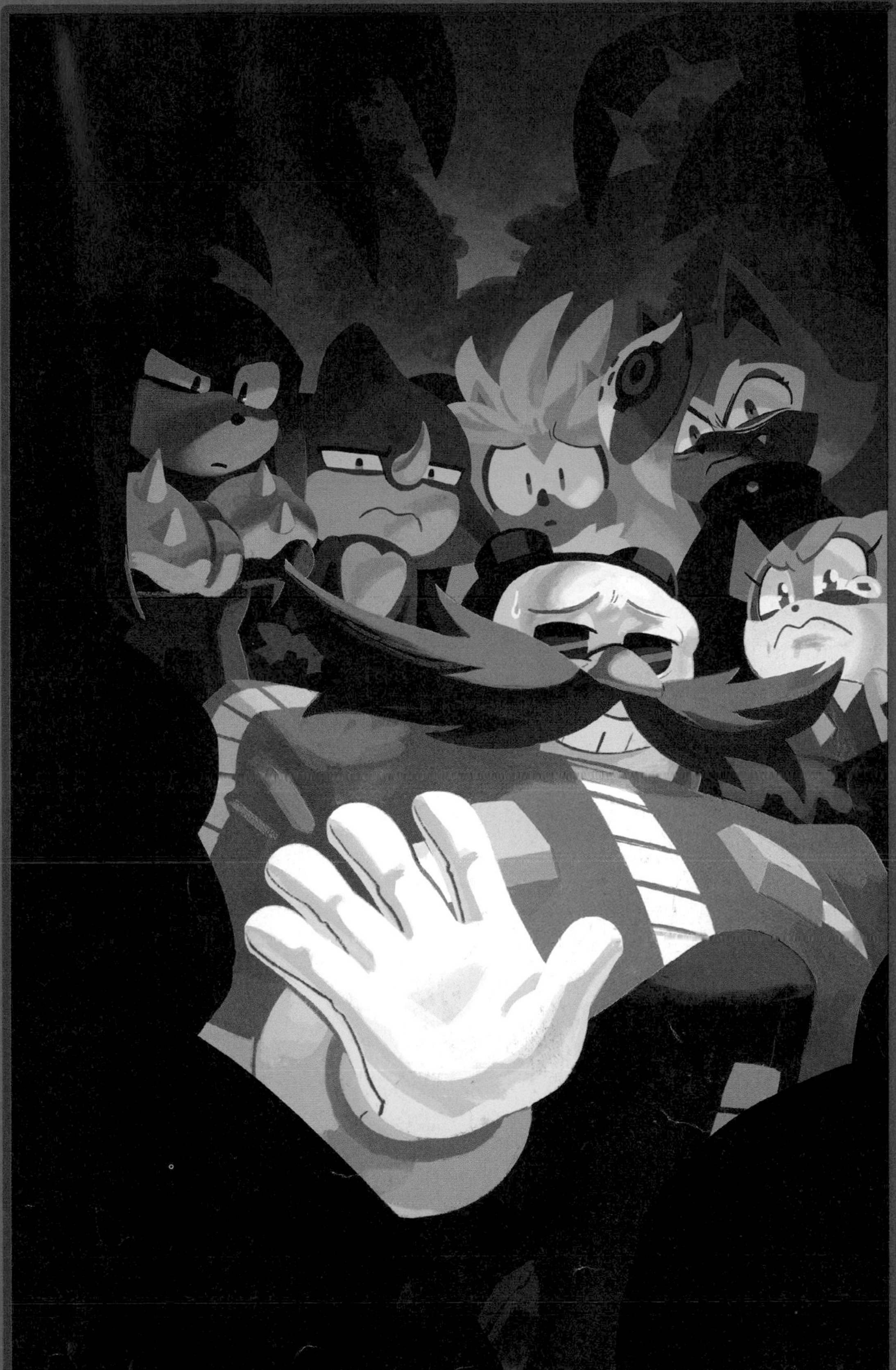

ART BY **NATHALIE FOURDRAINE**

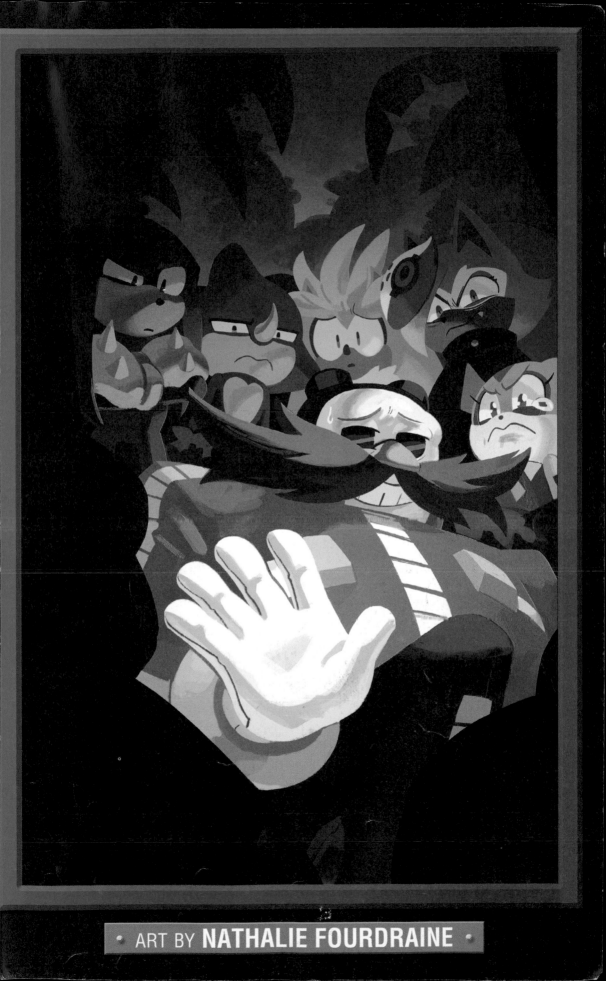

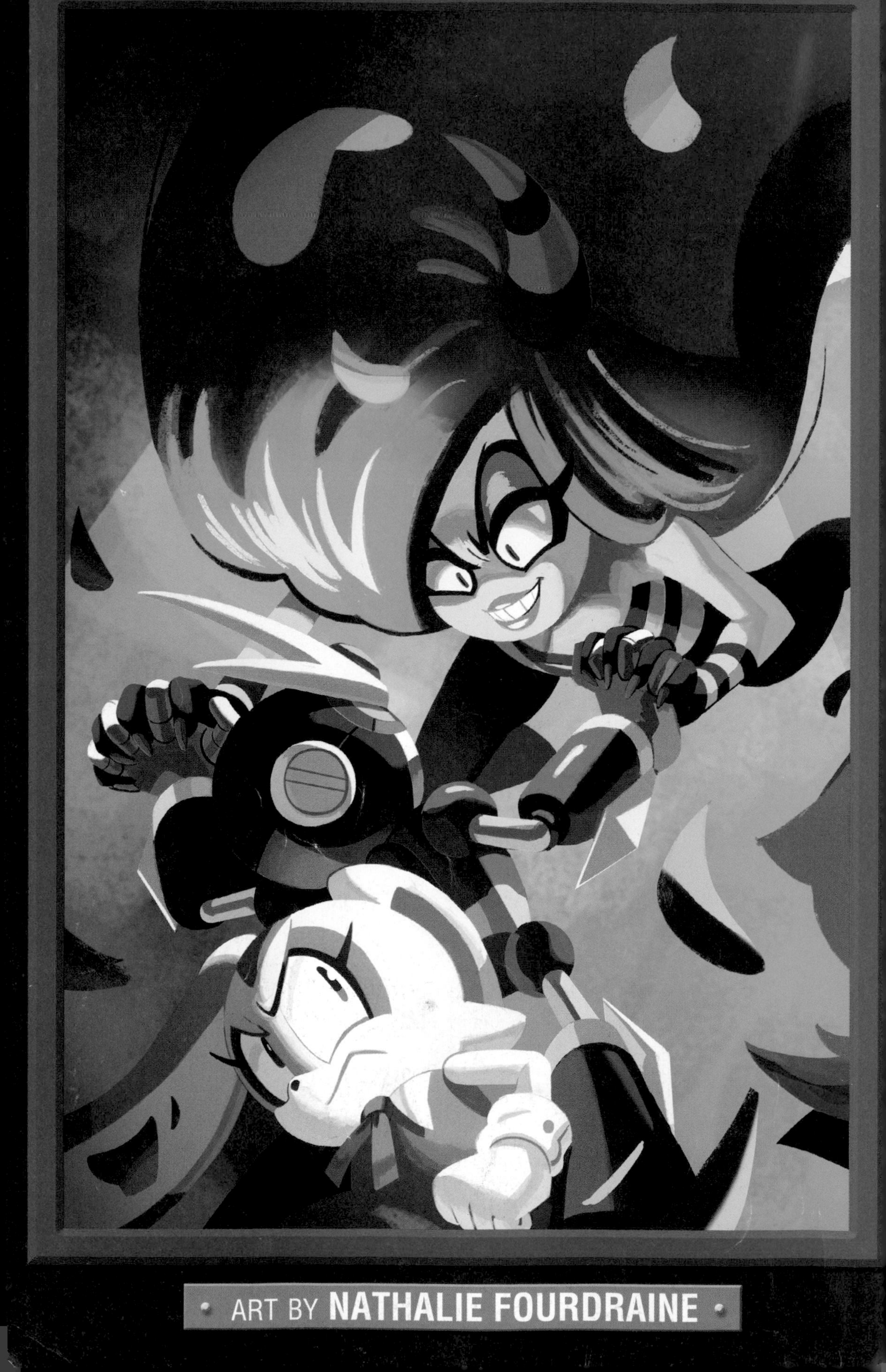

ART BY **NATHALIE FOURDRAINE**

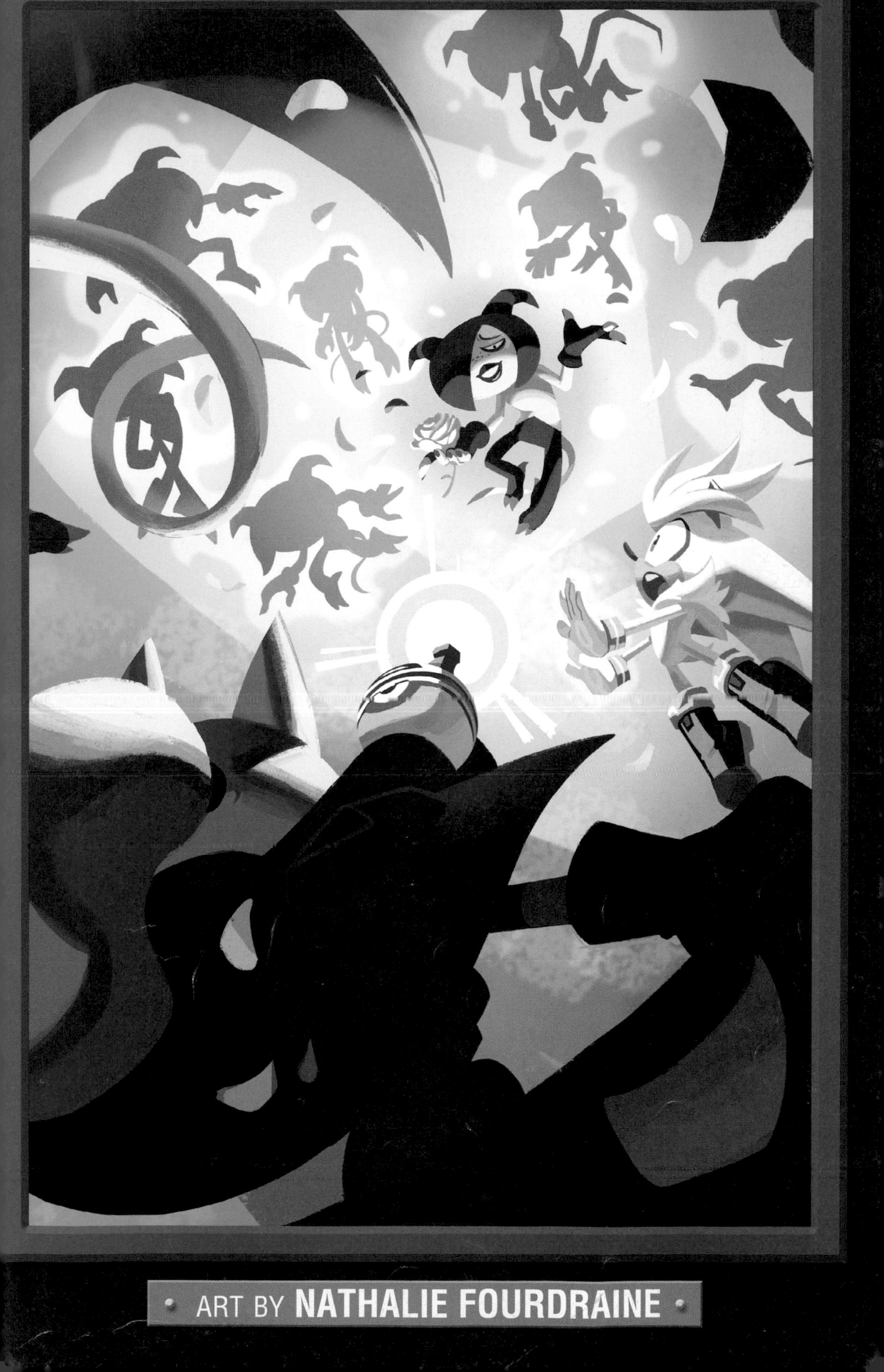

ART BY **NATHALIE FOURDRAINE**

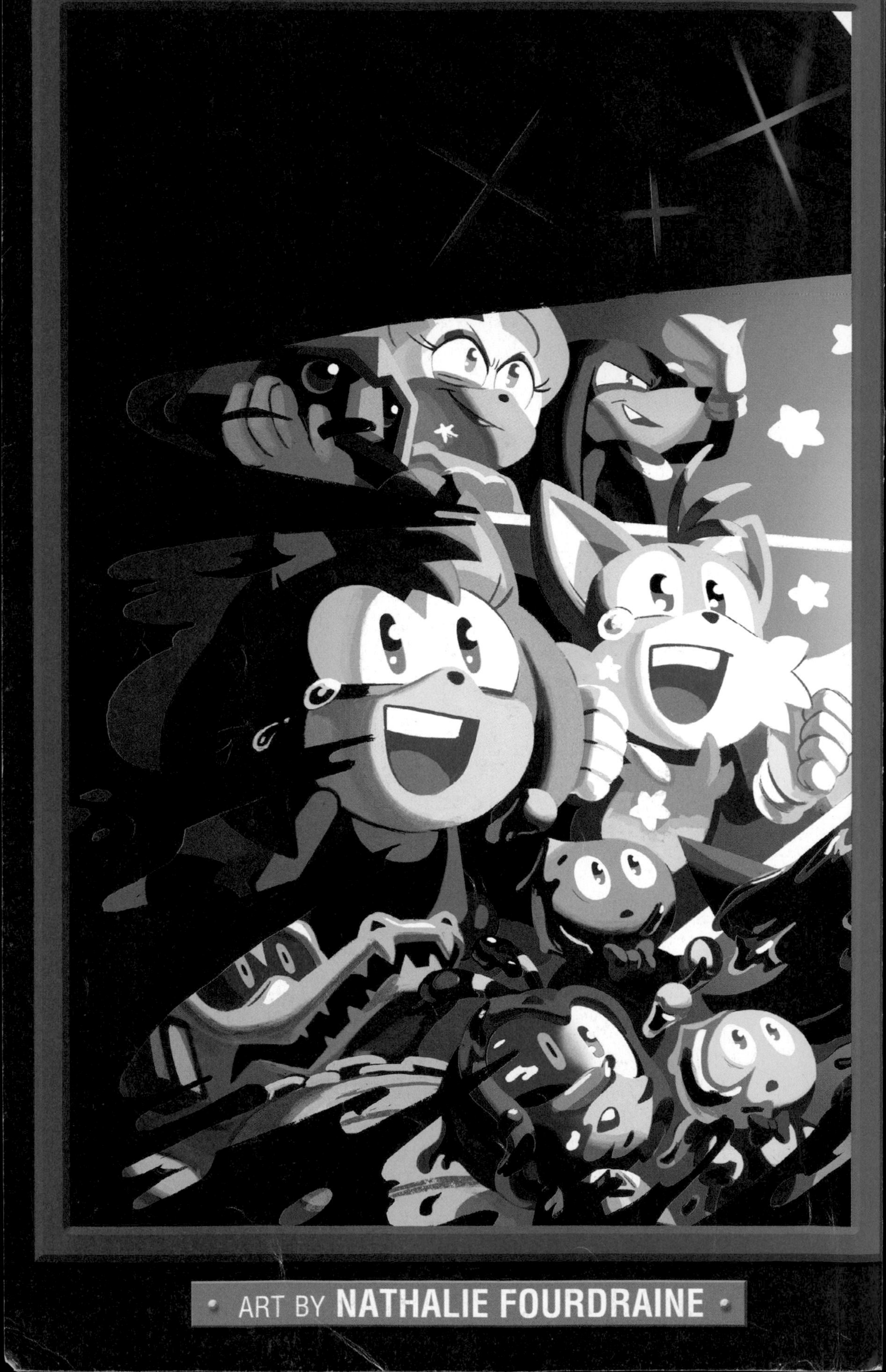

ART BY NATHALIE FOURDRAINE

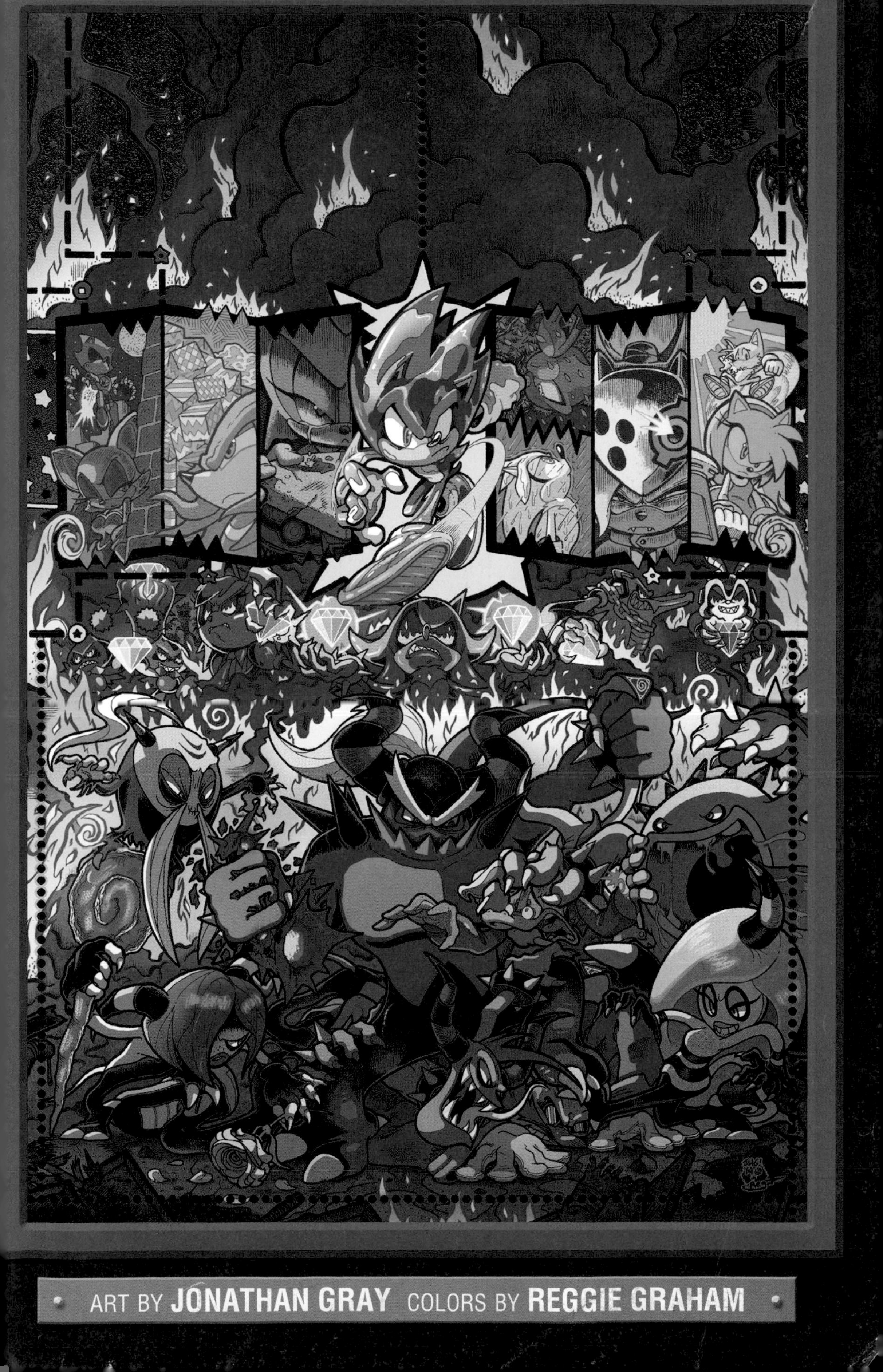

ART BY **JONATHAN GRAY** COLORS BY **REGGIE GRAHAM**

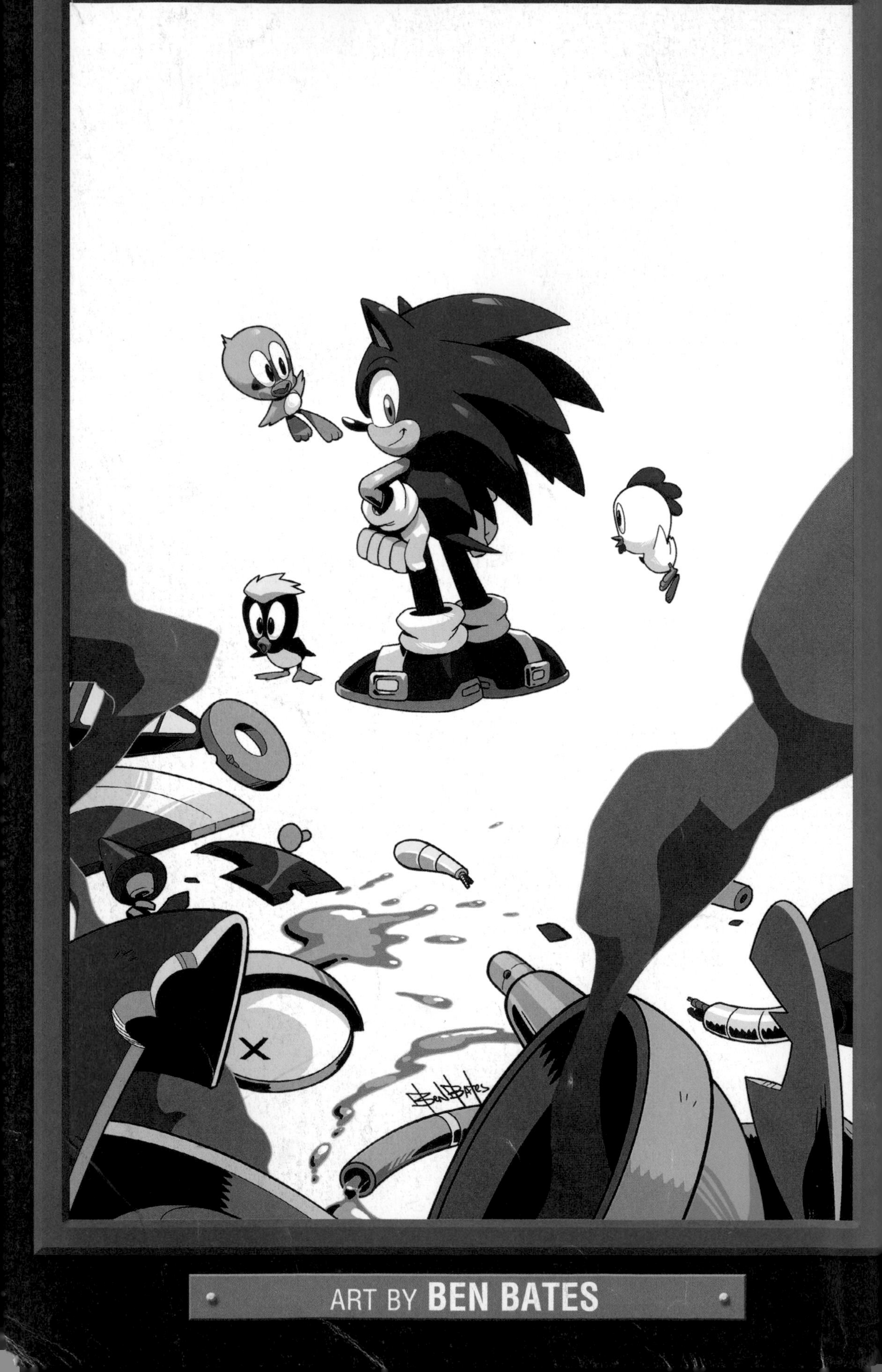
BEN BATES

ART BY **BEN BATES**

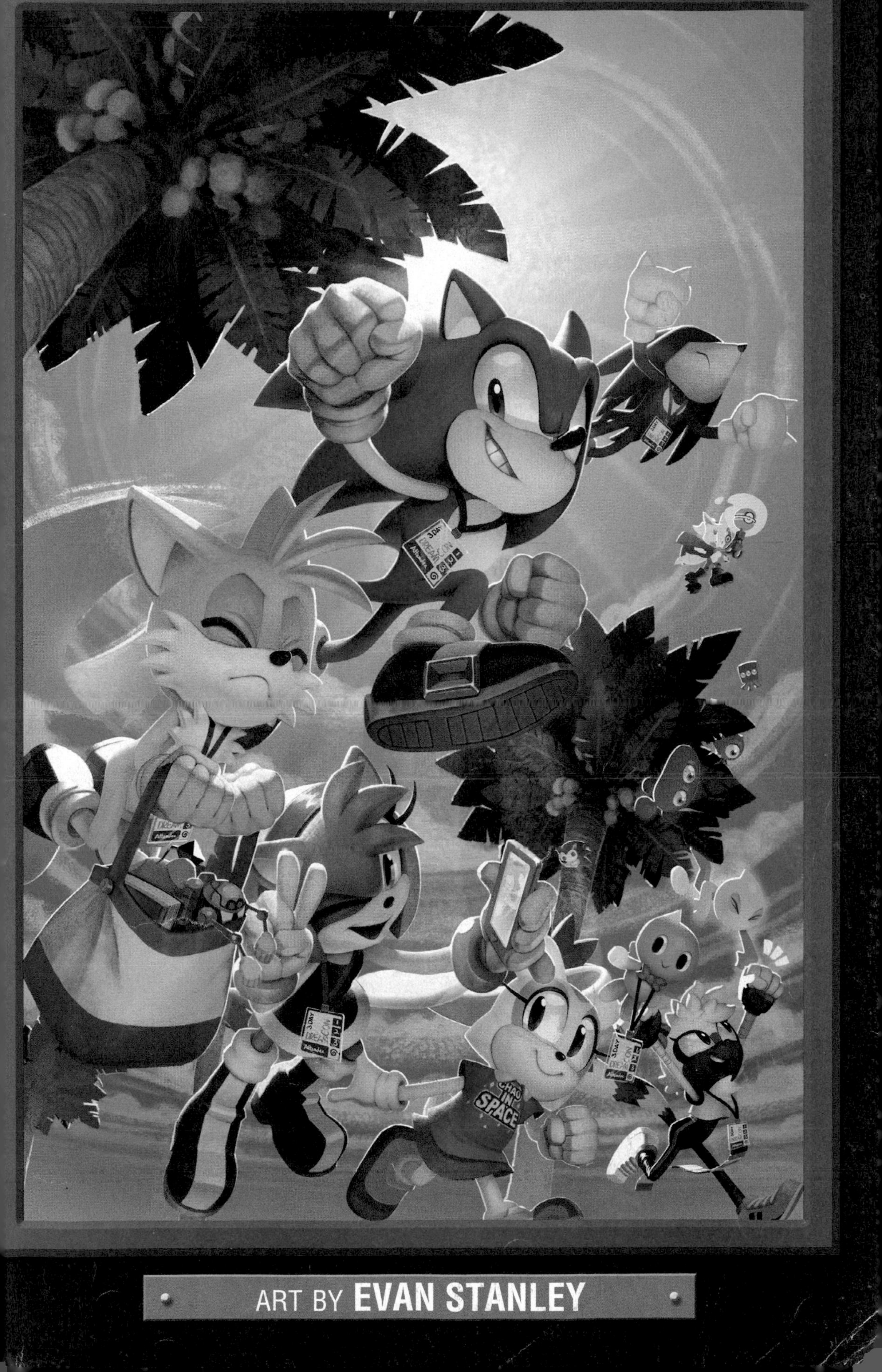
3 DAY
DREAMCON
CHAO IN SPACE

ART BY **EVAN STANLEY**

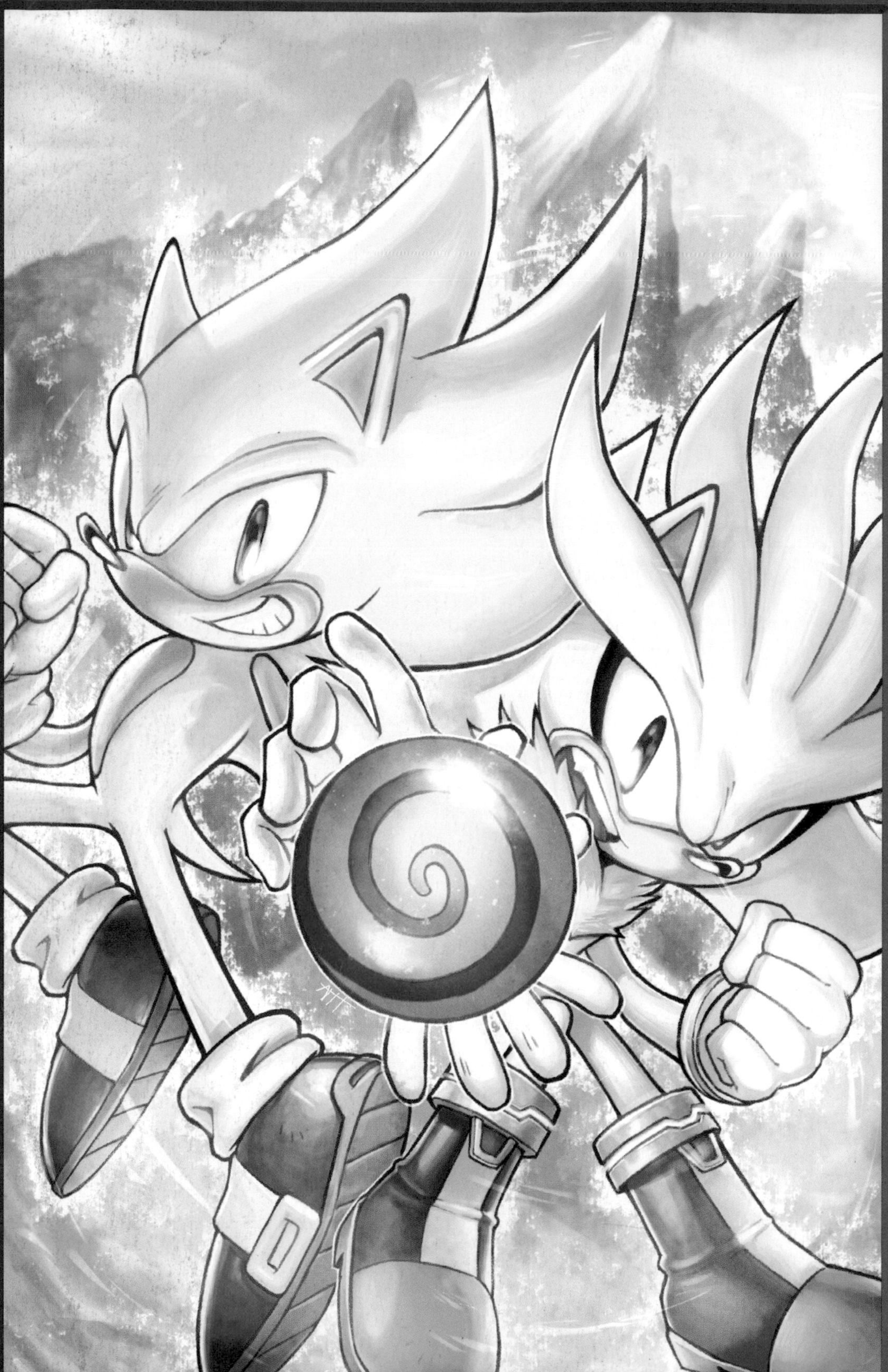

ART BY **AARON HAMMERSTROM**

SONIC™ THE HEDGEHOG

ALL OR NOTHING

SEGA®

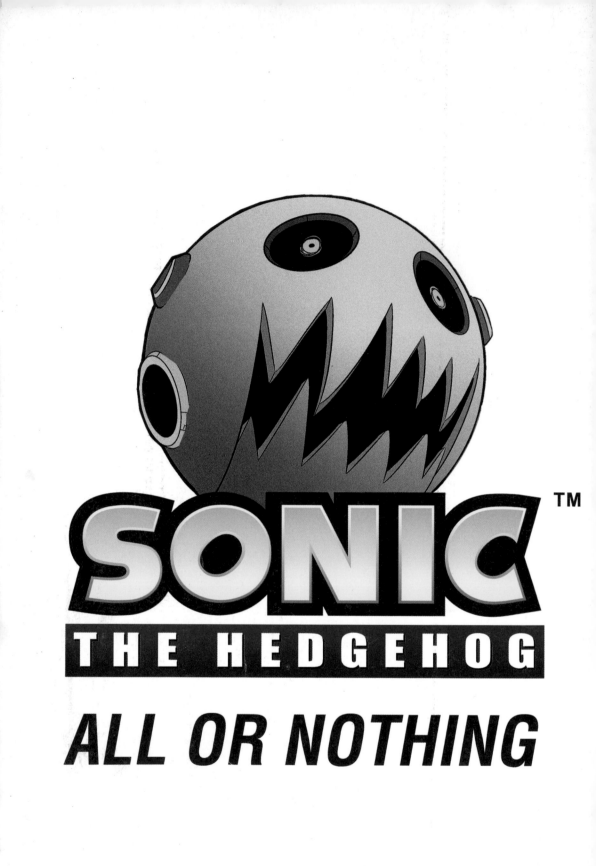

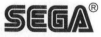